The All-Girl
FILLING STATION'S
Last Reunion

The All-Girl
FILLING STATION'S
Last Reunion

A NOVEL

FANNIE FLAGG

RANDOM HOUSE • NEW YORK

Published in the United States by Random House, an imprint of The Random House Publishing Group, a division of Random House LLC, a Penguin Random House Company, New York.

RANDOM HOUSE and the HOUSE colophon are registered trademarks of Random House LLC.

LIBRARY OF CONGRESS CATALOGING-IN-PUBLICATION DATA

Flagg, Fannie.

The all-girl filling station's last reunion : a novel / Fannie Flagg.

pages cm

ISBN 978-1-4000-6594-3

eBook ISBN 978-0-8129-9463-6

1. Women—Fiction. 2. Female friendship—Fiction. 3. Family secrets—Fiction. 4. Service stations—Fiction. 5. Domestic fiction. I. Title.

PS3556.L26A45 2013   813'.54—dc23   2013030030

Printed in the United States of America on acid-free paper

www.atrandom.com

246897531

First Edition

Book design by Susan Turner

For Sam Vaughan

PULASKI, WISCONSIN

JUNE 28, 2010

A few years ago, if someone had told me that
I would be at this reunion today,
I wouldn't have believed them in
a million years. . . . And yet, here I am!

—MRS. EARLE POOLE, JR.

Prologue

THE BEGINNING

———

Lwów, Poland
April 1, 1909

IN THE YEAR 1908, STANISLAW LUDIC JURDABRALINSKI, A TALL, RAW-boned boy of fourteen, was facing a future of uncertainty. Life in Poland under Russian rule was bleak and dangerous. Polish men and boys were being conscripted to serve in the czar's army, and in an attempt to destroy Polish unity, Catholics and priests had been jailed for anti-Russian sentiments. Churches were shut down and Stanislaw's father and three uncles had been sent to prison camps for speaking out.

But with encouragement from his older brother Wencent, who had escaped Poland five years earlier, Stanislaw arrived in New York with nothing but the ill-fitting plaid woolen suit he was wearing, a photograph of his mother and sisters, and the promise of a job. With the help of a Polish stevedore who he had befriended on the ship, he managed to hop a freight train.

Five days later, Stanislaw arrived on his brother's doorstep in Chicago, excited and ready to begin his brand-new life. He had been told that in America, if you worked hard, anything was possible.

The All-Girl
FILLING STATION'S
Last Reunion

A MOST UNUSUAL WEEK

Point Clear, Alabama
Monday, June 6, 2005
76° and Sunny

Mrs. Earle Poole, Jr., better known to friends and family as Sookie, was driving home from the Birds-R-Us store out on Highway 98 with one ten-pound bag of sunflower seeds and one ten-pound bag of wild bird seed and not her usual weekly purchase for the past fifteen years of one twenty-pound bag of the Pretty Boy Wild Bird Seed and Sunflower Mix. As she had explained to Mr. Nadleshaft, she was worried that the smaller birds were still not getting enough to eat. Every morning lately, the minute she filled her feeders, the larger, more aggressive blue jays would swoop in and scare the little birds all away.

She noticed that the blue jays always ate the sunflower seeds first, and so tomorrow, she was going to try putting just plain sunflower seeds in her backyard feeders, and while the blue jays were busy eating them, she would run around the house as fast as she could and put the wild bird seed in the feeders in the front yard. That way, her poor finches and titmice might be able to get a little something, at least.

As she drove over the Mobile Bay Bridge, she looked out at the big white puffy clouds and saw a long row of pelicans flying low over the

water. The bay was sparkling in the bright sun and already dotted with
red, white, and blue sailboats headed out for the day. A few people
fishing alongside the bridge waved as she passed by, and she smiled
and waved back. She was almost to the other side when she suddenly
began to experience some sort of a vague and unusual sense of well-
being. And with good reason.

Against all odds, she had just survived the last wedding of their
three daughters, Dee Dee, Ce Ce, and Le Le. Their only unmarried
child now was their twenty-five-year-old son, Carter, who lived in
Atlanta. And some other poor (God help her), beleaguered mother of
the bride would be in charge of planning that happy occasion. All she
and Earle would have to do for Carter's wedding was show up and
smile. And today, other than one short stop at the bank and picking
up a couple of pork chops for dinner, she didn't have another single
thing she had to do. She was almost giddy with relief.

Of course, Sookie absolutely worshipped and adored her girls, but
having to plan three large weddings in fewer than two years had been
a grueling, never-ending, twenty-four-hours-a-day job, with all the
bridal showers, picking out patterns, shopping, fittings, writing invitations, meeting with caterers, figuring out seating arrangements, or-
dering flowers, etc. And between dealing with out-of-town guests and
new in-laws, figuring out where to put everyone, plus last-minute
bridal hysteria, at this point, she was simply weddinged out.

And no wonder. If you counted Dee Dee's last one, technically
there had really been four large weddings, which meant shopping and
being fitted for four different mother-of-the-bride dresses (you can't
wear the same one twice) in less than two years.

Dee Dee had married, then promptly divorced. And after they
had spent weeks returning all the wedding gifts, she had turned around
and remarried the exact same husband. Her second wedding hadn't
been quite as expensive as the first, but every bit as stressful.

When she and Earle had married in 1968, it had been just a typi-
cal church affair: white wedding gown, bridesmaids in matching pas-
tel dresses and shoes, ring bearer, best man, reception, over and out.
But now everybody had to have some kind of a theme.

Dee Dee had insisted on having an authentic Old South *Gone
with the Wind* wedding, complete with a Scarlett O'Hara dress, large

hoop skirt and all, and at the last minute, she had to be driven to the church standing up in the back of a small moving van.

Le Le and her groom wanted an entirely red and white wedding, including the invitations, food, drinks, and all the decorations, in honor of the University of Alabama football team.

And Ce Ce, Le Le's twin sister, the last girl to marry, had carried her ten-pound Persian cat, Peek-a-Boo, down the aisle instead of a wedding bouquet, and the groom's German shepherd, dressed in a tux, had served as best man. And if that wasn't bad enough, someone's turtle was the ring bearer. The entire thing had just been excruciating. You can't hurry a turtle.

LOOKING BACK ON IT now, Sookie realized she really should have put her foot down when Ce Ce and James invited all their friends to bring their pets to the reception, but she had made a sacred vow to never bully her children. Nevertheless, having to replace an entire banquet room's wall-to-wall carpeting at the Grand Hotel was going to cost them a fortune. Oh, well. Too late now. Hopefully, all that was behind her, and evidently not a minute too soon.

Two days ago, when Ce Ce left for her honeymoon, Sookie had broken down and sobbed uncontrollably. She didn't know if she was experiencing empty-nest syndrome or just plain exhaustion. She knew she must be tired. At the reception, she had introduced a man to his own wife. Twice.

The truth was, as sad as she was to see Ce Ce and James drive off, she had been secretly looking forward to going home, taking off all her clothes, and crawling into bed for about five years, but even that had been put on hold. At the last minute, James's parents, his sister, and her husband had decided to stay over an extra night, so she had to quickly try and whip up a little "going away" brunch for them.

Granted, it wasn't much: Earle's coconut margaritas, an assortment of crackers, cream cheese and pepper jelly, shrimp and grits, crab cakes with coleslaw, and tomato aspic on the side. But still, it had taken some effort.

*   *   *

WHEN SOOKIE DROVE INTO the little town of Point Clear and passed the Page and Palette bookstore, it occurred to her that maybe tomorrow, she would stop in and pick up a good book. She hadn't had time to read anything other than her daily horoscope, the Kappa newsletter, and an occasional *Birds and Blooms* magazine. We could be at war for all she knew. But now, she was actually going to be able to read an entire book again.

She suddenly felt like doing the twist right there in the front seat, which only reminded her how long it had been since she and Earle had learned a new dance step. She had probably even forgotten how to do the hokey pokey.

All she really had left to deal with was her eighty-eight-year-old mother, the formidable Mrs. Lenore Simmons Krackenberry, who absolutely refused to move to the perfectly lovely assisted-living facility right across town. And it would be so much easier on everybody if she would. The maintenance on her mother's yard alone was extremely expensive, not to mention the yearly insurance. Since the hurricane, the insurance on everybody's house on the Mobile Bay had gone sky-high. But Lenore was adamant about never leaving her home and had announced with a dramatic gesture, "Until they carry me out feet-first."

Sookie couldn't imagine her mother leaving anywhere feetfirst. As long as she and her brother, Buck, could remember, Lenore, a large imposing woman who wore lots of scatter pins and long, flowing scarves, and had her silver hair teased and sprayed into a perfect winged-back flip, had always rushed into a room headfirst. Buck said she looked like something that should be on the hood of a car, and they had secretly referred to her as "Winged Victory" ever since. And Winged Victory never just left a room; she whisked out with a flourish, leaving a cloud of expensive perfume in her wake. Never a quiet woman in any sense of the word, much like a show horse in the Rose Parade, she could be heard coming a mile away, due to the loud jingling of the numerous bracelets, bangles, and beads she always wore. And she was usually speaking long before she came in sight. Lenore had a loud booming voice and had studied "Expression" while attending Judson College for women, and to the family's everlasting regret, the teacher had encouraged her.

Now, due to certain recent events, including her setting her own kitchen on fire, they had been forced to hire a twenty-four-hour live-in nurse for Lenore. Earle was a successful dentist with a nice practice, but they were by no means rich, and certainly not now, with all the money they had spent sending the children to college, the weddings, Lenore's mortgage, and now the nurse. Poor Earle might not be able to retire until he was ninety, but the nurse was a definite necessity.

Lenore, who was not only loud but also extremely opinionated and voiced her opinion to everyone within earshot, had suddenly started calling total strangers long-distance. Last year, she had called the pope in Rome, and that call alone had cost them more than three hundred dollars. When confronted with the bill, Lenore had been incensed and said that she shouldn't have to pay a dime because she had been on hold the entire time. Try telling that to the phone company. And there was no reasoning with her. When Sookie asked why she had called the pope, considering that she was a sixth-generation dyed-in-the-wool Methodist, Lenore had thought for a moment and said, "Oh . . . just to chat."

"To chat?"

"Yes, and you mustn't be so closed-minded, Sookie. One can certainly be on speaking terms with Catholics. You don't want to marry one, but a friendly chat can't hurt."

And there had been other incidents. At a chamber of commerce meeting, Lenore had called the mayor a pointy-headed little carpetbagger and a horse thief and was sued for defamation of character. Sookie had been worried to death, but Lenore remained unfazed. "They have to prove what I said was not true, and no jury in their right mind would dare convict me!" In the end, the judge had thrown the case out, but still, it had been very embarrassing. All last year, Sookie had to try to avoid running into the mayor and his wife, and in such a small town, it had been almost impossible. They were just everywhere.

Since the lawsuit, they had been through three different nurses. Two quit, and one left in the middle of the night, along with one of Lenore's dinner rings and a frozen turkey. But now, after months of searching, Sookie felt she had finally found the perfect nurse, a darling older Filipino lady named Angel, who was so patient and so sweet, even though Lenore continued to call her Conchita, because she said she looked exactly like the Mexican woman who had worked for her in Texas in the forties, when Sookie's father had been stationed there.

The good news was, now that Lenore had Angel, Sookie was finally going to be able to attend the Kappa reunion in Dallas, and her old college roommate, Dena Nordstrom, had promised to meet her there. They talked on the phone regularly, but she hadn't seen Dena in a long time, and she couldn't wait.

As SOOKIE SAT AT the intersection waiting for the red light to change, she pulled down the visor and looked at herself in the mirror. Good God, that was a mistake. She guessed that after fifty, nobody looked good in the bright sun, but even so, she really had neglected herself. She hadn't seen her eye doctor in over three years, and she clearly needed a new prescription.

Last month at church, she had embarrassed herself half to death. The correct quote was, "I am a vessel for God's love," but she had read out loud in front of the entire congregation, "I am a weasel for God's love." Earle had said that no one had noticed, but of course, they had.

Sookie glanced at herself in the mirror again. Oh, Lord, no wonder she looked so terrible. She had run out the door this morning without a stitch of makeup. Now she was going to have to drive all the way home and throw some on. She always tried to look somewhat presentable. Thankfully, she wasn't as vain as her mother, or she would never have left home at all. Outward appearances meant everything to Lenore. She was particularly proud of what she called "the Simmons foot" and her small, slightly turned-up nose. Sookie had gotten her father's longer nose, and wouldn't you know it, Buck got the cute one. Oh, well. At least she got the Simmons foot.

JUST AS THE LIGHT changed, Netta Verp, Sookie's next-door neighbor, whizzed by in her huge 1989 Ford Fairlane, probably on her way out to Costco, and tooted her horn. Sookie tooted back. Sookie loved Netta. She was a good old soul. She and Netta were both Leos.

Netta's house was in between their house and Lenore's. Poor thing. She had been stuck in the middle, with all the Poole children and animals on one side and Lenore on the other, calling her night and day, but she never complained. She said, "Hell, I'm a widow. What else am I going to do for fun?"

SOOKIE SUPPOSED SHE SHOULDN'T have been surprised that Ce Ce's wedding theme had been "Pets Are People, Too." At one point, there had been eleven animals living in the Poole house, including an alligator that had crawled out of the bay and up the back-porch stairs, three cats, and four dogs, one being Earle's beloved Great Dane, Tiny, who was the size of a small horse.

All the dogs, cats, and hamsters—and the one blind raccoon—were fine, but she had drawn the line with the alligator and insisted that it stay in the basement. She loved animals, too, but when you're scared to get up at night and go to the bathroom, it's time to put your foot down, and hopefully not on top of something that could bite it off.

The hard part of having animals, for her, was losing them. Two years before, Mr. Henry, their eighteen-year-old cat, had died, and she still couldn't see an orange cat without going to pieces. After Mr. Henry died she told Earle no more pets. She just couldn't take the heartbreak.

SOOKIE DROVE STRAIGHT ON through town, waved at Doris, the tomato lady on the corner, then headed down the hill, toward her house on the bay.

The old historic scenic route was lined on both sides with large oak trees planted before the Civil War. On the right side, facing the water, were miles of old wooden bay houses built mostly by people from Mobile as summer homes. Sookie guessed that if she had a penny for every time she had driven on this road over the years, she would be a millionaire by now.

She had been eight the first time her father had brought the family down from Selma to spend the summer. They had arrived in Point Clear on a warm, balmy evening, and the air had been filled with the scent of honeysuckle and wisteria.

She could still remember coming down the hill and seeing the lights of Mobile, sparkling and twinkling across the water, just like a jeweled necklace. It was as if they had just entered into a fairyland. The Spanish moss hanging from the trees had looked bright silver in the moonlight and made dancing shadows all along the road. And the shrimp boats out in the bay, with their little blinking green lights, had looked just like Christmas to Sookie. For her, there had always been something magical about Point Clear, and there still was.

ABOUT A MILE PAST the Grand Hotel, Sookie turned in and drove up her long crushed-oyster-shell driveway and pulled into the carport. Netta's house was almost identical to theirs, but Netta's yard was much prettier. As soon as she could get rested enough, one of the first things Sookie was going to do was prune. Her azalea bushes were a disgrace, and her limelight hydrangeas had just gone completely wild.

Their house, like most of the others along the scenic route, was a large white wooden home with dark green shutters. Most of the bay houses had been built long before air-conditioning and had a wide center hall that ran all the way to a large screened-in porch in back overlooking the bay. And like their neighbors, they had a long gray wooden pier with a small seating area with a tin roof on the end. When the kids had been much younger, she and Earle used to go sit there almost every evening to watch the sunset and listen to the church bells that rang up and down the bay. They hadn't done that in years. She was so looking forward to being alone with Earle again.

Sookie took the two bags of seeds out of the car and put them in the little greenhouse Earle had built for her, where she kept her bird supplies. A few minutes later, after she went inside, Sookie suddenly noticed how quiet the house was. Almost eerily quiet. As she stood there, all she could hear was the ticking of the kitchen clock and the cry of the seagulls out on the bay. It was so strange not to hear a door slamming or someone running up and down the stairs. How pleasant to have peace and quiet, and not hear loud music blaring from some-one's room. So pleasant, in fact, she thought maybe she would fix herself a cup of tea and sit and relax a few minutes before she headed out again.

Just as she was reaching for a tea bag, the kitchen phone rang. Now that the house was empty, it sounded like a fire alarm going off. She picked it up and looked at the caller ID number. It was a long-distance call, but not from an area code she recognized, so she just let it ring. She was too tired to talk to anyone if she didn't have to. In the past few days she'd had to smile and talk to so many people that her face still hurt.

Sookie stuck a cup of water in the microwave, grabbed her tea bag, and went out on the screened-in porch to enjoy it. She sat down in her big white wicker chair. The bay was as smooth as glass, not a ripple in sight.

She noticed that her gardenia bushes were still in bloom and thought she might cut off a few and float them in a dish in the living room. They always made the house smell so sweet. She took a deep breath of fresh air and was about to have her first sip of tea when the phone started ringing again. Oh, Lord, it was obviously somebody calling the wrong number or a solicitor trying to sell her something, and if she didn't answer they would probably drive her crazy all day. She got up and went back to the kitchen and picked up. It was her mother.

"Sookie, I need you to come over here right now."

"Mother, is something wrong?"

"I have something extremely important to discuss with you."

"Oh, Mother, can't it wait? I just got home."

"No, it cannot!"

"Oh, well . . . all right. I'll be there as soon as I can."

Sookie frowned as she hung up. That particular tone in her moth-er's voice always made her a little anxious. Had Lenore found out she had spoken to the woman at Westminster Village about assisted liv-ing? She had just been inquiring about the price, and it had only been one short call. But if someone had told Lenore she would be furious.

A few minutes later, Sookie walked over, and the nurse, who was in the front yard cutting fresh flowers, looked up and said, "Oh, good morning, Mrs. Poole," then added with a sympathetic little smile, "God bless you."

"Thank you, Angel," said Sookie.

Oh, Lord . . . it must be worse than she thought. As Sookie walked into the house, she called out, "Mother?"

"I'm here."

"Where's 'here'?"

"In the dining room, Sookie."

Sookie went in and saw her mother seated at the large Georgian dining room table with the twelve Queen Anne chairs. On the table, placed in front of her, was the large leather box with the maroon velvet inside that held her set of the Francis I silverware. Next to the box was the large Simmons family Bible.

"What's going on, Mother?"

"Sit down."

Sookie sat down and waited for whatever was coming. Lenore looked at her and said, "Sookie, I called you here today because I am not entirely convinced that you fully appreciate what you will be receiving upon my demise. As my only daughter, you will be inheriting the entire set of the Simmons family silver . . . and before I can die in peace, I want you to swear on this Bible that you will never, under any circumstances, break up the set."

Sookie was so relieved it wasn't about the call to Westminster Village, and said, "Oh, Mother . . . I do appreciate it . . . but really, why don't you leave it all to Bunny? She and Buck entertain much more than I do."

"What?" Lenore gasped and clutched at her pearls. "Bunny? Leave it to Bunny? Oh, Sookie," she said with wounded eyes. "Do you have any idea what was sacrificed to keep it in the family?" Sookie sighed. She had heard the story a thousand times before, but Lenore loved to tell it over and over, with large dramatic gestures included. "Grandmother Simmons said that at one point during the war, all that stood between them and the entire family going hungry was your great-grandmother's silver. And do you know what she did?"

"No, Mother, what?"

"She chose to go hungry, that's what! Why, she said there were days when all they had to eat was a pitiful little handful of pecans. And they had to bury the silver in a different spot every night to keep the Yankee soldiers from finding it, but she saved the silver! And now you say, 'Oh, just give it to Bunny'? Who's not even a Simmons—and not even from Alabama? Why don't you just cut my heart out and throw it out in the yard?"

"Oh, God. All right. . . . I'm sorry, Mother. It's just . . . well, if you want me to have it, then thank you."

Sookie certainly hadn't meant to hurt her mother's feelings about the silverware, but she really had no use for it. She didn't know any-body who used a pickle fork or a grapefruit spoon anymore, and you can't put real silver in the dishwasher. You have to wash each piece by hand. And she certainly didn't want to have to polish silver all day. The Francis I pattern had twenty-eight pieces of carved fruit on the knife handle alone, not to mention the tea service, the coffee service, and the two sets of formal candlesticks.

Sookie realized she probably should care more about the silver. After all, it had come all the way from England and had been in the family for generations. But she just wasn't as formal as her mother. Winged Victory would die of epilepsy if she knew her daughter some-times used paper plates and plastic knives and forks and just hated polishing silverware.

Lenore dearly loved to polish silver and, once a month, would sit at the dining room table wearing white cotton gloves with all of it spread out before her. "Nothing relaxes me more than cleaning my silver."

Oh, well. Too late now. The die was cast. Sookie was stuck with it. She swore on the Bible that not only would she never break up the set, but that she personally would polish it regularly. "Don't ever let tar-nish get a head start on you," Lenore said.

What could she do? Being Lenore's daughter meant she had come into the world with preordained duties. First, to proudly carry on the Simmons family line that, according to Lenore, could be traced all the way back to fifteenth-century England. Second, to protect the family silver.

It was such a beautiful warm day, and after Sookie left her moth-er's house, she took her shoes off and walked back home along the bay.

As she strolled along, she suddenly wondered how many times she and the children had walked back and forth to Lenore's house over the years. It seemed like only yesterday when all day long, the kids were running back and forth to her house and theirs.

Time was so strange. When the children were younger, she used to marvel at the tiny little footsteps they left in the sand, but those days were gone forever. They were all grown up now . . . and, bless their hearts, not a one of them had the Simmons foot, and three had the Poole ears. But that was another story.

A FEW MINUTES LATER, after she had thrown on a little makeup, Sookie drove back to town and was sitting in line at the drive-in bank waiting to make a deposit to cover yet another one of Lenore's unexpected expenses. About ten years ago, Lenore had suddenly started bouncing checks all over town and hadn't seemed the least bit concerned. "I hate fiddling with figures," she said. So now all Lenore's mail was delivered to Sookie to handle, including all her bills. Lenore's letters alone were almost a full-time job. She was always firing off editorials to the newspaper. The last one, suggesting that we do away with the vote for people under fifty-five, had brought in more than one hundred letters that Sookie had to answer. Lenore never looked at her own mail. "Just tell me if something is important," she said. The woman ordered almost everything she saw on television, and Sookie always had to send it back. Why would anybody over eighty want a ThighMaster?

Lenore was her mother, and she loved her, but *Lord,* she was a lot of trouble. When Earle had first bought the dental practice and they had moved down to Point Clear for good, Lenore insisted that before she would move with the family from Selma, Sookie's Great-Grandfather Simmons must be moved from the Selma Cemetery and transferred down to the Soldier's Rest Cemetery in Point Clear. "I would just die if I didn't have Grandfather Simmons to decorate. He was a general, Sookie!" And, naturally, Sookie was the one who ended up having to deal with all the endless red tape of trying to arrange it. After weeks of hassling back and forth with the cemetery people, having to sign paper after paper, she finally just begged them to please dig up anything—dog, cat, or horse—and send it on. At that point, she was so tired, she didn't care.

The car in front of Sookie moved one space closer to the teller, and she moved up with it. She looked at herself in the mirror again. She looked a little better with her makeup on, but, of course, she had forgotten to put on her earrings. Honestly, between the weddings and dealing with her mother, it really was a miracle she was still sane at all.

She had always had a delicate nervous system and a tendency to faint under pressure. And it was very stressful never knowing what her mother was going to do next. Lenore had shown up at Ce Ce's wedding wearing a large yellow hat with two live lovebirds in a cage sitting on top. God only knows where she got that.

Thank heavens, all Sookie's kids had been good kids, because when they were growing up, she had let them do pretty much what they pleased. She had wanted them to have a carefree childhood. Hers certainly hadn't been, with Lenore pushing her into everything. She had always been basically shy. She never wanted to be a Magnolia Trail Maiden or a cheerleader or to join all those organizations. But she had had no choice. Lenore ruled with an iron hand. "You owe it to the Simmons name to be a leader in society, Sookie!" she said.

Well . . . that certainly hadn't worked out. She knew she was a disappointment to her mother, but what could she do? She didn't know why, but in school, as hard as she tried, she had never been able to get more than a C average while Buck had made all A's. And those ballet lessons Lenore had pushed her into had been a complete disaster.

Sookie was finally at the drive-through window and handed the bank teller her deposit and suddenly noticed that she had developed a strange tic in her right eye, probably some leftover stress from the wedding. Thankfully, Earle had finally just picked the turtle up and handed it to James or they would probably all still be sitting there. The girl in the window pushed the drawer back out with her receipt and said over the speakerphone, "Thank you, Mrs. Poole, have a nice day."

"Oh, thank you, Susie. You, too."

"Tell your mother I said hello."

"I will."

After she left the bank, Sookie ran into the market and picked up a few pork chops and, as an afterthought, a can of sliced pineapple. Earle said he had a big surprise for her tonight, so she thought she might spice up the chops a bit.

SOOKIE WAS STANDING IN the "less than six items" checkout line when she heard someone call out her name. It was Janice, a pretty blond girl and one of Ce Ce's bridesmaids, who rushed over from the produce department, still holding a head of lettuce, and hugged her. "Oh, Mrs. Poole, I'm so happy to see you! How are you? You must be exhausted from all the excitement . . . but I just had to tell you, that was one of the nicest weddings I have ever been in. And such fun, too! Ce Ce and Peek-a-Boo looked so cute coming up the aisle—and it's always so wonderful to see your precious mother. I swear she never changes. She's still the prettiest thing . . . and funny. I wish you could have been at our table—she had us all just screaming with laughter. And that hat with those birds! How does she come up with these things?"

"I have no idea," said Sookie.

"What a character, and she was so sweet to bring her little Mexican nurse with her."

As Sookie moved one person closer to the checkout girl, Janice moved with her. "Oh, and listen, Mrs. Poole, I was going to drop you a note and apologize for Tinker Bell's terrible behavior at the reception. I don't know what got into him. He usually just loves cats to death."

Sookie said, "Oh, don't worry about it, honey. . . . After all, dogs will be dogs."

Janice thought about it for a second and said, "Yes, I guess you're right. They just can't help themselves, can they?" Then she made a sad face. "How are you holding up? You must be so blue with Carter and all the girls gone—but thank heavens, you still have your mother to keep you company . . . and I'll bet she just keeps you entertained twenty-four hours a day doesn't she?"

"Oh, yes, she certainly does," said Sookie.

Finally, it was Sookie's turn at the cash register, and Janice said, "Well, I'd better run. 'Bye, Mrs. Poole, so nice to see you. Be sure and tell your mother I said hey."

"I sure will, honey."

When she came out of the market, she saw that the Elks Club ladies had set up a bake sale, so she walked over to see what they had. Dot Yeager, sitting behind the table, said, "Don't they all look good?"

"Oh, they do."

"Your mother looked so pretty at church yesterday in that bright blue dress with her silver hair. I wish I could wear that shade of blue, but it just fades me out to nothing. I had my colors done, and I'm a fall, but Lenore is definitely a spring, isn't she?"

"Yes, I believe she is."

Sookie was standing there, trying to decide between the lemon icebox and the pecan pie, when her friend Marvaleen walked up. "Oh, hi, Marvaleen. What do you think would go better with pork chops? The pecan or the lemon icebox?"

"If it were me, I'd go for the key lime, but then, I'm a fool for key lime." Sookie bought the key lime.

Sookie was glad she had run into Marvaleen. She seemed so much calmer now. Marvaleen had recently gone through a divorce and, for a time, had been quite intense. She had been seeing a life coach over in Mobile named Edna Yorba Zorbra, and all she wanted to do when you saw her was tell you in great detail what Edna Yorba Zorbra had just said.

A few months ago, Sookie had been at the store and in a hurry, and she had tried to hide, but Marvaleen had spotted her and cornered her in the frozen food department. "Sookie, do you journal?"

"What?"

"Do you journal? Write things down?"

"Oh, like lists. Yes, I have to. I went to the store four times before I remembered to buy Parmesan cheese."

"No, Sookie, I mean seriously journal. Write down your innermost thoughts. Edna Yorba Zorbra says it's essential to maintain a healthy psyche. I can't tell you what a difference it's made in my life. I would never have divorced Ralph if I hadn't started journaling. I didn't realize how much I hated him until I saw it written down in black and white. Oh, you must journal, Sookie. I didn't know who I really was until I started journaling."

Well . . . that was fine for Marvaleen, she guessed, but she couldn't imagine anything she would rather not do than write about her innermost feelings. And besides, she already knew exactly who she was and, unfortunately, so did everyone else within a five-hundred-mile radius.

Driving home, Sookie passed by the cemetery, and sure enough, there was Lenore's car parked at the entrance. Every Monday, she put fresh flowers on her Grandfather Simmons's grave and inspected the grounds and made sure to call anyone whose relative's blooms were fading and lecture them about honoring the dead. Most people had moved on and were more interested in the recent dead. But not Lenore. The woman was obsessed with her ancestors.

Lenore's own mother had died in childbirth, and she had been raised by her grandmother. That probably explained a lot about Lenore and her propensity to live not just in the past, but in the distant past. Sookie's Great-Grandmother Simmons had been born during the Civil War, and her memories of that time were still raw and somewhat bitter. From early childhood, the message given to Lenore almost daily at her grandmother's knee was that in order to survive in this world, she was to remain strong and proud. The South had been bloodied and defeated, yes, but never bowed. They had lost everything but their pride and their good name.

At seventeen, Lenore was sent to Judson College and became president of her sorority, Kappa Kappa Gamma, and valedictorian of her class. It was at Judson where Lenore had met Sookie's father, Alton Carter Krackenberry. He had been a cadet attending the Marion Military Institute nearby. And from the first moment he met her in the receiving line, he had been blinded by love for life.

During World War II, Sookie's father had commanded an entire unit of men in Brownsville, Texas. But at home, Lenore always ruled the roost. He spoiled her terribly and did pretty much whatever Lenore wanted him to do. No matter how many insane things she did, he would just look at her and exclaim to his children, "Look at her—isn't she just wonderful?" To the day he died, he said that Lenore had been the most beautiful girl at the Senior Military Ball, a fact that Lenore had agreed with most wholeheartedly. And often.

* * *

AFTER SOOKIE GOT HOME and put the groceries away, she went into the sunroom with the paper and sat down to read when Peek-a-Boo jumped up in her lap. Oh, dear. She was perfectly happy to keep her until Ce Ce came back from her honeymoon, but she didn't want to get attached to her, so she picked her up and put her down on the floor. But the cat jumped right back up again. Sookie sighed and said, "Oh, Peek-a-Boo. Honey . . . don't make me like you. Go on now," and she put her back down again. But she jumped right back up. The poor thing was obviously starved for affection, and so against her better judgment, Sookie started to pet her. After a minute, Peek-a-Boo was purring and kneading Sookie's legs, looking up at her, happy and content. "Oh, well, bless your heart. . . . You miss your mother, don't you? But she'll be back, don't you worry. Do you want me to get you some more bites? Is that what you want, precious? Do you want to play with your little toy?"

Oh, Lord. She had only had the cat forty-eight hours, and she was already talking baby talk to it. But what could she do? She couldn't just ignore the poor thing . . . and she was so cute.

When Earle came home from work, Peek-a-Boo was happily chasing her mouse on a string that Sookie was pulling all through the house. Earle said, "Hi, sweetie. What did you do today?"

Sookie had been waiting for years to say this: "Nothing. Absolutely nothing."

THAT NIGHT IN BED, Earle was fast asleep, and so was Peek-a-Boo, who was now cuddled up next to her, but as usual, Sookie was still wide awake. Earle's big surprise was that he was going to take her on a second honeymoon and she was so happy about it. She wanted to spend as much time with Earle as she possibly could, while she still could. With her future being as uncertain as it was, Sookie really didn't know how much time she had left.

It was the curse of the Simmonses. When they reached a certain age, some of them (her Aunt Lily and Uncle Baby) had to be sent to Pleasant Hill Sanitarium. As the doctor said, "When a fifty-eight-year-old man goes downtown dressed up in a Dale Evans cowgirl outfit, complete with a skirt with fringe, it's time," and after Aunt Lily's unfortunate incident with the paperboy, it was obvious she needed to be committed. But with Lenore, it was hard to tell. When Sookie had called Dr. Childress in Selma about her mother's latest exploits and asked what he thought, he sighed and said, "Sookie, honey, I've known your mother all my life, and the problem with Lenore has always been trying to figure out what behavior is just 'delightfully eccentric' and what's 'as batty as hell.' I know it's not an official diagnosis, but every Simmons I ever knew had a loose screw somewhere."

Dr. Childress had been the family doctor for years, and Sookie wished he had told her this before, not after, she had had four children. Who knows what wacko genes she may have passed on? Being second-generation, the children could be safe, but she was a genetic time bomb waiting to go off any minute. She lived in fear and dread of one day embarrassing her husband and children, and at one of the weddings, having someone point at her and say, "That lady in the corner talking to herself and batting at imaginary flies is the mother of the bride."

When she tried to tell Earle how worried she was about the Simmons curse, he had always dismissed it. "Oh, Sookie, don't be silly. You're not going to lose your mind. You're as sane as I am." She hoped he was right. But a few weeks ago, she had gone for a dress fitting in Mobile and had left the dress at home. Hopefully, now that she was almost sixty, it was just a normal senior moment and not the beginning of something worse. She didn't know, but she had written her family a letter and put it in the safety-deposit box at the bank, just in case.

She also wished Carter would get married sooner rather than later. He had always been popular. A couple of his old girlfriends still called her, wanting to know about him, so she was hopeful. The other day, he had said, "Mom, I want to get married . . . it's just that I haven't found anybody, yet, and it's getting pretty discouraging."

"Oh, I know, darling, but I promise one day, you'll meet the exact right one, and when you do, you will know it."

"How?"

"You just will, that's all."

Sookie knew it was a stupid answer, but it had happened to her, sort of. She'd known Earle Poole, Jr., since grammar school. She just hadn't known he was the right one until years later. Granted, her life had not always been a bowl of cherries—but then, whose had? Even if her life were to end tomorrow, she still had so much to be grateful for. First and foremost, for Earle.

And her children had mostly been a joy. The twins, Ce Ce and Le Le, had never given her a minute's trouble. They had always been happy, probably because they had each other. From the moment they could talk, they just chattered away together. They were like their own separate little unit, and she was amazed at how well they got along. She had read that some twins hated to dress alike, but not hers. They loved it and had to have matching underwear and pajamas. They even spoke in stereo. One would start a sentence, and the other would finish it.

Raising Carter had been easy. He was just like her brother, Buck. Send him outside with a ball to play with, and he was fine. Dee Dee was the one she worried about the most. She had never been a particularly happy young girl, and her teenage years had been especially painful. She had always been a little on the chunky side, and unlike the twins and Carter, who had inherited Lenore's perfect complexion, she'd had terrible acne all through high school. Each new pimple brought on a new set of histrionics. Almost every afternoon, Dee Dee would come home from school, run to her room, and fling herself across her bed in tears, because some boy hadn't spoken to her or she hadn't been invited to some party or something equally as devastating. Sookie had spent hours sitting with her, holding her hand, while she cried and sobbed about how terrible her life was. "Oh, Mother," she would sob. "You just don't know how it feels to be me. Everybody's always telling me how cute and darling the twins are. All my life, people have fallen all over them and just ignored me." Then, inevitably, she would wail, "Oh, Mother . . . why did you have to have twins? Why couldn't you have just *one* like a normal person!"

Sookie tried to explain. "I'm sorry, honey. It wasn't anything I planned. It just happened. It was a surprise to me, too. They are the first twins on either side of the family. It was just a fluke."

"Well, I hope you're happy! You've ruined my entire life. I will always be some ugly fat lump with bad skin that nobody wants." And so it went, on and on. She tried to give Dee Dee special attention and be patient with her, because, unfortunately, what she said was true. Whenever the girls went anywhere, especially when they were younger, people made a huge fuss over the twins and left poor Dee Dee standing there, having to listen to them ooh and aah about how absolutely adorable they were. It broke Sookie's heart to see her suffer so. And she did know how it felt. Growing up with Lenore, she had always felt like a little brown wren, hopping along behind a huge colorful peacock.

TUESDAY

The next morning, Sookie woke up early, prepared to try to solve her bird problem. Earle had just walked out the door when the phone in the kitchen started ringing, and she wondered who in the world was calling her so early. It couldn't be Lenore; she was on her way to water therapy at the senior center. Oh, dear God, please don't let it be Dee Dee saying she was moving back home. She knew she was having marital problems again and today's horoscope had warned her to "Expect the unexpected." Sookie looked at the phone with trepidation and read the number on the readout. It wasn't Dee Dee. It was that same area code as yesterday, probably the same phone solicitor, so she didn't pick up. She didn't have time to talk to anybody now. She had to concentrate on her bird-feeding plan. It was going to be tricky. She'd seen how those blue jays could go through all their food in just a matter of minutes, so she was going to have to move very fast.

Sookie quickly rinsed off the breakfast dishes and stuck them in the dishwasher, but whoever was calling wouldn't hang up, and it was distracting. They used to have an answering machine, but Lenore thought it was an open mike for her to speak into on any subject at any time and had left fifteen- and twenty-minute messages on it, sometimes in the middle of the night, so they had to get rid of it.

As she finished up in the kitchen, she debated whether to put the sunflower seeds for the blue jays in the front yard or the back. If she put the sunflower seeds in the front, someone driving by might see her and want to stop and talk, and she didn't have a second to spare. So she decided she would start at the back and run to the front. Her success depended on how long it would take the blue jays to finish the sunflower seeds before they discovered the bird seed in front and how fast she could run from one yard to the other.

But what shoes should she wear? She looked down and realized she shouldn't try and run in her flip-flops; it was too dangerous. She went to her closet and found nothing suitable—practically every shoe she owned had a little heel.

She went down the hall to the twins' bedroom closet and started rummaging through a box of their old shoes. She found a pair of worn-out pink sneakers with pom-poms. Unfortunately, they were two sizes too large, but they'd be better than trying to run in flip-flops and breaking an ankle.

She put them on and laced them up as tightly as she could and went out to her greenhouse and filled her two large ceramic polka-dotted bird seed containers, one with sunflower seeds and the other with the wild bird seed. She went out and placed the container with the wild bird seed on the side of the house, ready to be picked up as she ran by, headed to the front yard. She then went back to the greenhouse, picked up the container with the sunflower seeds, took a deep breath, and ran to the backyard, filling up the feeders as fast as she could.

After Sookie finished filling the feeders in the backyard, she dropped the container on the ground and ran to the side of the house and picked up the other polka-dotted seed container and was running toward the front yard when she stepped in a gopher hole and lost her left shoe. She couldn't stop so she just went on without it.

And of course, the very same moment she hit the front yard, the new Methodist minister and his wife were driving by the house and saw Sookie, wearing one pink shoe with tassels, hopping around on one foot, throwing seeds from a large polka-dotted container at her feeders. They slowed down and, as a matter of courtesy, were going to stop and say hello, but thankfully for Sookie, decided against it and quickly drove on. They were from Scotland and didn't know if running around wearing one pink shoe with tassels while carrying a large polka-dotted container and throwing seeds was some kind of Southern bird-feeding ritual or not, but they were afraid to ask.

Sookie's neighbor Netta Verp was sitting out on her side porch in her robe, having her morning coffee, when she suddenly saw Sookie flying around the yard like a bat out of hell, with her polka-dotted bird seed container, slinging seeds every which way, and she wondered what in the world she was doing. Netta had never seen anyone in such a hurry to feed their birds in her life.

After Sookie had filled all the front yard feeders, she ran back into the house and stood looking out the living room window, waiting to see if her smaller birds would come to feed. She waited, but none came. Where were they? There was not a bird to be seen anywhere. She then ran down the hall and looked out the kitchen window and saw the blue jays happily gobbling up all the sunflower seeds in back, while as usual, all of her smaller birds flittered around in the bushes below. Oh, no. Those little birds didn't know what was waiting for them in the front yard. Oh, Lord. She hadn't planned on this. Now she didn't know what to do. She ran out on the back porch and started waving her arms and yelling at the top of her lungs, "Go to the front, little birds—go around to the front! Hurry up, little birds!" But how do you communicate with birds? It was so frustrating. Now not only were her little birds not getting anything to eat; all those sunflower seeds seemed to have attracted every blue jay in the entire area, and more were flying in by the minute.

Netta observed her neighbor out on her back porch, jumping up and down and waving her arms around like a crazy person, and she didn't know what to think. It was certainly peculiar behavior. She just hoped poor Sookie hadn't flipped overnight, but with the Simmons family you never knew.

After a moment, Sookie ran back to the living room window to see if, by chance, any little birds were there, but now a whole new gang of big blue jays were in the front yard, eating all the bird seed. It was so frustrating. The only other thing she could think of to do was to get Carter's old baseball bat and run out and try to scare the blue jays off. But she didn't want to get reported to the humane society for cruelty to animals, especially since she was on the board. Oh, God, the phone was still ringing off the hook. Whoever it was must have her on some computer redial. Between the blue jays and the phone, she was getting a headache, so she went in and picked it up.

"Hello!"

The person on the other end seemed surprised that someone had finally answered and said, "Oh, hello! Ahh . . . to whom am I speaking, please?"

"Well, whom were you trying to reach?" asked Sookie, as she saw three more blue jays swoop in.

"I'm trying to locate a Mrs. Earle Poole, Jr."

"Yes, this is she." As soon as she said it, she knew she had made a mistake. She should have pretended she was the maid and said Mrs. Poole wasn't home. She was stuck now. As she stood watching more and more blue jays show up at the little birds' feeder, she suddenly remembered that old BB gun of Carter's in the closet and wondered if she could fire off just a few warning shots from the porch without being seen.

The man on the phone was asking another question. "Are you the former Sarah Jane Krackenberry?"

"Yes, I was . . . am." Sookie realized that the idea that she would even think about shooting a gun at a helpless bird was not her normal way of thinking, but those blue jays made her so mad—the way they pushed the smaller ones around.

"Was your mother's maiden name Simmons, middle name Marion, first name Lenore?"

"Yes, that's right."

"Did your family live in Brownsville, Texas, from the years 1942 to 1945?"

"Yes, uh-huh."

"Is the current mailing address for Mrs. Lenore Simmons Krackenberry 526 Bay Street, Point Clear, Alabama?"

"Yes, all her mail and bills are sent to me." Sookie was still thinking whether or not she should get Carter's old BB gun and try and scare the blue jays away, but decided not to. If she were to accidentally hit one, she would never be able to forgive herself.

"Is your zip code 36564?"

Peek-a-Boo walked over and rubbed up against her leg. Then it suddenly occurred to her: Maybe Peek-a-Boo would like a big fat blue jay for breakfast. She could let her out. But on the other hand, if Peek-a-Boo ran away and anything happened to her, Ce Ce would have a fit.

"Ma'am? Are you still there?"

"Oh, I'm sorry, what was it?"

"Is your current zip code 36564?"

"Uh, yes. That's correct. You have to forgive me. I'm a little distracted. I'm having a little bird problem at the moment." Sookie sat down, held the phone against her ear, and retied her pink sneaker. She felt a dull pain start up in her right ankle. Oh, no. She knew as soon as she had stepped in that gopher hole, she had twisted something. She just hoped it wasn't sprained. She needed to put ice on it right away, before it could swell up, and she also had to get the man off the phone, but in a nice way. "Sir, I'm so sorry, but I think I've sprained my ankle, so I'm going to have to hang up now."

"I see . . . uh . . . Mrs. Poole, one more thing before you go. Will you be home tomorrow between ten A.M. and twelve P.M.?"

"Pardon me?"

"Will you be at this address tomorrow?"

"Yes, I guess so. I might go to the travel agency later. Why?"

"We are sending a letter to Mrs. Lenore Simmons Krackenberry— and we need to know if you will be home to sign for it."

It suddenly occurred to Sookie that this was certainly a weird call. Why did this man want to know where she would be tomorrow and at what time? She began to get a little suspicious and wondered if he might be some sex pervert or a burglar. So she quickly said, "Yes, I will be home, and so will my husband, the police chief. May I ask where you are calling from?"

"I'm calling from Texas, ma'am."

"Texas? Where in Texas?"

"I'm in the Austin area."

"Austin, Texas?"

"Yes, ma'am. And Mrs. Poole, the letter should arrive at your address tomorrow, sometime between ten and twelve."

Now Sookie really was baffled. Why would anybody in Texas be sending Lenore a letter? "Is this from the Gem Shopping Network? Are they in Texas? Has she ordered more scatter pins? I hope not. She has over a hundred now."

"No, ma'am."

"Is it from Barbara Bush? My mother thinks they have a lot in common, and she's always writing the poor woman, asking her to come down for a visit. I said, 'Mother, Barbara Bush is far too busy to come all the way down here, just to go to lunch with you.'"

"No, ma'am, it's not from Mrs. Bush."

"Oh . . . well, is it a telephone bill? Has she called somebody and reversed the charges again? If so, I apologize in advance. We have a wonderful nurse watching her, but she must have turned her back for five minutes. Anyway, I'm so sorry, and tell whoever she's called that we will be happy to pay for it."

There was a pause, and then the man said, "Mrs. Poole, we have a registered letter we are sending out overnight, and I just need to confirm that someone will be home tomorrow who is authorized to sign for it."

Sookie's heart stopped. A *registered* letter! Oh, no. That always meant something legal. Sookie winced as she asked the dreaded question. "Sir, when you use the term, 'we,' are you by chance a law firm?"

"I'm sorry, Mrs. Poole, but I'm not at liberty to discuss it over the phone."

Oh, God, it must be something serious, if the man can't even discuss it over the phone. "Listen . . . I'm so sorry. What is your name?"

"Harold, ma'am."

"Listen, Harold, is it about some editorial she's written? She watches the news and gets herself all riled up, and she's always spouting off about something. But believe me, if my mother has made any threats against the government or said anything stupid, I can assure you that she's a perfectly harmless old lady. Well, harmless as far as not being armed or anything. She's just not quite right, if you know what I mean. It's a family trait. You just have to know the Simmonses. They are all a little off. She has a brother and sister that are really off. You have no idea how much trouble the woman has caused. She's almost eighty-nine years old, and she won't go to assisted living, and she refuses to let us put in a walk-in tub for her, and I worry to death about her falling and breaking a hip." She sighed. "I'm sorry to be so upset. It's just that my poor husband and I have just gone through four weddings, and my little birds won't go around to the front yard. I'm just being overrun by blue jays, and another lawsuit is just not what I need right now. My nerves are all a jangle as it is. Can't you tell me what it's about?"

"I'm sorry, ma'am. I'm not authorized to give out any information over the phone."

"Oh, please, Harold, don't drag this out. You don't know me, but I really could go off the deep end at any moment. It's the Simmons family curse. It hit Uncle Baby overnight. One day, president of a bank, and the next, off weaving baskets over at Pleasant Hill. And Aunt Lily was perfectly fine and then for no reason, she shot at the paperboy. Thank God, she didn't hit him or she could be sitting in jail right now, instead of where she is."

"As I said, Mrs. Poole, you will be receiving the letter in the morning."

"Oh, Harold, can't you just open it up and read it to me now? I don't need to know all the details, just how much she's being sued for. We just went through our entire retirement account for a down payment for a house for our daughter Le Le and her husband. He's perfectly nice, but he plays the zither for a living."

"Oh . . ."

"Yes . . . that's what we said. But she loves him, so what can you do? Anyhow, we are mortgaged up to the hilt. Can't you at least tell me how much my mother is being sued for, so I can be prepared? I won't tell anyone. I promise."

"I'm so sorry, ma'am, but I don't have the authority to do that. I was instructed to locate the current mailing address and send it on, that's all. This is not even my department. I'm just filling in."

"Oh, I see. Well, couldn't you just take one quick little peek and tell me if it's over a hundred thousand dollars?"

Then she heard his muffled voice, obviously whispering behind his hand, "Mrs. Poole, the wife and I just married off our daughter, so I know what you've been through. Don't worry, she's not getting sued."

"No? Oh, thank God! Oh, bless you, Harold. I don't know why, but with Mother, I always assume it's going to be bad news, but then again, it could be good news, right?"

Harold didn't say anything, so Sookie's mood suddenly brightened. "Hey, wait a minute. Did she win a contest or something? Are you from Publishers Clearing House? Should I have her over here at the house in the morning, dressed and made-up or anything? I need to know, because she'll want to have her hair done. Will there be photographs? Or news people?"

"No, ma'am."

"Oh . . . well . . . can you give me just a little hint of what to expect?"

There was a long silence on the other end, then Harold said, "Mrs. Poole, all I can say is . . . you are not who you think you are," and then he abruptly hung up.

Sookie sat there with his last words ringing in her ear, and now there was someone banging away on her back door. As Sookie stood up, her ankle throbbed even worse than before, but she hobbled down the hall and opened the door, and there stood Netta in her robe, who looked at her strangely. "Honey, are you all right? I saw you running around the yard like you were in some kind of distress. I tried to call you, but your line was busy. You left one of your shoes out in the yard." Sookie took the shoe and said, "Oh, thank you, Netta."

"Are you okay?"

"I'm fine, Netta. I was just trying something new with feeding the birds, and this man just called about some registered letter for Lenore and I think I've sprained my ankle. Come on in."

"No, I can't, I'm still in my robe. I better get back home, but call me if you need me."

A FEW SECONDS AFTER Netta left, Sookie went and looked out in the front yard to check on her birds and, to her dismay, saw that her entire yard was now a veritable sea of blue. It looked like she was running a blue jay reserve. She'd been so distracted by the phone call that she didn't know if the little birds had gotten anything to eat at all. Oh, drat. She would just have to try again tomorrow.

She hobbled back into the kitchen and put some ice cubes in a hand towel and wrapped it around her ankle. As she sat there with Peek-a-Boo in her lap, she thought more about the phone call and what the man had said. "You are not who you think you are." Then it suddenly dawned on her. That man had probably been calling from the Jehovah's Witnesses or some other religious group. They were always leaving pamphlets at her door asking, "Do you know who you are?" or "Do you know who your father is?" Oh, Lord. Now she felt like a fool. What a complete idiot she had been, telling him all that personal stuff about the family.

But on the other hand, knowing her mother, he could be calling from ancestor.com or some other genealogy-tracing company. She'd also seen ads for them that said, "Who are you?" or "Who do you think you are?"

The more she thought about it, she thought that it must be Lenore trying to trace the Simmons family line again. "I just know we're related to the royal family in some way. I just feel it in my bones," she said. For as long as Sookie could remember, she had been tracing and retracing, but so far, no connection. Now even Dee Dee was obsessed with it and had the Simmons family crest hanging over the mantel in her condo.

As the morning wore on, Sookie tried to relax and just forget about the call, but she was still feeling a little uneasy. It was the word "registered" that bothered her. She hated to call Earle at work but she dialed the number anyway, and his receptionist answered. "Dr. Poole's office, may I help you?"

"Hi, Sherry, it's me. Could you get him to pick up? I need to ask him a quick question."

"Sure, hold on. I'll buzz him. How's your mother?"

"Fine, thank you."

"Well, good. Hold on."

A few seconds later, Earle picked up. "Hi, are you okay?"

"I'm fine. I just need to ask you something."

"Honey, I'm right in the middle of a root canal."

"Okay, I'll make it fast. A man from Texas just called and said he was sending Lenore a registered letter tomorrow. Should I be worried? He said he wasn't a lawyer."

"Well, then, no."

"What do you think it's about?"

"Oh, I don't know. It's probably just some come-on, trying to sell something or get her to join something."

"Then I shouldn't worry?"

"No, just forget about it."

"But it's registered."

"Well, honey. Just don't sign for it."

"Isn't that against the law?"

"*No.* Just tell Pete you don't want it. That's all. Sweetie pie, I've really got to go. I'll see you at home, okay?"

"Earle, maybe . . . I just won't go to the door."

"Fine."

"But won't he leave a note and try and redeliver it?"

"Honey, do whatever you want. Don't go to the door or just sign for it and throw it away. It's probably just junk. Okay?"

"Then I shouldn't worry?"

"No."

"And I don't have to accept it."

"No. Forget about it. I gotta go. Love you."

Sookie hung up and smiled. Earle always knew how to make her feel better. Even her ankle felt better.

WEDNESDAY

June 8, 2005

Sookie woke up and planned her day. She decided that this morning she would try a slight variation on yesterday's bird plan and put sunflower seeds into every other feeder. She hoped the little birds would figure it out and eat a little while the blue jays were still at the sunflower seeds. Then after she fed the birds, she was going downtown to the travel agency and check out trips and cruises. A second honeymoon—what fun! Her brother, Buck, and his wife were always going on cruises, so yesterday afternoon she had called Bunny in North Carolina and asked her advice. Bunny said that Prague was "the new Paris," but Sookie hadn't seen the old Paris, yet. She hadn't really been anywhere, except to college and to the store and back, so anywhere Earle wanted to go would be fine with her.

At 8:10, Sookie had filled all the feeders and was out in the backyard in the pink tennis shoes, hiding behind a tree with her binoculars, when suddenly someone walked up behind her and tapped her on the shoulder. She nearly jumped five feet in the air. It was Pete, the mailman. "Oh, my God, Pete," she said. "You nearly scared me to death!"

Pete, a tall skinny man in gray shorts, said, "I'm sorry. I knocked on the front door, but you didn't answer." He then reached into his bag and said, "I have a certified letter for you, but first I have to ask you, 'Are you Mrs. Earle Poole, Jr.?' "

Sookie sighed. Pete had only been her mailman for the past thirty years. "No, Pete, I'm the queen of Romania. Of course, it's me. You know who I am."

Pete took his job very seriously. "Oh, I know who you are, but it's an official letter, and I have to ask. Do you have power of attorney to sign for Mrs. Krackenberry?"

"Yes. What I want to know," Sookie said, "is *why* you are here so early? Don't you usually start your deliveries on the other side of the pier?"

"Yes, but I thought the letter might be important, so I came here first. I just need for you to sign right here on this line."

"Oh, Pete, I'm sorry you came all this way, but I don't want to sign for it."

He was completely taken aback. "But . . . it's a registered letter."

"I know, but Earle said I didn't have to sign for it, if I don't want to."

"Oh . . . well . . . huh . . . I've never had this happen before . . . so I guess I'll just write out a first attempt slip and try again tomorrow, then."

"But I won't want it tomorrow, either."

"Well, officially, I'm required to make three attempts to deliver it."

"Pete, I don't want it. I don't even know who it's from."

"Huh . . . well, that's up to you. But it does seem a shame—somebody sure went to a lot of trouble and expense to make sure you got it. And it could be important. . . . It looks like it's some kind of medical records."

"Pete! I really don't want to know. Right now, I'm busy trying to plan a vacation. Did you know that Earle and I have not been any-where alone since 1970? And what makes you think it's medical records?"

"It's from the Texas Board of Health, so I just figured it had some-thing to do with health information."

"Texas Board of Health? How weird. What could they want?"

"I don't know," he said, looking at the large envelope. "Did some-one ever get sick in Texas or hospitalized for anything there?"

"No. I was born in Texas . . . but . . ."

"Well, there you go. Maybe it's an outstanding hospital bill or something."

"Oh, I can't imagine it could be a bill at this late date. You knew Daddy. He always paid his bills."

"Yeah, that's true. Maybe it's a refund."

"Fifty-nine years later? I don't think so."

"Well, if you're sure you don't want it, I'll just leave you the at-tempted delivery slip on the door and go on then."

"Okay, thank you, Pete. Sorry."

As soon as Pete walked away, Sookie looked out in the backyard. Once again, it was full of blue jays. Not one little bird to be seen. Her plan was clearly a failure—not only a failure, but she might have made things worse. She wouldn't blame the little birds if they all just packed up and never came back. And it was so sad, because they were her fa-vorites, and they didn't even know it.

LATER, AS SHE SAT in the tub, she tried her best to forget about the let-ter, but it was still on her mind. It wouldn't have been so hard if Pete hadn't waved it around in her face and hadn't blurted out who it was from. It was so irritating. All she had wanted to do today was relax and not have to think about any more problems. She knew the letter had something to do with her mother, but what? She couldn't imagine. Had Lenore been sick or hospitalized when she was living in Texas? She had never said anything. Was there something her mother didn't want her to know? Everyone always said how young and beautiful she looked for her age. Maybe she had had a major face-lift in Texas. Or she could have hit somebody and put them in the hospital. Lenore was a terrible driver, and she had run into almost everybody in Point Clear at one time or another. Or maybe she had had some sort of mental break, like Aunt Lily, and been committed at some point. Could Lenore have been in a mental hospital? Oh, dear.

By the time Sookie had dressed and put on her makeup, her imagination had completely run away with her. The next thing she knew, she was downtown at the post office with the pink slip and had picked up the letter and was on the way home with it. She never did make it to the bookstore or the travel agency. She stared at the envelope it on the seat next to her all the way home. Sure enough, it had TEXAS BOARD OF HEALTH written across it, and stamped in big black bold letters across the front was PERSONAL AND CONFIDENTIAL MATERIAL ENCLOSED.

At 5:15 that afternoon, Earle walked in the house. "Hi, sweetheart. I'm home."

"Hi, honey," she said, not giving him a chance to sit down. "Earle, I know you think I'm silly, but I've been waiting for you to come home all day. Would you sit with me while I open this letter?"

"What letter?"

"The registered letter."

"Oh. I thought you weren't going to sign for it."

"Well . . . I tried not to . . . but anyhow . . . I wanted you to be here."

He smiled at her. "Okay, sweetie. Let me fix a drink, and I'll be right there."

Sookie sat down on the sofa in the sunroom and waited until he came back in and sat down across from her. "Okay, open her up, and let's see what we got."

Sookie took a deep breath and opened it and read the cover letter.

Attention: Mrs. Lenore Simmons Krackenberry
c/o Mrs. Earle Poole, Jr.
526 Bay Street
Point Clear, AL 36564

Our office has received the following, and as requested, we are forwarding to your present address.

H. Wilson

The envelope attached was postmarked Matamoros, Mexico, and handwritten in an almost uneven and childlike scrawl. Sookie read the letter inside, which was in the same handwriting.

May 20, 2005

Dear Mrs. Krackenberry,

Hello. I am the daughter of Conchita Alvarez, who worked for you in Brownsville, Texas, during the war. I am sorry to say my mother passed away last spring at the age of eighty-five. When we were going through her things, we found these papers she was keeping for you. They look important. They look like you might need them. I do not know where you live. I am mailing them back to where they came from so they can send them to you. My mother liked you very much. She said you were so pretty.

Sincerely,

Mrs. Veronica Gonzales

"Oh, for heaven's sake," said Sookie.

"What?"

"A lady in Texas that used to work for mother died and her daughter found some of Lenore's old papers and is sending them back. Well, that's very sweet of her."

"What kind of papers?"

"I don't know, yet. Let me see." Sookie picked up another piece of paper.

The next thing Sookie knew, she was lying on the floor, and Earle was standing over her, fanning her with a newspaper.

"It's okay, honey, you just fainted. Just relax and breathe. Don't talk."

Lying on the floor beside her was what she had just read.

October 8, 1952

Dear Mrs. Krackenberry,

Due to the military's recent lifting of certain restrictions in the Children's Medical Privacy Act, and in reply to your request of January 6, 1949, we are now at liberty to release photocopies of your daughter's original birth certificate, including all birth mother medical records in our possession, up to the date of her adoption from the Texas Children's Home. We hope this information will assist you and your daughter's health care professionals in determining her risk of any hereditary conditions. Please contact this office if you have any further questions.

Sincerely,

Cathy Quijano

Director of Public Health Services

Please find enclosed the following:

Birth certificate
Medical records
Adoption papers

A few minutes later, Earle had helped Sookie to the couch, and she was lying there with a cold rag on her head, trying to comprehend what she had just read. All she remembered were the words "her adoption."

Earle came back with a brown paper bag for her to breathe into, and a glass of brandy. "Here, honey, drink a little of this." He looked very concerned and kept patting her hand.

"Did you read it?" she asked.

He nodded. "Yes, honey, I read it. What a hell of a thing to spring on somebody."

"But what does it mean?"

He picked up the letter and read it again. "Well, sweetie . . . I'm afraid it means just what it says. Evidently, you were adopted from the . . . here are the papers . . . the Texas Children's Home . . . on July 31, 1945."

"But Earle, that can't be true. It has to be a mistake."

Earle looked at the papers again and shook his head. "No, honey . . . I don't think so. It looks pretty official, and they have all the right information."

"But it has to be a mistake. I can't be adopted. I've got the Simmons foot and Daddy's nose."

"Well . . . maybe not."

"Why? What else does it say? I don't understand."

"Honey . . . just keep breathing, and let me look at this again." He sat there reading the papers while Sookie continued breathing into the brown paper bag, but she didn't like the look on his face.

"Well?" she asked, between breaths.

He looked at her. "Are you sure you're up for this? This is a lot of information to get in one day."

"Yes . . . of course, I'm sure."

"I'm not going to read anymore, unless you promise me you won't get too upset and faint again."

"I promise."

"Well . . . your medical records look good. You were a very healthy baby."

"What else?"

Earle picked up the birth certificate. "According to this, it says that your mother's name was Fritzi Willinka . . . and I think the last name is . . . it looks like Juraaablalinskie. Or something like that."

"What?"

He spelled it out.

"Good Lord! What kind of a name is that?"

"Uh . . . let's see. Oh, nationality of mother . . . Polish."

"What?"

"Polish."

"Polish? I don't even know anyone Polish."

"Hold on . . . it says . . . birthplace of mother . . . Pulaski, Wisconsin . . . November 9, 1918. Religion of mother: Catholic."

"Catholic? Oh, my God. What does it say about the father?"

Earle looked again and then said quietly, "Uh . . . it says here, father unknown."

"Unknown? How can it be unknown? What does that mean?"

"I'm not sure. It could mean a lot of things. Maybe she didn't want to say or . . . I don't know."

Then Sookie said, "Oh, my God, Earle . . . I'm illegitimate. I'm an illegitimate Catholic Polish person!"

"Now, honey . . . calm down. We don't know that. We can't jump to any conclusions."

"Well, Earle, if you were married to someone, he certainly wouldn't be unknown, would he? Did she even give me a name?"

"Wait a minute. Yes, here it is. Your birth name is . . . Ginger Jaberwisnske or however you pronounce it . . . and you were born at 12:08 P.M., October fourteenth, 1944, weight . . . eight pounds, seven ounces."

Sookie slowly sat straight up and said, "Earle, that's not right."

"What?"

"1944."

"Well, honey, that's what it says. October fourteenth, 1944. Look . . . there it is in black and white."

Sookie looked stricken. "Earle, do you know what that means? Oh, my God, I'm sixty years old! Oh, my God—I'm older than you are! Oh, my God!"

"Okay, honey, now just calm down . . . that's no big thing."

"No big thing! No big thing? *You* go to bed thinking you are a fifty-nine-year-old woman, and the next day, find out you're sixty!" Sookie felt the blood slowly begin to drain from her face. Earle caught her just before she fell off the couch and hit the floor again.

A few minutes later, after she had come to again and had had a little more brandy, Sookie, who almost never cursed in her life, looked at Earle and said, "And *who* in bloody hell are the Jerkalawinskies?!"

WHO INDEED!

Stanislaw Ludic Jurdabralinski had arrived in Chicago on January 5, 1909. During his first few years in America, he had worked hauling beer barrels for a local brewery and learned English at night. Sometime later, Stanislaw got a better job building the Chicago and North Western railroad that went from Green Bay, Wisconsin, through a small town called Pulaski.

At the time, Pulaski, Wisconsin, was a tiny village of Polish immigrants who had been lured there by a savvy German landowner. After purchasing the land, he had spread brochures throughout the predominantly Polish neighborhoods in Chicago, Milwaukee, and the Pennsylvania mining regions, hoping to sell plots of land to the large number of Polish immigrants wanting to establish a "little Poland" in America, complete with churches and schools. He had even named the town after Count Casimir Pulaski, the Polish nobleman who fought with the American patriots in the War for Independence, as an added incentive. When the first group of new landowners arrived in Pulaski, they found that the churches and schools the man had advertised in his brochures were yet to be built, so they got busy and built them.

In the year 1916, Stanislaw Jurdabralinski arrived in Pulaski, working for the railroad, laying tracks. While he was there, he boarded with a nice Polish family who had a pretty eighteen-year-old red-headed daughter. In a few weeks, when the railroad moved on, Stanislaw did not. He stayed and settled down in Pulaski with his brand-new wife, Linka Marie.

Stanislaw, never afraid of hard work and always in a hurry to make money, held down a job at the local sawmill in the daytime and one at the pickle-canning factory at night. On Sundays after church, he began studying to become a citizen of the United States. As he sat in their little rented room above Glinski's Bakery, studying the Constitution and the Declaration of Independence, he would get so excited and would read out loud to his wife. "Linka, listen to this. It says, 'life, liberty, and the pursuit of happiness.' Imagine that, Linka. Our country wants us to be happy . . . and you will be. As soon as I get rich, I'll buy you a fur coat."

Linka laughed. "We have to buy a house first."

"And after I become a citizen, I can say anything I want, and they can't arrest me, and I can buy a house, and they can't take it ever away from me never."

Linka corrected his English. "Away from me, ever."

"That's right. And I can own my own business, like Mr. Spierpinski. Oh, just think, Linka, from now on, all our children are going to be Americans, and our grandchildren and their children, too."

Linka, who at the time was two months pregnant with their first child, said, "Stanislaw . . . slow down, and study."

THE PROUDEST DAY OF his life was the day Stanislaw went to Green Bay to be naturalized as a U.S. citizen. As soon as he was sworn in, he immediately grabbed his wife's hand and ran over to the big courthouse next door so he could apply for his American passport. Linka, trying to keep up with him, asked, "Why do you need a passport so fast, Stanislaw? We're not going anywhere for a long time."

"I know," he said. "But when I get back to Poland, I want them to see how long I've been a citizen."

A few weeks later, when his passport finally arrived in the mail with his smiling photograph inside, he walked all around town, showing it to everyone he met. He would point to his height listed and ask, "Do you know who else was six foot four? Mr. Abraham Lincoln, that's who."

A few weeks later, Linka gave birth to their first child, a dark-eyed little girl with black curly hair they named Fritzi Willinka Jurdabralinski, who was her father's pride and joy. To Linka's dismay, he would sometimes come home from work, pick her up from her baby bed, and take her to town to the Tick Tock Tavern and show her off.

Two years later came a son they named Wencent Stanislaw Zdislaw Jurdabralinski, and then a year later, twin daughters. One was born a few seconds before midnight on May 31, and the other thirty seconds later on June 1, so they named the first Gertrude May and the other Tula June. Two years later, their youngest, another baby girl, Sophie Marie, was born.

The twins and their baby sister had red hair like their mother, and Wencent, who they nicknamed Wink, was a sturdy little blond boy. Stanislaw was proud of all his children, but his firstborn, Fritzi, remained the apple of his eye. When she was five, he put her up on his shoulders, and they walked up and down Main Street, showing everyone they saw the deed to the land he had worked so hard to buy. "Look at this," he would say. " 'Sold to Stanislaw Jurdabralinski, two acres of land.' So I own land now . . . what do you think?" People in town liked Stanislaw. He was always cheerful and was a good man and could be counted on.

A few years later, with a loan from the bank and the help of his friends, Stanislaw built a large two-story brick house with a big kitchen and a long, wide front porch. Within a few years, in order to make a little more money, Linka, who was a wonderful cook, started selling her Polish pastries and sausages to lunchrooms and catering for big church events, while raising her children at the same time. And it wasn't easy. Her eldest girl, Fritzi, was turning out to be a handful. Always on the go, jumping and running here and there, playing ball with the boys, hanging from trees, jumping off twenty-foot ladders on a dare, she was, in fact, a show-off. But in her father's eyes, she could do no wrong. He would laugh when Linka told him what Fritzi had done that day. Even when the nuns called them in to speak about Fritzi's habit of getting into fights with the older boys on the playground, Stanislaw, being a good Catholic man, had nodded and looked serious. But later, he had said nothing to Fritzi.

So, what if she was a little wild? He had a feeling this girl of his was going to be something one day. He knew Linka was hoping one of the girls would be a nun, but Stanislaw was fairly certain it would not be Fritzi.

MEANWHILE, BACK IN POINT CLEAR

Earle was still sitting with Sookie, trying his best to calm her down, but he was having no luck.

"Oh, Earle . . . my life is over. I'll never be the same as long as I live."

"Oh, honey . . ."

"I'm not who I thought I was . . . and I never will be again."

"I know it's a big shock. It was to me, too, honey. But let's try to look on the bright side."

"What bright side?"

"Well, for one thing, aren't you just a little bit glad that you are not a Simmons?"

"No, I'm not glad! At least when I was a Simmons, I knew who I was and what I had to worry about. Now I don't know who I am . . . or what I have to worry about. I feel like I've just been abducted by aliens." Sookie suddenly became short of breath and clutched her chest. "Oh, my God . . . I think I'm having a heart attack. Oh, my God . . . I'm going to die and never know who I am!"

"Sookie, just calm down. You are not having a heart attack. You are just fine."

"No, Earle, I'm not just fine. . . . I'm a stranger in my own home!"

Earle had her breathe into the paper bag for a few minutes, and she calmed down a little, but her heart was still pounding, and she still felt dizzy. She suddenly grabbed his hand. "Oh, Earle, now that you know I'm not me . . . will you stop loving me?"

"No! You're my wife, and I love you. You'll always be the same wonderful person you always were. Nothing has changed."

"How can you say that? Everything has changed. I'm an entirely different person than I was, even a few minutes ago."

"No, you're not."

"I am so! Yesterday, I was a Southern Methodist English person, and today, I'm a Polish Catholic person with an unknown father."

"Oh, honey, think about it. If you hadn't found out anything, wouldn't you still be the same person?"

"But I did . . . and now I know I'm not myself. How can I ever be myself again? I was never myself in the first place! And I don't know why you're so calm about it. You've been married to me all these years, and you have no idea who I am or who my parents were."

"Sweetheart, it doesn't matter. You're the one I'm in love with. Not your parents."

"But . . . what about the children? I could be the daughter of a criminal or a mass murderer. You don't know." Earle laughed. "It's not funny, Earle. You can laugh, but I'm the one with two complete strangers' genes running all through my body. I know about DNA, and it does matter."

"Oh, honey . . ."

"No, really, how would you feel if you didn't know who you were?"

"But, sweetie . . . we do know. It says right here that you are the daughter of Fritzi—I can't pronounce the last name—but that's who your mother was."

"Yes, but I don't know her. I wouldn't know who she was if I fell over her. She could be Doris, the tomato lady, for all I know!"

LATER, EARLE WAS FINALLY able to get Sookie to sit up and eat a little hot soup and a piece of toast, but she cried and blew her nose all through dinner. "I can't believe I'm not a Simmons. No wonder I've never been pretty."

"Sookie . . . you are very pretty."

"Not like Lenore . . ."

"No, in a different way . . . but just as pretty, if not more so. I don't know why you never believed me."

But Sookie was not listening. "I'm not even a Krackenberry. No wonder I was never as smart as Buck."

"Sookie, honey, you are smart."

"No, I'm not. I failed algebra three years in a row. How smart is that, Earle?"

After she had her soup, Sookie sat up for hours reading and re-reading the papers, feeling just like she was in the Twilight Zone. It all seemed so unreal. She knew that the baby girl with the strange name listed on the birth certificate was supposed to be her, but she still couldn't quite believe it. Earle felt terrible and kept walking in and out of the room, asking what he could do, but there was nothing.

At about three-thirty, Earle came in and insisted that she come to bed. But even after Earle turned off the light, her mind was still racing a mile a minute. They say when you are dying, your whole life passes before your eyes. She supposed that was what was happening to her now. Every time she tried to calm down and sleep, something else from her childhood flashed before her eyes, and she'd think about all the things she had done to try and please her mother, trying to be what Lenore thought a Simmons should be. Her hair had always been dark red and straight, and she remembered all those mornings when Lenore had tried to fix her hair for school and how she always looked at it with disappointment and would say, "You don't have an ounce of curl." She thought about those hours she had spent at the beauty shop, getting all those horribly smelly permanents, having her hair fried into one big red frizz, trying to please her mother, or else her mother would get discouraged and have it cut in a short straight bob with bangs. All her life, she had either looked like Little Orphan Annie or the little Dutch boy on the can of paint.

Lenore hadn't liked how dark Sookie's hair was, either, and at least once a week, would always look at it and say somewhat wistfully, "Of course, when I was your age, I was more of a strawberry blond. I don't know why your hair turned so dark. It was blond when you were a baby. . . ."

Sookie had even tried dying her hair strawberry blond, but it had turned a really unattractive shade of pink. She had spent a good part of her freshman year of high school with bright pink hair, long before it was fashionable to have bright pink hair. And for what?

Surely, this was just some terrible nightmare she was having, and she would wake up tomorrow, and things would be normal again. It just *couldn't* be true.

LIFE CONTINUES

In the years following World War I, the sleepy bucolic world of rural America was beginning to change, and a man named Henry Ford was to blame. When he invented the first Model T automobile, he put America on wheels, and as more roads were built and cars were improved, people who had never traveled farther than the outskirts of their own towns started traveling by the thousands. Roads couldn't be built fast enough, and suddenly, family motor trips were all the rage. Americans were of pioneer stock and naturally adventurous and soon began driving all over the country. And if they could have built roads across the ocean, they would have driven all the way to Europe and on down to South America.

New businesses started popping up all over the country: auto courts, tourist camps, hotels, motels, and restaurants to accommodate the traveler along the way.

In 1920, there were 15,000 gas stations in the entire country, but by 1933, the number had jumped to 170,000.

It was clear the automobile was the future, and what better business to get in than owning a gas station? Gas companies were selling franchises left and right. And Stanislaw Jurdabralinski had the perfect spot for a filling station, on the empty lot right beside his house. So using their savings and another loan from the bank, and after finishing a two-week course in service station management, Stanislaw received his Phillips 66 uniform, complete with hat and black leather bow tie, and soon, a brand-new twenty-four-hour full-service filling station opened in Pulaski.

Stanislaw was so proud to have a family business at last, but when they were naming the station, he thought Jurdabralinski's Phillips 66 was too long, so he just named it Wink's Phillips 66, after his son, who would inherit it someday.

The first night the station opened, when the pump topper with the big, round, illuminated glass globe lit up, the entire family stayed up for hours and watched it glow in the dark. Poppa, who would now be sleeping on a cot in the back of the station, flicked the neon OPEN ALL NIGHT light in the front window on and off for them to say good night.

From then on, their lives revolved around the filling station on the side of the house. The cheerful ding of cars and trucks coming into the station day and night meant that Poppa was busy, and that was good. Wink and the girls grew up playing with hubcaps, air hoses, old spark plugs, and rubber tires, and the smell of gasoline. It seemed like fun to them. By the time Fritzi was eleven and Wink was nine, they already knew how to change a tire and pump gas and make change at the cash register. Soon the Jurdabralinskis were simply known as the Gas Station Family. Every town had one . . . or soon would.

IN 1936, AFTER THE Depression had hit the country, it had been devastating, but the Jurdabralinskis did better than most, with milk and cheese from the nearby farms and eggs from the chickens that Momma kept in the backyard. And thanks to Wink, who had grown into a big, strong guy, who loved to hunt and fish, there was always food on the table.

Stanislaw had worked out a contract with the county to supply all the official vehicles—fire trucks, police cars, snowplows, and all the school buses—with gas and repair service, so when many stations across the country had been forced to close, Wink's Phillips 66 managed to stay open.

In the summer of 1937, life at the Jurdabralinski house was anything but depressed. Momma played in the Thursday night Ladies Accordion Band of Pulaski, and they practiced in the living room four nights a week. The younger girls were all in the school accordion band, so they played along as well, and on most afternoons, the boys and girls from the high school would gather upstairs in the huge third-floor attic with the big record player on a table in the corner and dance and play Ping-Pong.

Fritzi and her sisters were of an age when boys were always either hanging around the station or sitting on the front porch of the big two-story brick house next door.

Even Wink, who worked at the station with his father after school, had female admirers who would pile into their cars and drive over to watch and giggle as he walked around and did a full service on their cars, washing the windows, checking the oil, water, antifreeze, and battery, and filling up the tires. They usually had only enough money for a fourteen-cent gallon of gas, sometimes just a half gallon. One local girl, Angie Broukowski, who was younger than Wink, borrowed her father's car, and she and her friends seemed to come in more than usual, even when she didn't have money for gas. Poppa said Old Man Broukowski's tires had been checked more than any other car's in the state of Wisconsin.

But at the Jurdabralinski house, Fritzi was the main attraction for both the boys and girls. She had just graduated from high school, and in her senior year, she had been voted most popular, best dancer, most athletic, biggest cutup, and most likely to succeed. Fritzi was definitely the personality kid of Pulaski High. Poppa was proud of her, but Momma worried that if Fritzi didn't slow down for five minutes, she was never going to get a husband. If she wasn't swimming, she was bowling or skating all night at the Rainbow Skating Rink or running up and down the roads to see how fast some car would go or running to the movies, and if she wasn't doing that, she was busy smoking cigarettes. Momma found a half-full pack of Chesterfields hidden in her top drawer. And as usual, when he was told what his daughter was up to, Poppa just shrugged. "She's a modern girl, Momma. They all smoke." Momma hoped that in the fall, when Fritzi went to work at the pickle factory, she would settle down with one of the local boys, so she wouldn't have to worry about her so much. Momma had already said a novena and prayed to Saint Jude about it.

NOW WHAT?

———

THE NEXT MORNING, EARLE BROUGHT SOOKIE BREAKFAST IN BED AND sat down beside her and said, "Honey, do you want me to cancel my appointments and stay home with you today? I will. I just don't think you should be alone."

"No, I want you to go to work. I need to think this out and decide what I'm going to do."

"Okay, whatever you want . . . but call me and let me know how you're doing."

After Earle left, Sookie did fall asleep for an hour, but when she woke up, she was still so devastated, she couldn't get up. She called Netta and told her she had the flu and asked her if she would feed the birds. She lay in bed and cried all morning. She knew she had to talk to someone else about this—someone she could trust not to tell Lenore—so she rolled over and called her old college roommate, Dena Nordstrom, in Missouri. Dena picked up right away.

"Dena, it's Sookie."

"Sookie! Hello—"

"Thank God you're home. Oh, Dena, something terrible has just happened."

"Oh, no, has something happened to Earle?"

"No."

"The children?"

"No."

"Your mother?"

"No . . . it's me!"

"Oh, honey, what's wrong? Are you sick?"

"No," she sobbed. "I'm Polish!"

"What?"

"Oh, it's a long story . . . but . . . oh, Dena . . . this man from Texas called and said I wasn't who I thought I was and at the time, I thought I knew who I was. But yesterday, I got a letter and found out that I was adopted—that Lenore is not my real mother and Daddy is not my real daddy either. And not only that . . . I'm a year older than I thought I was. I'm not even a Leo. All my life, I've been reading the wrong horoscope."

"Wait a minute . . . are you sure about this?"

"Yes, I'm sure. October is Libra."

"No . . . no . . . about being adopted?"

"Yes, it's all written down. I have it right in front of me. It says that on July 31, 1945, Mr. and Mrs. Alton Krackenberry adopted a baby girl named Ginger . . . Jurdbberlnske or something or other Polish. Anyhow . . . that's me. Or who I was supposed to be. Anyway, my real mother was born in Wisconsin, and I'm probably a Catholic to boot. You know how quick they are to baptize."

"Oh, wow . . . oh . . . what does Lenore say about it?"

"I haven't told her."

"Oh . . . well, have you said anything to the kids, yet?"

"No, you're the first person, besides Earle, that knows, and I knew you, being married to a psychiatrist, would understand. I just feel so confused and betrayed. Lenore knew I wasn't her real daughter, and she went ahead and pushed me into all these things . . . and all under false pretenses. She always made me feel so bad because I wasn't just like her. And I wasn't just like her, because I wasn't just like her! And now, thanks to her, I've been a card-carrying member of the Daughters of the Confederacy since I was sixteen, and I'm not even a Southerner. I'm a Yankee. And, Dena . . . here's the worst part," she sobbed. "I'm not even a Kappa."

"What do you mean? Of course, you're a Kappa."

"No, I'm not. I'm a fraud. I can't go to the Kappa reunion. I'll just have to resign. The only reason I got in was because I was a legacy through Lenore. I'll have to turn in my pin and everything."

"Oh, don't be silly, Sookie, you're a Kappa because everyone loved you. I went through rush with you, remember?"

But Sookie wasn't listening and continued to ramble on. "Oh, my God. I even made my debut at the Selma Country Club under false pretenses. I told Lenore I didn't want to be a debutante, and she went ahead and let me make a fool of myself. What will people think when they find out I'm not a Krackenberry or a Simmons—that I'm an il-legitimate Yankee Polish orphan?"

"Wait a minute. What makes you think you are illegitimate?"

"Because . . . it's written on my birth certificate: father unknown."

"Oh . . . well, Sookie, people don't really care about that kind of thing, anymore."

"Well, I do. I'll feel like an imposter, like some kind of social climber. Oh, I could just die of shame. I'm looking at myself in the mirror right now, and I have turned beet red with shame."

"But why, Sookie? You didn't do anything wrong. What are you ashamed about?"

"Because you know me, I have always prided myself on being honest and open and then to find out you are a fraud—that your en-tire life has been one big lie? I can never hold my head up again. I'm sure I need serious medication. I'm probably having a psychic break right now. Is Gerry at home? I might need him to send me some pills. How much are they?"

"Oh, Sookie, honey, you're not having a psychic break. You've had a shock. That's all. I'm shocked. It's understandable that you are upset. I mean, my God . . . who wouldn't be? What does Earle think?"

"Oh, he's being very sweet about it . . . but I'll tell you who is going to have a fit when she finds out: Dee Dee. She's always running out to the cemetery to help decorate Great-Granddaddy Simmons's grave . . . and then to find out the man is a total stranger. Oh, my God. And Dena, no wonder I didn't get Lenore's nose. I didn't get Daddy's nose, either. I got a total stranger's nose. I don't know why I thought I looked just like Daddy. I went through the photo albums last night, and I don't look a thing like any of them. I didn't get the Simmons foot. I got the Jaberwisnski's foot!"

"Well, what are you going to do now?"

"I don't know. I just feel all wicky-wacky. I'm just thrown for a loop and back. I can't even think about what to do. What can I do at this late date? I should have been told this when I was six, not sixty. All those Polish people I'm related to are probably all dead by now. And who would name their child Ginger? We had a golden retriever named Ginger. Anyhow, it's very upsetting."

"I know it is. And as upsetting as it is right now, you always told me you never wanted to be like your mother, and you're really not. Isn't that kind of good news?"

"That's what Earle said. And I guess it is, but right now, I feel like I've been hit by a train. Why couldn't I be a year younger? But no. Yesterday, I was only fifty-nine, and today, I'm already sixty, going on sixty-one! No wonder I look so old and tired. I am! I'm the world's oldest living orphan. Oh, God, how embarrassing. I feel like walking out and jumping off the end of the pier."

"Sookie, do you want me to come down there and be with you? I will. Just say the word."

"Oh, that's so sweet, but no, there's nothing anybody can do. I'll just have to figure this out by myself."

"Well, all right, but in the meantime, you won't do anything foolish, will you?"

"No, I've got to get Carter married and settled before I do anything foolish."

"Sookie, this is a lot to handle by yourself. Maybe it would be a good idea to seek out a professional to help you through this."

"Well, you're the lucky one. You married a psychiatrist. I married a dentist."

"Would you like me to ask Gerry to try to find someone for you?"

"No. This is not the kind of thing I would talk to a stranger about."

"But, Sookie . . . that's the point."

"Well, I'll think about it, but right now, I really don't want to tell anyone but you."

"All right, but I want you to call me and let me know what's going on, okay?"

"I will."

After she hung up, Dena thought about just getting on a plane and going down to Alabama, but Sookie had said she wanted to try and work it out by herself, and maybe she was right. Dena knew Lenore and had always gotten a big kick out of her, but she had also felt kind of sorry for Sookie, and finding out that she was adopted was going to be hard. Sookie had always viewed herself through Lenore's eyes. No matter how many times Dena had tried to tell her, Sookie had never understood what a great gal she was on her own. She had been one of the funniest and best-liked girls on campus, but she had never quite believed it. Everybody seemed to love Sookie but Sookie.

AFTER SOOKIE HAD SPOKEN to Dena, she realized that Peek-a-Boo needed to be fed, so she got up out of bed and went downstairs. As she opened a can of tuna, she thought about what Dena had advised. She was probably right, but there was only one psychiatrist in Point Clear, and it was obvious that Dr. Shapiro had never practiced in a small town before. His office was right next to the Just Teazzing hair salon, and you couldn't go in or out without everyone seeing you. She certainly couldn't go, or it would be all over town in less than five minutes.

Even Mobile was not far enough away for that, thanks to Lenore knowing so many people. At one time or another Winged Victory had been the chairman of every committee known to man, and was a clubwoman to the bone. If they didn't have one she liked, she started one, and she was always elected president. But as Netta said, "Lenore's damned good at running things, so why not?" Netta was right, of course. The woman seemed to have been born with a gavel in her hand.

The rest of the day, Sookie kept catching glimpses of herself in the mirror. She knew she looked the same on the outside. She walked and talked like the same person. But she didn't know who or what she was on the inside.

Finally, she called Earle, who came to the phone right away. "Earle, my ears are ringing. Does that mean I'm going to have a stroke? I feel like I might be having a stroke."

"No, honey, it's just stress."

"Yes, but my heart is racing. I could be having some kind of attack. Should I call an ambulance?"

"No, you're fine. Just breathe, sweetheart. Listen, my last patient cancelled, I'll be there as soon as I can."

She sure was glad to see him when he walked in the door. Later, she managed to fix dinner, but she still felt disoriented. Earle didn't leave her side.

When they got in bed, she tried to sleep, but she tossed and turned all night. Even Peek-a-Boo got fed up and went over to Earle's side of the bed. But she couldn't help it. All she could think about was that person she used to be . . . that woman in the mirror.

Earle finally rolled over and said, "Honey, it's four-twenty. Close your eyes, and get some sleep."

"I will, but Earle, are you sure I'm not having a heart attack? I can still hear it beating. Here, can you feel it? Shouldn't I go to the emergency room?"

Earle felt her heart and patted her hand. "No, baby, it's just anxiety. Try to get some sleep, and you'll feel better. I promise you."

Earle was right. After a few minutes, her heart did slow down. Thank God she had married Earle. He had been her strength and her rock through thick and thin. But with Lenore, even that hadn't been easy.

After she graduated from high school, her grades had not been good enough to get into a top college like Lenore had wanted, but not to be deterred, at the last minute, Lenore had pulled some strings with an old Kappa sorority friend of hers, and two weeks later, Sookie had been sent off to Southern Methodist University in Dallas with a new wardrobe and a note in her pocket.

Sookie, Dear,

If you can't be smart, be perky. Men love a happy girl, and date, date, date! Men love a popular girl.

Love,

Mother

The minute she hit SMU, she started rush week and, thanks to her being Lenore's legacy, had pledged Kappa right away. And, per her mother's instructions, she joined almost everything else in sight, as well. And God knows she had dated morning, noon, and night. By her sophomore year, she had almost wrecked her health trying to be popular, and it didn't help matters when her roommate, Dena Nordstrom, was voted the most beautiful girl on campus. All Lenore ever said after that was, "Oh, Sookie, why can't you be more like Dena? That girl is going to make something of herself." And as Lenore had predicted, Dena left college early and became one of the first female newscasters on television, while Sookie still struggled to make a passing grade.

At Christmas during her senior year at SMU, she had come home a complete nervous wreck and sick as a dog. And then two weeks later, when she had informed her parents that she was going to marry Earle Poole, Jr., from Selma, Lenore had thrown a complete fit.

The Pooles were a perfectly nice family. Earle's father was a doctor. But unfortunately, all the Poole men had big ears that stuck out a little on the side. "If you don't care about me, think of your future," Lenore had cried, waving her handkerchief in the air. "Those ears may be fine on a boy, but dear Lord in heaven, Sookie, think of those ears on a girl! You can't hide a thing like that. I've waited all my life to have granddaughters to dress up and to have their portraits painted, and I certainly don't want the Poole ears in the picture!"

Lenore had then flung herself onto the sofa sobbing. "I don't understand you. With your family background, you could have anybody you wanted. I sold my soul to get you into Kappa, so you would only meet the very nicest boys from the finest families, and this is how you reward me? By marrying Earle Poole, Jr.? Some dental student with big ears? Someone you went to grammar school with? Oh, why did your father and I bother to spend all that money on your debut and college? When I think of all those contacts wasted, oh, I just can't bear it. I feel like getting Granddaddy Simmons's sword off the wall right now and just falling on it."

It was usually at this point that Sookie had always given in to her, but probably because she was sick and still had a high fever, for the first time in her life, Sookie had stood her ground.

"Mother, I know you don't want to hear this, but I couldn't have married any boy I wanted. Don't you think I tried to find someone you would approve of? I dated everybody that asked me out. I had six dates in one day. Do you know how hard it is to be perky six times a day? I'm not pretty like you, Mother. The boys didn't fall all over me like they did you. I can't do it anymore. Earle loves me just the way I am, and no, we are not perfect. He has big ears, and I'm not smart or beautiful, and if you can't bear it, I'll go and get the sword, and you can do what you want with it. But I am going to marry Earle Poole, Jr."

Lenore had been so stunned at her daughter's sudden strength that she stared at her for a moment. Then she sat up and said, "Well, I can see that you are becoming more like your father every day." She sniffed a wounded little sniff. "This stubborn streak is certainly not from my side of the family. And if you refuse to listen to reason, there's nothing more I can do, but when you give birth to Howdy Doody, don't say I didn't warn you."

She had married Earle, but she had never heard the end of it. After Dee Dee, their first girl, was born, as Sookie was being taken back to her room, she had heard Lenore from all the way down the hall, standing at the hospital nursery window and wailing at the top of her lungs, "Oh, my God, Alton, she has the Poole ears! I knew it! I just knew it!" Unfortunately, the Pooles, who were in the waiting area around the corner, had heard Lenore as well. After that, family holidays were never pleasant.

When she told her mother she was expecting again, Lenore's reaction had been less than enthusiastic. "Oh, no," she sighed. "Well, let's just hope and pray it's a boy."

Eight months later, as Sookie was being rolled down the hall, exhausted and groggy from delivering not just one, but two more, baby girls, Lenore had come up alongside the gurney and whispered to her, "Mother doesn't want you to worry. I've checked into it, and my friend Pearl Jeff knows the very best plastic surgeon in New Orleans. She says it's a simple little procedure, and who's to know the difference?" My God . . . if Earle had not stepped in and stopped it, she might have let Lenore push her children into plastic surgery!

* * *

As for Earle, he had loved Sookie all through grammar school, and they had dated a little in high school, but he knew her mother had higher hopes for Sookie's future than him. So when Sookie had gone off to SMU, he had more or less given up.

But that Christmas in 1966, when he heard she was home for Christmas and was sick in bed, he screwed up his courage and went over to see her. Lenore had come to her door and begrudgingly let him in. "You can only stay for a short while, Earle, she needs her rest."

"Yes, ma'am."

Sookie had been propped up in bed, dozing on and off all day, when she thought she heard a knock on her door. A second later, there stood Earle Poole, Jr., wearing a blue suit and holding a bouquet of flowers and a box of candy. He said, "Hi, Sookie. I heard you were home, and I just wanted to say hello." The minute she saw him, Sookie suddenly burst into tears. He looked so goofy standing there in that bow tie and that bad haircut. She had always liked Earle, but it wasn't until that moment that she began to love him.

POINT CLEAR, ALABAMA

Friday, June 10, 2005

THE NEXT MORNING, WHILE SOOKIE WAS FEEDING PEEK-A-BOO, THE phone rang, and Sookie almost jumped out of her skin. She looked to see if it was Lenore calling. If it was, she would not pick up, but she saw that it was Ce Ce calling from her honeymoon at Callaway Gardens in Pine Mountain, Georgia.

"Hi, sweetheart," she said as cheerfully as she could possibly manage.

"Hi, Mother, how are you?"

"Oh, just fine, honey."

"I just called to let you know that we got here safe and sound, and we are just loving it. How's Dad?"

"Just wonderful."

"Is Peek-a-Boo giving you any trouble?"

"No, not at all. She's right here, honey, having her breakfast, and we're having a good time."

"Oh, great. Well, I love you. Tell Dad hey."

"Okay, darling. We love you. Have fun, and we'll see you when you get home."

After she hung up, she realized that at some point, she was going to have to tell the children that their grandmother was not really their grandmother. But it certainly wasn't the kind of thing you would tell someone on their honeymoon.

That afternoon, she took her binoculars upstairs and waited until she saw Lenore heading out to the end of the pier with her tea cart to have her usual five o'clock cocktails with her Sunset Club friends. Sookie then called Lenore's nurse, Angel, and told her that she had just come down with a terrible flu that the doctor said was highly contagious and could be fatal to older people, and he had advised her not to get anywhere near her mother for at least two weeks. She felt terrible about lying to Angel, but at this point, she didn't care if she ever saw or talked to Lenore again.

Just seeing Lenore from a distance was upsetting. All she really wanted to do was go downstairs and pull out a bottle of vodka and drink the entire thing. She thought about it, and it was very tempting, but she also had a big fear of becoming completely unruly and disgracing her husband and children in public. Unfortunately, she had always had a tendency to fall apart under stress and do something stupid. At her coming-out party, she had been so nervous, she had way too much to drink, and at the formal dinner afterward, she wound up flipping ice cream across the table with a spoon and had hit a good friend of her mother's in the back of the head. That same night, she had stepped on an olive and had skidded across the dance floor and wound up under someone's table.

And it wasn't just alcohol. In college, she had been heartbroken when some boy didn't ask her to the big fraternity party, and she had eaten two dozen Krispy Kreme doughnuts she had pilfered from the Kappa house kitchen pantry. Her roommate had come back from a date and found her passed out in the bed with a half-eaten jelly doughnut still stuck in her hair.

And she had always been accident prone. Coming down the aisle at her own wedding she had somehow managed to trip over her wedding veil, and she was the only person she knew who had broken a leg falling off a merry-go-round that was standing still at the time. Why Lenore ever thought she could become a ballerina was still a mystery to her.

As Sookie sat in her bed petting Peek-a-Boo, something suddenly occurred to her. All those years of feeling bad about herself, and it might not even be her fault! Polish people might not even be good dancers.

EARLE HAD BEEN ALMOST as surprised at the news as Sookie was, but driving to work that next day, he suddenly remembered a conversation he had once had with Sookie's father. And thinking back now, he wondered if Mr. Krackenberry had been trying to tell him in a round-about way that Sookie was adopted.

That night, Earle and his future father-in-law had just escaped the huge engagement party given for them at the country club and had gone out to the back patio overlooking the golf course to have a smoke.

As they stood there listening to the crickets, Mr. Krackenberry, a tall distinguished-looking man, had felt sorry for the boy. He could tell that Earle was scared to death of Lenore, but to his credit, Earle had hung in there, even after Lenore had thrown such a fit and continued to stare at his ears.

After a long moment, Mr. Krackenberry had cleared his throat and said, "Earle."

"Yes, sir?"

"You and Sookie are about to take a mighty big step. However, before you do, there's something about her that you should know."

"About Sookie?"

"Yes . . . and it could make a difference about how you feel."

Earle took a deep breath and faced him. "With all due respect, sir, I know her mother doesn't approve of me, but there's nothing you could tell me about Sookie that would make me change my mind. I love her, and I intend to marry her."

"I'm glad to hear it, son . . . but . . . how can I put this? You've heard the old saying, 'If you want to know what your wife will be like in twenty years, just look at the mother'?"

"Yes, sir. I've heard that . . . but I still love her. Oh, no offense, sir."

"No, none taken. And I assume you're aware that my wife has a brother and sister at Pleasant Hill and the family history."

"Yes, sir. Sookie told me."

"Ah . . . and so, naturally, you might have some concerns about

Sookie and any future children. But, if I were you . . . I wouldn't worry about it."

"Oh, I don't. Why?"

"Do you trust me, son?"

"Yes, sir."

"And do I have your word as a gentleman that this conversation will never be repeated to anyone—especially to Sookie's mother?"

"Yes, sir."

"Well, then . . . don't ask how I know, but I give you my word. Sookie is not a thing like her mother, or any of the Simmonses, for that matter. Do you understand?"

"Yes, sir. I think so. Oh . . . wow . . . well, that's a relief."

"Yes, I thought it would be."

"Oh, no offense, sir."

He laughed. "Again, none taken. I realize that Lenore may seem a little odd to you now and then, but I'll tell you, son . . . to me, she's still the most beautiful girl in the world. I haven't had a dull moment since the day I met her."

At that very moment, Lenore had whisked out on the porch in a tizzy, scarves flying behind her, and called out, "Alton . . . where are you? Oh, there you are. I need you. We have a tragedy. I just dropped my good ring in the punch. I just pray no one's swallowed it. It was Great-Grandmother's! Hurry!" Mr. Krackenberry looked at Earle and said, "See what I mean?" and started rolling up his sleeves as he followed Lenore back inside.

It's funny, but somehow, after that conversation, Earle had not worried about Sookie, nor had he ever really questioned what Mr. Krackenberry knew. But now he understood what the man had been trying to tell him.

THAT NIGHT, WHEN EARLE came home, he told Sookie about the conversation he'd had with her father at their engagement party.

Sookie was surprised. "Why didn't you tell me this before?"

"Well, honey . . . to tell you the truth . . . I just forgot."

"You *forgot*? Earle, do you have *any* idea how many sleepless nights I've spent wondering if I was going to wind up at Pleasant Hill?"

"No."

"No . . . you didn't! Because I didn't want to worry you. And now I find out you were never worried in the first place. I even wrote you and the children a good-bye letter with instructions, and now you say, 'I *forgot?*'"

"Well, honey, I also gave your father my word as a gentleman not to say anything. And he didn't tell me *why* you were not like Lenore."

"But why didn't Daddy ever tell me?"

"I guess he thought it would be better for you not to know."

"I wonder if Buck knows I'm adopted. I wonder if he knew all along and didn't tell me—"

"Oh, I would doubt it, honey . . ."

Now Sookie was even more shook up. What *else* did she not know that nobody had ever told her?

It was all so strange, and none of it made any sense. Buck was clearly related to Lenore, and yet, growing up, Lenore had always looked at him like he was something that had just dropped out of a tree. Whenever he would run through the house, she would exclaim, "Who is that odd creature that just ran through my living room with filthy feet? Surely, it can't be related to me!" Lenore had always paid much more attention to her than she had to Buck. And Sookie had always felt somewhat guilty about it. She had even asked Buck if he didn't resent her because of it, and he had said, "Are you kidding me? I'm just glad she has you to push around and not me." But why had she pushed her so hard? Was it because she was a girl? Lenore always said, "Men are necessary up to a point, but women are the natural leaders in society and in the home." Or was Lenore trying to make her into something *she* was not? Had Lenore almost wrecked Sookie's life just so she would look good?

Sookie realized she shouldn't be upset with Earle about not telling her about the conversation with her father. He thought he was doing the right thing at the time, and she could see he just felt terrible about it. But she was still confused about what she should do now, or if she should do anything at all.

WINK'S PHILLIPS 66

1937

Besides Wink Jurdabralinski, the six-foot blond dreamboat who filled your tank and cleaned your windshields, there was another reason Wink's Phillips 66 had more than its share of female customers. Clean restrooms! Momma had been ahead of the national mind-set on that score.

At the beginning, the care and maintenance of the station was mostly a male-dominated affair and as a result, most filling station restrooms were poorly maintained. The sinks and toilets were rarely cleaned, and the floors were usually filthy. As one horrified woman said upon leaving one in Deer Park, Michigan, "You could grow a garden in the dirt on the floor in there!" Women rarely felt safe using one and did so only in emergencies.

But at Wink's Phillips 66, Momma always insisted that both the men's and women's restrooms were kept as clean as the bathrooms inside her home. All four girls took turns making sure there was a fresh cake of white soap on the basin and a clean white towel, and that each customer that walked in would be greeted with gleaming white sinks and toilets and a white tile floor that had just been scrubbed with Lysol. A germ would not stand a chance at Wink's. All day long, you would see one of the Jurdabralinski girls scurrying to and from the house with a pail and scrub brush and a towel over her arm. Naturally, there were squabbles about whose turn it was to clean, but it was always done. Wink and Poppa and the other mechanics were never allowed to use the customers' bathrooms. "I don't want you and your greasy hands getting everything all dirty," Momma said.

As more and more women and girls were starting to drive cars, the gas companies finally caught up and started to compete with one another for female customers. A well-known nurse and nationally known health lecturer, Matilda Passmore, had said, "What better way to lure them into the stations than offering them a clean bathroom?" Texaco formed the White Patrol and maintained a fleet of White Patrol Chevrolets that carried trained cleanliness inspectors around the country looking for dirt in every corner. Texaco station owners hoped to pass inspection and win a White Cross of Cleanliness award and be allowed to add to their sign the words REGISTERED RESTROOMS. Soon, another company started sending out a group known as the Sparkle Patrol. And Phillips Petroleum Company, not to be outdone, came up with its own cleanliness campaign and hired a crew of attractive young registered nurses known as Highway Hostesses, dressed in light blue uniforms, white shoes and stockings, and a smart military-styled hat. Phillips executives hoped the Highway Hostesses would promote goodwill for the company by their "courteous manner, pleasing personality, and willingness to aid anyone in distress." They also gave directions, suggested restaurants and hotels, and found time to discuss infant hygiene with traveling mothers.

The hostesses started roaming the highways and byways in large cream-colored sedans with dark green fenders and the Phillips 66 logo on the door. Their job was to make sure each Phillips 66 bathroom lived up to the standards of Certified Restrooms. Unfortunately for the filling station owners, they picked stations for inspection at random, so you never knew when one might show up, a further incentive to "keep 'em clean" at all times.

WINK SAW IT FIRST. And as the huge cream-colored sedan with the dark green fenders quietly drove up and turned into the station, it might as well have been a shark. Wink felt the hair on the back of his head stand up. He blinked to make sure he was not seeing things, but no—it was real all right, and it looked exactly like the photograph in the Phillips 66 magazine. He walked over and asked, "May I help you, miss?"

The woman with a long, pointy nose said, "Yes, young man, I'd like to speak with the owner. Tell him that Registered Nurse Dorothy Frakes is here for restroom inspection."

"Yes, ma'am," he said and ran in the back and got Poppa.

Gertrude May, who happened to be looking out the window of the second floor, saw it next. "Oh, geez," she said and started running downstairs to get her twin sister, Tula June, and Momma.

By the time Momma looked out the kitchen window, the woman was out of the car, and Poppa was already talking to her. Momma had never been nervous before, but when she saw how official the woman looked, standing there in her crisp uniform, holding her clipboard under her arm, she suddenly panicked. "Oh, dear Blessed Mother of God," she said. "Whose turn was it to clean last?"

"Fritzi's," said the youngest girl, Sophie Marie, and Fritzi could have killed her.

"Oh, no!" Now Momma was really scared. Fritzi was terrible at cleaning. Momma grabbed her by the shoulders. "Fritzi, look at me. Did you remember the soap?"

"Sure, I did."

"Did you scrub the sink?"

"Yes, and it wasn't all that dirty anyway."

Momma looked out at Poppa, still standing there doing a lot of nodding. What was he saying? Then, suddenly, the nurse briskly turned on her heel and marched toward the women's bathroom with her clipboard held high, like she was headed for battle.

In the windows of the house, five pairs of eyes were fixed on the door, waiting for the nurse to reappear, but after several minutes, she still had not come out. Momma twisted her apron. "Oh, I wonder what's taking her so long?"

Tula June said, "Maybe she had to go to the bathroom or something."

Another minute went by and then they got a quick glimpse of her leaving the women's bathroom and entering the men's room. Momma said, "Sophie Marie, go and get my rosary. I'm a nervous wreck."

A short while later, Momma was still staring at the station and working her beads when the nurse came out of the men's room and spoke to Poppa. Again, there was lots of nodding, and he kept looking over and pointing at the house. "Oh, geez . . . what's he doing . . . for gosh sake," said Momma.

The nurse turned and walked over to the house, climbed up the steps, and knocked on the door. Sophie said, "She's at the door, Momma. Should we hide?"

."No, no—just stay where you are, girls," she said, as she took her apron off and smoothed her hair. She took a deep breath and opened the door.

"Are you Mrs. Jurdabralinski?"

"Yes, I am."

"Hello, I'm Nurse Dorothy Frakes from Phillips Petroleum. Congratulations on having scored a perfect 100 and having the cleanest restrooms I have ever had the pleasure to inspect. Why, you could eat off the floor in there, Mrs. Jurdabralinski, and so, at this time, I would like to personally present your official Certified Restroom emblem."

Momma was so overwhelmed, she burst into tears while Fritzi nattered in the background. "One hundred. I told you so. Ha-ha-ha," Fritzi said. "I don't know why people don't believe me."

After that day, Registered Nurse Dorothy Frakes became just plain Dottie, and the whole family loved it when she stopped by. She never bothered to inspect the bathrooms again. She just liked to go to the house and sit down, put her feet up, smoke a cigarette, relax a bit, chat with Momma and find out how all the girls and Wink were doing, and then head on out on her appointed rounds. "I'll tell you, Linka," she said one day. "I know being a Phillips Highway Hostess may seem glamorous to a lot of people, but it can get mighty monotonous at times. If you've seen one bathroom, you've seen them all. And if it weren't for nice people like you, I'd turn in my uniform tomorrow."

THE NEXT DAY

SATURDAY, JUNE 11, 2005

SOOKIE DECIDED TO CLOSE ALL THE SHADES AND LOCK ALL THE DOORS, and other than feeding Peek-a-Boo, she stayed upstairs. Her nerves were so on edge, every time the phone rang, her heart would start to pound, especially when she saw it was Lenore's number, so she finally took the phone off the hook.

At around twelve-thirty, she went downstairs. Lenore had her DAR meeting from twelve to one, so she was safe on that account. She was headed back upstairs when suddenly the doorbell started ringing. She heard someone calling out her name, and it wasn't Lenore. It was Marvaleen. Oh, Lord . . . just what she didn't need right now—a visitor.

She went over and unlocked the door and said, "Hi, Marvaleen."

"Oh, there you are. I was just about to leave. I was on my way to yoga, and I thought I might take a chance on finding you at home." Then Marvaleen looked at her intently and asked, "Sookie, do you get colonics?"

"What?"

"Colonics."

"No . . . I don't know what it is."

"They're like a very high-powered enema."

Sookie made a face. "Oh, Lord . . ."

"Oh, no, Sookie!" she said. "I've already had six high colonics, and I've never felt better in my life. Edna Yorba Zorbra says that before you can ever move forward with your emotional healing, having a clean colon is absolutely necessary. It's all part of learning to release the old negativity you've been holding on to."

"I see."

"Anyhow, I go to this terrific gal in Mobile." She opened her purse. "Let me give you her card. I'm telling everybody I know about her. And when you do call, be sure and tell her that I recommended you. She's giving all my friends a ten percent discount and a fifty percent discount on a series of ten. And you really need ten. Hey, maybe we can go together sometime . . . and then have lunch afterward. Call me."

"Oh, okay, Marvaleen. I sure will." She took the card and waved good-bye to her friend, but she couldn't imagine anything more she would rather not do than have a high-powered enema and then lunch with Marvaleen afterward. She would just stick with her two table-spoons of sugar-free orange-flavored Metamucil at night.

Marvaleen had always been somewhat of a spiritual seeker and was still seeking. Ten years ago, she had talked Sookie into going to a women's Bible study group, and Sookie had gone through a very short born-again period. She had been so happy, but Lenore had been hor-rified. "My stars, Sookie . . . you can believe in God, but you don't have to go around town telling everyone! You're embarrassing the fam-ily. The next thing I know, you will be handling snakes and speaking in tongues!" Eventually, Sookie told Marvaleen and the group she couldn't come anymore. She still went to church and still believed in something, she guessed, but she wasn't sure what.

But now after what had just happened, she wasn't sure of any-thing. She had always just assumed that a person's life was planned out somewhere, and that someone was in charge and paying attention. But the more she thought about it, the more Sookie came to realize just how random the events in her life had been. And in her particular case, alarmingly precarious!

As a baby, she had been just like some cat or dog at the pound put up for adoption, and the people in charge of her had quite obviously given her to a crazy person. Don't they check people out first, before they just hand over a baby? If they had known about Lenore's brother and sister, surely they would have found someone else. Sookie had a good mind to call those people in Texas and tell them they should have been more careful.

It was particularly upsetting when she realized that throughout her entire life, her every move had been controlled by Lenore saying, "Oh Sookie, a Simmons would never do this" or "a Simmons would never do that." She had no idea what a Jurdabralinski would or would not do.

She knew everybody had to have a mother, they even gave poor little motherless monkeys a ticking clock wrapped in a towel as a substitute. But now, thinking back on her life with Lenore, she wondered if she wouldn't have been better off with just the clock.

NEVER THE SAME AGAIN

It's funny how one event can change the entire course of a family's future. For the Jurdabralinski family of Pulaski, Wisconsin, that event took take place on August 9, 1938.

In the 1930s, hero worshipping and movie star crushes were in full bloom. Pictures of glamorous movie stars were plastered on the bedroom walls of most teenage girls, but a new craze hit when a tall, lanky flier named Charles Lindbergh had flown across the Atlantic Ocean. His picture had appeared everywhere. He was in the movies and on billboards, and every boy wanted to grow up and fly a plane like Lindy. All of America had fallen in love with the handsome young Charles Lindbergh, and a year later, they fell in love all over again with his female counterpart, Amelia Earhart, so bold and dashing with her auburn tousled hair and dressed in men's trousers. Girls sent off for her pictures and added them to their photos of their favorite movie stars.

Hoping to cash in on what Lindbergh and Earhart had started and take advantage of the new flying craze that was sweeping the country, Phillips Petroleum came up with an advertising promotion that was sure to be noticed. In a bold move, they hired skywriters to fly over their gas stations and write "Phillips 66" in the air. Most of the skywriters were old World War I pilots or barnstormers, the name given to the men who flew around the country performing aerial stunts, picking up a little extra cash on the weekends. But the pilot assigned to fly over Wink's Phillips 66 filling station in Pulaski, Wisconsin, picked up more than a little extra cash.

Billy Bevins's uncle had been a flier in World War I. He started his own flying school when he came home and taught Billy to fly when he was fifteen. Billy had been flying ever since. It was a good way to make a living, and in Billy's case, a good way to meet girls. He had done it all, from barnstorming to crop dusting, and had even flown a Davis Waco with the Baby Ruth Flying Circus. It was an advertising blitz unlike anything the country had ever seen. Billy would fly over county and state fairs, racetracks, and crowded beaches in his red and white plane, dropping hundreds of tiny rice paper parachutes—each one bearing a small Baby Ruth candy bar—on the crowds below.

It was a great job; however, one day, after too many drinks, Billy took it upon himself to fly in between the buildings in downtown Pittsburgh and it caused a riot in the streets. Several people almost fell out of office windows trying to grab the candy bars as they floated by. Traffic was snarled for the next two hours as people left their cars sitting in the streets to look for Baby Ruths. The next day, Billy was fired. Now he was back to barnstorming around the county and skywriting on the side.

THE PEOPLE IN PULASKI had been waiting for weeks for the skywriter to fly in. In preparation, Poppa and some of his farmer friends had brought in tractors and cleared out the large field in the back of the house, and Wink and all his friends got busy and cleared out all the rocks and made a long, smooth runway where the plane could land. When word got out that he was coming one Saturday morning, the entire town went out into their yards or stood waiting in the empty lot behind the filling station. Pretty soon, they heard the sound of a faraway motor. Fritzi was the first to see the plane and shouted for everyone to look up. Soon, a large white "P" was being formed in the sky. The entire crowd stood looking up in awe as the word "Phillips" was spelled out, then the number "66." As the icing on the cake, the pilot flew the plane straight down toward the ground and then back up and formed an arrow that pointed right down at the station. He then made a large circle in the sky, came back around, and landed the plane to wild applause from the waiting crowd.

But the pilot who opened the door and jumped down from the plane was not like anything they expected and a far cry from Charles Lindbergh. Billy was a short and stocky young man with a wide grin who clearly loved his work. "Hiya, pals!" he said as he made his way over to the filling station with the crowd following behind him. Fritzi was blown away. She had never seen anyone so confident, so self-assured, and she loved the way he had said "Hiya, pals!" with such flair. It was as if he had stepped right out of a movie.

Billy walked over to the station and posed for pictures and gave radio and newspaper interviews for about an hour. Later, he waved good-bye to the crowd with a "So long, pals," and went inside the house next door and was treated to lunch with the Jurdabralinski family.

During his visit, they learned that he had flown over that morning from Grand Rapids. Wink was enthralled as he sat and listened to Billy tell tales about his flying exploits as a barnstormer and stunt flier. After lunch, they walked him back to his plane and waved as he took off to the east. They all agreed it had been the most exciting day of their lives.

It had also been a very good day for Billy. He had flown away with a large paper bag full of good Polish sausage and homemade candy that the mother had packed for him, plus something else. He had learned the names of all four daughters.

NOT LONG AFTER BILLY's first visit, someone heard the sound of a plane circling above the town. They all came out and looked up and saw that it was the skywriter back again, but this time, after he had finished, they saw he had written in large white letters across the sky,

HEY, FRITZI, HOW ABOUT A DATE?

Billy had a hunch. Fritzi was not the prettiest sister. Sophie, the youngest, was the beauty, and the other two girls were swell looking, too, but there was something about Fritzi that he liked. She had real spirit, and he was looking for a gal with spirit.

When Momma stepped out and looked up and saw the message in the sky, she shook her head. She had been concerned about something like this happening. She was afraid that of all her children, Fritzi would be the one who would run off from home, looking for some wild new adventure. And she could tell by the way Fritzi had pushed her way past everybody to sit by Billy Bevins at lunch and how she had hung on to his every word, this might be it.

Two days later, when the family was having dinner, Billy Bevins called the phone number at the filling station, and Wink ran over to the house to get Fritzi.

After a few minutes, Fritzi came back to the kitchen looking flushed and excited and announced to the table, "Billy's coming to get me on Saturday and fly me to Milwaukee for dinner and dancing!"

Momma turned to her husband, waiting for him to put his foot down and say no, but he just nodded and kept eating. Wink and the other girls were as excited as Fritzi and started jumping up and down. Wink asked, "Can I go, too?" so Momma knew she was outnumbered. And, besides, what could she do? Stanislaw was right. Fritzi was a new breed of American girl with a mind of her own, and nothing she could say would stop her anyway. All Momma could do was go to Saint Mary's and light a candle to the Blessed Mother and pray Fritzi didn't fall out of the plane.

The next day, when Fritzi told her friends about it, one girl said, "Oh, Fritzi, I'd be scared to go off with a stranger like that." The other girl said, "Yeah, aren't you afraid he might get you up in the air and then try to get fresh?" But Fritzi wasn't worried. She had been on too many hayrides with over-six-foot-tall Wisconsin farm boys, and if she could handle them, she surely could handle him. Billy wasn't much taller than she was.

The following Saturday afternoon, Fritzi, dressed in a blue suit, white blouse, white shoes, and a white hat, climbed into the backseat of the plane and waved good-bye to her family, while Momma stood there making the sign of the cross over and over again. "Oh, dear Mother of God, let her live through this." But Momma knew, even if Fritzi did live, they were in danger of losing her. They always said that "Once you've been to Milwaukee, you're never the same."

THE LETTERS

IN THE PAST WEEK, SOOKIE HAD GONE THROUGH ALL THE FOOD SHE had stashed away in case of an emergency. She hadn't stepped out of the house. But now even she couldn't face another frozen shrimp. She really had to do a little grocery shopping. So she waited until noon, when she knew Lenore was safely at the Red Hat Society ladies luncheon. After she finished her shopping, she thought of something else she needed to do while she was out, so she whipped around the corner and parked in the back of the bank.

She went in and opened up their security box and removed the two letters she had written almost three years ago and reread them.

Dear Family,

If anything should happen to me as far as my mental health, I am saying good-bye to you now while I am still of sound mind. I want you to know that you are the very best thing that ever happened to me and that you have always been my constant joy and pride. I don't know what I ever did to deserve such a wonderful husband and children. Take good care of each other, and try and remember me when I was well.

I will love you forever,

Mother

Then, she opened up the one to Earle.

To My Darling Earle,

Promise me if something should happen, please feel free to divorce me and remarry. I want you to be happy, and you need someone to take care of you. Sweetheart, thank you for all the wonderful years we did have. When I'm gone, take care of Mother as best you can, and let Dee Dee help you. She is devoted to Lenore and will be happy to take over the paperwork.

Always,

Your loving wife,

Sookie

P.S. Pleasant Hill has recently raised their prices, so I have checked around for places a little less expensive. Try Brice's Institution in Tuscaloosa first. I think they may take Blue Cross.

P.P.S. Marvaleen told me on the QT that she thinks you are very handsome. Just a thought . . .

When Sookie reread the last letter, she was so glad Earle had not seen it. Marvaleen? What had she been thinking? Marvaleen was far too new age for Earle. Marvaleen wore thong underwear—not that there was anything wrong with that, but it would be a little too much for Earle. Sookie knew she really was the perfect wife for Earle. He had always said so, and now she could clearly see he was right. She knew exactly how he liked his corn bread: thin and crispy. He wouldn't be happy with anyone else but her. She tore both letters up and threw them away.

Sookie realized that starting today, she was going to have to reset her thinking. For years, she had lived with the fear of the Simmons gene, but now that was a worry she didn't have anymore. Of course, she didn't know about the Jurdabralinski genes, but she was fairly certain nobody could be crazier than the Simmonses.

As Sookie drove home from the bank, she suddenly remembered it was Monday and ducked down in her seat and hid as she drove past the cemetery. Her mother's car was there, but thank heavens, she hadn't spotted Sookie's car. That was another thing Lenore had put her through. It was so irritating to think that she had gone to all that hassle and trouble to move her great-grandfather there, and now it turns out she wasn't even related to him. The man was a complete stranger!

She felt like such a fool. Lenore had made her do all that stuff, knowing full well she wasn't a Simmons. Honestly!

And it wouldn't be so bad if the woman had ever once said thank you or even appreciated it. Lenore didn't even seem to have a clue or notice what all she had put her through.

Last year, after the mayor's lawsuit, when she was driving her mother home from the courthouse, Sookie had asked, "Mother, do you have any idea how hard it is to be your daughter?"

Lenore had looked at her completely puzzled. "Why, what an odd question. Hard? In what way, hard? I think I have been a wonderful mother. I would have loved to have been my daughter. Haven't I done everything humanly possible to see that you have every advantage?"

"Yes, Mother, you have. It's just that you come with an awful lot of drama, and you are never quiet."

"Well, I'm sorry if I'm not some dull and boring Sally-sit-by-the-fire. Yes, I talk a lot, but I happen to excel in the art of conversation."

"It's not just talking, Mother. It's just that you always have an opinion."

"Well, I should hope so."

"But it's always such a strong opinion."

"How can you expect me to have a weak opinion? Would you go into a restaurant and order a weak cup of coffee?"

"Yes, as a matter of fact, I would."

"You know what I mean, Sookie. Why have an opinion, if it's not

a strong opinion? Oh, I know the Good Book says the meek shall inherit the earth, but I don't believe it for one minute."

"But, Mother, surely there is something in between meek and
overpowering. Like . . . just normal." Sookie knew the minute she said
it, she had said the wrong word.

Lenore's eyes suddenly got very big. "Are you suggesting that I am
not normal? Granted, your Uncle Baby and Aunt Lily have their little
quirks, but I'm as normal as they come. Really, Sookie, you hurt me
to the quick."

If Lenore thought shooting at the paperboy was just "a little
quirk," then there was no point in expecting her to ever think anything was wrong with her. Lenore had never been normal in her life.
She certainly hadn't been a normal mother or a normal grandmother,
either.

One Christmas Eve, when the children had been quite young, she
and Earle had left them with Lenore while they ran out and did a little
last-minute shopping, and Lenore had served each child several cups
of the Simmons eggnog, which was 75 percent rum and 25 percent
nog. When they came to pick the children up, all four were stumbling
around her living room in a drunken stupor. "I don't know why you're
so upset, Sookie," Lenore had said. "My word, a little eggnog never
hurt anybody, and if we can't celebrate the birth of our Lord on Christmas Eve, then I don't know what the world is coming to."

That year, they had been the only children in town who had
opened their presents on Christmas morning with a hangover. And, of
course, no matter what Lenore did, the children just adored her. Especially Dee Dee. Whenever she was punished for doing something at
home, she would exclaim, "I'm going to live with Grandmother. She
understands me!"

Lenore had been so hard on her own children, but to Sookie's
great surprise, with her grandchildren, she thought whatever they did
or said was "Just darling! Just precious!" or "The cutest thing in the
world!" She had given them all the candy they wanted, even though
Earle, being a dentist, had asked her not to. So, of course, the children
loved being with her. Why not?

But then, they hadn't been raised by a woman who thought that
Sookie and Buck were the only two things that had stood between her

and winning an Oscar. She had said, "Oh, Sookie, when I saw Barbara Stanwyck in the movie *Stella Dallas,* I just cried my eyes out. I could have played that part to a T. Oh, well," she sighed. "Barbara Stanwyck had the career I should have, but it's all water under the bridge now." Oh, brother.

MILWAUKEE, WISCONSIN

1938

FRITZI DIDN'T LET ON, BUT SHE HAD ACTUALLY BEEN TERRIFIED AS Billy taxied the plane over to the edge of the field. She had never been in an airplane in her life, and when he revved the motor, ready for takeoff, she shut her eyes and held on to her hat for dear life. As the plane started rumbling down the field, her heart was pounding so hard she could hardly breathe, but if this is what it took to impress Billy, she would do it. She had been dazzled by Billy at first sight, the way he had jumped down out of the plane and sauntered through the crowd. Besides, she wanted to see something of the world before she settled down. She didn't want to marry one of the hometown boys and have five or six children before she was twenty-five. A lot of her friends had dropped out of high school, married, and already had a baby on the way. So when Billy had flown into her life, it seemed to her that she was to be rescued, not by a man on a white horse, but by one in a bright yellow plane.

AFTER A BUMPY RIDE, the plane lifted off the ground, and, suddenly, Fritzi felt the most amazing sensation. The loud roar of the engine became more of a hum, and she felt as if she were floating. When she opened her eyes, she was way up in the air and looking down at the small world below. Her family, still standing by the fence waving, became smaller and smaller as she and Billy flew up way above the town, headed over to Milwaukee.

Flying to Milwaukee was a revelation to Fritzi. Billy followed the railroad tracks all the way, and from up above looking down, the silos and water towers looked like some of Wink's old toys sitting on top of a patchwork quilt. Tiny tractors moved slowly through rows of corn and wheat, and the lakes that spotted the countryside looked like little round mirrors. The farmhouses, with sheets and overalls hanging from the clotheslines in the backyard, looked no bigger than the little wooden house pieces on a Monopoly set.

Fritzi didn't want Billy to know, but she had never been more than a few miles away from home before. When they landed in Milwaukee, they picked up Billy's car, and he drove her downtown for an evening of dining and dancing at the Oriental Room atop the Hotel Ambassador. Fritzi had never been in such a big city before, and as streetcars, taxis, and cars whizzed by, she felt as excited as she had ever been in her entire life.

Pulaski had pretty much shut down after dark, except for the roller rink and Friday night bingo at the church and an occasional polka night out at Zielinski's Ballroom. But here, everybody was wide awake and going somewhere. All the department stores, some a block long, were still open, and the windows were filled with smartly dressed mannequins wearing fancy clothes. Fritzi was amazed as they drove past flower shops, candy shops with little pink neon signs, and at least six or seven movie theaters with huge marquees.

Geez . . . if this was Milwaukee, what must Chicago or New York be like? She couldn't imagine, but she knew one thing: After this, she could never be happy just staying home and working at the pickle factory.

* * *

Once they entered the hotel, she did get a little nervous. This was the first time she had ever been to a hotel with a man. She hoped there really was a supper club, and she was not going to wind up in a hotel room. But she needn't have worried. As soon as the elevator doors opened on the twenty-second floor, they heard the music. And when they walked into the Oriental Room, Fritzi was overwhelmed. She felt as if she had just stepped inside a movie set, and she half-expected to see Fred Astaire and Ginger Rogers at any minute. She had never seen anything so glamorous. The room was lined with lime green leather booths. Little oriental red and green lanterns hung over the dance floor, and waiters dressed in yellow and black silk Chinese pajamas scurried around, serving drinks with tiny paper umbrellas. The dance floor was packed with people dancing to the Speed Hooper Orchestra. Fritzi noticed that there was not one accordion player. The girl singer, dressed in a long white sequined gown, wore a gardenia in her hair and just oozed sophistication.

As they were escorted to their booth and made their way through the crowd, everybody seemed to know Billy and would call out, "Hiya, Billy!" and he would say, "Hiya, pals!" Fritzi suddenly felt like a rube among all the beautifully dressed women in the room. When they sat down, Billy ordered her a champagne cocktail and a double scotch for himself.

Later, after Billy and Fritzi came back from the dance floor, a cute girl in a short skirt carrying a camera came up and asked Billy if he wanted a picture of the two of them. Another had a tray full of cigarettes and cigars and corsages for sale. Billy bought her a wrist corsage. All through the evening, Fritzi remained calm and pretended she had done this kind of thing before. She tried not to let Billy see it, but inside, she was impressed out of her mind. It was true. Once she had seen Milwaukee, she knew she would never be the same again.

That night, when Billy flew her back home to Pulaski, Fritzi looked down and saw the lights of the filling station below, and she was sorry the date was over. She wished it could have gone on forever. Long after they had landed and Billy was already back in Grand Rapids, Fritzi Jurdabralinski was still up in the air, in more ways than one. Somewhere along the way, she had lost her hat, but she didn't care. She had lost more than her hat; she had lost her heart. That night, Fritzi had fallen hopelessly in love with flying . . . and with Billy Bevins.

WHERE DID I GET MY TRAITS?

———

WHEN SHE WOKE UP THAT MORNING, SOOKIE REALIZED SHE REALLY needed to find out more about her ethnic background. She had always assumed that she had inherited either the Simmons or the Krackenberry traits. Now she wanted to try and figure out what behavior was from her Polish DNA and what was learned behavior. She wished she had paid more attention to world geography. She wasn't even sure exactly where Poland was. She knew it was in Europe somewhere, close to Russia or France, maybe? And she didn't know a thing about Polish people. As far as she knew, her only encounter with anything remotely Polish was eating those little Polish sausages they served at the Waffle House. And so after her bath, she fed Peek-a-Boo and turned on the computer. She typed up the words "Polish Traits," and clicked.

"The Poles are generally a fun-loving and hardworking people." Well, that was good so far, but she was curious about what they looked like, so she typed in "Famous Polish People." The first two names that came up were Frédéric Chopin and Liberace, both piano players. And she could see from Liberace's picture that they had similar noses. When she read on and saw that Martha Stewart was also Polish, she began to cheer up just a tiny bit.

*   *   *

LATER, SOOKIE WAITED UNTIL she knew Lenore was in water therapy and went outside and walked around her yard for the first time in days. When she saw Netta out in her front yard, pruning her azaleas, she wandered over and said, "Hi, Netta."

Netta looked up. "Well, hey there, gal . . . feeling any better?"

"Yes, I am. But don't tell Mother, okay?"

"I won't."

"Thanks, Netta. And thanks so much for feeding my birds."

"No problem, hon. Happy to do it anytime."

"Netta, let me ask you something. What do you know about Polish people?"

"Polish people?"

"Yes."

"Oh, well . . . let me think," Netta said, snapping off a dead branch in one of her bushes. "I know they like sauerkraut. And they love to sing, but they are not very good singers."

"Really?"

"Yeah. I heard that somewhere, but I've forgotten where. And, oh, they like their accordions and like to do the polka."

"Have you ever met any Polish people in person?"

"Not that I recall, no . . . or if I did, I didn't know it. Why?"

"Oh, no reason, I was just wondering. Well, I'll see you later."

Netta watched as Sookie slowly wandered back over to her house like she was in some kind of a daze. Between the pink sneakers and now this, she was getting worried. Maybe it was the flu, but Sookie just didn't seem like herself.

A FINE ROMANCE

Pulaski, Wisconsin

Billy Bevins thought Fritzi was a great gal. But as it turned out, he had had motives other than romance for taking her out. He hadn't told her yet, but he was really just looking for a new gal to join him in his flying act. The big draw at air shows were the female wing walkers, and Fritzi filled the bill. She had a terrific figure, a great smile, and a lot of confidence.

After they had gone out a few more times, and he had flown her over to see a performance of the Billy Bevins Flying Circus, he asked Fritzi whether she would ever be interested in joining his flying act if he trained her to do a few stunts. She answered with an emphatic "Yes!"

"Great!" he said, patting her on the back, then added, "Fritzi, gal, I'm going to show you how to do things in a plane you never dreamed about."

Fritzi shot him a look and said, "Yeah, I'll just bet you will!"

He had laughed when she said it, but to Fritzi's disappointment, and as much as she wished he would, he never so much as kissed her good night.

As time went by, Fritzi felt baffled. She knew he liked her, but something was wrong. She had never had a guy not try and get fresh with her. Maybe he thought she was too young or not worldly enough for him. So Fritzi tried acting a little older and tougher. She even plucked her eyebrows like Jean Harlow, but so far, nothing. She ordered a pair of tan jodhpurs, a white silk shirt, a leather cap, and a long white scarf. She put them on and strolled around town looking very much like a real pilot. Or so people in Pulaski said.

EVERY MONDAY, BILLY WOULD fly over to Pulaski and give Fritzi a flying lesson. He needed his wing walkers to be trained pilots, and as a favor to Fritzi, he threw in a few lessons for Wink as well.

Wink hero-worshipped Billy and started to walk like him and follow him around like a puppy. Wink did very well with his lessons, but Fritzi was the one whose progress Billy was interested in, and she didn't disappoint him. She was strong, athletic, coordinated, and—most important of all—as he had found on their first date, she was a damn good dancer. Before he trained any girl, he always took them dancing first.

Billy knew from experience, people with no rhythm made lousy pilots. Not only was Fritzi a good student and a fast learner, unlike a lot of girls, she was not afraid to get her hands dirty. After having watched her father work at the filling station all those years, Fritzi could take a motor apart and put it back together and change a tire in three minutes flat.

A FEW MONTHS LATER, when Billy flew in, Fritzi came running out, ready for another lesson, and he started off with his usual drill. "So, pal . . . what's your first rule?"

"Safety."

"Who's your best friend?"

"My mechanic."

"What do you do before you take off?"

"Check everything."

"How many times?"

"Twice."

"Right!" Billy was a highly skilled pilot, but he was also a real stickler on safety. That day, after they had landed, Billy turned to her and said, "Okay, kid. You're ready to solo. She's all yours. Take her up, do your stuff, then bring her on in. See you later," and he walked away and left her standing there.

Fritzi had no idea this was going to happen so soon, and she panicked, but she knew that if she didn't do it, she might not ever see Billy again. She walked around the plane with her heart pounding and did her safety check, twice. When she finally got in the plane, she was so nervous that her legs started to shake, and she wanted to jump out and run, but she took a deep breath and started the motor and taxied out, with her mind full of all the things Billy had taught her. To her amazement, before she knew it, she was up in the air, looking down at Billy, who gave her a thumbs-up. She stayed up in the air for about twenty-five minutes, flying in circles, and practiced landing in the air ten times, like Billy had taught her. "Go up and give yourself plenty of altitude, and envision that your runway is laid right out in front of you. Then, go through all your landing procedures, so when you do land, you've already done it so many times, landing for real will be a piece of cake."

And, sure enough, on her first solo landing, she did pretty well. The next week, Poppa drove her up to Grand Rapids to get her pilot's license. Poppa was so proud and showed it to everyone who came in the station. Fritzi was happy to have her license, but privately, her heart was broken. When she had gone to Grand Rapids, after she had gotten her license, she made Poppa drive her over to the hotel where Billy lived and had knocked on Billy's door to surprise him. A tough-looking woman with frizzy red hair had come to the door in her nightgown. She found out that the whole time she had known him, Billy had been living with Gussie Mintz, his second-string wing walker from Altoona.

What a fool she had been. He had never been the slightest bit interested in her and probably never would be. It was hard being around him after that, but Billy had never led her on, nor had he made any promises, so what could she do?

After that Fritzi started doing a few shows now and then. Billy would call her whenever Lillian Bass, his first-string wing walker, was not available and Gussie was too drunk to go on.

Soon, Billy began to see that not only had Fritzi taken to flying and performing stunts, she'd invented a few of her own. She didn't do the usual girl stunts. She went out on the wing and stood on her head, jumped through hoops, and did the jitterbug five hundred feet up in the air. As Billy told his mechanic one night at the hotel bar, "That crazy kid has more guts than brains. Damn," he said. "She reminds me of me at that age, and that ain't good." Billy took a swig of his drink, then said, "Now if I was a nice guy, I would send her packing, but I ain't a nice guy, I guess."

The mechanic, who had been with Billy for eleven years, said, "You'd better watch out, buddy. The next thing you know, that little gal is liable to have *you* jumping through hoops."

A few months later, when Lillian quit wing walking for good to get married, Billy called Fritzi in Pulaski and told her the first-string job was hers permanently, if she wanted it.

Did she want it? She jumped at the chance. Momma did not want her to go, but she could also see how unhappy she was. Her other three girls were homebodies, but not Fritzi.

Fritzi gave her notice at the pickle factory. One week later, Billy got her a hotel room where he lived and she moved to Grand Rapids for good and started traveling with the Flying Circus. To Poppa's delight, the move was headline news in Pulaski.

**MISS FRITZI JURDABRALINSKI,
PULASKI'S OWN AMELIA EARHART,
JOINS FLYING CIRCUS**

WHERE *IS* PULASKI?

———

POINT CLEAR, ALABAMA

THE NEXT MORNING, AFTER EARLE LEFT FOR THE OFFICE, SOOKIE WAS sitting at her kitchen table, looking at Earle's big road atlas of the United States, trying to find the town of Pulaski, when Netta knocked on the back door. Sookie got up and went to the door.

"Hey, Sookie, I saw Dr. Poole leave a little while ago, so I thought I'd run over and see if you needed anything from the store."

"Oh, thank you, Netta. I'm fine, but come in, and have some coffee."

"No, I can't stay. I'm still in my hairnet." Netta looked over at the table and said, "I see you've got your road maps out. Are you going on a trip?"

"No, I was just looking at a map of Wisconsin. Have you ever been to Wisconsin, Netta?"

"Nope, sure haven't. Have you?"

"No, I don't know anything about it. Do you?"

"Nothing much, except . . . isn't that where the horses with the big feet come from? I think they're pulling a wagon of Budweiser beer. Don't they call it Milwaukee's Finest?"

"I think you're right."

"And they like their cheese. And Wisconsin may be where Daisy the Contented Cow comes from, but I could be wrong. But if you're not going there, why are you looking at it on the map?"

"Oh, no reason. I just woke up and was curious about where it was, that's all. I'm surprised at how far up it is, almost as far up as Canada. I wonder how cold it gets in the winter?"

"I wouldn't know, honey. Well, I'll leave you to your map. Call me if you need me."

As Netta walked across the yard back to her house, she wondered why anyone in their right mind would just wake up one day and be curious about Wisconsin. But maybe Sookie wasn't in her right mind. Maybe poor Sookie had flipped. Oh, Lord. Another Simmons over at Pleasant Hill. Once that gene gets in there, it just hits them like a hammer, and off they go. Bless her heart. One day sane, the next day looking at maps of Wisconsin for no reason. Her poor kids are going to be very upset, and no telling what will happen to Dr. Poole. She never saw a man so devoted to his wife as he was. But it was to be expected, she guessed. With Lenore for a mother, that girl was probably driven to the brink. She liked Lenore, but she was glad she wasn't related to her.

Sookie sat back down and continued looking for Pulaski and finally found it. "Pulaski: Home of the largest polka celebration in the country." It was close to Green Bay, she could see that. Oh, dear, that was where those people painted themselves green and sat in the football stands in the freezing cold with wedges of cheese on their heads. Oh, well. Who was she to pass judgment? Carter and the girls had all gone to the University of Alabama, and Carter and his friends wore elephant hats to the games. To each his own, she supposed, but still, it was very strange to think that some of those people sitting in the stands with wedges of cheese on their heads might be her own relatives. Then another thought hit her. She had always liked cheese, especially pimento cheese sandwiches. Could that have come from her genetic background, or did she just love cheese? When Earle came home, she asked, "Earle, have you ever noticed that I eat a lot of cheese, or is it just my imagination?"

"Cheese? No, I haven't noticed you eating more cheese than anybody else. Why?"

"I was just wondering."

The next day, when she knew Lenore was busy playing bridge and that there was no danger that she would run into her, Sookie hurried downtown to the bookstore and spoke to the owner.

"Hi, Karin, how are you?"

"I'm fine, Mrs. Poole. You just missed your mother. She was here earlier with her little Mexican nurse, buying some birthday cards."

Oh, for heaven's sake. "Well, listen, Karin, I was wondering . . . where should I look for a book on Poland?"

"The country, Poland?"

"Yes. Or Wisconsin."

"Okay. Well, both of those would be in the travel section, but if you don't find what you want, let me know. I can always order it. Are you taking a trip now that all the weddings are over?"

"Well, you know, I just might be. I'm just not sure where, yet."

"Let me know if I can help you."

As Sookie searched through the books, it dawned on her that her mother always bought her greeting cards there, so she was probably in there earlier buying a birthday card for her, knowing full well that July 31 was not her real birthday. *Honestly!*

PULASKI, WISCONSIN

1939

In 1939, MOST AMERICANS, ESPECIALLY THE YOUNG, WERE BLISSFULLY unaware of what was happening outside of their own little world. But the citizens of Pulaski, young and old, were painfully aware of the horrible war that was raging across Europe. Every night, families sat glued to the radio, listening to the news of Poland. Most still had relatives and friends there, and each day, the men would gather at the bulletin board at the drugstore, reading the news of the day in disbelief. The Poles were fighting bravely, hoping to hold out for England or France to come and help. Stanislaw had a cousin who worked in the telegraph room at the Grand Hotel Europejski in Warsaw, and he had managed to send news of the bombing of the city by the Germans. He reported that each night, the Nazis sent more bombers, and each morning, whole new sections of the city were destroyed. Men, women, and children were being killed by the hundreds and left in the streets, along with the dead horses. And then, after September 1, the news abruptly stopped, and nothing more came out of Poland.

September the ninth was a cold, gray day, and the entire town of Pulaski was suddenly deadly quiet as the news was announced.

Father Sobieski, whose family was still in Warsaw, walked slowly up to the bell tower of Saint Mary's and rang the bell over and over with tears streaming down his face. Poland had fallen to the Nazis. Like so many, he had dreamed he would return home one day, but that dream was over. The Poland they loved was gone.

After a while, stunned people slowly began coming out of their homes into the streets, and, not knowing what else to do, they all walked over to the church, where a special mass was said entirely in Polish. When it was over, they all stood and sang the Polish national anthem.

Several weeks later, at the Pulaski movie theater, when they ran the weekly *Eyes and Ears of the World* newsreel, they showed films of the fall of Warsaw, and one woman screamed when she thought she recognized the man with his arms over his head being brutally shoved through the war-torn streets by a Nazi soldier. "That's my brother!" she screamed over and over, and she had to be taken home.

Poland had fallen, but life in America carried on as usual. Kids still played baseball, and the 1939 World's Fair in New York was being mobbed by people thrilled about seeing all the marvelous inventions that were in the works. The World of Tomorrow exhibit promised nothing but an exciting future. Elsewhere, across the country, women and girls sat in movie houses, swooning over Clark Gable in *Gone with the Wind,* while men and boys were enthralled watching John Wayne ride shotgun across the West in *Stagecoach.* At night, people were still laughing at their favorite radio shows, *Charlie McCarthy* and *Fibber McGee and Molly.* Teenagers everywhere were jitterbugging to Glenn Miller's "Little Brown Jug," and the Andrews Sisters had a big hit with "Beer Barrel Polka," a song that was especially popular in Pulaski.

BY THE SUMMER, GERTRUDE May and Tula June had graduated from high school. Both were well-liked and were members of the Thursday night Ladies Accordion Band of Pulaski and marched with them that year in the Polka Days parade. Tula and Gertrude both had steady boyfriends, lived at home, and helped Momma in the kitchen. The youngest girl, Sophie, was in her junior year at high school. The three girls were a joy to Momma. Gertrude was a big-boned, good-natured girl with a big laugh like her father. Tula was just plain silly and loved to giggle. Sophie was very pretty, and the boys liked her a lot, but she was shy and quiet and very much a homebody, which pleased Momma. She had already lost Fritzi, and she wanted to keep her last three little chickens close by, where she could keep an eye on them.

Momma hadn't said anything, but she had noticed that of all her children, Sophie Marie was the most devout and never missed mass, and she said her rosary every night. Momma would not be surprised if she turned out to have a religious vocation. She hoped so. It would be wonderful to have a nun in the family. She knew that with the way Wink fooled around with all the girls, particularly Angie Broukowski, he was never going to be a priest. Girls were now driving all the way over from Green Bay to the filling station just to flirt with him.

By the end of 1939, those in Washington, including Franklin Roosevelt, fearing that the United States would eventually be drawn into war, became concerned that the country was not prepared. The Army Air Corps was turning out only three hundred pilots annually, and so the government quietly and without much fanfare set up a new program, offered at colleges, called the Civilian Pilot Training Program, which turned out to be good news for the Jurdabralinskis. They already had the little airstrip they had built for Billy, and the local college needed a place to keep small planes and train students. When they asked Stanislaw if they could build a small hangar on the property and rent the land, he saw an opportunity for Wink and the girls and told the college they could use it rent-free. The only stipulation was that the instructor give Wink and his girls flying lessons in his spare time. The girls were thrilled. They idolized Fritzi and wanted to be just like her. But Momma was not happy. Having Fritzi flying all over the place was enough.

Dear Goofballs,

Poppa wrote and told me about your new venture. Can't wait for you to take me for a ride into the wild blue yonder. Billy says, "Be careful, be safe, have fun."

Fritzi

All three girls did fairly well—all except Tula. When she soloed, she came in far too low on the landing and brought an awful lot of cornstalks down with her. After that, Tula decided to just stick to playing the accordion and roller-skating.

THE INVISIBLE WOMAN

THE MINUTE CE CE GOT BACK FROM HER HONEYMOON, SHE RAN OVER
to see her mother and pick up Peek-a-Boo. "Oh, Mother, the honeymoon was just wonderful. And thanks again for taking such good care
of Peek-a-Boo."

"Oh, honey, I was happy to do it."

After they had visited awhile and caught up on Ce Ce's trip, Ce Ce
looked at her and asked, "Mother, is there something the matter? You
just don't seem like yourself today."

"Oh, no. It's . . . well . . . with all my children gone, I've been
doing a little reevaluating, that's all."

"About what?"

"Oh, how proud I am of all my girls. Le Le and Dee Dee have
such good careers, and now you're studying to be a veterinarian. And
I guess I'm feeling a little bit like a failure. I never did anything
with my life."

"Mother, what are you talking about? You worked and helped put
Daddy through dental school."

"Oh . . . not for that long, and I just did a little simple filing."

"And you raised four children. You were always there when any of us needed you. You cooked and cleaned and made sure we all had clean clothes. I don't know how you did it at all."

"Oh, honey, that's just housewife stuff. Anybody can do that."

"No, they can't. I can't. Grandmother sure couldn't. I don't know why you never give yourself any credit for all you did every day. And you never complained."

"Oh, yes, I did."

"Well, not to us. We never heard you complain about anything."

"No?"

"No. You were always so easygoing, so sweet. You just went along with everything."

"I did?"

"Oh, yes."

THAT AFTERNOON, SOOKIE CALLED Dena. "Dena, I want you to tell me the truth and feel free to be brutally frank. You were my best friend in college."

"Yes, I was."

"What would you say were my main personality traits?"

"Oh . . . well, you had a *great* personality. Everybody liked you, Sookie."

"But why?"

"Why? You were fun to be with and always so—"

"Agreeable?"

"Yes . . . and you always went along with everything."

"I knew it!"

"What?"

"I am a nonperson. I never had any real personality traits of my own. I'm traitless. I've just picked up things. If I hadn't been pushed into a personality by Lenore, everyone would have seen that underneath, I am nothing but a dull, traitless blob."

"Oh, Sookie, that's not true."

"Yes, it is. All these years, I've just been imitating other people. I'm just an empty suit."

"Sookie, what happened? You don't sound like yourself."

"That's just it. I'm *not* myself. I'm just one big piece of plasma floating around in space . . . the Invisible Woman. Why couldn't I have found all this out when I was young and still had a chance to change? Now it's too late. I'm already formed. I'm just a second-banana kind of person, and I always will be."

"Oh, Sookie, it's not true. And it's never too late to change, and do something different."

"Yes, it is. For me, at least. I don't think I've changed one bit since high school. I'm just older on the outside, that's all."

"Oh, honey."

"No, it's true, Dena. And there's nothing more unattractive than a sixty-year-old ex-cheerleader still trying to be perky. I just make myself sick. I don't even know if I really like people or if I'm just a big phony. Anyhow, thank you for being my friend."

Dena hung up the phone and felt so bad for Sookie, but she could understand how she felt. She had always thought that Lenore was hilarious and a lot of fun, but then she wasn't her daughter. And with Lenore, everybody was a second banana.

GRAND RAPIDS, WISCONSIN

BILLY BEVINS HAD MET PLENTY OF GIRLS, BUT NEVER ONE LIKE FRITZI. He was twelve years older, but pretty soon, when they all went out after the show, she could match him drink for drink, cuss word for cuss word—and lately, she had added a few new ones he had never heard of. Best of all, she had become almost as good a pilot as he was.

For the first few months in Grand Rapids, Fritzi had her own room at the hotel, and everything had been on the up and up. But as time went by, Gussie Mintz, the wing walker from Altoona that Billy was living with, had seen the handwriting on the wall. She saw how Billy looked at Fritzi and vice versa. He denied it, of course, but Gussie was not a fool. So one Saturday, while Billy and Fritzi were off doing the show, she up and packed her bags and moved back to Altoona. But she did leave Fritzi a note.

Dear Fritzi,

Well, I'm off. Good luck, and be careful. They say once flying gets in your blood, you can't ever get it out. I'm getting out while I still can.

Yours truly,

Gussie Mintz

P.S. I ain't mad at you, Fritzi, but you tell Billy I think he's a real shit.

Gussie may not have been the most refined of girls, but Fritzi had always liked her. When you got past all the makeup, booze, crying jags, and bad grammar, there had been something kind of noble about old Gussie, and Fritzi would miss her.

And no matter what Gussie had called Billy, Gussie was clearly still in love with him. She hadn't left because she *wanted* to. But, after all, she herself had kicked some other gal out before she and Billy had gotten together. Just the same, if she had had a gun, Gussie would have shot him right where it counted. It would have made her feel better and probably saved Fritzi a lot of heartache down the line. Billy was not the marrying kind, and he never would be.

As GUSSIE HAD PREDICTED, things with Billy and Fritzi progressed, and a few months later, she was spending more time in Billy's room than her own. He said, "Why pay for two rooms when you are only using one?" It was as close to a proposal as she was ever going to get. She knew by now there was never going to be a wedding. Billy didn't believe in marriage. The choice was hers. She knew it was a sin, but she had stopped going to church a long time ago, so she moved in with Billy. She only worried about two things: Momma and Poppa finding out, and getting pregnant. As Lillian, the other wing walker, had told her, "Honey, be careful. Once you get pregnant, your flying days are over."

WHO AM I?

———

SOOKIE REALLY WAS IN A DILEMMA. SHE KNEW WHO SHE BELIEVED SHE was for the past sixty (dear God) years. But it had all been a lie. The real question now was, if she wasn't that person . . . then who was she? And then she suddenly remembered something. She picked up the phone and dialed.

"Marvaleen, it's Sookie."

They chatted for a few minutes and then Sookie asked her, "So how are things going with your life coach, Marvaleen? Still going well?"

"Oh, yes. I see her for a private session twice a week and then once a week at her Goddess Within group. Oh, Sookie, I wish you would come with me to the group. It will just change your life. We meet every Tuesday in her backyard, in a yurt."

"A yurt?"

"Yes. She had it sent from all the way from Outer Mongolia, and I swear, Sookie, it has special powers. I feel it the minute we enter. We all enter the yurt completely naked in order to free ourselves of the superficial trappings of Western culture, then we drum and chant to awaken the female goddess within. And after just a few sessions, it's raised my consciousness to a higher level."

"I see. Well, let me think about it. What I was really wondering was . . . do you still journal?"

"Of course. It's a lifetime journey. Have you started, yet?"

"Not yet. But you said it really helped you find out who you were."

"Oh, it did, Sookie. You've just *got* to journal! First of all, Edna Yorba Zorbra says that all females have been raised in an oppressive society, and so our self-esteem is low, and so we start by doing an Appreciation Journal and build from there, then we go on to our Rage Journal. You can't get to primal scream until you do."

"I see."

"And it really works. At first, all my rage was at Ralph, and then it moved on to things I didn't know I was mad about—personally and globally—and after you release all your rage, you can begin to lift into a yin state of being. But, Sookie, I wish you would come to group or, at least, yoga."

"Well, let me see how the journaling goes first. How do you start?"

"Well, you start every morning making a list of ten things you like about yourself."

"Oh . . ."

"For instance, like . . . 'I like my breasts' or 'I like my feet'—things like that."

Later that afternoon, Marvaleen had printed out instructions and dropped them by for Sookie with a note.

Sookie,

I am thrilled you are embarking on this magical journey to your interior and honored to be your guide to self-realization and mindfulness. First, it is imperative that you create a private Sacred Space and set up an altar with a photo of yourself as a child, a candle, or anything else that speaks to you. I have a picture of the Dalai Lama and Oprah Winfrey. As a beginner, I would start with this simple self-esteem and appreciation journal. It helps open your chakras for more intensive work later. Each morning, write ten things you like about yourself and five things you would like to change. And, Sookie, be kind to your inner child. Remember, she needs reassurance from the adult you. Tell her you love her and that everything will be all right. Edna Yorba Zorbra says we must learn to parent ourselves as we trudge the road to Happy Destiny.

Blessings and White Light,

M

P.S. Just so you know, Edna Yorba Zorbra is doing a chant and meditation study this Thursday night, including a vegetarian potluck. Would you like to come? Let me know.

The next morning, Sookie went about creating her Sacred Space. She decided to set up her altar out in the greenhouse. She found a school picture of herself from the third grade and a candle and headed out with her journal in hand. She lit her candle and placed her photograph on the shelf. Lord, she really had looked like Little Orphan Annie. How pitiful. And then she sat down in her big rocking chair, opened her journal, and started to write.

Ten Things I Like About Myself

1. My husband
2. My children
3. My house

She had never even thought about body parts, one way or another, except her hair, and she had never liked her hair, but she needed seven more things. Earle always said she had pretty skin, but she had always hated her freckles. An hour later, she still had only three things. This wasn't going well at all.

Maybe she should just skip this and start with five things she hated. Aha—she had one.

1. Blue jays

Well, no . . . she really didn't hate them. She was just mad at them at the moment. And they couldn't help being how they were. And she couldn't be mad at nature, could she? Oh, Lord.

Two hours later, her candle had gone out, and Sookie was still sitting out in the greenhouse. It was clear the "journaling" wasn't working. As hard as she tried, she had not been able to get past number three on her "Ten Things I Like About Myself" list. Maybe tomorrow, she would try and reread some of the codependent books Marvaleen had given her.

A few years ago, before she had found the life coach, Marvaleen had been attending a twelve-step program for codependents and had dropped some books by. Sookie had read them and for a time she'd really tried to be a little more assertive where her mother was concerned, but it was hard to make any progress. Lenore was just so darned overpowering. And no matter what was going on, she always had to be the center of attention.

Every Mother's Day was a command performance, and it was all about Lenore. Never mind that Sookie was a mother herself and had four children. Lenore said, "Sookie, you may be a mother now, but remember, I was a mother first!"

God, when she thought about all those years she'd been sure to buy her a Mother's Day corsage and made sure all the kids had presents for her and had them get all dressed up, because they had to look just perfect for Grandmother, and they always had to go to the big Mother's Day buffet at the hotel, because it was where all Lenore's friends went, and she wanted to show off her grandchildren. As usual, Sookie had just been another person at the table while Lenore had held court.

On Lenore's birthday, Sookie always had to plan a huge celebration somewhere and make sure she received lots of presents. Even on Sookie's birthday, Lenore had hogged the spotlight, and they all had to hear about how she had been in labor with Sookie for over forty-eight hours and how Sookie had been such a large baby. But that was Lenore: the bride at every wedding, the corpse at every funeral.

Maybe the fact that Lenore hadn't had a mother herself was one of the reasons she had such poor parenting skills. Or maybe, as Buck said, she was as crazy as a loon. But whatever the problem was, Sookie was convinced that a lifetime with Lenore had wrecked her nervous system. Thank God, Earle had built her the greenhouse, where she could go out and sit and be quiet for a couple of hours.

Whenever she had complained to Buck about something Lenore

had done, he would say, "Oh, Sis, don't let her bother you. Just ignore her like I do." But Sookie couldn't just ignore her. She was far too close to ignore. Even now, she could hear Lenore sitting out on her pier and talking. No surprise. If the wind was right, people in Mobile could probably hear her all the way across the bay.

It wasn't fair. Her real mother was probably some nice, quiet, little Polish woman.

A STAR IS BORN

FOR THE NEXT FEW YEARS, BILLY AND FRITZI PERFORMED ALMOST every weekend all through the Midwest and did a few shows as far away as Canada. And because of Billy, Fritzi had met a lot of the great old-time barnstormers. She even took a plane ride with the most famous of all, Clyde "Upside Down" Pangborn, who taught her how to improve her spins and loops and how to pull out of a stall.

Sure, it was dangerous, and as she found out, flying with the circus was a hard-living, hard-drinking life. But it was also fun and exciting, and as Fritzi always said, "A hell of a lot better than my old job working at the pickle factory."

On most Monday mornings, after doing their show on the weekend, Billy was usually too hungover to fly, so Fritzi would have to fly by herself to the next town where they were performing and drop the flyers advertising their upcoming show. But she didn't mind. There was something thrilling about being up in the air all alone, just her and the plane, flying with the wind in her face. Sometimes, when she didn't get back until after dark, and it was just her and the stars, she felt like she could stay up there forever. She loved flying in and out of the silver clouds and seeing the lights of the little towns below. Of course, she missed her family something awful, but other than that, life was good and getting better all the time. After only a short while, she was already a headliner.

Come See
THE BILLY BEVINS FLYING CIRCUS

Featuring
FRITZI
The Most Famous Female in the Air Today

Performing
Death-Defying Aerial Stunts
&
THRILLS AND CHILLS!

See Famed Aviator Billy Bevins & Fritzi, the Female Daredevil
Perform Spectacular Stunts & Flying Demonstrations
&
BE AMAZED!

This Saturday at Legion Field
Starting at 2 p.m.
Fun for the Whole Family

Rides: $5.00 for 10 minutes

And they were spectacular stunts. Fritzi, dressed in her purple leather flying outfit with her long white scarf, tall boots, and helmet, would crawl out on the wings and do her stunts and dance for a while. Then, at a certain point, Billy, who was wearing a parachute, would level the plane and crawl out of the cockpit onto the other wing and walk to the end and jump off. People on the ground would scream in terror. "Oh, no! He's left the girl up there all alone! She'll be killed!" In the meantime, Fritzi would crawl back into the cockpit and take over the controls. And then, to the audience's surprise, she would perform rolls, loops, and tumbling spins almost all the way down, then, at the very last second, pull up and do the same thing again, leaving the audience screaming and breathless, thinking she would crash at any minute while Billy slowly floated to the ground in his parachute.

The crossover in the air looked dangerous to the crowd, but Billy, who left nothing to chance, had timed it to the last second.

When Fritzi would finally come in for a landing, her plane would be mobbed with fans. She liked that, and so did Billy. While Fritzi was still out on the field, signing autographs and posing for pictures and taking people up for ten-minute rides at five dollars a pop, Billy would be over at the airport bar, having drinks and "counting the gate." Some weekends, Fritzi's cut was almost seventy-five dollars.

Fritzi was glad she could send a little money home to help out. Momma still worried about her night and day, but Poppa said, "She's happy, Linka."

"Yes, she's happy she's showing off," Momma would say with a sigh. "But at least she's showing off for money."

POINT CLEAR, ALABAMA

SOOKIE WAS WORRIED ABOUT TELLING THE CHILDREN AND WAS TRYING to figure out the best way to do it. What could she do to soften the blow? She picked up her new cookbook, *Polish Cuisine*. Maybe she would have them all over for dinner and fix nothing but traditional Polish dishes, and if they liked it, she could say something like, "Well, I'm glad, because as it turns out, you all have Polish DNA." She read the recipes to see what she could do, but everything had too many beets and too much sauerkraut.

She knew her kids, and they would definitely not like golonka, pork knuckles cooked with vegetables, or zrazy, stuffed slices of beef and tripe. Besides, she didn't know what tripe was. She tried her best to find something fun she could make, but it was no use. She finally just gave up trying when she came to something called czernina, duck blood soup. Oh, dear. This was not going to work at all. She would just have to find another way. She supposed that when she did tell the children, she should probably start with Dee Dee first. And that was going to be very hard.

Lenore had filled Dee Dee's head with the Simmons family history and all that silly First Families of Virginia nonsense, and at times, Dee Dee could be a little snobbish. When Dee Dee was thirteen, Sookie overheard her saying to a new little girl in the neighborhood, "My grandmother is a sixth-generation Simmons from England. Who are your people?" She had made Dee Dee immediately apologize to the little girl. She also asked Lenore to please stop telling Dee Dee that she was better than everyone else. But, as usual, Lenore was absolutely no help. "Well, Sookie," she said. "Do you want me to lie to the child? Breeding counts in animals. Why not in people as well?"

As the days went by, Sookie started feeling a little steadier than she had. And, thankfully, after that one close call when she had driven by the cemetery, she had been able to successfully avoid seeing her mother. Then one morning she ran downtown for just a second to pick up the dry-cleaning and ran smack into her.

Sookie managed a pleasant hello, but Lenore just stared at her and said not, "How are you?" or "Are you feeling any better?" but "Good Lord, Sookie, your skin looks terrible. How long has it been since you've had a facial?" It was all Sookie could do not to strangle her right in front of the hardware store. As she walked away, her heart was pounding, and her hands felt all sweaty. It was at that moment she realized she must be more upset than she knew.

When she got home she called Dena.

"Sookie! I'm so glad you called. How are you, honey?"

"Terrible."

"Oh, no. Are you having problems?"

"Well, if you consider wanting to murder someone in broad day-light, only a half block from the police station, problematic, then yes."

"Oh, honey, that doesn't sound like you."

"No, it doesn't. I could be right in the middle of a nervous break-down and not even know it."

"Are you concerned?"

"Yes, I'm concerned. Considering the fact that I don't know about my real genetic makeup, who knows what I might be capable of doing? I could have relatives sitting in jail right now. I could be a danger to myself and others."

"Oh, Sookie, I'm sure that's not true."

"Really?"

"No, of course not. I'm sure that you come from a lovely, sweet family. You wouldn't be you if you hadn't."

After they hung up, Sookie hoped what Dena had said was true. She had done a little research on the subject and she knew that there were twenty-three chromosomes from each parent. She may never know about the unknown father, but she supposed for the kids' sake, for health reasons alone, she should try and find out a little something about her mother's side of the family—and for her sake as well. If by any slight chance she did have homicidal tendencies, she needed to know now, rather than later.

AFTER A FEW HOURS, Sookie finally got up her nerve and called information and got the number for the Pulaski, Wisconsin, Chamber of Commerce. She grabbed a small paper bag just in case she started to hyperventilate. When she dialed area code 920 and the number, a woman with a very blunt and definite accent that was alien to Sookie's ears answered and said, "This is Marian. Can I help you?"

"Oh . . . hello. You don't know me, but I'm calling to inquire about a family there named Jurdabralinski?"

"Who?"

She spelled the name for her. "J-U-R-D-A-B-R-A-L-I-N-S-K-I."

"Oh, the Jurdabralinskis. The Gas Station Family."

"Pardon me?"

"They used to run the gas station in town."

"Oh, I see. . . . Well, do you happen to know if the family was healthy?"

"Healthy?"

"Yes. Any history of diabetes, heart problems, any mental issues, cancer, or alcoholism?"

"Oh, geez. I never heard anything about that. My mom went to school with a couple of the Jurdabralinski gals, and as I recall, there were four girls and a boy, and two of the girls were twins."

"Twins? Really? Oh for heaven's sake."

"Oh, yeah. And one of the girls became a nun. And they were all healthy as far as I know."

"Do you know if any of them are still around?"

"Oh, let's see. . . . I think Tula Tanawaski was a Jurdabralinski before she married Norbert, but they moved to Madison. Are you a relative?"

"Oh, no, I'm just a college student doing some research on old Polish families."

"Well, we've sure got a lot of them in Pulaski. Now, I can find out more about the Jurdabralinskis for you, where they are and so forth, but it'll take a few days. We're awful busy here this week. We've got the Pulaski Polka Days going on, and we're up to our ears in activities, with the parade and all."

"Oh, well, I won't keep you, then. I'll call back next week."

"Give me your name, hon."

"My name?" Sookie panicked. "Oh, it's Alice. Alice Finch."

"Well, okay, Alice. I'll talk to ya next week, then."

She hated to lie to the woman, and she was sure she didn't sound like a college student, but she had to protect her real mother and Lenore as well. As she was quickly finding out, one deception begets a hundred others. At least she had gotten a little information. The woman said the Jurdabralinskis were healthy as far as she knew. That was all the information she really needed. Her hands were shaking as it was. What if her mother was the one who became a nun? Then she really wouldn't want me showing up. And if she found out that her child had not been raised Catholic, she wouldn't like that, either. She had enough information. Too much really. She was afraid to call back. Who knows what else she might find out?

Oh, dear. Dena was right. She really did need professional help.

HELP

POINT CLEAR, ALABAMA

"HELLO, DR. SHAPIRO?"

"Yes?"

"You don't know me, but I was wondering. I just live ten minutes from your office. Do you ever make house calls?"

"Oh, are you housebound?" he asked with some concern.

"Yes . . . well, sort of. I have a problem that, for many reasons, needs to remain anonymous."

"I understand, but I assure you that anything we discuss in session is confidential. Would you like to set up an appointment?"

"I would, but I can't. I know it's probably hard for you to understand, but my problem has to do with my mother. And if anybody saw me going in or coming out of your office, she would hear about it. She just knows everybody."

"I see. And are you still living at home with your parents?"

"Oh, no. I'm a fifty . . . uh . . . sixty-year-old woman with a husband and four grown children."

"I'm sorry. You sounded younger. Well, could you go into a little more detail?"

"This phone call isn't being recorded, is it?"

"No."

"Well, I've just had a terrible shock. I just found out I could be the daughter of a Polish nun from Wisconsin and that I am not who I thought I was at all. Dena, my friend, said I need professional help. She's married to a psychiatrist. Then today, when I wanted to strangle my mother, I realized she was right. Dena had already suggested that I call you, but I didn't. But now I'm worried that I could be having a nervous breakdown. I might need medication, but I'm not sure. Can you prescribe something over the phone?"

"No, I would need to see you first."

"Oh . . . darn."

"But I guess I could see you at your house, if you'd like."

"You could?"

"Yes."

"Wonderful. When?"

"Just a second . . . uh . . . I have an hour open at four o'clock to-morrow afternoon. Would that work?"

"Absolutely. Let me give you my address. It's . . . oh . . . you know, Dr. Shapiro, on second thought, that might not be a good idea. My mother lives just one house down from me, and she could just pop in any minute. And she never knocks. I know it's a lot to ask, but could we possibly meet somewhere else?"

"All right. If that would make you more comfortable. Where?"

"Uh, let's see—oh I know. How about the Waffle House on High-way 98?"

"Fine. And could you give me your name?"

There was a pause. "I'd really rather not . . . if you don't mind. I would prefer it not get around that I was seeing a psychiatrist."

"Okay, then. But how will I recognize you?"

"Oh, dear. Well, I'll tell you what. I'll be wearing a hat—and pink sneakers with pom-poms. Is that all right?"

"Okay."

"Oh, and how much will it be?"

"Well, let's just meet first and see where we need to go from there."

After Dr. Shapiro hung up, he was a little apprehensive. He had never met a patient outside of his office before and certainly never at a Waffle House, but the poor lady on the phone was either a paranoid schizophrenic or one of the craziest people he had ever talked to. Either way, she obviously needed help.

PULASKI, WISCONSIN

MAY 1941

WINK HAD GRADUATED FROM HIGH SCHOOL AND WAS NOW WORKING full-time at the filling station with his cousin Florian. He knew his parents needed him at home. His father was slowing down a bit and was not as strong as he used to be. Years of sleeping on a cot in the back of the filling station, being up and down all night, and going out in the freezing cold had started to take its toll. But secretly, Wink, who had his pilot's license, was chomping at the bit to get into the fight overseas. A few of his friends had snuck into Canada and joined the RAF and had been sent to England and were already in the thick of the fighting. But he had promised his girlfriend, Angie, who was two years younger, that he would take her to the senior prom, and at this point, anything Angie wanted, she got, and he didn't want to go off and leave her still single in a town full of bohunks like himself. He was not sure what to do, so he called Fritzi and asked her what she thought. She said, "Well, Wink-a-Dink, the old ball-and-chain bit's not for me, but if that's what you want, you've got yourself a great gal. You know I've always liked Angie, so I say full speed ahead."

"Okay! Thanks, Fritzi."

"Hey, do you have enough to buy a ring?"

"Oh . . . I forgot about that."

"Well, don't worry. I happen to be a little flush right now. Had some luck at a poker game up in Des Moines last week, so I'll send you a little when she says yes—and she will."

"Oh, thanks, Fritzi. But I don't know. I may have waited too long. She's been getting pretty popular lately."

"Well, get off the phone, knucklehead, and get over there."

WINK NEEDN'T HAVE WORRIED. Angie Broukowski had been madly in love with him since she was in the eighth grade. To her, Wink was the most handsome, most wonderful, sweetest boy in the world. She had only one goal in life: to become Mrs. Wencent Jurdabralinski, so of course she said yes, and they set a date in June. Between both families, there were to be more than two hundred relatives at the actual wedding, and the number of people coming to the reception afterward was so large that it had to be held at Zeilinski's Ballroom outside of town.

FRITZI CAME HOME A few days before the ceremony to help out with the festivities, and everybody in town was glad to see her. Since she'd started flying with the Billy Bevins Flying Circus, she'd had several write-ups in the local paper, and everybody was so proud of her. They felt like she was their very own Polish movie star. Her younger sisters, who had never been out of Pulaski and had grown up wearing mostly handmade dresses that Momma made, could hardly believe they had such a glamorous sister who had actually been to Chicago.

They sat in her room and stared at her in awe as she put on clothes that they had seen only in magazines. Fritzi even wore a tiny gold ankle bracelet, the height of sophistication, they thought, and just when they thought they had seen it all, the little white frilly cocktail hat she pulled out of a box was so elegant and saucy, they all screamed.

The next morning, Wink came into the kitchen and asked where Fritzi was, and Momma said, "Oh, you know your sister. She and your dad are already out walking around town, big-shotting it." Momma said it like she didn't approve, but she was really glad about it. She hadn't seen Poppa this happy in a long time.

Fritzi had tried to get Billy to come home for the wedding with her, but he'd refused. He said he was allergic to anything that involved church or him having to wear a tie.

However, on the day of the wedding, Fritzi figured that he either felt bad because he hadn't come or else he was drunk or both, because as the bride and groom came out of the church, Billy was flying around up above and had written inside a big heart "Congratulations, Wink and Angie," and then flew on back to Grand Rapids. As mad as she was at him, Fritzi had to laugh at the fool. He must have hijacked the plane right off the field, because he wasn't working that weekend. But that was Billy.

THE WAFFLE HOUSE

DR. SHAPIRO, A NICE-LOOKING YOUNG MAN IN GLASSES, WAS THERE A few minutes early and now wondered if the lady would even show up. But, suddenly, a woman wearing pink tennis shoes with pom-poms, large white plastic sunglasses in the shape of two hearts, and a man's fishing hat with lures all over it appeared at the plate glass window and was peering in. She then came in the door and quickly looked around the room, spotted him, hurried back to the booth, and said, "Dr. Shapiro?"

"Yes."

"It's me. Your patient."

He had the urge to say, "I never would have guessed," but his wife said people in the South didn't like his New York humor, so he said, "Please sit down."

She took her seat and slumped way down in the booth. The minute she did so, a large waitress in a pink uniform came over and said cheerfully, "Oh, hi, Mrs. Poole, I haven't seen you in here in a long time."

"Well, so much for anonymity," thought Sookie. "Oh, hello, Jewel," she said.

Jewel looked at Dr. Shapiro and asked Sookie, "Is this your cute son, the one your mother's always talking about?"

"No . . . just a friend."

"Oh. Well, what y'all gonna have today?"

"Just coffee, please. Decaf," said Sookie.

Dr. Shapiro added, "Make that two."

After Jewel walked away, Sookie said, "First of all, thank you so much for meeting me."

"Of course. How can I help you? You say you have a problem?"

"Yes, I do. And it's a very long story. Well, let me start at the beginning. A few weeks ago, I was feeding my birds. I have a terrible blue jay problem. I had thought I would try just putting sunflower seeds in the backyard and just the plain Pretty Boy small-bird seed in the front. . . ."

Thirty minutes and three cups of coffee later, when she finally got around to telling him just who her mother was, he suddenly understood. No wonder this lady was a nervous wreck. He'd met the mother. Who wouldn't be?

At eight A.M. the first morning after Dr. Shapiro and his wife had moved into their new house, they were awakened by what he thought sounded like a band of Hare Krishnas jingling up the front stairs. When he opened the door, he was greeted by a large, imposing-looking woman in a cape, holding a huge basket with a ribbon on it, who announced in a loud voice, "Good morning. I am Lenore Simmons Krackenberry, president of the Point Clear Welcome Wagon Committee, and on behalf of the entire committee, I want to say . . ." and then she sang at the top of her voice to the tune of "Shuffle Off to Buffalo," "Welcome! Welcome! Welcome! May we help ya, help ya, help ya! With your brand-new move!" Then she shoved the basket at him and said, "The rest of the girls will be along in a minute, but I wanted to get here first." And with that, she stormed right past him and into the house, calling out, "Oh, Mrs. Shapirooo . . . put the coffee on. You've got company!" He had spent only one hour with her, but it seemed obvious that the mother was the one who needed medication, not this poor woman. But he let Sookie continue to talk, because she seemed to be in such distress.

"So as I told Dena, I just feel all wicky-wacky. One minute, I'm mad at my mother and then I feel guilty and then I get mad at her all over again. So do you think I'm having a nervous breakdown?"

"I think under the circumstances, anger and confusion are perfectly natural."

"You do? You think it's *natural* to want to strangle your mother?"

"Under certain circumstances, yes. You feel betrayed and hurt and, naturally, you want to lash out."

"That's right. Yes, I do."

"Nobody likes to be lied to."

"No, they don't, do they? Oh, I feel so much better already. Dr. Shapiro, you're a professional, so you would know if someone was having a breakdown, wouldn't you?"

"Yes."

"So in your opinion, I'm not getting ready to flip out or anything?"

"I think it's highly unlikely."

Sookie sighed a huge sigh of relief. "Well, I just can't thank you enough. And this wasn't nearly as scary as I thought it would be. I'm sure you've heard this before, but you're such a good listener."

"Well, thank you."

"And you must think I'm very rude. Here I am going on and on about my problems, and I haven't asked you a thing about yourself."

"That's perfectly fine, Mrs. Poole. I'm here to listen to you."

"Oh, before I forget, how much do I owe you for this? And do you mind if I pay you in cash? I don't want the people at the bank to know that I had to see a psychiatrist. They might not say anything, but you never know. I've enjoyed this so much, could we do it again? Same time next week, same booth?"

To his surprise, Dr. Shapiro found himself agreeing.

After Dr. Shapiro got back to his office, he jotted down a few notes.

New patient: Mild situational anxiety and very nice lady.
Mother of patient: Narcissist with mild to severe illusions of grandeur.

WAR

Before the Sunday mass started, Father Sobieski had gone to the side door of the vestry and motioned for Stanislaw Jurdabralinski, who always sat in the first row, to come around to the back of the church. His altar boy had not shown up, and he needed him to fill in. It was kind of funny to see the five-foot-nine-inch priest enter the altar with the six-foot-four Stanislaw, wearing a black-and-white altar boy vestment that, on him, looked more like a blouse, but the mass came off without a hitch. After mass, the Jurdabralinskis walked home together, except for the youngest, Sophie, who always stayed and helped the nuns wash and iron the vestments for the next week's service.

Later that day, Gertrude and Tula were over at the Rainbow Skating Rink, practicing their routine for the big skating contest that was coming up, when Mrs. Wanda Glinski, the organist, abruptly stopped playing, right in the middle of "Blue Skies," and everyone wondered what had happened. A few seconds later, an announcement was made over the loudspeaker that the Japanese had just attacked Pearl Harbor and that the rink was closing. As stunned skaters slowly started heading off the floor, Mrs. Glinski began playing "God Bless America."

A few blocks away at the Pulaski theater, people were watching *How Green Was My Valley,* starring Maureen O'Hara and Walter Pidgeon. Wink's wife, Angie, and a girlfriend were seeing it for the second time, when the screen began to slowly fade, and the house lights came on. The theater manager walked out on the stage and said, "Ladies and gentlemen, we just got word that the Japanese have attacked Pearl Harbor, and all servicemen are to report to their bases immediately." As confused people got up out of their seats, gathering their things and silently beginning to file out down the aisles, a picture of the American flag suddenly appeared on the screen.

Most of them had no idea where Pearl Harbor was or why it had anything to do with them, but those few who did were somber. One man said, "Well, we're all in it now."

Over at the church, one of the nuns came in and told Sophie that she was to go home to her family right away, but did not tell her why. When Sophie got to the house, Momma and the other girls had all gathered in the kitchen, and the minute she saw her, Momma grabbed her and held her close. Poppa was sitting at the table with his ear to the radio and kept shaking his head in disbelief as he listened to the same report repeated over and over. After a moment, he looked up at his wife with a stricken expression on his face. "Oh, Linka, we can't lose America. If we lose America . . ." Then his voice cracked and the big strong man, who had always been their tower of strength, put his head down on the table and sobbed. All the girls quickly gathered around their father and hugged him, while his wife stood by, helpless and unable to do anything. She knew he was right. If America was lost, then there was no hope—not only for them, but also for the world.

Fritzi and Billy had just done an air show outside of Akron, Ohio, on Saturday, and as usual on Sunday morning, Billy stayed in bed with a hangover. Fritzi was up and already downstairs in the hotel coffee shop when she heard the news from a bellboy who ran in the door and yelled, "The Japs just bombed Pearl Harbor! It looks like war!" and ran back out, on his way to tell everyone in the hotel and up and down the street.

When Fritzi got back upstairs with his coffee, Billy was wide awake and sitting up. She sat down on the bed and handed the coffee to him. "Honey, have you heard?"

He nodded. "Yeah, some kid just ran down the hall, so I guess it's true, then?"

Fritzi said, "Yeah, it seems to be."

He took a few more sips of his coffee, then looked at her and said, "Well, that's it for me." He got up, showered and shaved, put his clothes on, and headed out to find the nearest recruiting office. Fritzi tried to call her family back home, but all the circuits were busy.

By the time Billy got downtown, he saw that a line had already formed, and the office had not yet opened, but one of the guys said someone was on the way. Billy was older than most in line, but he was more than willing to go. In fact, he couldn't wait. Like all the other guys that day, he was mad. How dare those bastards attack America. Just who the hell did they think they were fooling with?

That Sunday, as the news spread across the country, people who hadn't thought much about it suddenly felt things they hadn't just a day before. At the big hockey game at Madison Square Garden, after the announcement was made and as all the men in uniform stood up and started filing out of the stadium, headed back to their bases, everyone suddenly stood and gave them an ovation that didn't stop until the last man had left the stadium.

From that day forward, the National Anthem was not just something Americans had to get through before a game started. Now hats came off, hands were held over hearts, and the cheer at the end was heartfelt. They had just gone through one war and a Depression, and nobody wanted war, but now that it was here, there was nothing more to do, except get in there and win it as fast as possible.

Sunday night, Wink came over to the house with a teary-eyed Angie beside him. They sat in the living room with Momma and Poppa, and Wink, just a year out of high school and for the first time looking like a grown man, said, "Poppa, I hate to leave you to run the station, but you know I'm going to be drafted sooner or later, and if I sign up now, I have a shot at getting into the Army Air Corps."

Momma said, "But, Wink, Angie is going to have a baby."

Angie looked at Momma. "I tried to talk him out of it, but he won't listen to me."

Poppa looked at Wink. "You do what you think is right, son. Don't worry about the station. We'll get by."

"Thanks, Poppa, and listen, while I'm gone, can Angie move into my old room upstairs and stay with you guys until I get back?"

"Of course," said Momma. "We would love to have her."

"I can help with the cooking," said Angie. "I just don't want to move back home. I think I won't miss him so much if I'm here."

AT SIX A.M. THE next morning, Wink, along with almost every boy in his senior class, stood outside the drugstore in the snow, waiting to be picked up by the school buses that were driving them to Green Bay to sign up.

Billy took his army physical in Grand Rapids and would have been 4F because of his liver, but they needed all the experienced pilots they could get and as fast as they could get them, so he and his bad liver were ordered to report to Pensacola, Florida, on December 15. In the next few days, he officially disbanded the Flying Circus and, luckily, was able to sell the planes to a flying school.

On the afternoon of December 12, Fritzi saw him off at the train station, and when he stepped up on the train, he said, "I don't know when I'll see you again, pal, so take care of yourself, and write me a letter every once in a while, okay?"

"I will."

As the train started pulling out, he shouted over the noise of the engine, "Hey, who's your best friend?"

"You are!" she yelled.

He gave her a thumbs-up, and that was the last glimpse she had of him. When she left the train station, the streets were packed, and she couldn't get a cab, so she had to walk back to the hotel in the snow. As she walked, she noticed a lot of the store windows had already been decorated for Christmas, and some had been left only half done.

She and Billy had been together for a long time but had made no commitments. She had realized that Billy was not the marrying kind, and evidently, neither was she. But still, she was already feeling a little lost without him. When she got back up to the hotel room, she saw the envelope on the dresser he had left. Inside was a hundred-dollar bill and a note.

Merry Christmas, Squirt. Buy yourself a new hat.

Billy

Fritzi sat on the bed, wondering what she was going to do now. She didn't want to just hang around, waiting and doing nothing. And damn it to hell, it wasn't fair. She could fly as well as most of the guys she knew. She had tried to enlist in the army and showed her pilot's license to the man at the recruiting office, but he informed her that neither the Army Air Corps nor any of the armed services would take female fliers.

"Why not?" she asked. "The plane doesn't know if it's a man or a woman flying it."

"Regulations," he said. "Now, if you could just step aside and let me get on with my business. We're at war, little lady, and war's no place for women."

One guy standing behind her piped up. "I've got a place for you, honey, anytime," as the other guys laughed.

Fritzi picked up her license and stuck it back in her purse and said, "Well, okay, if that's how you feel. It's your loss." As she walked out, she said, "So long, knuckleheads, see you in the funny papers." But she was mad and hurt, and when she got back to her room, she sat down and cried her eyes out.

She knew from the magazines that England and Russia were using female pilots to ferry planes, but here, it was a no-go. So that afternoon, she packed up her purple leather flying suit and the rest of her clothes and went home to Pulaski, just in time to say good-bye to Wink. He had been accepted into the Army Air Corps and was being sent to Scott Field in Illinois for training.

Now she had even more reasons to hate the Japs. They had knocked her out of a swell career, Billy and Wink were gone, and she was stuck on the ground for the duration. It was quite a comedown. But flying and doing stunts was all she knew how to do, so after a while, she signed up for the job on the canning line, back at the pickle factory.

LUNCH WITH LENORE

———

POINT CLEAR, ALABAMA

IT WAS GOING TO BE A VERY HARD DAY. IN THE PAST, SOOKIE AND Lenore had a standing lunch date every Wednesday, and Sookie really couldn't put it off any longer without causing even more trouble. Lenore had already left a picture of herself in Sookie's mailbox with a note attached. "In case you have forgotten, this is your mother. Where are you?!"

Sookie sighed and looked at the clock and dialed the phone. After a moment, her mother picked up. "Hello, this is Lenore. To whom do I have the pleasure of speaking, please?"

"It's me, Mother."

"Oh . . . hello, you."

"How was your water therapy?"

"Very wet. Where are you?"

"I'm at home, why?"

"I thought maybe you had moved to China. Are we finally going to lunch today? Or have you called to tell me you have suddenly come down with some other mysterious disease?"

"No, Mother, we are going to lunch. Where do you want to go?"

"Oh, I don't care. You pick."

"Well, how about the Fairhope Inn?"

"No, I'm tired of that."

"Okay. The Bay Café?"

"No, let's go to the Colony. I'm in the mood for crab cakes."

"Fine. I'll pick you up."

When Sookie hung up, she noticed her stomach was hurting. Just the tone of Lenore's voice was already irking her last nerve.

LENORE SWEPT INTO THE restaurant and waved at everybody she knew. And as usual, if there was someone there she didn't know, she went over and introduced herself. As head of the Welcome Wagon Committee, she was sure they wanted to meet her.

When she sat back down, she said, "That cute couple over in the corner are visiting all the way from Canada, can you imagine? Anyhow, she was very nice and said she loved the color of my hair, and I said, 'Well, if one must go gray, it's just as easy to go silver.' I gave her Jo Ellen's number. Did you order my crab cakes?"

"Yes."

Lenore waved at the couple again and turned back to Sookie. "She really could use a new rinse. But look at you, Sookie. You're fifty-nine years old, and you don't have a gray hair on your head. Count yourself lucky, my girl. When I was your age, I was already completely white, but I think it's an English trait. Queen Elizabeth went gray early as well."

"So you said."

"As you know, I used to be a strawberry blonde."

"Yes, Mother, you have told me that almost every day of my life."

"Well, it's true. I was known far and wide for being the only strawberry blonde in south Alabama. At the Senior Military Ball, when they played, 'Casey Would Waltz with a Strawberry Blonde and the Band Played On,' everyone in the room stopped and stared at us. Your father was a wonderful dancer. We both were, and they played it over and over again. And all the other boys would cut in, and I remember one said, 'Lenore, dancing with you is like dancing with a feather.' But, then, I was always light on my feet." She looked over at Sookie and sighed. "Oh, Sookie, I wish you just hadn't given up on your dancing lessons."

"I didn't *just* give up on them, Mother. If you remember, Miss Wheasly told me it would be best for the class if I pursued other interests—something I had a natural talent for."

Lenore made a face and looked away. "Mrs. Bushnell's daughter, Gage, is a prima ballerina in New York. That could have been you, Sookie."

"When every time I went up on a point, I fell over? I don't think so, Mother."

"I don't think you tried, that's all."

Sookie looked at her. "What?"

"Well, I'm very sorry, but it wasn't me that gave up a promising career to marry Earle Poole, Jr."

"Mother, what promising career? As what?"

"Oh, Sookie, you could have been anything in the world if you had wanted to. You had a real chance to be something, but no. You threw it all away to marry Earle Poole, Jr. I didn't have the opportunity like you did. When I was at Judson, I excelled in dramatics. Dr. Howell said that I could have been a professional actress if I had wanted to, and he taught Tallulah Bankhead, so I guess he knew a talented actress when he saw one. Of course, Tallulah's daddy let her do what she wanted, but Daddy wouldn't let me go on the stage. And it's a shame, really, because I always wondered what would have happened if I had. There's no telling what I could have done if I had been allowed to follow my natural bent. I might have gone straight from the stage to the movies, but I married your father and settled for being just a housewife."

"Mother, you were never just a housewife."

"Well, I was so. I cooked and cleaned and raised two children, and if that wasn't me, then who was it?"

"Mother, you never cooked, and you never cleaned."

"Well, I oversaw everything, and anyhow, that's not the point. That's why I pushed you to be something. But you just never had any ambition, and I don't understand it. You are descended from a long line of leaders. Your great-grandmother single-handedly saved the family home from the Yankees, and you are just content to sit around all day and fiddle with those birds. You will be sixty years old soon, and what have you done? If I told you once, I have told you a hundred times. You need to think about your duty as a Simmons, and at least try to accomplish something to be proud of before it's too late."

Sookie had heard this same speech a hundred times, but today was obviously one time too many. "Mother, just stop it. All that Simmons stuff is just a bunch of baloney, and you know it!" Sookie was stunned at her own outburst.

Lenore was shocked as well and just looked at her for what seemed to be a long time and then said, "I don't know what you mean, Sookie. It's obvious that you are just not yourself today, and so I am going home." Lenore stood up, walked out, and got into the car and waited.

Sookie, still a little shaken, paid the bill and went out, and drove her mother home in silence. When they arrived at her house, Lenore got out of the car and said, "Call me if and when you regain your senses."

Sookie felt terrible about snapping at her mother like that and immediately called Dr. Shapiro, and he met her for an emergency meeting. But he did not find her behavior alarming at all. "It's to be expected," he said.

Sookie understood that that kind of behavior might be expected somewhere else, but in Point Clear, Alabama, upset or not, she should never have raised her voice in public. It just wasn't ladylike, and besides, she was married to a dentist, and a certain amount of decorum was expected.

CHRISTMAS

———

PULASKI, WISCONSIN
1941

MOMMA HAD TRIED. SHE STILL BAKED THE OPLATKI—POLISH CHRIST-mas wafers—as usual, but it was a bleak old Christmas in 1941. All of the songs about peace on earth and goodwill toward men that played in between the grim news of the war rang a little hollow that year. It seemed the whole country was preoccupied with one thing. Every large company in America was busy changing over, mobilizing, and gearing up to put all their resources toward the war effort. Everybody wanted to do something to try to help win the war and get the boys home again.

Fritzi had been home for only about a month when their old friend, bathroom inspector and nurse Dottie Frakes, came by for a visit and informed them that after today, she was taking a leave of absence from Phillips Petroleum to become an army nurse. After a big lunch, Poppa went back to work, and Momma and the other girls started to clean the kitchen. Dottie offered to help clean up, but Momma said, "No, you two just go relax."

Dottie got up and said, "All right, then, Fritzi, let's you and me go sit in the parlor and have a little catch-up chat."

As they went in, Dottie turned and pulled the wooden sliding doors shut and turned to Fritzi with a concerned look. "How long has your father had that cough?"

"Oh, quite a while, I think. He's had a bad cold. Why?"

"I didn't want to alarm your mother or the girls, but I don't like the sound of that cough."

"What do you mean?"

"I've worked in hospitals, and I know what that sound means."

"Oh . . . what?"

"He needs to see a doctor as soon as possible."

That afternoon, Fritzi tried to get her father to go see the doctor, but he said, "Oh, Fritzi, I can't leave the station for that kind of foolishness. You know how shorthanded we are now. I'm fine. I'll be better tomorrow."

She put her hands on his shoulders and pleaded with him. "Please, Poppa. Just go for me."

He laughed. "If I'm not better in a week, I'll go. I promise."

When she had first arrived home, Fritzi had noticed how thin and tired her father looked, but when she felt his shoulders now, there was nothing there but skin and bones.

She hated to do it to Poppa, but she had to tell Momma what Dottie had said and see if Momma could talk some sense into him. Before she even finished the sentence, Momma had her apron off and her hat and coat on and was headed next door to the filling station. Five minutes later, she and Poppa were downtown, sitting in Dr. Renschoske's office. Momma was an old-fashioned wife and rarely questioned her husband in any way, but not this time.

The tests came back, and the diagnosis was as Dottie had suspected: advanced tuberculosis that had to be treated right away. But when the doctor started talking to him about the different sanitariums that specialized in TB treatments, Stanislaw would have no part of it. "Just give me some medicine. I have a business to run."

"Stanislaw, you won't be alive to run anything if you don't do what I tell you. You will go home and get in bed and rest until Linka and I work out where you are going and when."

He did, and in the meantime, his nineteen-year-old nephew Florian was put in charge of running the station. Three days later, the arrangements for Stanislaw had been made at the sanitarium. The hard part was getting him there. All the trains and buses were full of servicemen trying to get to bases. So Fritzi called a flying pal of hers and Billy's in Grand Rapids, who flew over and picked up Poppa to fly him all the way down to Hot Springs, Arkansas. Poor Poppa. He had flown off with two sets of clean pajamas, a sack full of sausages, and a rosary that Sophie had slipped into his pocket. When the plane had taken off, Momma, who had never been separated from him for even one night, had stood and cried into her apron and wondered if she would ever see him again.

AND AS IF THINGS couldn't get worse, Florian soon received his draft notice, as did Poppa's mechanic. The other fellow they had just hired to fill in quit to work in Sturgeon Bay, where he could make more money, and Momma was worried to death.

A week later, after Fritzi came home from work, Momma went into her room and closed the door behind her and told her about an offer she had received from a man in Oshkosh to buy the station. Fritzi was stunned that her mother would even think about selling. "You can't do that, Momma."

"But Fritzi, what will we do when Florian and the boys leave for good? We have to close down. There will be no one left to run the station. When I think how hard Poppa worked to get this place . . . it will kill him for sure."

"You can't sell it, Momma."

"But Fritzi, the hospital costs so much. We have to. Who knows how long Poppa will have to stay away or how long the war will last. And there are no men left to hire. They will be all gone—either to the service or working at the factories. We have no choice."

Fritzi said, "Yes, we do."

"What?"

"I'll run it!"

"Oh, Fritzi, by yourself? You can't do that."

"No, not by myself. The whole family—all of us. Now that you have Angie to help cook, Gertrude, Tula, and Sophie can help."

"But, Fritzi, you can't have all girls running a filling station. Nobody would come."

When Momma said that, something suddenly clicked in Fritzi's mind, and she said, "Momma, you just wait and see."

Later, Fritzi called a meeting in the kitchen with all the girls and told them her idea. They seemed skeptical. "But we don't know how to fix a motor or anything about carburetors and things like that," said Gertrude.

"No, but I do."

Tula said, "But it's so dirty over there. I don't want to get grease all over me."

"Oh, come on, girls. We can't let Poppa down now or Wink. We've all worked at the station at one time or another, and what we don't know, we can learn. Florian isn't leaving for a couple of weeks. He can teach you what you need to know, and I can teach you the rest. I know we can do it. Whatta ya say?"

The sisters all turned to Momma. "What do you think, Momma?"

Momma said, "I think you should listen to what Fritzi says. She's the man of the house now."

THE NEXT DAY, FRITZI gave her notice at the pickle factory. That night, she rooted around in the gas station files and found Poppa's old study materials from the service station management course he had taken. She sat down and studied all night long. It didn't look too hard. All you had to do was follow instructions.

1. Welcome greetings and windshield service
2. Gasoline solicitation
3. Radiator check, oil check, battery test, tire pressure check— including spare tire—lubrication check, vacuum service offered
4. Itemized collection and friendly farewell and thanks for stopping
5. Attendants must be neat and clean at all times, fingernails, uniforms, etc.

"Oh, hell," thought Fritzi. This was going to be easy. She knew most of this stuff already.

The gals would need uniforms, so Momma took all of Wink's and

Poppa's old uniform pants and shirts and cut them down to fit the girls. Just for an extra added touch, she embroidered in red on each individual shirt the words "Hi, I'm Fritzi" or "Hi, I'm Gertrude," and so on.

Fritzi had learned a little about organizing a work team from her old Flying Circus days, so she sat down and worked out a plan. And at the end of the week, everybody had a designated assignment.

Tula would do most of the mechanical work. Gertrude, the strongest girl, would be in charge of changing tires and fixing flats. Fritzi would pump gas and check under the hood and drive the tow truck when needed. Sophie was good at math, so she would work as the cashier. Inside the station, they sold candy, potato chips, cold drinks, hot coffee, and Momma's sausages and home-made sandwiches and pastries. They also sold trinkets, key chains, lighters, glass ashtrays, and toys and gave away free maps and free postcards.

In three weeks' time, Fritzi and her sisters, wearing brand-new uniforms with hats and cute little black bow ties, were ready to start. When word got out that four good-looking sisters were now running a filling station, business suddenly started to pick up. Doing the air shows with Billy, Fritzi had learned a lot about advertising, and pretty soon, ads started appearing in local newspapers that featured a photo of the four smiling girls standing in front of the station with a caption above it that said:

WHEN IN PULASKI, STOP AT WINK'S PHILLIPS 66
THE ALL-GIRL FILLING STATION

They had signs put up along the highway that, underneath their logo, said:

Is your car ailing? Let us kiss it and make it better.
Car dirty? Let us houseclean your car.
The prettiest mechanics in the state of Wisconsin.
Let us put the spark back in your plugs.

Fresh coffee, sandwiches, homemade candy, and Polish sausage inside.
Mothers, we'll change your wipers and your baby's diapers.

As an added attraction, a day before he left for the navy, Gertrude's boyfriend, Nard Tanawaski, had come to the station and rigged up the record player to four big outside speakers. After that, they played big-band swing music all day long. It added some cheer to the cold winter days.

As word continued to spread about the "All-Girl Filling Station," long-haul truck drivers suddenly made it a point to reroute their runs through Pulaski, and a lot of men all the way from Green Bay and as far away as Madison mysteriously developed car trouble.

Carloads of guys and gals carpooling to factories stopped in to fill up on their way to work. The music made them feel happy, and so did the four friendly girls with the big smiles. Before long, they even had big logging trucks swinging down across the border of Canada just to get a look.

Secretly, Fritzi had been worried whether her sisters would be able to handle it, but they surprised her at how they had jumped in and helped. Even though Sophie Marie was still a little shy, she was very pretty and, therefore, a big asset. Nothing helped sales faster than a pretty girl, and the All-Girl Filling Station had *four*.

Dear Wink-a-Dink,

I am sure you know by now that yours truly and your sisters are running the station, so don't worry. We will hold the fort down until that happy day when you come back and take over for good. Soon, I hope.

It's sure hard to look pretty and get dates with grease under your fingernails and with your hair smelling like gasoline. Momma and Angie are cooking almost day and night. We are selling sausages as fast as they can make them. But with the sugar rationing starting . . . no more paczkis or pastries of any kind, and Gertrude is not happy about it.

Love,

Fritzi

P.S. Heard from Billy. He's down in Pensacola instructing naval cadets and says they are scaring the hell out of him. Sure do miss him and wish I was in Florida today enjoying the sunshine, that's for sure. I am sending you a photo of the four of us taken at the station for the newspaper. Don't we look cute?

THE WAFFLE HOUSE

POINT CLEAR, ALABAMA

SOOKIE WAS DEEP IN THOUGHT IN BOOTH NO. 4 AND THEN LEANED IN
and said, "The thing is, Dr. Shapiro, I can understand her not wanting
me to know I was adopted, but all those years of her telling not only
me, but my poor children, how lucky we were to be a Simmons. All
that was a lie, and she's put us in a terrible position. I can't tell the
Daughters of the Confederacy or the Kappas that Dee Dee and I are
not really Simmonses without Lenore finding out. I hate being a
fraud, but I don't want to upset her, either. You don't know me, but
I've never really been this mad at anybody before, and it makes me feel
so bad, but I just don't know how to get over it. I seem to be stuck."

"Well, first of all, as we've said, your anger and hurt at your mother
are perfectly normal, and yes, it was a terrible thing to do to a child,
but I think it might help you to know that most of her behavior was
probably unintentional. Think of a person being born without a foot.
In other words, your mother has a little something missing, and in her
case, it's the ability to see or feel beyond oneself or empathize with
another person's feelings, even one's own children. And in most cases
they're not even aware they are doing it."

"Maybe . . . but I still just don't understand how she could keep
on lying to me all these years."

"I'm not so sure she was lying—at least not in her own mind—and as you have said, when your mother believes something, facts don't mean a thing."

"Well that's true. She's convinced she's related to the queen of England."

"Exactly, and sometimes this kind of delusional thinking is a survival skill gone wrong. What do you know about her childhood?"

"Not much . . . just that she was raised by her grandmother. Her mother died in childbirth, and she said that when she was growing up, her daddy was hardly ever home. He was a state senator so he spent most of his time in Montgomery."

"I see. And has she ever mentioned her mother?"

"Only one time . . ."

"Just once?"

"Yes."

After Sookie left the Waffle House, she realized it was strange. As obsessive and preoccupied as Lenore had been about the Simmons family line, she had never discussed anything about her mother, where she was from, or how old she was when she died. Her name hadn't even shown up in the family Bible. And whenever Sookie had asked about her, Lenore had made it quite clear she didn't want to talk about her. Lenore had never even mentioned her mother at all until that one day after the twins were born. Sookie had been exhausted, and all she wanted to do was stay in bed and rest, but Lenore had stormed into her room and thrown open the blinds. "I'm here to announce the good news. You are going to get up, and we are going out to lunch."

"Mother, not today, please. I'm too tired."

"Oh, come on, Sookie. You'll feel so much better if you do."

"But I don't feel like it. I don't think I ever want to get up again."

"Oh, don't be such a baby. I'm your mother, and you have to do what I say. It would be rude not to. Besides, haven't I always been right? You're just lucky to have a mother who cares. And don't forget you come from a long line of military leaders, and we always advance. We never retreat."

This was a conversation they had had many times, but on this particular day, for some reason, right in the middle of it, a strange faraway look had crossed over Lenore's face—one that Sookie had never seen before. It was as if she suddenly remembered something. Then she said rather sadly, "Oh, Sookie, you just don't know what it's like growing up without a mother. I even used to envy those poor little white-trash sharecropper families that lived out in the country. As poor as they were, at least they had a mother. We only get one chance in life, and I missed mine, and once you miss it . . ." Just for a split second, Sookie thought she saw tears start to well up in her mother's eyes, but then Lenore quickly changed the subject.

Sookie tried to get her to talk more about it, but Lenore said, "There's nothing more to say, except that you and Buck need to get down on your hands and knees and thank your lucky stars you have me. Nothing stings more than an ungrateful child, you know. Now you get up out of that bed and get dressed, and put on something nice. We are going out to lunch, and let there be no ifs, ands, or buts about it. Your life awaits you out in the world, my girl, and you're not lollygagging your life away in bed."

PULASKI, WISCONSIN

FRITZI HAD BEEN HOME FOR ONLY A SHORT WHILE, BUT SHE SOON found out that old Gussie Mintz back in Grand Rapids had been right. Flying was now in her blood, and as busy as she was running the station, she was becoming restless. She missed Billy, but there were still a few good-looking guys left who were doing war jobs. And that big Irish redheaded trucker, Joe O'Connor, from Manitowoc, who was always trying to get her to go out with him, *was* a good-looking son of a gun. She liked him a lot, but she was not in love, and she certainly had no interest in getting married or, God forbid, ever having children. She and Billy had too much to do after the war was over, but Joe was a great dancer, and she was not against having a little fun. After all, she had been to Milwaukee, and knew the score. And as Billy said, "Life is too short for regrets."

As the days went on, the filling station became the center of the war-drive effort in Pulaski. Uncle Sam needed all the supplies he could get for the troops. As an incentive, Fritzi set up a kissing booth outside, and anything that Uncle Sam needed, from a bundle of paper to tin cans, would get you a kiss from one of the girls. And like all filling stations, theirs was an official drop-off place for the huge rubber drive, and considering the reward, all the guys from near and wide collected all the rubber they could—everything from old tires and water hoses to sink stoppers and canning jar tops. One man, eager to get a kiss from one of the girls, even stole his wife's rubber girdle and brought it down, and Mrs. Luczak wasn't happy about it, either. She marched down to the station and got it right back. She said, "Fritzi, I'm as patriotic as the next one. They can have everything else, but I *need* my girdle."

That night, Momma sat down as she always did and wrote to her husband at the sanitarium.

Dear Poppa,

We miss you, but we know you are busy getting well, and we can't wait for you to come home. Oh, Poppa, you would be so proud of your girls. They are all working so hard to help win this old war as fast as possible so Wink and all the boys can come back home soon. They all seem so grown-up now. Even Sophie Marie is such a different girl now. She has realized how pretty she is. All the boys want a kiss from her, but she is the same sweet girl who never misses mass. Wish I could say the same for the other girls, but I know God will forgive them for sleeping in on Sunday. They work so hard during the week. I may have gotten good news about Fritzi. She has been seeing a lot more of that nice Irish boy I told you about. I just pray she will get all that flying planes out of her head and marry him and stay home. We got a nice long letter from Nurse Dorothy Frakes today. She is overseas somewhere and says so many of our poor boys are being killed and hurt, but she says all the nurses are working as hard as they can to save as many as they can. Rest up, Poppa, and don't worry about a thing. We are all fine.

Love,

Momma

THE WAFFLE HOUSE

Point Clear, Alabama

This week, Dr. Shapiro had a cancellation, and they were meeting earlier than usual. Jewel greeted them with a big smile. "Here you two are again. Two coffees?"

Dr. Shapiro said, "Yes, and you don't happen to have a bagel, do you?"

"A what?"

"A bagel?" He could tell by her expression that she didn't and said, "Just give me an English muffin."

"Okay. You want anything, Mrs. Poole?"

"No, thank you, Jewel, I'm fine. I just had breakfast."

After Jewel left, Dr. Shapiro asked, "How are you doing?"

"Oh, a little better, I think, but every time Lenore starts on the Simmons stuff, it's hard not to say anything. It makes me remember all those years growing up and how bad she made me feel. The woman never let me forget anything. She always brought up everything I did wrong."

Dr. Shapiro said, "I understand, but you know, those are your mother's behavioral patterns."

"And then I start to think that I'm just remembering only the bad things."

"Do you have any positive memories about your mother?"

Sookie sat there racking her brain, but nothing came to her.

Jewel brought the coffee and muffin. "Thank you," said Dr. Shapiro.

Sookie put cream and Sweet'N Low in her coffee and frowned. "Hmmm . . . positive memories. Well, I had a wonderful father and brother, and in high school, we were the state football champions my senior year."

"No, I mean positive memories about your mother."

"Well, life with Lenore was never dull, I'll say that. And she is funny. I have to admit she can say and do some of the funniest things. When Buck and I were little and lost a tooth, we would put it under our pillow for the tooth fairy to find, and later, Lenore would always dress up as the tooth fairy, with a tall hat and a wand, and come in our room and dance all around and sing some silly little song and leave us a present under our pillow. And I remember feeling good when everybody said that Buck and I had the prettiest mother in school. And she always smelled so wonderful. One time, I must have been four or five, I was sick with a terrible fever, and I remember she sat by my bed all night and petted my head. Every time I woke up, she was right there. And she would say, 'Don't worry, Mother's right here.'" Suddenly, tears welled up in her eyes, and she was embarrassed and grabbed a napkin. "Oh, Lord, I'm sorry. I don't know why I'm crying."

"Why do you think you are?"

"I guess I just remembered how happy I was to wake up and see her sitting there. I just wish I hadn't disappointed her so much. What about you, Dr. Shapiro, did you have a happy childhood?"

"Let's go back to your last statement for a moment, about disappointing your mother. Did your brother ever disappoint her?"

"Oh, yes, but in a different way. She didn't particularly like Bunny, the girl he married."

"What about earlier? When you were younger?"

"She more or less let him alone. I think the problem was that I was a girl, and she wanted me to be more like her, but I couldn't. And now we know why."

"And if your mother had had a biological daughter, do you think she would have lived up to all her expectations?"

"I think so. Yes."

"How?"

"Well, she probably would have been prettier and smarter. Not had straight hair. She probably would have had talent and certainly been more ambitious."

"*Or* she could have been none of those things. Just because she would be related by blood doesn't guarantee she would have any of these attributes. Did it ever occur to you that Lenore was lucky to have you? I'm amazed you turned out as strong and sane as you did."

"*Me?* I don't feel very strong . . ."

"But why would you? Your mother formed an incorrect opinion of you and, naturally, you agreed with her. Children always think their parents are right. But in this case, your mother was entirely wrong. Think about it. Your mother is an overpowering individual, and yet, you managed to have a stable marriage and raise four children."

Sookie said, "Well, yes, I did, didn't I? And knock on wood, not one of them got on dope that I know of. At least, that's something, isn't it?"

"Yes, it is. You may not be the person your mother wants you to be, but you are you. Our job here is to try and separate the wheat from the chaff and figure out who *you* are and not who your mother thinks you are."

Sookie looked concerned and said, "Oh. And will that require me having to journal?"

"Not unless you want to," he said.

"No. I like just talking."

"Good. Same time next week?"

"I'll be here."

THAT AFTERNOON, SOOKIE CALLED her friend Dena. "I'm so sorry. I know I promised, but I can't go to the Kappa reunion this year."

"Oh, no . . . why?"

"Well, first of all, I just couldn't face everybody, knowing that I am an imposter."

"Oh, Sookie. You know that's not true."

"Well, even so. I can't leave now. I really need to keep seeing Dr. Shapiro, the poor thing. He's so sweet and, honestly, Dena, I think I may be his only patient, and I can't let him down. He depends on me to show up."

THE ALL-GIRL FILLING STATION

Pulaski, Wisconsin

That spring, when the station got busy, Gertrude and Tula came up with an idea of their own to help speed up customer service. They presented it to Fritzi, and she approved.

After that, the minute a car pulled in, Gertrude and Tula, wearing cute little caps and short skirts with fringe on them, would fly out of the station on roller skates, and while Fritzi was filling the car with gas, they would clean all the windows, the lights, and the tag in less than two minutes. And, sometimes, if the boys inside the car were cute, they added extra little twists and twirls and skated backward as they cleaned.

Momma watched them out the window one day and later said to Fritzi, "Don't you think that all that skating around is a little too show-offy?"

"No, I don't."

Momma laughed. "No, you wouldn't."

"And it brings in the customers like crazy."

"Well, whatever you think, Fritzi. I don't know what we would have done without you. If anything happens to me or Poppa, I can die happy, because I know you'll take care of the girls."

"Sure, Momma."

"But I worry about you sleeping in the station all night. Are you sure you want to do that?"

"Sure, I'm sure. Don't you worry about a thing, Momma."

Fritzi didn't tell Momma, but being on roller skates at a gas station could be dangerous. One day, Tula had shot out of the station to the tune of "Boogie Woogie Bugle Boy" with a rag in her hand and had hit a grease spot. To everyone's amazement, she skidded underneath a big eighteen-wheeler truck, came out the other side, and ended up all the way across the street. Without missing a beat, she had skated back across the street to the station and finished cleaning the windows of a Packard.

After all their initial bellyaching, Gertrude and Tula came to love working at the filling station. Gertrude's boyfriend, Nard, had proposed to her in a letter, and she had written back and accepted, so she wasn't dating, and all the boys Tula had been dating were in the service, so there wasn't much else to do but work. And Fritzi always made sure there was something fun going on all the time, including weekly Friday night dances out on the big platform on the side of the filling station. One week, Fritzi got Quiren Kohlbeck and his Orange Crush Orchestra to come all the way from Manitowoc, Wisconsin, and play on the back of a truck, and that night, the town of Pulaski bought more war bonds than the next five towns over combined, and they were very proud of that fact.

It was mostly girls jitterbugging with other girls, but they did have a good turnout from the guys still home working at the factories nearby and some of the Coast Guard boys stationed over in Sturgeon Bay. Sometimes the music went on until after midnight, but nobody in town complained. Everybody was working hard, and they deserved a little recreation. Even the nuns from Saint Mary's came over and sat with Momma on the porch and watched the fun.

It was a busy time for everyone. When Momma and Angie weren't cooking, they were rolling bandages for the Red Cross or tending to the big victory garden in the back. In their spare time, all the girls wrote to the servicemen and sent packages of good Polish food to all the boys from Pulaski.

The youngest girl, Sophie Marie, had just graduated from high school and was still torn about what to do. She felt she had a religious vocation, and she had planned on entering the convent right away, but she also knew her sisters needed her at home to help at the filling station. She cried when she told Sister Mary Patricia that she would have to wait until her brother, Wink, came home after the war to take over. Sister Mary Patricia was very understanding. She said, "Sophie, it could be for the best. I entered at seventeen, and not that I regret my decision, but I often wish I had lived a little more out in the world. I think it might have helped me understand more what the girls are going through. And, sometimes, we can serve Him best by serving our families and our country."

Fritzi hadn't said anything, because she hadn't wanted to be a bad influence on the kid, but she was glad Sophie was staying. She was a big draw with the customers. And as Fritzi figured it, after the war, none of the girls would ever have the chance to run a gas station again. Besides, Sophie had the rest of her life to be a nun, so why not have a little fun while you can? The only downside with Sophie was that Fritzi had to watch her language around her, and she hated that. She just loved to cuss a blue streak and shock the truck drivers.

All the Jurdabralinski girls, including Momma and Angie, were kept busy morning, noon, and night, but they were not too busy not to be worried about Wink. They had not heard from him in a while. When they finally received a V-mail letter from him, they were so relieved they called Poppa in Hot Springs and read it to him over the phone.

Dear Folks,

Guess what? I am writing this letter to you from the deck of a troop ship. Our entire unit is being shipped overseas. Don't know where we're going yet, but I am sure it will be where Uncle Sam thinks we can do the most good.

This ocean is something else. I didn't know there was that much water in the world. A lot of the guys are pretty seasick, but I am OK so far. Sure wish I had my rod and reel with me. There must be some pretty big fish swimming around under there. Don't worry about me. I am in good hands and the grub is pretty good. Not as good as Momma's, though. I think this war will be over soon and I will be home again before you know it.

Love,

Wink

P.S. I really appreciate you girls taking over the station for Poppa and me. I have shown the guys in my unit the photo you sent, and they all say I sure have some swell sisters. And pretty, too. A few of them said after the war, they were headed to Pulaski to see you in person.

PULASKI, WISCONSIN

Dear Wink,

Don't know where you've ended up, but we all really miss you, buddy. Momma is still keeping that candle lit for you over at church, and she and Sophie never miss daily mass, so you are in good hands on that score.

I just wish I was there with you so I could keep an eye on you. I know you are a big-shot flyboy now, but I can't help it. You're still my little brother you know, and, despite it all, I am quite fond of you, so don't go being a hero on me. OK?

Fritzi

P.S. We hear that Poppa might be coming home soon. Not too soon, I hope. It was eight below zero here today, and the pumps froze again. Well, gotta go. Take good care of yourself, Winks. We are so proud of you . . . and give them Krauts hell for me, will ya?

HAPPY BIRTHDAY

———

POINT CLEAR, ALABAMA

EVERY MORNING, SOOKIE WALKED AROUND AND FILLED HER BIRD feeders. She couldn't let the blue jays go hungry, but she still missed her small birds. They wouldn't come to the small-bird feeders she'd tried, either. Every once in a while, one or two would come and feed on the seeds that had fallen on the ground, but she still had more blue jays than anything. Mr. Nadleshaft at the Birds-R-Us store said it was a common problem, but so far, nobody seemed to have an answer.

When Sookie came in from the yard, the phone in the kitchen was ringing. It was Lenore, who sang into the phone, "I know a little girl who's having a big birthday on the thirty-first."

Sookie wanted to sing back, "No, I'm not," but she didn't.

"What I want to know is where are we going this year? Have you thought about it? I know where I think we should go."

"Mother, I have thought about it, and I really don't want to do anything this year. I just want to skip it."

"What? Skip your birthday? Don't be silly."

"I'm not being silly. I really just want to be with Earle and spend a quiet evening at home."

"A quiet evening at home? On your birthday? Sookie, what in the world is wrong with you? Are you over there drinking? I swear, you are just getting more peculiar every day. You can have a quiet evening alone with Earle anytime, but you are not going to skip your birthday, for heaven's sake. And, anyhow, it's not just about you. I'm the one who gave birth to you. So don't make me have to come over there and spank you. Besides, I've already written the funniest poem, and I've set it to music. 'Roses are red, my dear, violets are blue, after forty-eight hours, then there was you!' Oh, and it goes on and on."

A thousand smart replies went through Sookie's mind, but what was the use? No matter what she said, the woman was determined to continue perpetuating this lie to the grave.

"Sookie, are you still there?"

"Yes, Mother."

"I think we should have the party out on my pier this year."

"I see. Are you going to cook?"

"Of course not. We'll have it catered. And you need to start thinking about who all you want to invite."

She supposed she would just have to go along with the charade. She was still confused about how to handle the situation and she wasn't up for a fight with Lenore over it. And so once again, she would be celebrating the wrong birthday. Oh, Lord what a mess.

SOOKIE FOUND HERSELF IN a strange position. She was grateful to Lenore for adopting her, but now that she knew she was not a Simmons, it was hard for her to keep on pretending. She went back and forth between being grateful and wanting to kill her, but as Dr. Shapiro had said, it was natural to feel that way. Still, it did make it hard when Lenore blathered on and on about how proud she was to have the small and delicate Simmons foot.

Lenore hadn't had the Simmons foot for years. She just didn't know it. Lenore was so vain she wouldn't wear her glasses, and so when Sookie took her shopping and she would ask to see a shoe in a size 6, Sookie would quietly walk back to the storeroom and ask the clerk to bring her mother the same shoe, only in a size 7½. It was a small white lie, but Sookie knew that any other way Winged Victory would cause a scene and insist they were all wrong. Once Lenore believed in something, you could never convince her otherwise.

She believed she was perfectly self-sufficient, too, but she wasn't. Lenore wouldn't even be going to water therapy three times a week if she had let them get her a walk-in tub. "Those are for invalids," she had said, and then she proceeded to fall getting out of her bath, knocked herself out, nearly broke her hip, and wound up at the emergency room. When she woke up in the hospital, Lenore thought she was dying and called everyone and told them if they wanted to see her alive, they needed to get there right away. "I doubt I will live through the night," she said. All the kids had dropped everything and run home from college, and Buck and Bunny had flown in all the way from North Carolina. The next day, when she woke up alive, Lenore turned to Sookie and said, "Sookie, call Jo Ellen and tell her I need her to come over here and fix my hair, and tell that orderly she needs to water these flowers."

That afternoon, when everyone had gone home, Sookie had asked her, "Mother, do you know how much trouble you caused? You scared everybody half to death, calling them like that. Carter almost killed himself speeding to get here in time."

Lenore said, "Well, you're just lucky I survived, but if I had died, they needed to be here." Then she added, "Good heavens, Sookie, you sound like you're *sorry* I didn't die."

"That's not what I meant, Mother, and you know it."

But Lenore wasn't listening. "I don't think I like this room. Sookie, go down the hall and ask them if they have something with a better view."

THE MISHAP

WORKING AT A FILLING STATION COULD BE REALLY DANGEROUS. GAS was highly flammable. Hubcaps could pop off and hit you in the face. You could burn yourself on overheated engines. Tires could blow up if you put too much air in them. And when slamming down hoods, if you weren't careful, fingers could be broken.

Fritzi had told the girls a hundred times that they needed to keep their minds on what they were doing. So far, there had been only one serious mishap at the station. And, of course, a man was involved.

TULA WAS ALL ATWITTER, because Arty Kowalinowski, the handsome six-foot star football player from Pulaski High, was home on a four-day furlough from the army. And thrill of thrills, he had asked her out to the movies that Friday night. He had not known it, but Tula had spent most of her junior and senior years writing "Mrs. Arty Kowalinowski" all over her notebooks and dreaming about him at night. But this was the first time he had asked her out, and so she was over the moon. Tula had not even gone on the date yet, but she was already hearing wedding bells and planning what she would wear. Something with a lot of white netting, she thought.

That Thursday night, she spent hours washing her hair over and over again—trying her best to get the gasoline smell out—scraping the grease out from under her fingernails, and picking out her outfit. The next morning, she didn't want to chip one of her newly painted bright red fingernails, so she showed up at work wearing big, thick workman gloves.

She was in such a daze all day that it was hard for Fritzi to get her to do much of anything. And Tula was not happy when late that afternoon, a huge black 1936 Chevy with transmission problems came in for service. Tula wanted to wait and do it the next day, but Fritzi wouldn't let her. Tula was their main mechanic, so she rolled under the car on the wooden dolly, grumbling about it, but she still wouldn't take her gloves off.

Tula was an excellent mechanic, but that day, she must have been thinking about her date with Arty Kowalinowski, because when she was underneath the car working, she somehow unscrewed the wrong valve, and suddenly an entire pint of thick five-year-old filthy oil gushed out and landed all over her face.

Tula screamed so loudly that Momma heard her all the way over at the house. Gertrude got to her first and grabbed her by the legs and pulled her out sputtering and spitting out black oil.

Her screams were so loud that the fire truck and the police showed up. Five minutes later, Tula was still hysterical and dripping oil as they led her over to the house to try to clean her up.

It was already five o'clock, and she had a date in two hours. She knew Arty was leaving the next day, and she might not ever get another date with him again.

But the oil was everywhere: in her hair, her eyelashes, up her nose, and in her ears. After being scrubbed for at least an hour, her face was still stained a strange gray color. She and Momma had shampooed her hair three times with Oxydol soap, but even so, she still reeked of old, rancid oil. Tula looked in the mirror and realized it was no use. She couldn't possibly go. "I look like a dead rat," she said.

THIRTY MINUTES LATER, ARTY Kowalinowski was standing in front of the Pulaski theater waiting for his date, when Fritzi and Gertrude showed up instead. Tula had threatened to kill both of them if they told him what had happened, so all they said was, "Tula's not coming."

He was disappointed, but they all went inside anyway and had popcorn and saw the movie *Kitty Foyle* with Ginger Rogers and a cartoon.

While they were sitting in the theater enjoying the movie, Tula was upstairs at home, sitting in the big claw-foot tub, soaking her hair and bemoaning her fate to her mother and Sophie. "I begged Fritzi to let me wait until tomorrow, but she's so bossy. She wouldn't let me. She said, 'No, it has to be done today.' I hate her. I just hate her."

"Now, Tula, she's your sister. You don't hate her. That's a sin."

"I don't care. Arty Kowalinowski is the only boy I ever really loved, and she made me miss my one chance to go out with him. Now he'll probably meet some other girl, and I'll wind up an old maid, and it's all her fault."

When Gertrude and Fritzi got home later that night, they went upstairs to see Tula, who unfortunately, still looked gray. "We brought you some popcorn," said Gertrude. "And Arty said to tell you he was just heartbroken not to get to see you this time."

"He did?"

"Yes," added Fritzi. "And when we gave him your picture, he said he would be looking at it and thinking about you every day until he got back."

"He did?" said Tula, reaching for the popcorn.

"Oh, yes . . ."

It was a bold-faced lie, but it made Tula feel better.

THE WAFFLE HOUSE

BOOTH NO. 7

AT THEIR NEXT SESSION, DR. SHAPIRO SUDDENLY LOOKED UP FROM his notes and asked Sookie a question that surprised her.

"What about your father?"

"What about him?"

"I've heard a lot about your mother, but you haven't mentioned him."

"I haven't?"

"No."

"Oh . . . well, he was so sweet, bless his heart."

"He must have seen your mother's behavior. Did he ever try and stop it?"

"No. But you didn't know Daddy. He thought she was the most wonderful woman in the world. And when I would complain that she was pushing me around, he would say, 'Oh, honey, I know you don't want to join that club or do whatever, but she's only pushing you because she loves you, and it means so much to her,' so no, he was never very much help."

"How did you feel about that?"

"You mean, did it make me mad? Oh no. He couldn't help it. Poor Daddy always had a blind spot when it came to Mother. When they met she had evidently been the belle of the ball . . . and I don't think Daddy ever got over the fact that she married him. Every year on their anniversary, he would play the song they had danced to at the Senior Military Ball . . . and they would waltz all around the living room."

"So in other words, you and your brother grew up in a house with a domineering mother and a father who gave you little or no protection."

Driving home, Sookie thought about what Dr. Shapiro had said. It was true. Her father had seen how unhappy Lenore had made her, and he really had not stood up for her. Should she be mad at Lenore for that or mad at Daddy? Or mad at both? Oh, Lord. She didn't want to be mad at anybody. There was a part of her that just hated sitting around, whining about her childhood. It was embarrassing at her age. But Dr. Shapiro said it was important. Still, it made her feel creepy, like she was doing something bad, betraying the Simmons family secrets, and there were a few.

THE SIMMONSES, LIKE MOST families in the South, had lost everything during the war, and all they had left was their pride and stories of the "glorious past." Her grandmother told tales of how her mother, Sookie's namesake, Sarah Jane Simmons, had single-handedly saved Greenleaves, the family plantation, by charming the Yankee soldiers and dazzling them with her beauty, and how after the war, three Yankee officers had written and begged her to marry them, which was, of course, out of the question . . . and on and on.

As a child, all these stories had enthralled Lenore. But in Lenore's case, with each passing year, the "glorious past" had become more and more glorious until in 1939, she had confided to a friend, "I could have written *Gone with the Wind* about Greenleaves, but Margaret Mitchell beat me to it."

When Buck and Sookie were growing up, Lenore had waxed poetic, ad nauseam, all about the grandeur of the old Simmons family plantation, "almost a complete replica of Tara," she said, "only much better furnished." But when he was in high school Buck had looked it up in the Selma Civil War Archives over at the courthouse.

The truth was that Greenleaves was never a plantation. It was just a nice two-story farmhouse located on a few acres of land, and the Simmons family's only encounter with the enemy during the war was when one little skinny half-starved Union soldier, who was lost, stopped by and asked for directions. But to hear Lenore tell it, hundreds of Yankee soldiers had marched through the county, looting and stealing and digging up every inch of their land, looking for buried silver and gold. The fact that the man her grandmother later married got drunk and burned the place down was somehow never mentioned.

GOOD-BYE, MR. HATCHETT

PULASKI, WISCONSIN
1942

ALL THAT YEAR, EVERYBODY IN TOWN WAS BUSY PITCHING IN TO HELP with the war effort. Housewives were saving grease for bullets, and were collecting all the rubber and aluminum and scrap metal they could scare up. The Jurdabralinski girls, like all the others, had given up their nylon stockings, which were needed for parachutes, and now everybody had a victory garden.

The good news was that Poppa had come home from the hospital, and they all celebrated. But the war news was not good. Pulaski had already lost three of their boys, and Fritzi was worried about Wink and all the other guys she knew who were now in the thick of it.

They got another letter from their friend Dottie Frakes, who was tending to wounded soldiers in the Pacific. It made Fritzi feel so damn useless. Momma and Sophie went to mass every morning and prayed for the boys overseas, Gertrude and Tula rolled bandages for the Red Cross in their spare time, and all she did was pump gas. And since gasoline was now being rationed, she pumped less and less of it every day. The posters down at the post office had a picture of a soldier and read "They do the fighting, you do the writing." Fritzi had written to all the guys she knew, but she wanted to do more.

So a few weeks later, when Mr. Hatchett, the Civilian Pilot Training instructor over at the college, was drafted, and they asked Fritzi if she would step in and take over his job while he was gone, Fritzi said she was more than glad to do it.

Teaching would give her a chance to fly again. The college knew they were taking a chance on trusting a former female stunt pilot with their students; however, they needed a replacement for Mr. Hatchett. But Fritzi turned out to be an excellent instructor, and her students loved her—especially the boys. Between running the gas station and teaching, she was pretty busy, but sometimes after a lesson, she would take off and fly for a while by herself. It was wonderful to be up in the air again, even if it was in a Piper Cub.

PULASKI, WISCONSIN

Dear Wink,

We are OK here. Hope you are the same. Not much news except that the CPT instructor you and the girls took lessons from was drafted. And yours truly has taken over his job. Just for a laugh, I gave Sophie and Gertrude a few lessons, and I was surprised. They've both gotten pretty good, especially Sophie. She aces her landings like a pro. It almost put me to shame . . . but not quite. Ha-ha! But it makes me wonder if after this is over, you and me and the two girls and Billy might start our own Flying Circus? But I'm just dreaming, I guess. I have a feeling when you get home, your bride is going to nail your feet to the ground and never let you go upstairs again. Can't say as I blame her. There is not a man left here that's not under 16 or over 60. They're either too young or too old. And it sure is lonesome here. So come home soon.

Fritzi

P.S. How does it feel to be a daddy? He's a fine little boy, Winks. Looks like you.

PULASKI, WISCONSIN

My Darling Husband,

I hope you got the package I sent. I knitted them all myself. I am over at the station filling in for Fritzi for a few hours and things are pretty slow. I'd rather be busy. It seems if I have time on my hands I do too much thinking. I know we are told our letters must always be cheery and gay but, honey, sometimes I do wonder, why us? We were so happy for such a short time. Why did this war have to happen now? Why couldn't we have been born five years earlier or even five years later? It isn't fair. I had you for such a short time and I'm scared I'm not the same girl you left and when you come home, you won't love me anymore, and I'm scared this war will change you, too, Wink. We can never get back to those two kids we used to be, and that's what hurts. It's hard to believe that just last year I was a silly teenage girl playing house, and now I'm a grown woman with a baby to raise and my husband is across the world, and I don't know when I'll see him again. Oh, honey, please don't be brave and take any chances. Just do what you have to do and come home to me. I kiss your picture every night. Do you feel it? Everybody here asks about you.

All my love,

Angie

PULASKI, WISCONSIN

Dear Wink-a-Dink,

Woke up on the wrong side of the world this morning, grumpy
as hell. Was a bear all day until I figured out what was wrong. I
forgot to say thank you to the man upstairs today for being
born in the good old USA, for Momma and Pop, the rest of the
girls, and especially for you, Wink, the grandest guy I know and
who is my very own brother. After I had a good talking to
myself, I felt better. Anyhoo, pal, things here are status quo.
With all this darn gas rationing, folks are just dribbling into the
station, not more than one or two a day now, and then not
spending much. Had a kid come in the other day who could
only afford to buy a nickel's worth, but your Angie, with the
big heart, shot him a little more.

Angie's holding up pretty well, Wink, but do write her
when you can. I swear, that gal just lives from letter to letter.
She's fighting this war with you, Wink, and is being brave. The
whole town is fighting this war with you. You should see the
kids. They have collected everything but their Momma's kitchen
sink, no joke, and Poppa and Mr. Rususki are now in the home
guard, helmets and all. We had a blackout drill the other night,
and Poppa was so excited he walked off the back stairs and fell
in the bushes. Momma was in the kitchen and heard him

cussing in Polish and ran out and fell off right on top of him. Before it was over, all of us girls wound up in the bushes, laughing our heads off. Nothing was hurt but Poppa's pride. Good thing it was just a drill. Don't know what would happen if it was the real thing.

Fritzi

LONDON, ENGLAND

DECEMBER 25, 1942

Hi, Gang,

Merry Christmas all the way from England. Sure was strange not being home at Christmas. It really stirs up a lot of memories, especially today. I sure have learned something in these last months. All the guys here are very quiet tonight, including big-mouth me. We had a special Christmas Day broadcast from the States, and it sure was good to hear their voices, especially Frances Langford. At the end, when she sang, "I'll Be Home for Christmas," a lot of the guys had to leave the auditorium pronto, including me. The British people have been swell to us. Last night, every family here invited two or three of us to spend Christmas Eve at their house with them. My family was not Catholic, but the father drove me and Kracheck over to the next town for midnight mass and waited, then drove us back to the base. There sure are a lot of nice people here, but it's not home. I know after we clean up all this stuff over here, I will be back next year to enjoy Christmas with you for real.

Winks

THE END OF AN ERA

1943

WINK'S PHILLIPS 66 WASN'T THE ONLY STATION THAT WAS HIT HARD BY gas and rubber rationing. People just weren't driving much anymore, and filling stations all over the country were closing down every day. Fritzi and the girls kept theirs going longer than most, but finally, Poppa and Fritzi came to the same conclusion. It was costing them more to stay open than they were making, so the decision was made that at the end of the week, they would close down. It had been snowing on that last day the station was open. The weather outside was cold and gray and more or less matched the mood inside. The girls were sad as they cleaned out the counters and took down the pictures on the walls. Sophie packed up all the old maps and postcards and took them over to the house. Poppa said it was only temporary. He was sure that after the war, they would open right back up, and everything would go back to normal. But the girls wondered if anything would ever be the same.

Running the all-girl filling station had been a lot of hard work, but now that it had come to an end, they began to realize just how much they would miss it. For a short while, thanks to Fritzi, they had sort of been famous, and now it was all over.

It was around five when they finished and already dark outside.

The girls had gone home, and Fritzi walked around and locked all the doors and turned the lights off for the last time. When she came back over to the house and handed Poppa the keys, Gertrude said what they had all been thinking: "Oh, Fritzi, I wonder if we'll ever have as much fun again."

SHOULD SHE OR SHOULD SHE NOT?

———

POINT CLEAR, ALABAMA

SOOKIE FELT SHE HAD MADE SOME PROGRESS SINCE HER FIRST THERAPY session. She was finally able to be around Lenore without having such a strong emotional reaction (like wanting to strangle her), but it was still so strange seeing Lenore in a brand-new light—not as her mother, but as a total stranger—and she was torn about what to do.

Sometimes she'd wonder whether she should she tell Lenore she knew she was adopted. If she did, what good would it do? The woman was eighty-eight years old, and she obviously didn't want her to know. She had gone to great lengths to keep it from Sookie, and telling her now would only upset her. And it's not like they could work anything out at this late date. The damage had already been done. Sookie still felt hurt and angry, but at the same time, she was also beginning to feel grateful to her. Other than Lenore pushing her into everything known to man, her family life had been wonderful. She couldn't have asked for a better father or brother. She had grown up in a lovely home and certainly had never gone without a thing. And if she hadn't been adopted by them, who knows where she might have ended up? A Texas family could have adopted her, and she could have grown up on a ranch, and that would have been a disaster. She was absolutely terrified of horses. Or she might not have been adopted at all and never left the orphanage, just sat there until she was eighteen and then been kicked out with nowhere to go. And if she hadn't grown up where she had, she certainly would never have met Earle Poole, Jr. She would have been a totally different person with a completely different husband and an entirely different set of children, or maybe she wouldn't have married at all. It was mind-boggling to think about just how random her life had really been.

If her real mother had kept her, she might have grown up in Wisconsin speaking Polish or at least speaking with a Yankee accent. She may have even played the accordion or, who knows, she might have become a nun. And if she had been that other person and had passed herself on the street, she probably wouldn't even have recognized her. She supposed she would have still looked like herself on the outside, but she would have been someone entirely different on the inside. She would have been herself, but an entirely different version of herself. Of course, she might not have been as nervous, or she might have been just the same. Maybe her bad nerves had nothing to do with Lenore. It was hard to know what parts of her personality had been formed by DNA and what parts had been the result of her environment. She had always assumed she had gotten her height and her nose from her father and the Simmons foot from Lenore, but now who knew where anything came from?

Oh, Lord. Just when she thought she was going to be able to relax and enjoy her life, this had to happen. How could she relax with all these questions running around in her head all day and night?

As the days went by, she found herself thinking more and more about her real mother. One night, in the middle of dinner, she said to Earle, "I wonder what she looked like."

"Who?"

"That lady. Fritzi. My real mother. I wonder if she had red hair?"

"I don't know, honey, but I'm sure we could find out."

"Oh, it's probably too late. If I'm sixty, she would be at least eighty-something. She's probably dead by now."

"Well, honey, maybe not. We could at least try to find out, and if she is still alive, I'm sure she would love to meet you. Think about that."

Sookie thought about it for a minute. "Oh, I don't know, Earle. Even if she is still alive, you wonder why would she just give up a baby like that."

Earle shrugged. "I don't know, honey, but I'm sure she had a very good reason. We don't know the circumstances."

"No, you're right. But still, I think I might be too scared to meet her."

"Well, you could always just talk to her on the phone."

"That's true. But what would I say? 'Oh, hello, this is the daughter you gave away sixty years ago, just calling to say hi,' or 'Hi, guess who this is.'"

"No, sweetie, just tell her the truth. That you just found out and you wanted to make contact; you could do that, couldn't you?"

"Yes, I suppose, but I could give the woman a heart attack, calling out of the blue like that. And don't forget she's never tried to find me. And it's been so many years, she might have even forgotten she had me."

"Well, just think about it. But if it were me, I'd want to at least try to find out."

THAT NIGHT IN BED, she did think about it. And it occurred to her that even if the woman was still alive, she might not want to hear from her. She could have married and had a completely new family and might not want them to know anything about her. The woman was Catholic and, who knows, she could have seven or eight or even more half brothers and sisters out there somewhere! Oh, my God . . . and if she did find her mother, and they all wanted to meet her, the entire family might come out to Point Clear and bring all their children and grandchildren. She could have hundreds of Polish relatives piling in on her from all over the country. Where would they stay? You couldn't keep a thing like that quiet. If all those Polish people hit town all at once, Lenore would be sure to hear about it in five minutes. So, no, she'd better just leave well enough alone. Who knows what a hornet's nest she might stir up?

But still, she was curious, and it really was a mystery. Why had Fritzi Jurdabralinski, who was from Wisconsin, wound up all the way across the country? And what was she doing in Texas? Had she married a cowboy? Or a soldier? Or had she married at all?

RESTLESS IN PULASKI

—

PULASKI, WISCONSIN
1943

SINCE MOST OF THE BOYS FRITZI HAD BEEN TEACHING WERE NOW going into the service, the Civilian Pilots Training program at the college was shut down and the plane was sold to the military.

And now that the filling station had closed, Fritzi had nothing to occupy her time and she just hated to sit around doing nothing.

That good-looking Irishman had been somewhat of a distraction, but he had joined the marines and was off in North Carolina. She was not content to just be a sideline spectator in the war. She wanted to do something other than roll bandages and write soldiers. She could apply for a job at one of the big airplane factories out in California like a few of her friends had, but even that wasn't enough for Fritzi. She didn't want to build planes. Hell, she wanted to fly them. Day after day, she paced back and forth on the airstrip in the back and cussed a blue streak where Momma and the girls couldn't hear her. Damn it to hell and back, there were times she just hated being a female.

FRITZI DIDN'T KNOW IT, yet, but things were starting to move in her direction. Even before the war started, two highly skilled American women flyers, Jackie Cochran and Nancy Harkness Love, had started to plant the idea with the military higher-ups that if war came, the United States should seriously consider training women to fly military planes so that they could perform ferrying missions, flying new planes from the factories where they were built to the military bases. This would free the men up for combat service. England already had women flying ferrying missions and were successfully completing assignments. Russia even had female combat pilots. Eleanor Roosevelt said publicly, "Women pilots . . . are a weapon waiting to be used."

But in the United States, when the subject was approached with the top brass, they said that the idea of women ever flying planes for the military was absurd and completely out of the question. Women were far too high-strung and emotional. Flying was and always would be a man's job. This was their attitude, until the war actually started, aircraft production increased, and a shortage of male pilots ensued. In late 1942, these very same men suddenly had a change of heart and had to admit that maybe it was not such a bad idea after all.

A list was compiled of all the women in America with flying experience and a pilot's license, and telegrams were sent out asking if they would be interested in flying military planes for the U.S. government, and if so, to please report to the Howard Hughes Airport in Houston, Texas.

Fritzi opened her telegram and read it. Was she interested? She was not only interested, she couldn't wait. She talked it over with Poppa, and he gave her his blessing. Momma cried in her apron again and said, "It's all Billy Bevins's fault that Fritzi won't stay home."

When she told the girls she was leaving, they were sad to see her go. But they were also proud and excited to think that their big sister was going to be flying planes for the United States of America government.

PULASKI, WISCONSIN

Dear Winks,

A great big yahoo! Looks like you won't be the only Jurdabralinski flying for the good ol' USA. I passed all my preliminary tests with flying colors, and it's now official. Excuse me, but I am writing this letter while jumping up and down with excitement. A bunch of us have been chosen to train the army way, so we can ferry airplanes in the States and free up more of the guys for combat duty, and so, my boy, have no fear. More help is on the way. I am headed out for Houston in two days to begin training. We are starting out as civilian volunteers, but the scuttlebutt is that as soon as we get up and going, we will be military for real, and I am hoping to outrank you, buddy . . . so watch out. Texas, here I come!

Fritzi

AN OLD FRIEND

FRITZI ARRIVED AT THE TRAIN STATION IN HOUSTON AND WAS PICKED up, along with a bunch of other girls from all over the country. They were driven over to either the Bluebonnet Hotel or the Oleander Motor Court, where they would be staying until they could get into the new barracks out at Avenger Field in Sweetwater, Texas.

The next morning, they were all out at the base for orientation. On their first break, Fritzi walked into the rec room to get a Coke, and she suddenly heard a familiar voice say, "Well, lookie at what the cat done drug in."

Fritzi looked over, and she couldn't believe her eyes. Sitting over in the corner at a table was Gussie Mintz, Billy's old girlfriend from the Grand Rapids days. "I heard you were coming in today," she said.

"Well, my God . . . Gussie! How are you?"

"Honey, I feel like a tired old poker chip, but don't you look smart and sassy. You haven't changed a bit. Have a seat, gal."

Fritz threw her bag down and joined her at the table. Gussie poured her a Coke and shoved it over.

"Well, is that son of a bitch Billy Bevins still alive?"

Fritzi laughed. "Oh, yeah, he's still with us."

"Well, shit, and I was hoping to hear some good news. Where is he? In jail, I hope."

"No. He's down in Pensacola, teaching cadets."

"Really? Well, they must be desperate if they took that fool. You two ever get hitched?"

"No. You know Billy."

"Yeah, I know Billy. But still together?"

Fritzi nodded. "On and off. You know Billy."

"Well, at least you hung in there. But enough about him. What do you think about the gals getting to fly? Isn't it great?"

"It's terrific. Finally, they came to their senses."

"Too bad they won't let us go military officially, yet. Hell, if they did, them Japs and Krauts wouldn't last a day between me and you. If nothing else, I could cuss them to death."

Fritzi laughed. "You could for sure, but from what I heard on the bus coming in, it could be happening any day now. Are you down here training?"

Gussie shook her head sadly. "Naw . . . I still have my pilot's license, but I can't fly no more, Fritzi. I lost my nerve."

"Oh, no."

"Yeah, after I left the act and sobered up a little, I just couldn't do it no more. When I got the letter, I told them I couldn't fly, but that I wanted in on it even if it ain't no more than sweeping out hangars or cleaning toilets, so here I am . . . a lot older and not one damn bit wiser, but still here."

"I'm glad you are, pal," said Fritzi.

"Yeah, me too. After all these years, I wound up right back where I started out. I'm slinging hash over at the mess hall, but I'm doing it for Uncle Sam and the gals, so it ain't so bad."

TELLING THE CHILDREN

—

After talking it over with Earle, and as much as she was dreading it, Sookie decided she really had to tell the children. They had a right to know about their genetic background. As planned, she would start with Dee Dee, and it was not going to be easy. Dee Dee was devoted to her grandmother and had always dined out on being a Simmons. Sookie was afraid that when she found out the news, she would throw a complete hysterical hissy fit. So she decided that Miss Busby's Pink Tea Room in downtown Mobile, near Dee Dee's office, would be the perfect place. Nobody ever raised their voices in there. At least she hoped not.

Sookie screwed her courage to the wall and called Dee Dee at work. Two days later, they were seated in a lovely little pink booth over in the corner. After they had been served their tea, Sookie said, "I haven't been here in a long time. I forgot what a pleasant place it is."

"Yes, Grandmother loves it here."

"I can see why. Such lovely little watercress sandwiches. We should meet like this more often. I think it's important that mothers and daughters stay close, don't you? Speaking of that, I was doing a little reading, and did you know that as a rule, Polish people are good-natured, hardworking, and loyal?"

"Really?" said Dee Dee, clearly not engaged.

"Yes, I thought it was very interesting. And were you aware that Chopin and Liberace were of Polish descent?"

"Yes, I know."

"And here's another little fun fact. The Poles excel not only at the piano, but on the accordion as well."

"Yes, so? Who cares, Mother?"

Sookie paused. "Well . . . you might."

Dee Dee looked at her. "Mother, why are you talking about all this stuff? You're beginning to worry me. Are you all right? You just don't seem like yourself today."

"Well, it's funny you should say that, Dee Dee . . . because that's exactly what I wanted to talk to you about. The truth is, honey, I really am not myself—or at least who I thought I was—and here's the bad news: Unfortunately, neither are you."

"What?"

"Oh, Dee Dee, this is so hard for me. And believe me, it was a shock to me as well, and I thought about not telling you . . . but you need to know, especially if you have children."

"Mother, what are you talking about?"

"Well . . . a few months ago, Lenore received a letter, and naturally I read it, thinking it was a bill or something."

"Yes?"

"Well, it was from the Texas Board of Health, and I found out that your grandmother—now promise me you won't get upset."

"Okay, you found out that . . . what?"

"That my mother—your grandmother—is not really my real mother, and when I say 'real,' I mean that we are not related to her . . . that, in fact . . . I was adopted."

Dee Dee smiled. "You are kidding me. This is a joke, right?"

"No. I have the letter right here and my birth certificate. And you can read it if you want—but only if you promise not to scream and make a scene. Do you promise?"

"Okay, I promise. Let me see it."

Dee Dee took it and read it, and her mouth dropped open. "Oh, my God! Oh, my God!"

"Honey, keep your voice down."

"Mother, do you realize what this means?"

"Yes, among other things, it means we are not related by blood to either Uncle Baby or Aunt Lily. At least that's some consolation."

"No, Mother! It means that if you are not a Simmons, then I'm not a Simmons!"

"That's true, but considering the heredity factor in—"

"But it can't be true—I've *always* been a Simmons!"

"I know . . . it's very shocking, and I'm still having a hard time believing it. But evidently, it's true."

"Have you told Daddy?"

"Of course."

"What did Daddy say? Was he upset?"

"Well, he was surprised . . . but not upset."

Dee Dee suddenly looked ashen. "But how can I not be a Simmons? I feel like a Simmons. I've *always* felt like a Simmons."

"I know you have, honey, and I also know how much that has always meant to you, and that's why I hated to tell you."

Dee Dee continued staring at the birth certificate. "Your real name is Ginger Jurdabralinski? Like our *dog*, Ginger?"

"Yes."

Dee Dee looked at her with horror, and her voice was getting louder and louder with each new discovery. "Your real mother's name was Fritzi Willinka Jurdabralinski?"

"Evidently."

"Your mother was *Polish*? Born in Pulaski, Wisconsin? Oh, my God!" After she continued to read on, Dee Dee almost yelled, "Father unknown?" Three ladies at the next table turned and looked over at them.

Oh, dear, Sookie knew Dee Dee was not going to like that part. "Honey, please . . . try and keep your voice down."

Dee Dee dropped her voice level down to a whisper. "Oh, my God, Mother. That means you are a—you haven't told anyone about this, have you?"

"No, no. You and your father are the only two people that know. And I wanted to tell you first, before I tell the other children."

Sookie knew Dee Dee would be upset, but she had no idea how much. Dee Dee had just come completely undone, and so they left the tea room and made their way to a bar down the street. Dee Dee was on her second drink, still rattled to the bone by the news, when she said, "And Grandmother knew about this all along—and she let us all think we were real Simmonses. My God, Mother, I'm the recording secretary of the Alabama chapter of the Daughters of the Confederacy."

"I know."

"Why . . . *why* would she do such a thing?"

"Oh, sweetie, why does she do anything she does? Your father thinks she just wanted us to feel like we really belonged to her."

"What did she say when you told her you knew?"

"I haven't told her. And Dee Dee, I've given a lot of thought to this, and I don't think we can ever let her know that we know. I'm afraid it would kill her. Remember, she is eighty-eight years old."

Dee Dee's eyes suddenly filled with tears. "But she always said I was her favorite. Why wouldn't she have at least told me?"

"Sweetheart, I don't know. But I'm so sorry. I knew you would be upset."

"Upset? I'm just thinking about staging my own death is all. My life is over. I hope you know that. Why live?"

"Oh now, sweetheart, I think you're making too much of this. After all, we're talking about my parents, not yours. You know who your real mother and father are. And don't forget, you know for sure that you are half a Poole. That's something, isn't it?"

Dee Dee sighed. "Oh, the Pooles are all right, I guess. But what about my Simmons family coat of honor? And who are these people anyway—the Jurdabralinskis? Or however you say it. Do you know anything about them?"

"Well, a little . . . yes."

"What?"

"Well, I know that they were evidently a very nice family, four girls and a boy, and two of the girls were twins, just like ours. Isn't that funny?"

"Were they cheese farmers or what?"

"Oh, no . . . no, honey. The father was a very well-respected businessman."

"What did he do?"

Sookie knew Dee Dee really wasn't going to like this, so she soft-pedaled it for a moment. "He was in the automobile business." She didn't dare tell her he ran a gas station.

SHE WAS GOING TO tell the twins next, but she wanted to wait until Ce Ce had been home from her honeymoon for a while so she could tell them together.

After she told them, they were surprised, but they took it very well. Ce Ce said, "We love you, Mother. We don't care that you are adopted, do we?"

Le Le shook her head. "No, we don't care if we're not really related to Grandmother."

"No," said Ce Ce. "We don't care."

"Yes, but I know how much you both love Grandmother, so I hope it won't change how you feel about her."

"No, not at all," said Le Le. "She's still our grandmother, and we will always love her."

"But you're our mother, Mother. You're the one we love the most," added Ce Ce.

"Yes," said Le Le, "and we always wondered why you let her push you around so much."

"You did?"

"Yes," Le Le said.

"We did," said Ce Ce. "She was always nice to us, but she pushed you around something awful."

"And it made us mad, too," said Le Le.

"It *did*?"

"Yes, it did," said Ce Ce. And they both nodded in agreement.

SHE WAITED TO TELL Carter until the following weekend, when he came home from Atlanta with a guy friend of his. They were going to go deep-sea fishing with Earle and watch the Alabama game. That Sunday, a few hours before he was supposed to leave, she took him in the den and told him. After he got over his initial shock, Carter said, "Wow . . . Mom. From the look on your face when you said you had something you wanted to talk to me about, I thought it was really serious, like you and Dad were getting a divorce or something." Then he looked at her with wide eyes. "Wow . . . so you were adopted. How about that."

"I know it's pretty shocking to find out after all these years that none of us are related to Grandmother. How do you feel about it?"

He sat there for a moment and then said, "Well . . . I think it's really kind of great news. Now none of us have to worry about winding up over at Pleasant Hill."

Sookie was surprised to hear him say that. "Oh, honey. I never knew that ever worried you."

"Sure it did, Mom. You know I love old Winged Victory to death and always will . . . but let's face it. She is as nutty as a fruitcake. I was always afraid that one day, you might wind up just like her."

Sookie smiled. "Well, honey, it could still happen. And I'll tell you, if I get any more big shocks like this one, who knows?"

"So," said Carter, "your real mother worked at an all-girl filling station? How cool is that?" Then he grinned. "Oh, boy, I'll bet Miss Dee Dee had a flying fit when you told her."

"Pretty much," said Sookie. "But you know, honey, your sister really surprised me. She seems to be coming along pretty well."

IN THE PAST WEEKS, all her children had surprised her in some way. She found out things she never knew about them. Dee Dee even called her a few days after her meltdown at Miss Busby's Pink Tea Room and said, "Mother, I just want you to know that no matter what your background is, I still love you."

"Well, thank you, Dee Dee. I appreciate that."

"After all, it's not your fault you are not a Simmons. You can't help it, and you must be as disappointed as I am. So if you need to talk, call me anytime, night or day. I'm here for you . . . and Mother, I just want you to know that I've taken down the Simmons coat of arms."

"Ah . . . well, I know how hard that must have been for you."

"Yes, it was. But I've ordered the Poole family coat of arms, and I'll put it up as soon as it arrives."

"Oh, how nice. I'm sure your father will be so pleased."

"And Mother, just so you know . . . about your people. I've looked them up, and the Polish are considered to be extremely intelligent and good-looking people, so you mustn't feel too bad about yourself, okay?"

"Okay, honey, I'll try not to, and thanks for the information. I feel better already."

Poor Dee Dee. At least she was trying to move on, and much faster than Sookie had expected.

AVENGER FIELD

Billy Boy,

Sorry I haven't written for a while, but we left Houston and arrived at our new base in Sweetwater and have been kept busy twenty-four hours a day. This is the hottest place I have ever been. If hell is this hot, then I ain't going. It hasn't been under a hundred degrees since I've been here, and the dust storms are terrible. I have red dust in my hair, teeth, ears, and everywhere the sun doesn't shine. I don't know if I'll ever be clean again. And, oh, have I mentioned the snakes and scorpions and the bugs? It's so hot, a lot of us gals pulled our cots outside to sleep, but you never know what might crawl in bed with you. These damn snakes even try to get in the planes for a little shade . . . not happy about that. I make them do a good check on mine— don't want any snake copilot.

And they don't make it easy on us girlies. We are doing everything the army way. We train like the big boys, including calisthenics, and we march everywhere . . . I'm even marching in my sleep. No fun, but we do it. My new pal Willy says it's just more proof that they will be taking us in the Army Air

Corps for real pretty soon. The grub is pretty good. Had my first hominy grits. Mmmm . . .

Other than dodging tumbleweeds and spiders and water bugs, I'm just fine. The other girls I have met here are all swell as far as I can tell. We have six girls to a bay. I'm in with Pinks, this real cute little Jewish gal from New York. Her dad runs a big brassiere factory, and we are all sporting new undies, compliments of Mr. Pinksel. I really get a kick out of her and Bea Wallace from Oklahoma, who wears steel-toed cowboy boots and carries a .45 on her hip. What a snazzy-looking dame she is . . . brunette, about five foot nine with a million-dollar smile and all legs. She is the only one of us who still looks good in these god-awful overalls they gave us. None of them fit worth a damn. The crotch in mine hits me at the knees, but when she walks by, all the guys' eyes pop out of their heads. And no, you ain't meeting her, so stop drooling. Anyhoo, she must be loaded. She started flying so she could check out the cattle on her family's ranch. Her dad was a great pal of Will Rogers, so we call her "Willy" just to razz her. The other three gals in my bay are nice, but kinda not in my league: girls finishing school, rich debutante types, all college grads, one from Vassar and two from Smith, and they sorta have a snooty air about them, always talking about their la-di-da schools.

Anyhoo, the other night, when we were all sitting around chewing the fat, did I pull a good one. Willy and Pinks were in on the joke, and I casually let it drop that I was a recent graduate of the Phillips School for Young Ladies.

One of the Smith gals looked puzzled and was about to say something when Pinks piped up and said, "Oh, Phillips. Why, I heard Phillips was so exclusive it was almost impossible to get in. How did you ever manage to do it?" And I said, "Daddy did have to pull a lot of strings." Well, that shut them up.

Boy, did the three of us have a big laugh later. Quite a feat for someone who barely made it out of high school, eh?

Fritzi

P.S. I see what you mean about cadets. We have a lot of ninety-day wonder boys flying around Texas now. They just got out of flight school and don't have near the flight time hours that the gals do, but they still feel superior to us and like to hotdog it and show off in front of the girls, and it's pretty damn dangerous. Some of the boys have been buzzing the gals, playing fighter pilot and trying to scare them. None of us have been given formation training, and a plane flying that close does scare them. When they complained, their CO said, "Boys will be boys, and some of them may be tempted to fly on your wing and horse around a bit with the gals, but it's to be expected." But after a few close calls, he ordered that they were to stay five hundred feet away from us at all times. That rule applies on the ground as well. Our barracks are off-limits to all males. Mrs. Van de Kamp is a nice local lady who acts as a house mother to all the girls here and she makes sure that law is strictly enforced!

AVENGER FIELD

Sweetwater, Texas

Dear Billy,

We are training every day now. I saw my first real live Mexican
and had my first tamale. Pretty good. I am sending you a
ceramic sombrero ashtray and a picture of me in the flying rig.
They have issued us men's flight suits—they look more like zoot
suits on us. Took your advice and made friends with the
mechanics. Have a swell one by the name of Elroy Leefers who
is looking out for me. I miss you, and congrats on your new
commission. Guess I'll have to salute you now.

Fritzi

P.S. The town of Sweetwater gave us gals a barbecue—sure was
fun. These Texans are some of the friendliest people I ever met.

AVENGER FIELD

Billy Boy,

I thought I was a tough guy, but from now on, you have my permission to call me a sissy. Yesterday, Willy and I took off and were in the air no more than five minutes when I look over and see the biggest rattlesnake I have ever seen crawling right toward me. It must have been sleeping in the side compartment, and the vibration of the plane woke him up in a hurry.

Well, you always wonder how brave you will be in a crisis. I've pulled planes out of spins, I've danced on wings in a windstorm, I've done a lot of things . . . but Billy . . . when I saw that damn snake headed toward me, I froze as stiff as a starched collar. My head was telling me . . . jump out . . . move . . . do something . . . but I just sat there with my eyes as big as two platters. Then Willy looks over, sees it, calmly reaches across me, grabs that thing by the tail, and slings it out the window into the wild blue yonder. When I could breathe again, I see that Willy is as calm as a cucumber. She looks at me and starts laughing. She says she never saw a person turn green before. She tried to make me feel better and said I did the right thing by not moving—little did she know it wasn't planned. If I could have moved, I would have. Willy is one swell gal and my hero, but I didn't tell her that.

Fritzi

P.S. I'll bet that snake was surprised to find itself flying.

AVENGER FIELD

Billy Boy,

Long time no hear from. Hope you're sending lots of good
pilots over the pond to kick their asses. We are busier than hell
here. By the way, remember those three college gals I told you
about? I have to take it all back. After being around them for a
while, I found out they are regular fellers. In fact, they really
have the goods. Damn good fliers. They work hard. Don't
complain. And can slug it out with the best of them. Ain't this
old war funny? Here I am living and flying with gals that I
would never have met in a million years, and I was wrong about
thinking they were snooty. I think it was me that had my nose
out of joint. Oh, well, wouldn't be the first time . . . eh?
Anyhow, after a few bars, I finally broke down and told them
about Phillips being the name of my old man's filling station
back in Pulaski, where the Jurdabralinski sisters majored in
grease monkeying, and they had a good laugh. Turns out they
were fascinated and made me tell them all about it. Go figure. I
think this war is going to change a lot of people's thinking. It's
changed mine already. Okay, Billy Boy, time for me to hit the

hay. Take care of yourself, and I'll see you real soon, if I get anywhere near you. Even if it is only for a night, and you know what I mean.

Me

P.S. I read that in Pensacola the boys outnumber the girls about a thousand to one. No wonder you are lonesome for me. I hate to report that the opposite here is true. Five thousand men to one girl. We sure don't lack for dancing partners. But don't worry, I am being good. Well, as good as I can be.

HELLO, ALICE

Point Clear, Alabama

Sookie had already fed the birds, still mostly blue jays, and done a little gardening before it got too hot. August was deadly, and by eight A.M., it was already so hot and humid outside, you wound up soaking wet. It was Monday, and she thought she would get dressed and run out to the Walmart and do her weekly shopping early and get it over with.

She had just stepped out of the tub when she heard the phone in the bedroom ringing. Her mother was at her garden club meeting, so it was probably Netta. She usually wanted Sookie to pick something up for her at Walmart, so she wrapped herself in a towel and ran in and picked up.

"Hello."

"Alice?"

"Pardon me?"

"Is this Alice? I'm trying to reach Alice Finch."

Sookie suddenly recognized the voice and quickly said, "Oh, yes! This is Miss Finch, yes."

"This is the lady from Wisconsin calling, from the chamber? You called a while ago wanting to know about the Jurdabralinskis. I kept waiting for you to call back, but you never did, so I got your phone number off the phone bill. Where is area code 251?"

Sookie panicked and lied and said, "Georgia," and immediately realized that was stupid, but it was too late.

"Oh, well, listen, I have some information for ya, hon. Real interesting tidbits about the Jurdabralinskis. Mom says that three of the Jurdabralinskis were WASPs. How about that?"

"WASPs?"

"Yeah, kinda unusual, don't you think?"

"Yes, I thought they were Catholic."

"They were Catholic, but they were WASPs—ya know, girl fliers during the Second World War?"

"Girl fliers?"

"Oh, yeah. Mom says there were a bunch of write-ups in the paper back then. They were known as the Flying Jurdabralinski Girls of Pulaski. She says at one time, three of the Jurdabralinski girls were in the service, and the one girl that was killed . . . died in a plane crash."

"Oh, no."

"Oh, yeah. They had a big funeral for her over at the cathedral and everything, and she was a big hero and all."

Sookie felt her heart sink. "Which sister was it? Do you know . . . was her first name Fritzi?"

"Hold on, I've got all the stuff written down. Okay. Hmmm . . ." As Sookie waited for her to find it, she felt her heart start to pound. "No . . . that's not it. Wait a minute. Oh, here it is . . . no, it was another Jurdabralinski sister who died."

Sookie suddenly felt strangely relieved. "Do you have any information on the sister named Fritzi—about what ever happened to her?"

"Hold on . . . let me ask Mom. She's right here. Hey, Mom, do you know what ever happened to Fritzi Jurdabralinski?" Sookie heard mumbling in the background. "Mom says she moved off years ago. She thinks to somewhere in California."

"Does she know where?"

"Hold on. Mom . . . Mom! Alice wants to know where she moved to in California . . . . She says she doesn't remember, but it was a Danish town."

"A Danish town?"

"Mom, a Danish town? . . . Yeah, she says she got a postcard from her sometime in the fifties, and it had windmills on it."

"I see. Does your mother happen to know if she's still alive?"

"Is she still alive, Mom?" More mumbling in the background. "She says she must be or it would have been in the papers. Mom reads all the obituaries. But now here's the other really interesting tidbit. One of the girls went on to become quite a celebrity in her own right. She and her twin sister. They had an accordion act and used to play locally, and Mom says she wrote an awful lot of good polkas. I know she wrote 'I'm Too Fat to Polka' and 'The Wink-a-Dink Polka' and a lot of others. I can get you a list. I can go down to the newspaper and look up those articles and send you a packet of what all I find."

"Oh, that would be wonderful."

"Okay, then. I'll dig up what I can and send it on to ya. What's your address, hon?"

Oh, dear, now she was caught. "Uh . . . send it to Alice Finch, in care of Mrs. Earle Poole, Jr. 526 Bayview Street, Point Clear, Alabama."

"Huh. I thought you said you lived in Georgia."

"Yes, but it's very close to the state line, and I get my mail in Alabama."

"Oh. Well, okay, then. I'll get this off to you as soon as I can get it all gathered up. Nice talking to you, Alice."

"You, too. Thank you."

AFTER SHE HUNG UP, Sookie sat there and noticed her hands were shaking. She knew the woman was talking about her real mother and her real family, but it still seemed so unreal and scary. She didn't even know that women flew planes during World War II. She thought there had only been men pilots.

The phone rang again, and she picked it up. This time, it was Netta. "Are you going to Walmart?"

"Yes, I sure am."

"Could you pick me up a six-pack of paper towels and a carton of Diet Dr Pepper?"

"Of course."

"And a pound of frozen shrimp. If you're coming right back."

"I sure will. No problem."

"Are you okay? You sound funny."

"No, I'm fine. Listen, Netta, do you know anything about the WASPs?"

"What wasps?"

"The girl WASPs that flew planes during the Second World War."

Netta thought to herself, "Uh-oh, here she goes again." "No, honey, I didn't know wasps flew planes."

"Well, I didn't either . . . until just now . . . isn't that strange?"

"Yes . . . I would say so."

"Have you ever heard of a town in California that's Danish and has a lot of windmills?"

"No, honey, sure haven't." After Netta hung up, she was worried again. She had thought Sookie was getting better, but evidently not.

LATER, AS SHE WHEELED through Walmart, Sookie asked a few people if they had ever heard about the WASPs, and not one person had. Mr. Lennon, one of the Walmart greeters, said he thought he remembered something about them, but he wasn't sure. But then, he was ninety-two. Sookie couldn't wait for Earle to get home.

THE MINUTE EARLE WALKED in the door, Sookie said, "Earle, you won't believe this, but I just found out my mother was a WASP and flew planes in the Second World War!"

"What?"

"A woman from Wisconsin called and told me. And her sisters did, too."

"Hold on. Slow down. Now what?"

"My mother was a WASP. Like a WAC, only they flew planes. Have you ever heard of them?"

"No. I knew there were WACs and WAVES, but no."

"Can you look them up on the Internet for me? I'm too nervous."

"Sure, honey." They walked back to the den, and Earle sat down and turned on the computer. He typed in "Women Fliers," "World War II," and the word "WASPs," and suddenly, something came up. "Here it is," Earle said.

The Women Air Force Service Pilots (WASPs) were the first women to serve as pilots and fly military aircraft for the United States Army Air Forces during World War II. The original twenty-eight women were under the direction of Nancy Harkness Love, who was an advocate of using experienced women fliers in domestic service to ferry airplanes in order to free up male pilots for combat or overseas ferrying.

WASP FACTS

1. The WASPs served in the Army Air Forces from September 1942 to December 20, 1944.
2. More than 33,000 women applied. 1,830 were accepted. 1,074 graduated from the training program.
3. Governed by the Civil Service Commission, although under military discipline order, the WASPs were originally stationed at the Howard Hughes Airport in Houston, Texas, but were transferred to Avenger Field, Sweetwater, Texas, in February 1943.
4. WASPs received seven months of training, the same as male cadets.
5. WASPs were stationed at 120 Army Air Bases within the United States.
6. WASPs flew 78 different types of aircraft, every plane the Army Air Corps flew, including the B-29.
7. WASPs flew sixty million miles of operation flights.
8. Types of flying duties included ferrying aircraft from factory to bases, flight instruction (basic and instrument), towing targets for antiaircraft, towing targets for aerial gunnery, tracking and searchlight missions, simulated strafing, and radio-controlled flights.
9. Thirty-eight died while flying for the Army Air Corps.

"Wow," said Earle. "This is pretty impressive. I had no idea. This is really something, isn't it?"

"Yes, and now I know why she was in Texas, and my two aunts were there, too. One of those girls that died was my aunt."

"Oh, no. Really?"

"Yes. The lady is sending me newspaper articles."

"Really? Does she know if she's still alive?"

"She thinks so. The last time she heard from her, she was in California. Look up a town in California that's Danish and has windmills."

"Oh, okay, but could you get me a drink? An iced tea or something?"

SOOKIE WAS IN THE kitchen when she heard Earle call out. "I found it!" Sookie brought him his iced tea, and he pointed to the screen, and sure enough, there was a picture of a town with lots of big windmills everywhere. "Here it is. It says, 'Solvang, California. Two hours north of Los Angeles, nestled in the beautiful Santa Ynez Valley. Come and discover the charming little town of Solvang, California. History: In January 1911, the Danish-American Colony Corporation, looking for farmland and impressed by the area's abundant year-round sunshine, bought nine thousand plus acres of land. The new settlement was named Solvang, which means "Sunny Field" in Danish. The corporation advertised in Danish-language newspapers, and soon both U.S. Danish immigrants and those still in Denmark bought land in the colony. Many descendants of the original settlers still populate the area today.' This has to be it."

"I'm sure it is. But I doubt if she's still there."

"Don't you want to find out?"

"Oh, I don't know, Earle. I'm not sure. Even if I did meet her, what good would it do? What if she's just horrible, and I hated her? Or what if, after she met me, she decided to move here with us? And I couldn't say no, and then Lenore would find out. I don't know, Earle. I still think it might be better to just leave well enough alone."

"You do what you want, but if you don't, and she dies, you might

regret not meeting her when you still had the chance, or at least talking to her on the phone."

"But why?"

"Well, you could find out why she gave you up. Don't you think
she at least deserves a chance? Don't forget you just found out about
her, but I'm sure she has been wondering about you for fifty-nine
years."

"Sixty," added Sookie.

LATER IN BED, SOOKIE said, "Just imagine, Earle, I'm scared to go on
a Ferris wheel, and my real mother actually flew a plane."

Earle smiled. "It's pretty exciting."

"Yes . . . I guess it really is."

Earle was glad to see Sookie start to take some sort of an interest.
He hoped she would change her mind after reading about the WASPs
and all that they did. He would like to meet the old gal himself. But
it was Sookie's decision.

NOW, THINKING MORE ABOUT it, Sookie realized that another reason
not to meet her real mother was that when she found out that her
daughter had never really accomplished anything and was just a
housewife, she could be terribly disappointed in her. Good Lord. She
had already disappointed one mother, and that was bad enough. She
didn't know if she wanted to take a chance on disappointing two.

AVENGER FIELD

Billy,

What's wrong with the damn male race? We are getting a lot of flack from a bunch of disgruntled flyboys. As if things weren't tough enough, a group of them here are not happy that girls are doing the same thing they are, and in some cases (mine), doing it better. We could ignore it, but they have started enough rumors about us to sink our entire program. They are telling people that we are a bunch of man-hungry females who joined up just so we could sleep around with the male pilots and are generally a no-good lot that should be sent home. Two weeks ago, we found out that they brought in a group of prostitutes and put them up at the Sweetwater Hotel and told everybody they were WASPs. I can tell you that didn't endear us to the townsfolk.

Finally, it got straightened out, but we are now being forced to live like nuns. Our director Jackie Cochran says we can't afford a hint of scandal. No dating instructors, no cussing, and ladylike behavior at all times while the flyboys do what they want. But Cochran says that our morals are to be above reproach. It's hell being a guinea pig, but as our house mother Mrs. Van de Kamp said, if we can prove ourselves, it will all be worth it in the end. Then maybe the next group won't have it so bad.

I know you are not reading about it in the paper. They don't want it getting out, but we lost three girls this month, and one was a bay mate of mine and a really nice gal. She was married to a marine serving in Guadalcanal and has two kids at home. A few days ago, she came in too low and crashed on landing right outside the barracks.

I know you see a lot of this, and it's all just part of training, but I am still not used to it and hope I never will be. It makes me so mad when all the newspaper reporters that come here only want to show the gals putting on lipstick or posing like models . . . all this phony baloney stuff. If anybody thinks this is a glamorous job and that we are just in it for the fun, they haven't watched them pull a friend out of a burning plane and die right in front of them. Nobody here is saying much, but the mood is pretty glum.

Fritzi

THE CHECK RIDE

SWEETWATER, TEXAS
1943

MOST OF THE MALE INSTRUCTORS AT AVENGER FIELD WERE NICE, BUT some bitterly resented being assigned to Sweetwater, and they went out of their way to make the girls' lives miserable. They would yell at them, call them "stupid" and "incompetent," and do everything in their power to try to make them wash out. One, a surly lieutenant named Miller, was particularly rough on them. Day after day, girls would come in after their lessons with him in tears. One girl had been so devastated by his bullying, she quit and went home. And he made no bones about how he felt. It was clear he thought women had no business flying planes.

One afternoon, over at the club, he was sitting at the bar, talking to the bartender in a loud voice, so he was sure to be heard by the girls that were there. "God, I hate this job. When people ask me what I did in the war, what am I gonna say? That all I did was teach a bunch of Goddamned women? Shit . . ."

FRITZI WAS STANDING AROUND, waiting to go up and take her first military check ride, when Miller walked up and said, "Okay, Jurdabralinski, let's go. I'm gonna take you up and see what you can do. And when I tell you something, don't talk, just do it."

"Yes, sir," she said.

As she was climbing up to her altitude, he reached over her from behind and yelled at her, "Jesus Christ, pull the damn stick back . . . don't ease it back," and he grabbed it and jammed it against her leg as hard as he could. "You're not in some powder puff derby. Pull the damn thing. Jesus Christ, what idiot taught you to fly?"

Fritzi desperately wanted to pass this inspection, but something snapped. She gunned the engines and as soon as she got her altitude, she suddenly flipped the plane over and flew upside down while Miller, who was now suspended in midair and hanging on to his shoulder straps, screamed for dear life, "Turn over! Turn over! Goddamn it!" When she did, Fritzi did a barrel roll, shot straight up, and then did her famous death drop into fifteen spins straight down. She then pulled up at the last second, shot back up, and went into a hammerhead stall just for good measure.

DOWN BELOW AT AVENGER Field, all the ground crew was standing there and looking up and watching what was happening and yelling. Pretty soon, everyone on the ground was looking up, and people were running out of the hangars and barracks to see what all the noise was about.

Gussie Mintz came out of the mess hall with a cigarette hanging out of her mouth to see, and she looked up just as Fritzi did another barrel roll, and she started to laugh. "You show 'em how to do it, gal," she said.

After another series of amazing spirals and loops, mechanic Elroy Leefers started grinning. "Give him hell, Fritzi!" After a few more minutes, she did a double loop, came in for a perfect landing, drove the plane to the main hangar, and stopped. She turned around and said to Miller, who was red-faced and fuming with rage, "Compliments of Billy Bevins, the greatest flight instructor alive."

"Get out of the plane!" he said.

"Yes, sir! Right away, sir!" she said as she jumped down. She undid her parachute and left it lying on the ground. Fritzi knew she had washed out, but nobody called Billy Bevins an idiot and got away with it, not while she was alive.

As FRITZI WALKED AWAY, Willy and Pinks ran up to walk with her, and when Pinks looked back, Miller was still sitting in the plane. Fritzi went straight to the barracks and started packing her things. Once a girl washed out, they left as soon as possible. It was too painful an ordeal for everyone to drag it out.

Her bay mates who had witnessed her flight were not happy and stood there and watched her pack. Pinks said, "The bastard had it coming, but damn, Fritzi . . . what are we going to do without you?"

AFTER FRITZI HAD PACKED, Willy and Pinks walked with her to the gate. Just as Fritzi was about to get on the truck, a girl came running up, panting, "The captain wants to see you in his office right away." Damn. She was hoping to get out before the report was finished and she had to face the music, but she hadn't made it.

A few minutes later, when she walked into the commanding officer's office, she saw Captain Wheeler sitting at his desk with an extremely grim expression on his face. Mrs. Van de Kamp sat in a chair behind him and looked as if she had been crying. Captain Wheeler glanced up from the report, looking furious, as he barked at her, "Young woman, that was one of the most reckless and irresponsible displays of complete disregard of rules and safety that I have ever witnessed. Do you realize you endangered the life of an instructor and yourself and risked destroying a military plane?"

"Yes, sir."

"And if that wasn't bad enough, you also put the reputation and the future of the entire WASP program in jeopardy today. You, of all people, know how hard Mrs. Love and Mrs. Cochran are working to ensure that this program continues, and then to pull a stunt like that."

"I understand. I'm sorry, sir. I wasn't thinking. I lost my head."

"This program is not about you. It's about all the girls and the ones that will follow them."

"Yes, sir."

He picked up the report from Lieutenant Miller and said, "You obviously didn't pass the inspection."

"No, sir."

"Mrs. Van de Kamp has informed me of some of the problems you girls have had with Lieutenant Miller, but that's no excuse, and according to official military protocol, you should be court-martialed."

"Yes, sir."

Captain Wheeler put the report down on his desk, leaned back in his chair, and looked out the window. After a long minute, he turned back around and looked at her and said, "I know military rules, and by all rights, I should throw you out on your ear." Then he sighed, "But I think anybody that can make that sour little son of a bitch Miller mess his pants deserves another chance, so I'm grounding you for two weeks or until we can ship Miller out of here. But if you ever pull a stunt like that again, you are out. And I will personally make sure you never fly another plane as long as you live. Do you understand?"

"Yes, sir."

"Now get out of here."

"Yes, sir. Thank you, sir."

"And Jurdabralinski . . ."

"Yes, sir?"

"Tell Billy I said hello."

Now she knew why Miller didn't get out of the plane. They told her later, Miller made the mechanic taxi the plane over to another hangar and then ordered everyone out. But word got around. The mechanic was Elroy Leefers. As for Fritzi, she didn't know how much she really loved being a WASP until she almost wasn't.

THE AFFAIR

Winged Victory was at the Just Teazzing beauty shop having her hair done when her friend Pearl Jeff came in looking for her. Pearl had just heard something from a friend, and she couldn't wait to tell Lenore.

Thirty minutes later, Lenore came storming in Sookie's front door and marched back to the kitchen where Sookie was sitting and having her lunch. "I want to talk to you, young lady, and I mean right now. I am just appalled at your obvious complete lack of discretion. Have you forgotten you're a married woman?"

Sookie looked up. "What?"

"I wondered why you were never home anymore and why I could never get you on the phone, and now I know."

"What?"

"You know what. Word has just reached my ears about what's been going on between you and that Dr. Shapiro, and I want you to put a stop to this nonsense right now."

"But, Mother—"

"Don't you 'But, Mother' me. Why, the very idea of you having . . . whatever you are having . . . is disgraceful. Earle Poole, Jr., is one of the finest men I have ever known in my life, and now you do this?"

"Do what? What are you talking about?"

"Everybody knows you two have been meeting all over town. I simply will not allow you to treat Earle this way. Earle has been nothing but an ideal husband and father, and you're lucky to have him. I just hope and pray I'm not too late, and he doesn't find out. Remember, what's good for the goose is good for the gander, and with his looks, why, he could have any woman he wanted, so I would suggest you just nip this little thing in the bud right now, before you wake up and find yourself a divorced woman."

Sookie sat there completely flabbergasted. "I don't believe what I am hearing. First of all, it's not true. I am not having an affair with anybody, and I can't believe you would even think that of me. And secondly, I thought you didn't like Earle."

"What do you mean? I've always liked Earle, and you know it. And if it isn't true, why are you meeting this man all over town? It certainly looks suspicious to me. Nobody's that crazy about waffles!"

"All right, Mother, since you insist on knowing everything, yes, I am meeting Dr. Shapiro all over town. And do you know why? Because I happen to be a patient of his, and I was trying to keep it a secret, so I wouldn't embarrass you or, God forbid, besmirch the precious Simmons family name, even though two of them are sitting over in the loony bin right this minute!"

Lenore looked at her with shock. "Sookie, Pleasant Hill is not a loony bin. And they are being treated for a simple nervous disorder. Why would you say such a terrible thing?"

"Okay, Mother, have it your own way. You always do."

"And, anyhow, why are you seeing a psychiatrist? Is this one of Marvaleen's ideas?"

"No, it isn't. I'm sure it's hard for you to imagine, Mother, but every once in a while, I actually have an idea of my own."

"Well, it's just plain silliness, and I want you to stop it right now. Do you hear me, young lady?"

"Mother, you do understand that I am a grown woman?"

"I don't care how grown you are. You're still my daughter, and I won't have you causing a scandal."

There was long pause while Sookie debated whether to just let her have it once and for all . . . but she didn't. "Okay, Mother."

"Good. I just hope and pray that Earle doesn't hear about this. That poor man is under enough strain as it is, having to fiddle with all those teeth all day, without you acting a fool in public."

"Yes, Mother."

"Well, now that we have settled that . . . I'll take a cup of coffee."

Lenore sat down and stared at Sookie while she made the coffee, then said, "I must say, Sookie, I am very concerned about your behavior lately. Has that doctor been giving you pills?"

"No, Mother."

"Hmmm . . . well . . . something's wrong with you. He could be hypnotizing you, and you just don't know it. You've never been very smart about your friends. I always said if Marvaleen said, 'Let's jump off a building,' you'd be right behind her. Don't forget what happened when she drug you to that Bible study."

"No, Mother."

A FEW DAYS LATER, Marvaleen heard the rumor about Sookie and had an entirely different reaction. When she saw Sookie get in her car at the parking lot at Walgreens, she ran over and knocked on her car window. Sookie rolled down the window. "Hi, Marvaleen, how are you?"

"Open the door," she said, pulling on the handle. Sookie unlocked the door, and Marvaleen jumped in and playfully slapped her on the leg. "Oh, you sly dog, you devil you. They always say it's the quiet ones you have to watch out for. Why didn't you tell me? I think it's all just so exciting, and he is sooo cute."

It suddenly dawned on Sookie what she was talking about. "And young, too. I told you journaling would change your life, and I was right. What is he—thirty?"

"Oh, Lord, Marvaleen, whatever you've heard is not true. I am not having an affair."

Marvaleen winked at her. "Uh-huh, of course not, but honey, you don't have to be embarrassed with me. I approve wholeheartedly. Edna Yorba Zorbra says it's really what nature intended. We should all be with younger men. She says it's only fair. She says we don't hit our sexual peak until sixty. Our sex drive is going up while the men our age are going down."

"But, really, Marvaleen, Dr. Shapiro is just a friend."

"Uh-huh, well, do me a favor. See if your friend has a friend."

"Marvaleen, believe me. I am not having an affair. I'm only seeing him professionally. He's helping me with a few issues, that's all."

"Sure you are, and of course, that's what I'll say if anyone asks. You can trust me. But between us, I'm so proud of you. I always thought you were just one of those dull little housewife types that would never change."

"What? Do you think I'm *dull*?"

"Not anymore."

"But you used to think I was dull?"

"Yes, but not in a bad way. Just conventional. You know—"

"I see, and what else did you think? Don't be afraid to hurt my feelings. I really want to know. Seriously, if you were to describe me to someone, what would you say?"

"Oh, well, I would say you were just as nice and sweet as you could be, that's all."

"That's all. Is that what most people think?"

"Well, yes . . . I guess so. But it's all positive."

"But isn't there something about me that's negative? I have to have some bad faults."

"No, I really can't think of anything, except . . . but even that's not bad."

"No, no—tell me. Except what?"

"Oh, I suppose if you had any fault, I guess it would be that you let people push you around."

"You mean Mother."

Marvaleen nodded. "And me, too. But Sookie, that's not a bad thing. Edna Yorba Zorbra says there are leaders and followers, and the secret to happiness is to embrace your role in life."

"I see."

"Edna Yorba Zorbra says that I'm a perfect combo of student and teacher combined."

"Really?"

"Yes. She says I could morph into becoming a professional life coach any day now if I followed my goddess within. But anyhow, what I really wanted to tell you was that if you and—you know who—ever need a little privacy, I do have that guesthouse in back, and the key is under the mat. Feel free to use it anytime. After all, we cougars have to stick together."

Sookie realized there was no convincing her otherwise, so she said, "Well, thanks, Marvaleen, I just might take you up on it. A couple of sailor friends of mine are shipping in next week."

"Sailors?"

"Uh-huh. Twins."

"Twins?"

"Uh-huh. They do everything together." Sookie winked at Marvaleen. "If you know what I mean."

Marvaleen opened the car door in a daze and got out, stood in the parking lot, and stared at Sookie as she drove away. "Wow. Talk about still waters running deep."

After Sookie drove off, she realized she really shouldn't have said that about the sailors. She would call Marvaleen when she got home and tell her she had made it up. But at least she had found out that people thought she was dull, and what she had suspected all along was true. She had heard of a man without a country. She was a woman without a personality. She had absolutely no personality.

How *do* you get a personality after sixty? She didn't even know where to begin. And why didn't she have one? Had Lenore squashed it? Or had she just been born that way? Her kids all had their own unique personalities—where did they get them? Now she wondered what her personality would be like if she had been raised in Wisconsin by Polish people. She might have been a whole lot of more fun . . . and played the accordion, done the polka, and everything.

When she got home, Sookie was still upset to think that anyone would believe that she, of all people, would be having an affair. Honestly. It was so embarrassing. But obviously, the Waffle House was out. She picked up the phone and made a call. "Dr. Shapiro, do you by any chance know where the Ruby Tuesday out on the four-lane is?"

GRADUATION DAY

――――

AVENGER FIELD

WINTER OF 1943 HAD BEEN ROUGH. A BITTER BATTLE WAS RAGING IN Europe, and Uncle Sam needed all the gas it could get to help fuel the necessary planes and military vehicles. After talking it over with Poppa, Gertrude was the next Jurdabralinski girl to sign up for the WASPs.

Momma wasn't happy, but there was nothing she could do, so Gertrude arrived in Sweetwater, Texas, on May 4 with sacks filled with homemade bread and sausages and two large jars of sauerkraut for Fritzi. The next day, Willy, Pinks, and Gertrude had a picnic on Fritzi's bed with six bottles of Jax beer that Gussie Mintz had smuggled out of the officers' mess.

FRITZI WAS IN HER final phase of training and anxious to finish and get her assignment. The girls had hoped that by the time they graduated, they would be taken in the Army Air Corps and get their real wings, but it had not happened. At the last minute, Jackie Cochran, at her own expense, had Neiman Marcus in Dallas make up special wings for the girls. Graduation Day was pretty special. A lot of the top military brass flew in from Washington, and the entire town of Sweetwater turned out to cheer them on as they marched in. As disappointed as they were not to have real Army Air Corps wings, it was pretty funny for all of them to watch General Hap Arnold try to pin the wings on each girl's chest. He got pretty flustered trying to figure out what was chest and what was not. And on some of the girls, especially Pinks, there was an awful lot of what wasn't chest. Before it was over, the general was red-faced and sweating, And it wasn't from the heat.

That night, before she went to bed, Fritzi sat down and wrote her brother a letter.

Dear Wink,

I got your last letter, but it was mostly blacked out. Those censor boys are really on a tear, so I don't know where you are now or what you are up to, but I get the idea that you are in it pretty good. Not much news is coming out of Europe, but we know our guys are letting them have it.

Just so you know, I graduated today, and we got our assignments, and my pal Willy and I sure are happy. We found out we will both be stationed at Long Beach, California, and will be ferrying planes straight from the factory for shipment overseas. Our pal Pinks has been kicked upstairs and is staying on here at Avenger Field to assist Captain Wheeler. And she is going to make one hell of an administrator. Pinks had never mentioned it to us until today, but she has a law degree. I didn't even know there were women lawyers. Those New York gals are smart as hell. We sure will miss her, but we will be stopping in at Sweetwater from time to time to check up on her and Gertrude and the rest of the gals.

Well, gotta go. Keep 'em flying! California, here I come!

Fritzi

LONG BEACH, CALIFORNIA

Dear Billy Boy,

Flew over to Palm Springs, California, headed back to Long Beach, air smooth as glass. I never knew there were so many mountains and oil wells in California. Just for fun, flew with one wing in Mexico and one in California. Wow.

When this thing is over, I'm thinking about pulling up roots and heading out west. Billy, this place was made for flying. And the rest ain't so bad, either. Palm trees, movie stars, and you can pick an orange or a lemon right off a tree. Everybody here has a tan and the whitest teeth I have ever seen. And speaking of movie stars, I was walking down Hollywood Boulevard, headed for the canteen, when I heard someone tooting their horn at me. I looked over, expecting to see some fresh guy, but it was this snazzy-looking blonde in sunglasses driving a big blue convertible who pulls over to the curb and says, "Hi, soldier, need a ride?" And when I jumped in, Billy, I'll be darned if it wasn't Ginger Rogers, my favorite actress, and I said, "Hey, the last time I saw you was at the Pulaski theater in *Kitty Foyle,* and you were swell in it, too." "Thanks," she says and then looks at my wings and wants to know all about it, and despite being so famous, is real down to earth. When I got out of the car, I said, "So long, Kitty, thanks for the ride," and she got a laugh out of that. She is one sweet gal, but then everybody here is just swell to us. I haven't paid for a drink or a meal since I've been here. And the place is crawling with famous people. Willy and I went to the Brown Derby for lunch, and when we asked for the check, the waiter said, "The two gentlemen in the corner have already taken care of it." We looked over and there sat Mr. Bob Hope and Mr. Bing Crosby. Then Bob Hope comes over and gives us two free tickets to his radio show and invites us to come to dinner at his house in Toluca Lake after the broadcast. All strictly on the up and up. His wife and kids were there, and so was Martha Raye, and after dinner, the doorbell rang, and I swear, Willy and I about died. It was Edgar Bergen and Charlie McCarthy, and old Charlie said, "I hear there are some beautiful pilots here." Anyhow, we had one swell time. They sure make us feel appreciated, and it's not only here, it's everywhere. People bend over backward to make you feel at home. I know it's not me, it's the uniform, but it still feels good. Billy, after the war is over, you need to come out here and look into doing some stunt flying for the movies. We met a few of the guys here, and they say the pay is great.

Fritzi

P.S. An hour later.

Billy, I just read this letter. Yikes! Boy, do I sound like one big jerk going on and on about Hollywood. When I think about the gals that got killed, I feel ashamed of myself for still being alive and having such a swell time. But I don't know what else to do, and I still miss them like crazy.

PENSACOLA, FLORIDA

Fritzi Gal,

Great to hear about Hollywood. I sure will put the stunt-flying idea in the hopper. Sounds good to stay in one place. I am getting too old for barnstorming anymore. These kids here are scaring the living hell out of me. A little training, and they think they are hot shots. They are cracking up planes left and right, and a lot of them are determined to take me down with them. You tell that guy bellyaching about teaching a bunch of women, I'd be happy to swap places with him. I would rather fly with a woman anytime.

Listen, Fritzi, I know it's a rough deal losing your pals, but you just enjoy every minute you have, and that's an order.

Billy

LONG BEACH, CALIFORNIA

Dear Billy,

Your pigeon landed back in Long Beach, tired and happy. It sure
was great to see you, honey, even if it was for just two days. Maybe
next time, we will actually leave the room for some sightseeing.
Ha-ha. I doubt it. I'll tell you, Billy, when I saw you standing there
at the gate in Newark, I almost fainted. A visit with you was just
what the doctor ordered. But the next time you have a few days
off, let me know, so a gal can at least throw on a little lipstick and
comb her hair. I must have looked terrible, but it's hard to look
pretty after ten hours of flying. You look great. The navy must
agree with you, and those stripes you are sporting don't hurt, either.

The P-38 I picked up in Newark today had parts falling off of
it, but tonight, all the way across the desert, the stars twinkled like
diamonds in a dark blue velvet sky, and coming in and seeing all
the lights of L.A. spread out for miles, whew! So beautiful. Foul
weather, bad gas that funked up the engines, mechanical
problems . . . all forgotten.

Love,

Fritzi

RUBY TUESDAY

———

Dr. Shapiro got a little lost on the way and was late for their appointment. And when he did find the restaurant and walked in, he almost didn't recognize Sookie. She was wearing a long blond wig and big black sunglasses. "It's me," she said. He sat down and apologized for being late. "Oh, that's all right. It's my fault. I should have given you better directions." After the waitress had taken their order, Sookie leaned in and said, "Dr. Shapiro, I'm sure you're wondering why I asked you to meet me here and not at the Waffle House."

"Well . . ."

"I didn't want to tell you this over the phone in case your wife or someone was listening."

"Ah."

"But the thing is—we have somewhat of a sticky situation. It seems we have been spotted by somebody. This is such a small town. Anyhow, my mother's friend Pearl Jeff has evidently heard a rumor . . . about us . . . and told Lenore, and she had a fit."

"Oh?"

"Yes, I know it sounds ridiculous, but someone must have seen us together a few times, I guess, and now Mother has the idea that I am running around town, having an affair with a younger man behind my husband's back. Can you believe it? And it's not only my mother, but Marvaleen has heard it, too. Of course, she was thrilled about it. She thinks I'm dull. Anyhow, she even offered me her guesthouse, for an illicit tryst, I guess. Anyhow, I don't want you to worry about it. They have no idea who you are. It's me they are talking about. But isn't it just the silliest thing you ever heard of? I told them it wasn't true, but they wouldn't believe me. And, of course, the first thing I did was tell Earle."

"Oh?"

"Yes, and he thought it was the funniest thing he had ever heard, you and me having an affair."

"Really?"

"Oh, not that he thinks you're funny. It's me. I've always been sort of a prude about these kinds of things. Marvaleen had always been the racy one. Anyhow, Earle said that I should let them go on thinking it. Of course, I didn't tell him about the twin sailors I mentioned to Marvaleen, either, but as I said to Earle, I have Dr. Shapiro's reputation to think about, too. Anyhow, that's why I'm wearing this wig and the reason I asked you to meet me way out here, in case you wondered."

"I see."

"Lenore said that I had to stop seeing you or I would ruin my reputation, but I certainly don't want to stop being your patient. But after hearing this, if you feel we should not go on, I will certainly understand."

"No, I don't want to stop. I'm still game, if you are. And I think the fact that you're here at all shows great progress."

"You do?"

"Yes, you are not allowing what someone may or may not think deter you from doing what you want."

"Even though I wore the wig?"

"Yes."

Sookie sat back in the booth and thought about what he just said. "Well, I guess that's true, isn't it?"

"Yes. Under the same circumstances, some people might not have the courage to continue."

"No, they wouldn't, would they?"

Sookie drove home feeling really good about herself. She really must be doing better. But still, just to be on the safe side, next week, she and Dr. Shapiro were meeting at Mrs. Minor's Café and Truck Stop on Highway 98.

NEW CASTLE ARMY AIR BASE

Dear Billy,

How's by you? Excuse the handwriting. It is 3 A.M., and I am sitting in the nurses' quarters john, where they put us for the night. Stopped in at Sweetwater the other day to check up on all the gals, and Gertrude is doing just fine. She says she got a letter from Sophie, and Sophie is thinking about joining up as well, but I am going to discourage her. This rough-and-tumble life is not for her. Too bad, though, because she is a damn good pilot.

    In the meantime, yours truly is busy. Made six deliveries in five days, setting a record. Ahem, gloat, gloat. I did have a laugh along the way. Had one woman ask me if I was in the Mexican Army. Best yet, people still don't know what to make of the uniform. We have been taken for everything from Girl Scout leaders to stewardesses to Red Cross volunteers. And most good restaurants won't let us in. When we arrived in Wilmington, looking forward to a steak with all the trimmings, one snooty puffball says to us, "We don't accept women in trousers," to which Willy says, "Would you accept a boot in your behind?"

But she said it to us, not him. We are to be on our best behavior, damn it.

Worst of all, the other day when a few of the gals had to land on a base in Georgia, they were held at gunpoint by an eager MP. This yo-yo thought they had stolen a U.S. military plane. When they finally got it straightened out, he said, "Nobody told me about no women flying." We still seem to be the best-kept secret in the country, even to the army.

Fritzi

LONG BEACH, CALIFORNIA

Dear Sophie,

I hear from home there are still some rumblings about you threatening to sign up for the WASPs. Hmmm . . . I know you didn't ask for my advice, but you are getting it anyway.

Here's the deal. It ain't easy. Once you get to Avenger Field, you will be sharing a room with six other girls and a bathroom with twelve others. No privacy. They will work you until you drop. The instructors here are strictly army and tough, and if you don't wash out and do start delivering, it is worse. You are up before dawn and head out in the cold so you can get to the airport, ready to take off at light. You will most likely be flying in an open cockpit in snowstorms, sleet, and rain or in weather so hot you are a baked potato when you land. And not to be crude, but these planes are designed for men with a built-in tube. Once you're up, there is no way we can wiggle out of forty pounds of heavy flying suits and parachute, and go to the bathroom, and on those four- and five-hour trips, this can be hell.

Once you deliver, you are on your own to get back to base. Now, because they don't want any talk about fraternization, they won't let us hop a ride back on a military plane with the guys, so we have to go commercial or any way we can. And here is my other big worry. Guys. As good-looking as you are, you are bound to be swamped by every guy here wanting to date you. We are outnumbered by the guys about five thousand to one, and I'm not sure you are ready to handle that. Gertrude is a big gal, and as you know, I have a big mouth, so we can take care of ourselves. But knowing you? You are a sucker for a sob story. In other words, I don't think this is the place for you. You have always been on the delicate side, and I am not sure you could even get through the physical training. I know you want to help out, but there are a lot of other things you can do. You mean too much to Mom and Pop and all of us, and if anything ever happened to you, I would never forgive myself. Okay?

I've had my say and told you the worst, and you have to make your own decisions, but at least you have been warned.

Love you, kid,

Fritzi

THE DECISION

SOPHIE HAD READ THE LETTER SHE RECEIVED FROM FRITZI, BUT EACH day, as she sat in the kitchen with her father listening to the war news, she felt more and more that she had to do something. She knew she was a good enough pilot to at least try to join up at Sweetwater.

Besides, working at the filling station with Fritzi, she had heard bad language and had guys make passes at her. She assured her mother that nothing could change her mind about her religious vocation. "But, Momma, I really believe they need me. I can fly as well as Gertrude, and she went. And if I can free up just one man to fight overseas, it could make a difference."

Momma sighed. "Well, if you think so, then I guess you should go. It means that now I'll be lighting four candles, instead of three. Oh, dear Jesus in heaven, I hate this war. It's taking all my children. Thank God, your sister Tula doesn't fly or I'd be losing her, too."

FIVE DAYS LATER, WHEN Sophie Marie arrived in Sweetwater, Gertrude was waiting for her as she got off the bus. Gertrude was so happy to see Sophie, even though it meant she would have to start getting up early on Sunday mornings again. Since Gertrude had been away from home, she had been slacking off on going to mass every week, but she had promised Momma to take good care of Sophie. Now that Fritzi had left, she was the oldest sister, so she was going to be on her best behavior, but oh she had loved sleeping in on Sundays.

LENORE'S AT IT AGAIN

Point Clear, Alabama

After she had repeatedly been asked not to, Lenore started watching the local late-night television news again. "It only upsets you, Mother," said Sookie. And sure enough, a few mornings later, Lenore called Netta and woke her up out of a sound sleep.

"Hello," said a groggy Netta.

"It's Lenore. Listen, dear, I want to run something by you before I call the newspaper."

Netta looked at the clock. It was 6:18 A.M. "All right, go ahead, Lenore."

"This country is a mess, and it's not getting any better."

"I agree with you there, hon, but what can you do?"

"That's just it. I know exactly what we can do and where we went wrong."

"Well, good for you, Lenore," said Netta, as she slowly got up out of bed and put Lenore on speakerphone and headed to the bathroom.

"Looking back now, it is clear that our first big mistake was ever doing away with the monarchy. This democracy thing is just not working. And we've certainly given it a fair chance for how many years now?"

"Two hundred and something, at least," called out Netta from the other room.

"More than a fair chance, wouldn't you agree?"

"Oh, yes, more than fair."

"It sounded like a good idea at the time, and I hate to say it, but the majority of people in this country are simply just not capable of governing themselves. My Lord, look who they just reelected mayor. That man doesn't have enough sense to tell time, much less run an entire town."

"You're right about that," said Netta as she flushed the toilet.

"I know I am! And something has to be done before he runs us all into the ground. Nobody wants to spend all that money for those stupid bicycle paths."

Netta came back to her bedside table and took Lenore off speakerphone. "I agree, hon, but what do you propose?"

"People just have to step aside, and let someone who knows what's best for them take over."

"Sounds good, but who?"

"Well, this is where I need your feedback, Netta. Not to toot my own horn, but you know I have excellent organizational skills."

"You wouldn't be president of all those clubs if you didn't, Lenore."

"Right. So I'm thinking about just stepping in, bypassing the entire election thing, declaring myself mayor, and just be done with it."

"Well, I don't know why not, Lenore. You sure couldn't do any worse."

"That's right. I say throw the bums out. Start small, on a local level, and then we can decide where to go from there. I don't see where we have any other choice *except* absolute rule. Do you?"

A FEW SECONDS LATER, at 6:21, Sookie picked up her phone. "Hey, Sookie, it's Netta. I'm sorry to call so early, but your mother's at it again."

"Oh, no. What's she done now?"

Netta chuckled. "Nothing yet, but she says she wants to declare absolute rule, appoint herself mayor, and overthrow the city government."

"Oh, *God* . . . is she serious?"

"I don't know. It could be just one of her whims, but just in case, you'd better get over there and stop her, before she calls the newspaper."

"Thanks, Netta. I'm so sorry she bothered you again."

"Oh, that's all right, I'm used to it by now. But you know, Sookie, as crazy as it sounds, she just might have a point."

SOOKIE DRESSED AND HEADED straight over to her mother's house. She found Lenore in the kitchen.

"Good gracious, what brings you over so early in the morning?"

"Mother, I am here because you cannot be calling up the newspaper and causing any more trouble."

"Trouble? What are you talking about?"

"Netta just called me."

"Oh, well. You know I'm right."

"Mother, you may be right, but let me remind you one more time. Earle has to practice in this town, and I cannot have you stirring up another hornet's nest. We haven't finished paying for the last lawsuit."

"But somebody has to do something. The man is going to ruin us all."

"Fine, Mother. Just let someone *else* do it. Please—let's just try and get through Thanksgiving without some big drama. Promise?" Lenore looked pained. "Please, Mother? For the family's sake?"

Lenore sighed. "Well, all right. I promise. But you know I could whip that city council into shape in twenty-four hours."

"I'm sure you could, but just let it be."

"All right, Sookie. If you insist on interfering with my freedom of speech, then I have no choice but to be muted. But I must say you have certainly become very demanding of late. Are you sure that doctor didn't give you pills?"

"No, Mother, he didn't give me pills. I wish to God he had."

LATER, SOOKIE STOOD IN the kitchen, thinking about what all she had to do to get ready for Thanksgiving. She had never been a particularly good cook, and yet, for the past twenty-something years, she had somehow managed to prepare three meals a day plus meals for all the dogs, cats, hamsters, and—for a short while—the alligator. She had always tried her best to provide good nutrition and balanced meals, but there were times when she had given in and let them all eat pizza. After all, when some boy with a lit "Pizza" sign on top of his car would deliver it right to the door, who was she to object? Her girls were not very good cooks, either. Her only hope was that Carter would marry a girl who cooked. Not only cooked, but who would just love to do Thanksgiving for the entire family.

Thanksgiving was always stressful. This year, Buck's wife, Bunny, had invited the family to come up to their house in North Carolina for Thanksgiving, but Lenore had refused to go. She said, "Sookie, I don't even like to have to write the word 'North' on a letter. Why would I go there?"

"Mother, please tell me you're kidding."

Lenore laughed and said, "Oh, I suppose I am . . . but I'm not sure." Nevertheless, they didn't go to North Carolina.

So, once again, Sookie was cooking. And, as usual, Lenore would arrive shortly before the meal, looking fresh and beautiful in some lovely outfit and sit and hold court all through the meal. It was so irritating. But one thing Sookie vowed she was not going to do this year was make the stuffing for the turkey from scratch. It took too much time, and it never turned out right. This year, she was going to order it from Bates House of Turkey, and she didn't care who knew it. And if Lenore said one word about it, she would say, "Well, Mother, if you don't like the stuffing, then next year, you can bring your own."

NEWARK, NEW JERSEY

Dear Billy,

Hit Newark late Monday night, rain, sleet, zero visibility, and had to land at alternative airstrip in Tenafly. Landed in mud up to our you-know-whats. We had some damage, but at least we landed. The guys in the two planes before us flipped over, and one hit a fence. Whew. Anyhow, we were stuck here for a few days, and Pinks found out and called her dad and managed to get us tickets to a Broadway show called *Oklahoma,* and boy, was Willy happy about that. She sat up all night polishing her boots.

It was our first Broadway show, and what a show! Being from Oklahoma, Willy got pretty excited about the whole thing, and every time anybody on stage said, "Oklahoma," Willy stood up and yelled, "Hee-haw!" It was pretty funny. I'm just glad she didn't shoot off her gun. We went backstage afterward and met the cast, and Alfred Drake, the leading man, took one look at long tall Willy and asked her out, and I got to go along for the ride.

He is one snappy dresser. Offstage, he is strictly Fifth Avenue. He took us to Sardi's, where all the big shots go, and we got a table right up front. And pretty soon, in walks George

Raft with six feet of blond bombshell in gold lamé hanging on
his arm. Then on to the Rainbow Room and the Copacabana.
What a night. And the next day, we went ice-skating at
Rockefeller Center. I skated. Willy watched. They don't ice-
skate in Wapanucka, Oklahoma. Rode on a bus and a subway
and had drinks at the Plaza Hotel. Oh, brother. How are you
gonna keep Willy down on the ranch after she's seen New York?
She took to that town like hot cakes, and it took to her.
Cabbies almost wrecked their cabs, waving and honking their
horns at her.

Miss you,

Fritzi

AVENGER FIELD

———

Sweetwater, Texas

Dear Wink-a-Dink,

On a trip across, Willy and I stopped in at Avenger Field, and just so you know, after all my warnings, it seems our little sister Sophie showed up here a few weeks ago and is now in training. I was not happy about it, but Pinks said not to worry about her and that Gertrude and Sophie were both doing great. And I guess she is right. My mechanic, Elroy, said he overheard another mechanic say that "those Jurdabralinski girls sure know their motors. They can tell you what's wrong, even before we check it out." Our grease monkeying days are sure paying off here. I heard all the instructors are pretty impressed with them as well. One told me Sophie was a natural fly-by-the-seat-of-her-pants pilot. I wanted to tell him I taught her everything she knows, but for once, Miss Show-Off didn't. Momma would be surprised.

I am sending you an article that was in the newspaper telling how our family now has four pilots flying for the good ol' USA. Momma says Poppa is so proud, he is about to bust. Me, too!

I have no idea what you are up to, so the next time you write, tell the censor boys to lay off for just a line or two, will ya? Get this war over with and come home soon. I need to see your ugly face.

Fritzi

P.S. Gertrude brought her accordion and is pretty popular around the barracks. My pal Willy from Oklahoma said she had never even heard a polka in her life and is teaching Gertrude some country western tunes. Ever heard "Back in the Saddle Again?" Ouch. Pretty corny, but I didn't tell Willy this.

LONG BEACH, CALIFORNIA

Dear Billy!

Now the tale can be told. It seems that the new big B-29 was having a lot of problems with engine fires, and a lot of the boys were afraid and refusing to fly the thing. It seems like Lieutenant Colonel Paul Tibbets must be anxious to get it up and going, because he secretly trained a few WASPs to fly it. He then painted "Lady Bird" on the side along with the WASP symbol, and they toured it all around the country to air bases. When they landed and the boys gathered around the plane and saw two females step out of the cockpit, it shamed them into flying it. No more refusals. I am proud as punch to tell you that those two little gals were bay mates of mine. Don't know what Tibbets has in mind with the B-29, but it must be something pretty darned important.

Love,

Fritzi

THANKSGIVING DAY

Having everybody home for Thanksgiving was wonderful, and Sookie was glad to see all her children and Buck and Bunny, of course. But it was also a strain. When Lenore found out that Carter was bringing a girl home, she insisted that Sookie use the Simmons silver. "We don't want her to think we don't know better."

On Thanksgiving Day, Sookie watched as Lenore took her first bite of the Bates House of Turkey stuffing, and she was ready with her rehearsed reply, but Lenore didn't even seem to notice the difference. Next year, she just might order the turkey from there as well.

After dinner, when all the dishes were done and everyone else was busy watching football, she asked her brother, Buck, if he would come and take a walk with her outside. "Sure," he said. "I need to walk off some of the turkey," so they headed out the back door and down the stairs into the yard. As usual, the weather on Thanksgiving Day was warm and balmy. People in Point Clear were often still in their short sleeves until at least December, sometimes later. And today was just perfect. They walked out to the end of the pier and sat down.

Buck took a deep breath and smiled as he looked out at the water and the big white clouds floating over the bay. "God, I love this place. Sis, do you remember all those summers when we slept out on the screen porch and listened to that old radio?"

"Oh, yes."

"And remember those big thunderstorms and watching the lightning over Mobile? What a show. I sure miss this old bay, but"—he sighed—"Bunny loves North Carolina, so what are you gonna do? But it's sure nice to come home once in a while. I know it's a pain in the behind to have all of us and have to do all that cooking."

"Oh, no. Not at all. I'm just glad you could come."

Buck suddenly looked over at Sookie. "Sis, are you okay? You seem worried about something. Is Winged Victory being sued again?"

"No, thank God. But I do need to ask you something."

"Sure, what?"

"Well, it's something that might come as quite a shock to you . . . or maybe not . . . I don't know."

"What?"

"Buck, did you know that I was adopted?"

Buck blinked and looked out at the water again and thought awhile before he answered. "Oh, I might have heard something about it. Why?"

"Then you knew?"

"Yeah, I guess so . . ."

"You knew that I was adopted? It didn't bother you?"

"No. Not a bit. Why should it?"

"You didn't resent me?"

Buck looked shocked. "Resent you? Good Lord, no. Like I said, I was always just glad you were there to help keep Lenore off my case."

"But, Buck . . . we were always so close. Why didn't you ever tell me?"

He sighed. "Well, Sis, I didn't find out myself until I was in high school. And Dad said not to tell you, because he thought it might upset you or make you feel bad. So I didn't. But when did you find out?"

"About five months ago. The Texas Board of Health sent Lenore a letter and I opened it. My adoption papers were inside."

"Oh, I see. Did you tell Lenore?"

"No, I didn't."

"Are you going to?"

"I don't know yet. But why did Daddy tell you?"

"Oh, I guess he was worried. It was after he had his first heart attack. He said that just in case anything were to happen to him, he wanted me to have a letter he had written. He said if anybody ever came around asking anything about your birth certificate in the future, I should give the letter to them."

"Why would anybody ask about it?"

"Well, it seems after you were adopted Lenore wanted to make sure you had a birth certificate with her listed as the mother, so she and the Mexican lady who worked for her drove over the border and had a fake one printed up in Mexico. The thing had been done illegally, and I guess Dad was worried that if somebody ever found out, Lenore might be hauled off to jail or something, so he wrote out a confession saying that he did it."

"Oh, no."

"Yeah, poor guy. He was going to take the rap for her. Anyhow, Sis, I'm sorry you had to find out like that. But honestly, I'd really forgotten all about it. To me, you were always just my sister, and I just felt lucky to have you."

Sookie looked at her brother and smiled. "Buck, you may just be one of the nicest guys in the world."

"Yeah, I probably am."

He put his arm around her, and they strolled back to the house. Suddenly he laughed. "You know, the thought of Winged Victory being thrown in the slammer is pretty funny."

"Yes, can you imagine? I'll bet after two days, they would be begging us to take her back."

"Yeah," said Buck. "And after three days, she'd be running the joint." They both laughed.

*   *   *

THE NEXT MORNING AT breakfast, Bunny looked at Sookie and said, "Well, all I can say is that Buck sure can keep a secret. In all these years, he never told me you were not his real sister."

"Bunny, for God's sake," Buck said. "She is my real sister!"

"Oh, you know what I mean. Sookie, he never said one single word to me about you being adopted, so I can tell you it makes no difference to him, or I would have known it. But I still can't believe it. It's just amazing how you two act so much alike, and yet you're not even related."

Buck rolled his eyes. "Bunny, I think you just need to drop it, okay?"

Buck was upset with Bunny, but Sookie wasn't. After all, what she said was absolutely true. They were not related by blood, but it really didn't matter. They would always be brother and sister, no matter what.

They were two different people thrown together for life by some odd twist of fate and random coincidence. In 1945, Lenore had wanted a daughter, and Sookie had been available. And as to what had caused her to be there on the exact day that Lenore had walked in, she didn't know. Lenore could just as easily have picked out another little girl, or if she had even come a day later, she might have already been adopted by somebody else. She guessed it was just supposed to be.

A FEW DAYS AFTER everyone left, Sookie got a letter from Buck.

Sis,

Thanks for having us. We had a great time, and Bunny and I are still full of turkey. Honey, here is the letter Dad gave me. Thought you should have it. It might come in handy if you ever wanted to blackmail Winged Victory.

I love you, Sis.

Buck

Enclosed was a note written in her father's hand.

To Whom It May Concern:

This is to verify that I, Alton Carter Krackenberry, am fully responsible for the illegal forgery of my daughter's birth certificate.

A. C. Krackenberry

BROWNSVILLE, TEXAS

LENORE SIMMONS HAD RARELY FAILED AT ANYTHING IN HER LIFE, BUT after eleven years of marriage, she had failed to have a child. She had hoped that something would happen while they were stationed in Texas during the war, but it hadn't. And now with the war almost over, the thought of returning home to Selma, where all her friends were now happily raising children, was humiliating. It was actually her housekeeper, Conchita, in whom she had confided this, who had suggested she go to Dallas to the Gladney Home and just take a look. On the first day Alton could get away, they flew to Dallas.

The staff was very nice, and there were plenty of wartime one-, two-, and three-year-old children to see, and Lenore saw them all, but at the end of the day, when the lady came back in the room, Lenore said, "Well, they are all really darling, but I was wondering . . . do you have anything smaller?"

"Excuse me?"

"I was really looking for a baby, preferably a little girl."

"Oh, I see."

"Do you have any more in the back that we haven't seen?"

"No."

"No little babies at *all*?"

"Well, we do have one little nine-month-old girl, but we already have an interested couple that are coming back to see her tomorrow."

Lenore's eyes lit up. "You mean she's on hold?"

"Well, I guess you could say that. Yes."

"Oh, couldn't we just look at her? Just in case the other couple doesn't work out? Please? Sometimes people change their mind."

"Well, I suppose I can show her to you if you like, but remember . . . she's pretty well spoken for."

"Oh, I understand, don't we, Alton? We'll just take a quick little peek."

FIVE MINUTES LATER, AS Lenore held the baby, she exclaimed, "Oh, Alton, look at these eyes. Why, if she isn't the spitting image of myself at that age, I don't know who is. And look," she said, when she pulled back the blanket, "she even has the Simmons foot!" From the first moment Lenore saw her, she was in love, and the other couple never stood a chance.

THE FORGERY

BROWNSVILLE, TEXAS

ALTON KRACKENBERRY HAD BEEN VERY UPSET WHEN HE FOUND OUT about the baby's forged birth certificate. "I can't believe you did something like this behind my back. My God, Lenore, what were you thinking? I'm an officer in the United States Army. I could get court-martialed over a thing like this. You tear that up right now."

Lenore clutched it to her breast. "No, I can't. Oh, please, Alton . . . it's just a little white lie, and it will mean so much to Sarah Jane down the line to carry the Simmons family name. Think about *her*. And imagine that poor little thing having to go through life with a birth certificate with 'father unknown' written on it. It would destroy her self-confidence forever."

"Do you realize that this is an illegal document? If people found out you paid for it, you could be arrested for forgery."

"But nobody is going to find out. Oh, Alton, think about your daughter's future. I did it for her sake, not mine. What nice boy from a nice family is going to marry a girl with an unknown father? She could never be a Kappa or make her debut, and, really, what girl wouldn't want to be a year younger, if she had the chance?"

"What?"

"You want her to have all the advantages she can, don't you? It's

hard enough for a young girl to succeed in society—and then to bur-
den her with this stigma, over something she can't help? Yes, it may be
bending the law just a tiny bit, but this little piece of paper will make
all the difference in the world to her."

"But Lenore, it's a lie—"

"Yes, but it *could* have been true. She could have been our daughter. And you have to admit, she looks more and more like a Simmons
every day. Don't you believe in predestination? I think God meant for
us to have her."

"Lenore, don't bring God into this. This is a criminal offense."

After more pleading, ending with Lenore flinging herself onto the
sofa sobbing and screaming, "You don't love me!" Alton, against his
better judgment, finally agreed, but with one stipulation. "Lenore, if
we get caught, don't say I didn't warn you."

"Oh, I won't." She smiled and dried her tears. "And don't worry,
Alton, I'll take full responsibility. As her mother, I would gladly serve
time sitting in a lonely prison cell if it meant protecting my daughter's
future. A mother's love knows no sacrifice." This last sentence was
delivered while looking at herself in the mirror.

TWO MONTHS LATER, WHEN Lenore and Alton arrived back home in
Alabama with their new daughter, Sarah Jane, everyone noticed she
was rather large for a two-month-old baby, but Lenore had wanted the
baby's official birthday to be the day she was adopted. And so it was,
with the help of a rather good fake birth certificate that Lenore had
bought in Mexico, thanks to Conchita, who had a friend who specialized in these things. Lenore had really wanted only one child, and a
year later, Buck had been a complete surprise. Oh, well.

LENORE HAD NO QUALMS about making things up. Her father and
grandmother had done the exact same thing. Lenore's mother had not
died in childbirth. The truth was that when Lenore was five, her
mother, whom she had adored, had come home from a trip to New
Orleans and announced to her husband that she hated him and Selma,
Alabama, and was leaving for good.

As the carriage had driven away, Lenore ran after it, calling out to her mother to stop, but she had not turned around, and the carriage kept going. She had never seen her mother again. Lenore never knew why she had left. She could have been unstable or had simply not loved her children enough to stay. Either way, it was easier to pretend it had never happened. As far as she was concerned, Sookie was her daughter, and she really had been in labor for over forty-eight hours.

THE IRISHMAN

SCOTT FIELD, ILLINOIS
1944

IT WAS LATE WHEN FRITZI ARRIVED ON BASE, BUT SHE SAT DOWN AND
wrote a letter to Billy. He had been on her mind.

Dear Billy,

Landed at Scott Field a few hours ago, and the place was
packed. Finally got a bed in the nurses' quarters, so am
dropping you a quick line before I hit the sack. I'm feeling a
little worse for the wear tonight, after flying all day in
headwinds and fighting with a faulty odometer that I had to
kick all the way across the country.

Also, too much fun the night before. When I was in
Wilmington, I ran into two old flying pals, Nancy Batson and
Teresa James, who were headed to Orlando. Boy, did we do that
place up good. Nancy is the beautiful blonde from Alabama I
told you about, so we didn't lack for dancing partners . . .
mostly guys waiting to dance with "Alabama." And Jamsie's
from Pittsburgh and a real kick in the pants . . . and she can
hold her liquor. I was doing okay until we went to some joint
and Jamsie ordered us some concoction called a gin rickey.

Don't remember much after that. Didn't get in until four A.M. and had to leave at six. But it sure was great to see those gals again. Besides Sharpie, they are two of the best fliers in the entire outfit, and when we go military for real, I wouldn't be surprised if both don't turn out to be generals. As for me, I'll be happy just being a plain private. Wouldn't know what to do if I couldn't go on cussing officers.

Me

What Fritzi failed to mention to Billy was at one of the last bar stops, she had run into that big redheaded Irishman Joe O'Connor from home. He was now in the marines and was shipping out the next day on his way overseas. It really was good to see him again. She just wished they hadn't wound up at the Pink Cloud Motel. But as he said, the way the war was going, he might not ever see her again.

WARTIME ROMANCE

Long Beach, California

As the war progressed, Fritzi started delivering the P-47, the heaviest fighter plane that the WASPs flew. It weighed 12,500 pounds and had a 2,400 horsepower engine. It was twice the size of a British Spitfire. The cockpit had enough room for only a single pilot, so her first flight had to be solo. She had flown the smaller AT-6, but it had a much smaller 450 horsepower engine, and so she was a little nervous the first time she flew the P-47. It had so much power on takeoff that it pushed her back in the seat. But after she got the gear up and leveled out, she found that it was actually easy to handle. She had heard so many tales from the guys about how hard the P-47 was to fly, but to her, the thing was a pussycat. From then on, it was her favorite plane.

In Long Beach and Newark and at all the stops at the air bases in between, Fritzi and Willy met a lot of cute guys. Many of the fellows they met and danced with were headed overseas, and a few thought they were in love and tried to get serious, but Willy was engaged to her hometown boyfriend, who was a captain in the army, and Fritzi had decided no more Pink Cloud Motel situations. Even so, the guys really got a kick out of them. Word got back to the states that a lot of the bombs being dropped over Germany had either "Willy" or "Fritzi" written on them.

It seemed that romance was in the air that year, even back home in Pulaski. The next time Fritzi landed in Long Beach, she had four letters waiting for her: three from Tula and one from Momma.

LONG BEACH, CALIFORNIA

Dear Billy,

How's by you, honey? Sorry I haven't written much lately, but have been up to my ears. Then we had a love crisis going on back at home, and I got stuck right in the middle. It was touch and go there, and it could have blown up into a pretty serious situation.

A few months ago, Nard Tanawaski, Gertrude's fiancé, came back home from the army on a hardship leave and was missing Gertrude so much, he started hanging around our house all day. They said they hadn't meant for it to happen, but he and Tula fell madly in love with each other and want to get married. What a big mess! And everybody, even Momma, was afraid to tell poor Gertrude. So you guessed it. They tapped yours truly to do it the next time I stopped in at Sweetwater. I sure was dreading giving the poor kid the bad news, but when I told her, it turns out she was as happy as could be about it. She says she realized she wasn't in love with Nard a long time ago and had been trying to think of a way to let him down easy, and if Tula wants him, that's just fine with her. So it looks like it will be the same brother-in-law, just a different sister.

Whew! I'm glad that's all over, but speaking of love, it looks like Sophie has it bad for some English pilot she met. Sure surprised me. I didn't know she had any interest in guys at all. Oh, well, we'll see. In the meantime, I'm not telling Momma.

I'm a little tired, so I will sign off for now. I need to hit the hay. Hughes Aircraft had a backlog, so I am making three or four deliveries a day to San Francisco from Long Beach. I know each one is headed out to our boys in the Pacific, so I leave a little good luck note for the lucky pilot. I swear, Billy, those planes are flying off the assembly line every ten minutes now, but we need them, so no complaints.

Love,

Fritzi

YOGA SOUP

Marvaleen was terribly disappointed when Sookie told her the truth. "You mean all that stuff about the sailors wasn't true, either?"

"No, honey, and the young man I'm meeting every week is not my boyfriend."

"Well, who is he then?"

"If I tell you, will you promise not to tell anyone?"

"Of course."

"Well, I've started seeing a psychiatrist."

"At the Waffle House?"

"Yes, among other places. It's not that I'm ashamed, it's just that I'd rather not have it get around town. And there is no way we could meet at his office without being seen. So he agreed to meet me outside for my sessions."

"Oh. But why are you, of all people, seeing a psychiatrist?"

"Well . . . uh . . . I've just been under a lot of stress."

"Childhood issues?"

Sookie said, "Yes, that's right. Childhood issues."

"You know, Sookie, when I first started seeing Edna Yorba Zorbra, I had a stiff knee, and she said that sometimes the body holds stress from early childhood trauma and that yoga is one of the best ways she knows to release it. And, really, it's done wonders for me."

After that, Marvaleen started dropping brochures by the house from Yoga Soup, the yoga studio she went to. Sookie usually threw them out, but lately she had been feeling a little stiff, and she wondered if maybe it *was* a holdover from early childhood trauma. Lord knows she'd had her share.

And it had started at a very early age. Sookie remembered being only seven when Lenore, true to form and ignoring all facts, had taken it upon herself to write, direct, produce, and star in an original historical pageant entitled *The Saga of the Simmons of Selma.* The opening scene had taken place on a large Southern veranda where Lenore (playing her own grandmother) was discovered with her two grandchildren (played by Sookie and Buck) at her feet. To this very day, Sookie could still remember how terrified she had been when the curtain had gone up at the big auditorium. She had only one line, "Oh, Grandmother, you fought off all those Yankees all by yourself. How brave." But when the time came for her to speak, she had such a bad case of stage fright, she froze. Luckily, Buck had said the line for her. And then there was the Junior League Mother-Daughter Beauty Pageant. That hadn't gone very well, either. No wonder she was so stiff. So she thought she might give yoga a try. She bought a mat and leotards and signed up for Yin Flow for Beginners.

Bright and early the next morning, she showed up for class ready to begin. She did just fine during the sun salutations part, but she must have done something wrong during the hip opening stretch, because that afternoon when she went for her session with Dr. Shapiro, she could hardly walk.

Dr. Shapiro was already waiting for her at the new spot she had found called A.J.'s Steak and Ale House, located on U.S. Route 78. He was alarmed when she limped in the door and over to the table. "Are you all right?"

"Oh, yes." She sat down and winced in pain. "Have you ever done yoga?"

"No."

"Well, if you ever do, take my advice, and watch out for the hip opening stretches."

"Thanks, I'll keep that in mind," he said.

LONG BEACH, CALIFORNIA

Dear Wink,

Sorry I haven't thanked you for the great Brown Betty teapot you sent all the way from merry old England. You will be happy to know that it arrived here safe and sound. I would have written sooner, but time's just gotten away from me. The last few months have gone by so fast, I even forgot to send something for Poppa's birthday, and I could kick myself around the block and back for that.

Speaking of time going by, Angie sent me the latest photo of little Wink. What happened? In the last one she sent six months ago, he was still a baby, and now he is a little boy in short pants. We all sure miss you over here, buddy. Momma said that Angie is just counting the days until you get back. Me, too. And if we have our way, it shouldn't be too much longer. The whole country is throwing everything they have behind the war effort.

Seriously, Wink, I wish you could see with your own eyes how hard people at the factories are working around the clock to get as many planes to you boys as possible. Tell your guys that they would be proud to see how the whole country is pulling together and doing everything they can to help get this war over and get you boys home safe and sound.

All of us in uniform get all the glory, but my hat's off to all those guys and gals showing up day after day, working on an assembly line, doing their job. And you never hear a complaint. Poppa always said this was the greatest country in the world, and now I see how right he is.

Fritzi

LONG BEACH, CALIFORNIA

Dear Billy,

It is late here, but I can't seem to sleep tonight. Flew through a big rainbow today. Was delivering another sweet new P-59 to San Francisco, and it was foggy and gray all the way down, until I hit the Santa Ynez Valley, north of Santa Barbara, and then bang, all of a sudden, the sun comes out. I looked down, and the hills below me have turned a bright lemon yellow, and there was a big rainbow right in front of me, and when I flew through it, I swear, Billy, I looked out, and my wings were glowing pink and green and blue, and I felt so damn happy I wanted to stay up there all day.

I feel sorry for the poor people that don't fly, don't you? Anyhoo, this sure is beautiful country. After my ride on the rainbow, I circled around a bit and saw some windmills and scared a few cows, but what a sight. I just wish you could have been there to see it with me. You have been on my mind so much lately, Billy, and I wonder if you ever feel that way. Things that used to seem important to me, like being famous and just having a good time, don't seem to matter all that much anymore. I used to laugh at all those gals who talked about wanting to put down roots and settle down somewhere. But lately, it doesn't seem like such a bad idea at all. Didn't mean to get all corny on you. Guess I might still be up there flying around in that rainbow or it could have been all those damn cows. Anyhow, honey, as you might have noticed, I miss you.

Fritzi

LONG BEACH, CALIFORNIA

Hi, Momma,

All is well. Still busy as ever. Stopped in at Sweetwater the other day to see Sophie and Gertrude, just in time to share the box of goodies you sent from home. Sure do miss your cooking. All the girls in Sophie and Gertrude's bay started hanging around, hoping to get a homemade doughnut. We shared some, but hid the rest.

Sophie says to tell you not to worry. Seems like she caught a bug down here. Got a little run-down and needs to take it easy for a while. Darn it all, why couldn't I have caught that bug, so I could loll around in bed and be waited on hand and foot? That gal gets all the luck. But the docs say it shouldn't be too long till she's up and at 'em again.

Also, Gertrude won't tell you, but she has been chosen to go to Camp Davis and fly tow target, so the boys on the ground can practice their shooting. Don't worry. They won't be shooting at her, just at the target she will be pulling behind her. A pretty swell job, and only the best gals were chosen. Tell Poppa hello for me. Gotta run.

Fritzi

P.S. Don't know if it's all this Mexican food out here in California, but you will be happy to know that I am gaining weight. If I don't slow down, I could give Gertrude a run for her money.

LONG BEACH, CALIFORNIA

Dear Billy,

I just got word that I am coming out your way. On the fourteenth, I am taking a B-24 Liberator across to Biloxi, Mississippi, and will have a few days off before I have to pick up another and fly it back. Can you meet me somewhere in between? I know you are busy, but I sure do need to see you, honey. Let me know.

Fritzi

THE BUBBA GUMP SHRIMP CO.

SOOKIE AND DR. SHAPIRO WERE MEETING IN THE BACK ROOM OF THE Bubba Gump Shrimp Co. restaurant out on the Causeway. After he came in and sat down, she looked at him and asked somewhat apologetically, "Dr. Shapiro, would you think I was terribly rude if I ordered something to eat? I don't know if it's all right to eat a meal during a session or not."

"Of course it is. Order anything you want."

"Oh, thank you. I was so busy working out in my yard all morning, I lost track of time and completely forgot to eat breakfast, and I'm just starving. I got so behind I didn't even have time to change."

The waitress who took their order informed her that, unfortunately, it was too late to order breakfast.

"The grill's already off, hon. We just have what's on the luncheon menu."

Sookie looked it over. She knew shrimp was their specialty, but she had just made shrimp and grits last night, so she ordered the fried oysters, hush puppies, coleslaw, and a side order of fried zucchini sticks.

Dr. Shapiro stuck with his usual cup of decaffeinated coffee. He had not quite come to terms with Southern cuisine. You could hardly get a thing that wasn't fried.

After Sookie's food came she took a few bites and was in the middle of telling him what she had said to Marvaleen about the twin sailors. "Honestly, Dr. Shapiro, I just don't know what possessed me to say a crazy thing like that. I've never even dated a sailor, much less—" Suddenly Sookie's eyes flew wide open and she turned white as a sheet. "Oh, my God," she said. "I've got to go." She then jumped up from the table and ran back to the ladies' room as fast as she could.

Dr. Shapiro had no idea what was wrong, and she didn't have time to tell him. Sookie was sitting facing the door and had suddenly spotted Pearl Jeff, her mother's friend, coming in the door with a group of ladies. Other than her mother, Pearl Jeff was the last person in the world she wanted to run in to.

When Sookie did not return to the table after fifteen minutes, Dr. Shapiro became concerned. She must have eaten a bad oyster, and it could be a case of seafood poisoning, because it had certainly hit her fast. He waited a little while longer, then walked over to the table of women sitting in the corner. "Excuse me," he said. "My friend is in the ladies' room and I think she may be ill. Could one of you please do me a favor and check and see if she is all right?"

"Why, certainly," said Pearl Jeff, as she picked up her purse and headed back to the restrooms. One door was marked "Buoys," and the other said "Gulls." She entered the door marked "Gulls."

Sookie was hiding in a stall, and the minute Pearl spoke she recognized the voice.

"Hello," she called out. "Is there a lady in here?" When she didn't get an answer, Pearl marched over to the stall where she saw two feet and banged on the door. "Hello? Are you all right in there? Your gentleman friend is worried about you."

Sookie panicked. She didn't know what to do, so she just kept flushing the toilet over and over again.

A FEW MINUTES LATER, Pearl came back out and asked Dr. Shapiro, "Was your friend wearing pink tennis shoes with pom-poms?"

"Yes, I think so," said an anxious Dr. Shapiro.

"Well, she's in there all right, but from the sound of things, I don't think she'll be out for quite a while." Now he didn't know what to do. He couldn't just leave, so he sat there and waited.

Finally, after the table of women left, he went up to the counter and asked the waitress if she would go in and check on his friend. After a moment the waitress came out and handed him a note that Sookie had just scribbled on her check pad.

Dear Dr. Shapiro,

I am so sorry! I know my time is up for today, but I will see you next week and explain. Don't worry. I am not sick.

The waitress had informed Sookie that the table of ladies had left, but she was afraid to come out too soon. Pearl and her friends could still be out in the parking lot.

By the time Sookie did think it was safe to come out, the place was empty. Her lunch was ice cold and she had missed her session. Sookie sat in the booth almost in tears. There was just no escaping, no matter how hard she tried. Being Lenore Simmons Krackenberry's daughter in a small town was like having a tracking device attached to your body. Somebody was always going to know where she was at all times. She had always felt so sorry for poor Princess Anne of England. No wonder she lay low. Sookie knew just how she felt.

A SAD DAY

It was a Tuesday in October. Fritzi walked into the barracks and greeted everyone as usual. "Hiya, pals, I'm back and ready to eat. Who wants to—" She stopped talking when she noticed that they had barely looked up, and some of the gals looked like they had been crying. "What's the matter?" Willy pointed to the letter on Fritzi's bed.

She picked it up and saw that it was from the Army Air Forces headquarters in Washington. She quickly opened it and read the news that General Hap Arnold had directed that the WASP program was to be deactivated on the twentieth of December. Fritzi was stunned. "Is this a joke?"

"No, read on."

Fritzi sat down on the bed and read the letter. "When we needed you, you came through, and you served most commendably. Blah blah blah." Then she cut to the end. "But now the war situation has changed, and the time has come when your volunteer services are no longer needed. If you were to continue in service, you would be replacing, instead of releasing, our young men. I know the WASP wouldn't want that. Blah blah blah. My sincerest thanks, and happy landings always." That day, WASPs stationed on ninety different bases all over the country received the letter.

It seemed that thousands of civilian male flight instructors had been excused from joining the army as long as they trained military pilots. But now that the army had all the pilots they needed, they had started closing down flight schools across the country. However, the army didn't have enough infantry troops for the ongoing war in the Pacific and in Nazi-controlled Europe. Suddenly, these civilian flight instructors found themselves subject to the draft and could end up in combat not as fliers, but as regular foot soldiers. And just as suddenly, a lot of these same instructors wanted to take over the WASPs' jobs, so they could remain in the States.

Many would have to be trained at great expense to the government to handle the advanced planes the women were now flying, but, nevertheless, the men got together and organized a huge publicity blitz to try to defeat the bill that was now in front of Congress that would militarize the WASPs and keep them flying.

The public was told that it wasn't patriotic for women to be military pilots if they would be taking jobs away from men, and it was suggested that if they wanted to serve in the military, the women could join the WAC and become nurses, where they were really needed. And then the VFW and the American Legion jumped on board, and the bill to militarize the WASPs was defeated. This meant that the families of the girls who had been killed would be receiving no death benefits, and at the end of the war, the WASPs, unlike all other discharged veterans, would be left with no GI Bill, no medical, no nothing.

PENSACOLA, FLORIDA

Fritzi,

Honey, just heard what happened. What a raw deal. And what a damn stupid move on the army's part. It's gonna cost the army a fortune to train all those guys to replace you. Arnold says the main flack was caused by those guys that didn't want to be drafted and have to go into combat, and they did a bang-up letter-writing blitz. He said they even got their mommies to write Congress. What a bunch of pantywaists. My friend Barry, who trained some of the WASPs, says there wasn't a thing wrong with you gals, except that you were gals. Wish I was running this man's army and could help, but dammit, I ain't. Anyway, I know how bad you must be feeling right now, but the hell with them. Go out and get yourself a stiff drink. Oh, hell, get as many as you want, and know that I am always in your corner.

Love you, pal,

Billy

It was the first time he'd ever said he loved her, and she really needed to hear that right now. It softened the blow a little. And she did take his advice about the drinks.

HAPPY LANDINGS

DECEMBER 17, 1944, FRITZI LANDED THE BIG FOUR-ENGINE BOMBER for the last time, and before she walked away, she stopped and gave it a pat. "Well, good-bye, old gal. You're one hell of a plane."

On December 20, all the WASPs who were stationed all over the country were called back to Sweetwater, and after they had turned over their equipment—gas masks, goggles, leather flying suits, and boots—the government gave the women a dinner to say "Thanks again for your service, good luck, and happy landings." Fritzi sat there and thought to herself, "Well, that's a hell of a note." After the dinner was over, when she'd said all her good-byes, she wandered out on the field and found a plane, gassed and ready to go, and decided if she was being kicked out, the government owed her at least a free ride home.

Fritzi knew she was drunk, but she didn't care. She had done something she would never be able to forgive herself for. And now that the WASPs had been disbanded and she wasn't needed anymore, it really didn't matter to her one way or the other if she lived or died, so she started the motors, took off to the left, and headed in the direction of Wisconsin. She didn't really want to go home, but she had no other place to go.

She made three or four stops along the way, and the army finally found the missing plane a week later, parked outside a hangar at Blesch Field in Green Bay. After calling a cab, Fritzi was home. A little hungover, but home. Hijacking a military plane was a serious offense, but no charges were ever filed.

Pinks had been left in charge of cleaning up inventory back in Sweetwater and agreed with her. She knew what Fritzi had been through. And Pinks figured that after what all those gals had done, the government should have flown all of them home.

After the war was over, the WASP records were sealed, and it was pretty much forgotten that they had ever existed at all.

It would be another thirty years before another woman would fly a military plane.

VICTORY

On VJ Day, a neighbor ran out in the street and waved his arms and shouted, "The war is over!" Suddenly, there were church bells ringing all over town and horns blowing and kids running around banging pots and pans. They knew it was the end of an era for the entire world.

But most people who had been in it, like Fritzi, just sighed a big sigh of relief. For her, it meant that Winks had made it through alive and would be coming home for good.

The war was over, but it had taken its toll. More than 400,000 Americans had been killed and 1.7 million had been hurt in some way. And most people didn't know about the 39 WASPs who had been killed or that 16 Army nurses had died by enemy fire, and 67 had been taken prisoner, including Nurse Dottie Frakes, who was held in a Japanese concentration camp for more than three years.

But in August 1945, Americans were in a jubilant mood. Finally, their world could get back to normal. As the headlines said, "Hooray! Rosie the Riveter can finally go home and be Rosie the Housewife again!"

The problem was that a lot of women didn't want to be just housewives again. Fritzi was hoping to join Billy and go to California for employment, and Gertrude hoped to get a good, high-paying job at the big Ford Motor Company plant in Willow Run, Michigan. But in the summer of 1945, Kaiser-Frazer Corporation took over the plant to prepare for the postwar years, and it had no room for women. It wanted the best of the jobs to go to the returning GIs. Wink came back home and reopened the filling station, and Angie was happy to go back to being a housewife and mother again. But Gertrude still wanted to work. She tried to get a job flying, but quickly found out that the only job open for women in aviation was that of a stewardess, and when she applied she was told she was too fat to be a stewardess, so she wound up teaching accordion over at Saint Mary's school.

SOOKIE HAS THE BLUES

SOOKIE AND DR. SHAPIRO STILL MET ONCE A WEEK, DESPITE THE FACT that they had almost run out of meeting places. But even with all the hassle of having to change restaurants, she knew it was doing her a lot of good. However, she was finding out that self-examination was not easy. They say the truth can set you free, but sometimes it can really depress the hell out of you. Sookie woke up one morning feeling a little blue, and when Dee Dee came to pick her up for lunch that day, Sookie was still in her nightgown.

When she answered the door, she said, "Oh, honey, come on in for a minute. I'm sorry. I didn't realize how late it was. I should have called you sooner, but I don't think I'm up for lunch today."

"Why?"

"Oh, I don't know. I just feel a little down today. Do you mind?"

"No, I guess not. But what's the matter with you? Are you sick?"

Sookie sat down in her chair and shook her head. "No, I'm not sick."

"Then, what is it?"

"Oh, sweetheart, I don't want to bother you. It's nothing. I've just been thinking too much lately is all."

"Thinking about what?"

"Oh, stupid things . . . about my life . . . things like that."

"What about your life?"

"Oh, sometimes I think maybe your grandmother was right about me all along. I've had two fantastic mothers—one a hero who flew planes—and I turned out to be just a big nothingburger with no courage at all."

Dee Dee looked at her in utter disbelief. "What? You must be kidding. You were our hero. Don't you know that? You were the best mother in the world. And you did so have courage."

"Me? I don't think so."

"Yes, you did. Don't you remember that day when we were little when Daddy's Great Dane fell off the end of the pier? You're not a good swimmer, but you jumped right in the bay and pulled him out. Don't you remember that?"

"Yes, I guess so—but your daddy loved that stupid dog."

"And that time we went to Disney World, and you were scared to death, but you got on that roller coaster, just so you could ride with us?"

"Yes, I do remember that. And I wouldn't do it again, I'll tell you that."

"But you did it once. That's something, isn't it? And I don't care what you say, it takes great courage to have four children and sit by and watch them make mistakes. Look at me. I've obviously married the wrong man twice, and you never made me feel bad or said a word about it. And when I needed you, you were always there. So I won't have you thinking you are a nothingburger. Nothing could be further from the truth. Now, Mother, don't make me have to spank you. You just get up out of that chair right now and get dressed, because we are going to lunch. Do you hear me? The world awaits!"

Sookie looked at her daughter and smiled. It was at that moment that she realized that her little girl, the one she had been worried about the most, had quietly grown up.

Sookie got up and did what Dee Dee said. As she was upstairs getting dressed, she had to laugh. Dee Dee may not be a Simmons by birth, but she was certainly Lenore's granddaughter, all right. They went to lunch and had a marvelous time.

LENORE'S BIG DAY

Point Clear, Alabama
January 2006

LENORE HAD A BIRTHDAY COMING UP, SO IT WAS TIME TO START PLAN-ning, and she always had a list of instructions for Sookie about how she wanted to celebrate.

Sookie got out her notebook and walked over to her house. Angel told her Lenore was back in her little den off the alcove. When she went inside, she found her mother fully made up but still in her floral dressing gown, sitting at her desk looking forlorn. "Hey, what are you doing? I came over to find out what you wanted to do this year to celebrate your birthday."

"Nothing. Absolutely nothing. When you're my age, there's nothing to celebrate."

"Why? What's the matter?"

"I'm so upset."

"Why?"

"Oh, Sookie, it's so awful to be old. Look at my phone book. Almost everyone I know is dead. Nobody is left that remembers me when I was young. I don't have anybody left to reminisce with. If it weren't for you and Buck, nobody would remember me at all. I'm being pushed into the past. Oh, it's terrible when you don't have a future or anything to look forward to. I used to think that after you and Buck were grown, I'd go on the stage, but then your daddy got sick, and I had so many club obligations, I guess I just misjudged time. And when your daddy died, it was too late. Oh, I could write a book. I'd call it *A Life of Regret* or *The Things I Didn't Do*. And I could have done so many things. I was always good at anything I put my mind to, you know that."

"That's true. You could do anything and do it better than anybody else. But you know, Mother, I have always wondered: Did it make you happy?"

"What?"

"Have you ever been happy?"

"Oh, Sookie, why do you ask me these silly questions? I must say I liked you better when you were busy raising children. Lord, all you do now is sit around and think, and thinking is not good for you, Sookie."

"Thank you, Mother."

"Well, Sookie, your mother is the only one who will ever tell you the truth. You know I'm right, Sookie."

"Okay, Mother. Whatever you say. But what do you want to do about your birthday this year?"

"Oh, I suppose I owe it to the children to have some sort of celebration. It means so much to them, and who knows? I may not be here next year, so maybe we should do a little something."

Sookie sighed. "How many people?"

"Oh, no more than thirty. I'm just not up to it this year."

"Yes, Mother."

"And if we do go to Lakewood, don't let them talk you into putting us in the smaller room."

"Yes, Mother."

That meant she wanted to go to Lakewood and be in the big room. And knowing Lenore, she would start adding more and more people as it got closer.

But that was Lenore. Her birthday was a big thing to her and she assumed it was for everyone else in town as well.

As Sookie walked back home, she began to think about the situation regarding her own birthday. Her real birthday, in October, had quietly come and gone. She wondered about the woman listed on her birth certificate. It was strange to think that somewhere out there, someone she had never met might have been remembering that day too.

GETTING TO KNOW YOU

SOOKIE HAD ALWAYS WORRIED THAT SHE AND DEE DEE HAD NEVER been as close as she would have liked, but Dee Dee had started calling and asking her to meet for lunch almost every week now. And it was nice getting to know her daughter just a little better.

They were sitting outside at Sandra's Sidewalk Café one afternoon, when Dee Dee said, "Oh, Mother, did I tell you that I finally got the Poole family crest reframed?"

"No, you didn't. Are you pleased with how it looks?"

"Oh, yes. I think I like the gold even better than the red."

"Oh, good." Sookie took a sip of her iced tea and said, "You know, Dee Dee, I just realized something."

"What?"

"Well, just think, you are a Poole by blood, and I only married a Poole, so you are even more related to your father than I am. And none of us are related to the Simmonses at all. Isn't that strange? I mean, what is genetics, and what is environment? And why am I the way I am?"

"Oh, Mother, who cares? We certainly don't. The only thing that matters is who you are now. And besides, this is America, and you are free to be anybody you want to be. You can even change your name legally, if you want to, and not be a Simmons or a Jurdabralinski. You can be whoever you want to be."

Sookie smiled. "Can I be Queen Latifah?"

Dee Dee laughed. "No, but you could call yourself Lucille Flypaper or Tiddly Winks McGee, if you want."

"I know you're kidding, but you know, it might be fun to be someone different, just for a change. 'Sookie' is way too babyish for a sixty-one-year-old woman, don't you think?" Sookie took a bite of her salad and then said, "Virginia Meadowood."

"What?"

"From now on, I want to be known as Virginia Meadowood."

"Yes, Mother."

"Do you think I'm too old to start over?"

"No, Mother, sixty-one is young."

"I wish I could start over. I would do things so differently if I had the chance."

"Oh, what?"

"Oh, I wouldn't have let so many things bother me, and I would have stood up to your grandmother more, of course. But then if I were someone else, I might never have been a Kappa, and I wouldn't have married your father. You would have had a completely different father or else you might not have been born at all or I could have had four totally different children. I can't imagine. It just boggles my mind thinking about all the what-ifs, wondering why things turned out how they did and if it was supposed to be that way or is your life just an accident."

"It's a mystery, isn't it? But, Mother, you may want to change and be someone different, and we will support you in anything you want to do, but we've all talked about it, and we're really glad you married Daddy, and we admire you for having so much patience with us and with Grandmother."

"Really?"

"Oh, yes. But seriously, Mother, you are not who you think you are."

Sookie had heard that before. "How so?"

"Well, it's true that Grandmother is flashy and flamboyant and all that, but she's a little shallow. You think you're not important, but you are. You have heart, Mother. You are a real human being."

Sookie was suddenly overwhelmed to be hearing this from her daughter, and tears sprang up in her eyes. "Well, thank you, honey. That means a lot to me."

LATER THAT AFTERNOON, SOOKIE called Dena. "I'm telling you, Dena, when you live long enough to see your children begin to look at you with different eyes, and you can look at them not as your children, but as people, it's worth getting older with all the creaks and wrinkles."

PACKAGE FOR ALICE

PETE THE MAILMAN WALKED TO SOOKIE'S DOOR and knocked just as Lenore was coming up the stairs with a sack of B & B pecans she had picked up for Sookie. When Sookie opened the door, she saw them both and said, "Well, good morning!"

Pete said, "Good morning. I've got another package for Alice Finch."

"Oh, thank you, Pete. I'll take it."

"She's been here for quite a while now. She must like it here."

"Yes, she does. Thank you, Pete," Sookie said. "Have a nice day."

As Lenore walked in the door, she asked, "Who's Alice Finch?"

"Just a friend."

"What friend?"

"You don't know her, Mother."

"Why not?"

"I don't know."

"I know everybody who's moved here. I've never heard of anyone named Alice Finch."

"She's a friend of Marvaleen's."

"Oh, well, no wonder. Why are you getting her mail?"

"Mother, do you have to know everything?"

"Yes, I do. Here are your pecans."

"Thank you."

"Do you have any of Earle's coffee left? I need a little more. Conchita makes the weakest cup of coffee known to man."

"No, but I can make some. Did I tell you I spoke to Carter?"

"No."

"He has a new girlfriend, but he isn't serious about her, he says."

"Well I certainly didn't like the last one he brought home. She was far too loud and aggressive for my taste."

ALTHOUGH SOOKIE REMAINED PLEASANT on the outside, the next hour and a half was sheer torture. She was dying for her mother to leave so she could open her package, and the minute she heard the front door shut, she tore into it.

Dear Alice,

Here are a few articles and other stuff. Some of the pictures are a little faded, but I thought you might want to see them. Will send more when I find it.

She opened the folder and saw a newspaper clipping with a picture of a slender young woman wearing jodhpurs, lace-up leather boots, and a white shirt standing by a plane with her hands in her pockets.

Sookie knew this was a special moment in her life. She was looking at a picture of her real mother for the very first time. The pretty dark-haired girl smiling at the camera couldn't have been more than seventeen or eighteen, but she looked so confident and self-assured. Underneath the picture was the headline:

MISS FRITZI JURDABRALINSKI OF PULASKI
BECOMES WISCONSIN'S FIRST GIRL PILOT
Pulaski News
1939

Miss Fritzi Jurdabralinaki, Pulaski's own Amelia Earhart, will be appearing with the famous Billy Bevins Flying Circus.

Then Sookie saw a clipping with another photo of Fritzi.

SISTER JOINS HER BROTHER IN THE AIR, FLYING FOR THE USA
Green Bay Journal
1943

Miss Fritzi Jurdabralinski, a licensed pilot, has joined a group of
women fliers who have volunteered their flying services to the
United States government. She will be going to Houston, Texas,
for training. "I am very happy and hopefully, with women
taking over the domestic ferrying of planes, we will be able to
get this war over sooner." Fritzi is the daughter of Mr. and Mrs.
Stanislaw Jurdabralinski of Pulaski, Wisconsin.

Sookie sat staring at the glamorous girl in the photos. She liked
her face and the way she stood, looking like she was ready to go out
and conquer the world.

Before that, Fritzi had just been a name on a piece of paper, but
now that Sookie saw that she was a real person, the enormity of it all
hit her. This was her mother, who had carried her for nine months.
This pretty girl was the one who had given birth to her. Had she held
her, she wondered? Or had she not even looked at her? Why had she
handed her over to strangers? Had she done something wrong? Had
her mother not liked her? Earle was right. She had to try to find her.
She might not like the answers, but she couldn't go on not knowing.
Now she was worried she had waited too long.

When Earle came home, he was glad about the decision. "I know
it's a hard thing to do, but like I said, if you don't try, you will always
regret it."

Earle went to the computer and started searching for websites per-
taining to former WASP pilots and found one. After a few days, he
had an answer and a telephone number. Mrs. Fritzi Bevins of Solvang,
California, was still very much alive.

SOOKIE SAT THERE WITH the number in her hand. "Earle, could you
call her?"

"No, sweetie, that wouldn't be right. You're the one she wants to hear from, not me. Do you want me to dial the number?"

"No."

"Do you want me to be here with you?"

"No, it would make me too nervous."

"All right, but I'll be right outside on the porch, okay?"

"But Earle, what if she hangs up on me?"

"Honey, she's not going to hang up on you."

"Okay, but what if I faint?"

"You're not going to faint."

"I feel like I might."

"All right, I'll tell you what. I'll go and get the smelling salts, and if you start to feel funny, just take a few whiffs. But you're not going to faint." He came back and handed her a small bottle. "You can do this, sweetheart. And you'll be so glad you did. I'll be right outside."

Earle left, and she stared at the phone. She had the same feeling she had when she was eight and had climbed up on the high diving board at the swimming pool and had looked down. It had been so embarrassing. She'd had to turn around and crawl back down the ladder and make her way past all the other kids who just couldn't wait to jump.

She went over all of Earle's pep talk points in her head. Okay, you have nothing to lose . . . everything to gain. She will be glad to hear from you, and even if she isn't, you at least tried.

She closed her eyes and dialed. 805-555-0726. Oh, God. As the phone was ringing, she suddenly felt her mouth go dry. She might not be able to speak. Should she hang up?

"Hello."

"Hello . . . is this Mrs. Fritzi Bevins?"

"Yes, it is."

"From Pulaski, Wisconsin?"

"Yes."

"Uh . . . you don't know me, but I recently received some papers. From Texas. And, well . . . I think I might be your daughter?"

There was a long silence on the other end, and then after a moment, the woman in a softer voice said, "Hiya, pal. I've been waiting for this call for a long time."

*   *   *

A FEW MINUTES LATER, after she hung up, Sookie screamed, "Earle!" He jumped up and ran in, and Sookie said, "I just talked to her."

"You're kidding."

"No!"

"How did she sound?"

"Very nice. And she's invited me to come to see her."

"No! Wow."

"Can you believe it? She said she would love to meet me."

"See? Now, aren't you proud of yourself?"

"Yes."

"Are you going to go?"

"Well, maybe . . ."

A FEW DAYS LATER, Sookie went up and knocked on Lenore's door, and Lenore opened it just a tiny crack. "Mother, it's me. I just wanted you to know that I will be gone for a little while, so if you need me to do anything before I leave, let me know."

"Well, come in, don't stand out on the porch. You're letting all the air-conditioning out."

"Okay, but I can't stay."

"Come in. Now, what do you mean you're going to be gone? Where are you going?"

"To a health spa."

"A health spa? What for?"

"Earle thinks I've put on a few pounds, and I just need a little rest . . . after the weddings."

"Where?"

"Oh, I guess my hips."

"No, where is the spa?"

"California."

"*California?* What's the matter with the hotel spa right up the street?"

"Nothing. I just need a change of scenery."

"You don't look fat to me."

"Mother, please!"

"All right, all right. But I just hope this trip is not another one of Marvaleen's harebrained ideas."

"No, Mother, she has nothing to do with it."

"Well, good. That girl is just not up to you, socially or otherwise. Don't forget you have your reputation to think about. When will you be back?"

"I'm not sure, but call Earle if you need anything."

Lenore looked at her as she walked toward the door and called out, "Sookie!"

"Yes?"

"Make sure your luggage matches." Lenore had not said anything to anybody, but she was still concerned about her daughter. She just hadn't seemed herself lately.

MEETING MOTHER

SOLVANG, CALIFORNIA

THE CAR PICKED SOOKIE UP AT THE SANTA BARBARA AIRPORT AND drove her about forty-five minutes up the 101 Freeway and into the small Danish town of Solvang. Sure enough, there were windmills everywhere. She had never been to Europe, but she felt like she was there. The driver, who had the address, went through town and made a right turn on Alisal Road and drove about three blocks, and there was the sign, RANCHO ALISAL ESTATES. As he turned right on the street, she suddenly said, "Stop! Please, may I just sit here for a minute?"

"Yes, ma'am," he said and pulled over to the side of the road.

She took her small bottle of smelling salts out and took a few sniffs and sat and waited. There was a moment when she just wanted to turn around and go home. But she pulled herself together and said, "All right, I'm ready."

FRITZI HAD SAID SHE lived in a trailer park, but this was no ordinary trailer park. This one was beautiful, with a lovely little golf course in the middle. They found her street and pulled up to a pretty light blue mobile home, and the driver said, "This is it."

Sookie got out and walked up the three steps covered with green felt leading to the front door with her heart pounding, but before she could knock, an older woman with dyed blond hair worn up on her head in curls, wearing a sleeveless striped cotton dress and white plastic earrings, opened the door. And after all the mental rehearsing of just what she would say, at this very moment, all Sookie could manage was a weak little, "Are you Mrs. Bevins?"

"You bet I am," said the woman in a definite Midwestern twang. "You must be Sarah Jane. Come on in. I was kinda worried you wouldn't find me, but here you are."

"Yes, well, I had someone drive me."

"Ah, smart. Come on in the living room, and have a seat. You must be tired coming all this way."

Sookie walked over and sat down on the brown plaid sofa and placed her purse by her side.

The woman sat across from her and said, "Well . . . you made it."

"Yes," and after an awkward silence, Sookie said, "Uh . . . you have a lovely place here."

"Thanks. It's not much, but it's paid for. You need to use the facilities?"

"Pardon me?"

"The bathroom."

"Oh, no, I'm fine. Thank you." Sookie couldn't help but stare at her. The lady was older, but she still recognized her from the old photos. And now seeing her in person, she could see a definite similarity to her own face. "Well . . . so here we are, after all these years," said Sookie.

"Yeah, here we are."

"Yes."

"Is this your first time in California?"

"Yes."

"Would you like some coffee or a drink? I've got some beer or wine and some hard stuff in there, I think."

"No, thank you, but I would love some water, if you have it."

"Oh, sure. It's not bottled, though. Is that all right?"

"That's fine." Sookie looked around and noticed the photographs that almost filled the fake brown wooden walls in the living room and all the way down the hall. "This certainly is a lovely spot, Mrs. Bevins.

Driving in from Santa Barbara was just beautiful. All the mountains and trees."

"Call me Fritzi, honey, everybody does. Yeah, I'm from Wisconsin, but hell, after you've seen California, I couldn't live anywhere else." She walked over and handed Sookie a glass of water.

Sookie took it, but her hands were shaking so much she spilled some of it on the rug. "I'm so sorry. I think I'm just a little nervous."

"Don't worry about it, kid. We both are. Don't forget the last time I saw you, you had no hair or teeth and weighed eight pounds, and now look at you. A grown woman with four kids. And good-looking, too."

"Really? Well, thank you."

"I know I'm not much to look at now, but believe it or not, I used to be somewhat of a looker."

"Oh, you were. Absolutely. I've seen pictures of you. You were wonderful looking and still are. Your hair is different, but I would have recognized you anywhere."

"Yeah? Well, I guess I look pretty good for an old bag. Where did you see my picture?"

"In the newspaper articles. I read all about you, and I'm just in awe of what you did during the war. You were so brave."

"Well, honey, it was a job that needed to be done, and we did it, that's all. What about you? Have you had a good life?"

"Oh, yes, and as I mentioned, I have a wonderful husband and four wonderful children, and well, you have four wonderful grand-children."

"And the people who adopted you, were they good to you?"

"Oh, yes, just wonderful. I have no complaints."

"Are they still alive?"

"Just my mother—well, the lady who adopted me. My father passed away in 1984."

"I'm sorry to hear it. Does your mother know you're here?"

"No. She doesn't know that I know I was adopted."

"Ah."

"I didn't see any reason to upset her. She's not . . . well, anyhow . . . no, I didn't tell her. I hope you don't mind that I came. I can understand that meeting me must be very difficult for you, but I really needed to see you in person and, well, come to terms with . . . well, as you can imagine, it was quite a surprise to find out after all these years."

"Ah, yeah, and I'll bet you have a lot of questions you need me to answer. So ask away."

"Well, yes I do. I have a list somewhere here." Sookie fished in her purse. "Oh, here it is. I guess I need to know about family health issues. If there was anything genetic we should be worried about, any heart or diabetes or mental issues. Things like that."

"No, everybody mostly died of old age. Everybody was pretty hardy." She laughed. "Some a little too hardy. Momma and Gertrude got pretty fat in their old age."

"Oh, well, that could explain my oldest daughter, Dee Dee. She's always had a tendency to put on weight. So, umm . . . no dementia or Alzheimer's?"

"No, everybody—Momma, Poppa—were as sharp as tacks right up until the day they died. And just so you know, all of us Polacks are pretty healthy."

"Well, that's certainly good to know." Of course, the elephant in the living room was who her father was. Fritzi didn't seem to be forthcoming with that information, and Sookie thought it might be rude just to ask her outright so soon. "I guess I have so many things I've wondered about."

"Yes?"

"I guess I wondered, during all these years, did you ever think about me?"

Fritzi nodded. "Oh, sure, kid. All the time. I always wondered how you turned out. What you looked like, what you were up to. Things like that."

"I see . . . and did you ever think about trying to find me?"

"No, I never did. I figured it was best not to. To tell you the truth, after the war, I went through a pretty rough patch. Drank too much, stuff like that."

"Oh."

"Did you bring pictures of your kids?"

"Oh, yes."

After Fritzi looked at all the pictures, she said, "Great-looking kids. And your husband looks like a regular nice guy."

"Oh, he is. And he said to be sure and tell you that he would love to meet you one day, but he thought that maybe I should come by myself the first time. And, of course, if you ever need any dental work, he'd be glad to do it. To tell you the truth, I really wanted him to come with me. I was kind of scared to come by myself, but I'm so glad I did. I'd love to see some photographs of your . . . well, *my* family."

"Oh, sure, kid. I got all of them hung up." As they walked down the hall, Sookie saw a picture of the four sisters standing in front of the all-girl filling station taken in 1942. Sookie was surprised at how much her girls looked like the Jurdabralinski sisters.

Sookie said, "I just can't imagine how hard it must have been to run a gas station."

Fritzi nodded. "It was, but it was also a hell of a lot of fun. And this is your Uncle Wink when he was in the Air Corps over in England."

"Oh, wow, he looks a little like my son, Carter."

"Yeah?"

"He has the same smile."

Then Fritzi pointed to another photograph. "And here's a picture of your grandmother standing in front of the house. You can't tell here, but Momma was the one with the really red hair."

"Really?"

"You bet. Even redder than yours."

"Is this the house where you grew up?"

"Yep. Poppa built it for us in the twenties. But after Wink died, Angie sold it to a real nice family in town."

"Is the filling station still open?"

"No, it closed down a long time ago. I think they just use it for storage or something now, but it's still there."

After they had visited for a while and Fritzi had made them a cup of coffee, Fritzi picked up the pictures of Sookie's family and looked at them again. "Real nice house. Right on the water."

"Oh, yes. Our backyard is the Mobile Bay."

"You're not far from Pensacola or the Gulf of Mexico."

"No."

"I know that area. Very pretty. I used to fly around there."

Fritzi placed the photos down and nodded. "Yeah," said Fritzi. "I can see that after having such a nice quiet settled life all these years, finding out about this must have knocked you for a loop."

"Well, yes, it did. You can imagine my shock after all these years. I mean at age sixty, to meet your real mother for the very first time is pretty extraordinary."

Fritzi reached over and took a cigarette out of a pack, lit it, and looked at her for a long time, then said, "Damn, I hate to do this to you, pal, but I'm afraid I have another shock for you."

"Oh? What?"

"I'm not your mother."

Sookie was not quite sure she heard right. "Pardon me?"

"I'm not your mother."

"But . . . your name is on my birth certificate."

"Yeah, I know. But just the same I'm not your mother." Sookie felt herself suddenly getting light-headed. Fritzi looked at her. "Hey, are you all right? Sarah Jane?"

Sookie realized she must have blacked out for a second, but said, "Yes, I guess so, but I don't understand. If you're not my mother, then who was?"

"Well, it's a long story, kid. You probably should have a drink; you don't look so good." Sookie did slug down a scotch and took her smelling salts out of her purse, just in case, and waited with her heart still pounding for Fritzi to continue.

AVENGER FIELD

Sweetwater, Texas
January 1944

Fritzi was in Sweetwater for a few days to catch up with Pinks and Gussie Mintz and have a little visit with her sisters. The first night she was there, Sophie came in from her date with her cheeks flushed and her eyes glowing, smiling and laughing to herself. Fritzi was sitting in a chair, painting her toenails. She looked at Sophie and said, "Somebody must have had a good time. If I didn't know better, I'd say you were as boiled as an owl."

Sophie sat on the other cot and smiled at her. "No, I haven't had a drop to drink. Oh, Fritzi, I never knew I could be so happy. I'm in love with the whole world. He's so wonderful!"

"Who?"

"Jimmy. Jimmy Brunston. He's the RAF pilot here on special assignment I introduced you to."

"Oh yeah. I remember."

"Well anyway, he's picking me up late Friday night, and we're going to Houston for the weekend."

"Whoa. Oh, no, you're not."

"Oh, Fritzi, it's all on the up and up. I promise you. He's already booked a room for me at the Shamrock Hotel, and he's staying with some English friends across town. It's our last weekend together. He's going back overseas next Tuesday. Oh, Fritzi, I've just *got* to go. He's gone to so much trouble to arrange everything, and he's so wonderful."

"Well, all right, if you're so crazy about him, go on, but look, kid, don't do anything you shouldn't. These guys will say anything. Just remember, they're all here today and gone tomorrow. Have fun, but be careful."

"You don't understand, Fritzi. Jimmy's not like that. He's a perfect gentleman. He really loves me, Fritzi. He's asked me to marry him, and he said the minute the war's over, he's coming back to get me."

"Does he know your family ran a filling station? He seemed like the snooty English type to me."

"Of course, he knows. I've told him everything, and he thinks it's just charming. That's what he said. He's not snooty at all. He's told me all about his parents, and they're just regular people, and he said as soon as they met me, they would love me."

"Fine, but tell Lieutenant Brunston if he does anything he shouldn't, he'll have to answer to me."

THE NIGHT JIMMY AND Sophie flew over to Houston was warm and clear. The clouds below them were like huge silver balls of cotton. When they were halfway there, Jimmy switched channels on the radio and picked up a big band station. As they listened to the Glenn Miller Orchestra play "Moonlight Serenade," Sophie felt like they were the only two people in the world, all alone up in the clouds, so much in love.

SOPHIE DIDN'T UNDERSTAND WHEN, after a couple of months, Jimmy's letters from overseas became less and less frequent, and then they stopped altogether. It wasn't like him not to write. He had written her every day. Something must be wrong. She knew he was going on bombing raids over Germany almost every night and that there had been losses. She held her breath every time the casualty report with the names of the pilots came in, but it wasn't until after three of her letters were returned unopened that she started to panic. She was desperate and sick with worry. He had to come back.

The next morning, she went to the Red Cross office in Sweetwater and spoke to Mrs. Gilchrist, a nice older woman, and showed her the returned letters. She gave Mrs. Gilchrist his regiment number, where he was born, the names of his parents, the name of the town they lived in, and the date he had last called her.

Mrs. Gilchrist wrote it all down and said, "I'll do my best, but I can't promise anything. As you can well imagine, overseas communications are very difficult right now. But try not to worry. I can't tell you how many girls have come here expecting to find out the worst, and it was all a mix-up. So don't give up hope. Tomorrow, you may get five letters."

TWO DAYS LATER, BACK in the bay, Sophie heard someone yell across the room. "Sophie Jurdabralinski! Phone call!"

Sophie ran over to the phone, hoping it might be Jimmy, but the girl made a face and said, "It's a female."

"Oh . . . . Hello."

"Sophie?"

"Yes?"

"This is Mrs. Gilchrist from the Red Cross. Can you come by my office? I have some good news for you."

"Have you located Jimmy?"

"No, but we contacted our office in London, and we have his parents' phone number, and I have arranged a transatlantic call for you. I'm sure they know where he is and will be happy to hear from you, so come to my office when you can."

Sophie immediately went to Mrs. Gilchrist's office. The Red Cross operator on the switchboard placed the call for her and then motioned for her to pick up.

After a few rings, a woman answered, "Hello?"

"Is this Mrs. Brunston?"

"Yes?"

"Oh, hello. This is Sophie Marie, and I'm calling from America."

"Oh, hello."

"I don't know if he has mentioned me or not, but I'm a friend of your son's, and I haven't heard from him for quite a while. I was wondering if you knew where I could contact him."

"Oh, yes, I see, but I'm afraid you've reached the wrong number. James's mother's line was bombed out."

"Oh, no."

"Yes, but not to worry. No injuries. She's quite safe with friends in Hampshire. But this is his wife speaking, and he's due home on a short furlough any day now. Hush, darling, Mummy's on the phone. I'm sorry. Is there a message or a number where you can be reached? Hello? Are you still on the line?"

"Yes, I'm here. Uh . . . no message."

"I'll be happy to tell him you called. Was it Sallie?"

"No, Sophie, but it really wasn't important. Thank you anyway."

After she hung up the phone, she just sat at the desk, and when Mrs. Gilchrist walked back in the office, she assumed by the look on the girl's face that her young man had been killed. She went over, sat down beside her, and took her hand. This was the heartbreaking part of the job she hated. "I'm so terribly, terribly sorry, dear. I was hoping . . . well. Oh, how I hate this old war, so many young people lost. Is there anything I can do—anyone I can call for you?"

"No, but thank you." Sophie went back to the barracks and said nothing to anybody for three weeks. But when Fritzi came through Sweetwater again, Sophie knew she was going to have to tell her.

FRITZI WAS QUIET FOR a moment, then sighed. "How long?"

"Three months."

"Damn. I know some people, but it's too late to do anything now. Why didn't you tell me sooner?"

"I guess I thought if I told him, maybe he could get a leave, and we could get married. I don't know. I guess I was just too ashamed. I don't know what to do."

"Well, you're not the first or the last gal that this has happened to. I figured that guy was up to no good." Fritzi lit a cigarette and blew the smoke up in the air and then said, "You know this kind of thing is not good for the WASPs. We have a reputation to uphold. How soon will you start showing?"

"I don't know. Another couple of months, I guess."

"Well, the good news is the way those flying suits fit, nobody will be able to tell for quite a while, so you can keep flying. But at the first sign, when you reach the point you think you can't go anymore, call me. And let me take it from there."

Fritzi walked into the office of a friend, who was the head nurse of the base hospital. Nurse Joan Speirs looked up, happy to see her. "Fritzi! Hello, you old slug. How are you?"

"Hiya, pal," Fritzi said, then she closed the door behind her and sat down. "Listen, I've got a situation, and I need a little help."

A year earlier, before Joan's husband, Don, was shipped overseas, Fritzi had taken a big chance and smuggled him on a flight from Grand Rapids to Dallas and had gotten Joan and Don a room off base so they could spend the weekend together before he left. He had been killed a month later. She was more than glad to do Fritzi a favor.

About three and a half months later, after a visit to Nurse Speirs, Sophie was officially put on sick leave. Diagnosis: unknown viral infection. Nurse Speirs arranged for her to stay in a private clinic in Amarillo until the baby girl was born.

A couple weeks later, Gussie Mintz asked around and found a couple in Sweetwater who would keep the baby, and as soon as she could, Sophie returned to flying. But every free second she had, she spent with her baby. She said after the WASPs were disbanded, she would probably just go somewhere and get a job. She knew she couldn't go home, but she couldn't give up her baby, either. As she told her sister, "Oh, Fritzi! I've never loved anything so much in my life."

Then, just three weeks before the WASPs were to be sent home for good, the accident happened. It was a midair collision, and Sophie Marie had been killed instantly.

SOLVANG, CALIFORNIA

FRITZI COULD SEE THAT SOOKIE WAS UPSET AT THE NEWS. "I'M SORRY to have to tell you this, but you needed to know."

"Yes."

"And I did wonder about you a lot. But to come totally clean with you, I guess the other reason I didn't look for you was that I didn't want to have to face you. The truth is, your mother should never have been in Sweetwater in the first place, and it really was my fault that she was there at all. Oh, I wrote her a letter and told her how rough it all would be, but I could have stopped her if I had tried hard enough, and I didn't. And I should have. I always knew deep down she didn't belong there, but I think there was another part of me that thought it would be great to have three Jurdabralinski girls flying for the WASPs. It was a show-off kind of a thing. I was always such a damn show-off. If I had been thinking about her, instead of me, she might be alive today.

"Anyway, after I got back to Sweetwater from your mother's funeral, I found out that the couple that had been taking care of you were moving back to Ohio, and I couldn't take you home. I had promised Sophie I would never tell our parents what happened. She was always Momma's good girl. Hell, we always thought she was going to be a nun, and it would've broken Momma's heart if she had found out. So I didn't know what to do. God knows I couldn't take care of you, and I wanted you to have a shot at a good life with a real family, ya know?

"Anyhow, my pal Pinks had just seen some movie called *Blossoms in the Dust* about some woman in Texas that ran an orphanage, so she checked it out. They were full up, but they gave us the name of another place, so she called and set it up, but they told her she had to get there as soon as possible, because they only had room for one more. So that night around two A.M., a friend of mine named Gussie Mintz picked you up and smuggled you onto the base. It was freezing that night, so Pinks and I wrapped you up in a leather flying suit, and Elroy gassed up a plane and had it ready to go. The two of us flew you over to Houston and got back before anyone noticed a plane was missing. I won't lie to you. I was going to walk in and hand you over and say we didn't know who you belonged to—that we'd just found you somewhere—but when the time came, I couldn't do it. You were just so damn little, ya know, and I guess I wanted you to know that you had belonged to somebody, so I put my name down on the birth certificate. I figured if for any reason Momma and Poppa ever did find out about you, it wouldn't have been such a shock. I was always a wild hare. It's kinda funny now, because I was never the maternal type, you know? Did I hate to leave you? You're darn tootin'. But the way things were going, I didn't know what else to do, so for better or worse, I did what I thought was best. And there you have it."

"I see."

"Oh, pal, believe me. You were better off. Maybe if it had been a different time, things might have been . . . different. But I tried to do the best I could for you."

"Oh, I'm sure you did. And I've had a wonderful life. So . . . you're really my aunt."

"That's right. I didn't know if I was going to tell you. But after meeting you, and seeing what a nice sweet kid you are . . . you deserve to know the truth."

"I see."

"Your adopted parents were nice? You liked them?"

"Oh, yes, very much."

"Took you to church, did they?"

"Oh, yes. And that was another question. Am I Catholic?"

"No. Your mother and I tried to have you baptized, but that damned Irish priest said he wouldn't do it unless we had a marriage certificate. I've been a lapsed Catholic ever since, but now that I'm older, I go every now and then. Take what you like and leave the rest behind, you know. I'm sorry to have thrown so much at you. I could have let you go on believing I was your mother, but you need to know about your real mother. She wasn't a tough old broad like me. And I'll bet you're just like her. A true-blue lady to the core."

"Oh, I don't know. I've tried to be a lady, whatever that means."

"No, you're a good girl. I can tell. You're more like your mother than you know. She never tooted her own horn, and as pretty as she was, she was never stuck up. If she had a fault, it was that she was too tenderhearted. We used to call her Saint Francis of Pulaski. She was always bringing stray cats and dogs home, taking care of sick birds . . ."

"Oh, did she like birds?"

"Oh, yeah. One time, she had this old crow that used to eat right out of her hand."

"Really? I like birds, too."

"See? And I want you to know something else about your mother. She loved you."

"She did?"

"Oh yes. You were her entire world, and if she had not had the accident, she would have kept you. She never for one moment thought of giving you up."

"Really?"

"Absolutely. No question about it. Your mother loved you more than you will ever know."

LATER, SOOKIE CHECKED INTO her room at the little Solvang Gardens Hotel, not far from Fritzi. It was a sweet little room with a small kitchen, and it had a small garden in the back. That night, she looked at the photograph of Sophie that Fritzi had given her. My God, she was, as Fritzi said, the prettiest sister, and she did look shy. Sookie knew that look so well. She had seen it on her own face so many times before.

Fritzi had let her take some books that had been written about the WASPs back to the hotel, and she sat up that night and read all about them and what they had done, and she was in awe of all of them.

When she finished, she gave them back and said, "Thank you for letting me read these. Wow, I had no idea. Just think, Fritzi, you are all legends."

Fritzi laughed. "Well, I don't know about that."

"But you are. It must have been quite an exciting time in your life."

"Oh, yeah, it was, but you ask any veteran of World War II, and they will tell you the same thing. I try not to live in the past like some of these old geezers. I'm pretty happy with the present. But looking back now, I can tell you, those years were pretty damn special. I used to hate it when I heard all that talk about us being the greatest generation. But now, looking back at how young we all were, and when you think about how we started the war with almost nothing, and how everybody pulled together . . . the soldiers got most of the glory, but it was also those gals and guys working day and night, cranking out all those planes and tanks and ships that won the war. And you know, it's funny. It never occurred to any of us that we wouldn't win. So now when I think about all we accomplished in just four years, I have to agree, we were great. We didn't know it at the time, of course. I was one of the lucky ones. I got to do what I loved and serve my country, too. None of us felt like a hero. We were just doing what everybody else was doing, only we were doing it in the air.

"It was a magic bubble of time. You knew you had to live for the moment, and we all felt so alive. The music seemed like it was written just for us. Hell, we thought we were saving the world, and in a way, we did. Who can say what would have happened if we hadn't come into the war when we did? We could all be speaking German or Japanese right now. Who knows? But as hard as it was, I wouldn't have missed it for the world.

"It seems like we were always moving. I don't remember ever getting more than two or three hours' sleep. None of us did. I think we lived on adrenaline. We were too excited to sleep. None of us thought much about what would happen after the war, and then when we were told the WASPs were being disbanded, and it was all over, it was tough. Of course, it wasn't only us. It was all the gals that had stepped in during wartime and gone to work at the factories and everywhere else where they were needed. And now we were being told to go home and be happy to be housewives again. Some of them were glad to go home, but a lot of the gals found out they liked being independent and on their own and wanted to keep working, but they were told that it was unpatriotic to take a job away from a returning soldier. It was quite a kick in the teeth, particularly for the WASPs. All that we did to prove ourselves didn't mean a thing. They just wanted us to go away and pretend it never happened. Even our records were classified.

"Then back in 1976, when ten women began flight training for the U.S. Air Force, a Pentagon press release touted them as 'the first women military pilots,' and I called Jamsie and Nancy and Dinks and they hit the roof. 'Hell, no. We were the first.' None of us were whiners, but we knew what was fair. So a group of us got together again and decided we weren't going to let all those gals who died, your mother or any of them, just be forgotten."

THE NEXT DAY, FRITZI picked Sookie up and took her to lunch at the Alisal River Grill, where Fritzi often played golf. After they had ordered, Sookie asked her if she had ever met her real father.

"Just once. A real quick hello and good-bye. But I can tell you his name. It was James Brunston. I don't know his middle name."

"What did he look like?"

"He looked very healthy, if that's what you're worried about."

Sookie laughed. "No, I mean was he tall? Short?"

"Geez, honey, it was over sixty years ago now, but I remember that he was a tall, good-looking blond guy with blue eyes. You got your mother's hair, but I think you got his nose."

"What was he like?"

"Oh, he seemed nice enough. Of course, later when I found out what he had pulled on Sophie, I changed my mind.

"But you know, looking back on it now, I realize that it was a different time. People were scared, and all bets were off. We all sort of lived for the moment. We had to. That's all we had. None of us knew if we even had a future, so we grabbed for every little slice of happiness we could. I know I did. And who's to say? He could have loved your mother, and maybe he would have come back. Who knows? Not to excuse him, but this kind of thing happened. Boys fell madly in love with girls they didn't even know. Boys were desperate to get married. Hell, I could have married a hundred different boys if I had wanted to. All they knew was that they could be killed any day, and I guess they wanted to leave something or someone behind to prove that at least they had been here.

"Me, I got lucky. After the war, me and Billy moved out here and started a little flight school, and we had forty good years together. After we retired, we traveled. We had a little plane, and I flew us wherever we wanted to go. I can't complain. I've had a damn good life, and I've lived long enough to see the gals fly jets and finally get a chance. And it feels good to know you helped open up a little window for them, ya know?"

SOOKIE STAYED ON IN Solvang for a week and visited with Fritzi every day. They usually had either lunch or dinner together, and the rest of the time, she just wandered around town, talking to people, and it was wonderful. Here in Solvang, she wasn't Lenore Simmons's daughter. For the first time in years, she was just herself. She met a lot of Fritzi's friends, and she even made some friends of her own. Two nice ladies visiting from Japan invited her to have dinner with them, and she had breakfast with the sweetest couple, Susan and Michael Beckman from Tenafly, New Jersey. And she met the cutest lady, named Linda Peckham, in the hotel spa.

She called Earle every night, and in one conversation, he said, "Honey, I haven't heard you sound so happy in a long time." And it was true.

ON HER LAST DAY in California, she and Fritzi went to the old Spanish mission for mass and had dinner at Bit o' Denmark restaurant.

When they had finished dinner, Sookie said, "Uh . . . Fritzi, before I go home, could I ask you one more question? I'm really curious about the name Ginger. Did you name me after someone in your family?"

Fritzi laughed. "No, sorry about that, kid. The night we took you in, when they were filling out the birth certificate, and they asked me what your name was, it was the first name I came up with. I was a big fan of Ginger Rogers."

"Oh, as in Fred Astaire and Ginger Rogers?"

"That's right."

"Oh, how nice. I love her."

"Yeah? Me, too. I met her once, and she was a pretty swell dame on the screen and off. But you did have a real name—the name your mother gave you."

"Oh?"

"Yeah, and you're probably not gonna like it, but she named you after me."

"My real name is Fritzi?"

"Yeah. Fritzi Willinka Jurdabralinski. Can you take it?"

Sookie smiled. "Yes, I can. And not only that, I am honored to be named after you."

THE NEXT MORNING, WHEN Sookie was leaving to go home, Fritzi walked her to the car, and Sookie said, "Thank you for a wonderful time."

Fritzi said, "Kid, I wouldn't have missed meeting you for the world. And oh, before you go, here's a little present for you."

"Oh, thank you."

"You keep in touch, ya hear?"

"I will."

AS SOOKIE'S CAR DROVE away, Fritzi walked back in the house and thought to herself, "That poor kid. Such a nice sweet gal, and she's been lied to all her life. And now I'm doing the same damn thing." She hadn't told her what had really happened to her mother. Sookie had been through enough already, and what good would it do for her to know anyway? Nothing could be proved.

IN THE CAR, SOOKIE opened the little package that Fritzi had handed to her. Inside was a small blue rosary and a note.

Dear Sarah Jane,

This belonged to your mother, and I know she would want you to have it.

Fritzi

THE ACCIDENT

November 23, 1944

ALTHOUGH THE WASPs HAD ONLY A FEW MORE WEEKS BEFORE THEY would be officially disbanded and would return to civilian life, there were still a lot of guys wanting to get a date with Sophie. But dating was the last thing on her mind. All she wanted to do was fly the remainder of her ferrying trips and, in between, spend time with her baby.

None of the fliers were having any luck with her. But one guy in particular was having a hard time taking no for an answer. He wasn't used to it. Bud Harris had a certain reputation to uphold. He was known as the Lady Killer. He was handsome, was a smooth talker, and had always had success. He'd been so sure he could get a date with Sophie, he made a bet with his buddies that not only would he go out with her, but he would have her in the sack in two weeks.

He tried everything he knew, including the old "Oh, honey, I may never come back alive. Won't you give me just one date?" line. He sent flowers, he wrote notes, he used all of his tricks of the trade. But she still had no interest, and he wasn't happy about it.

He wasn't about to lose his bet over some dumb little Polack bitch who didn't know how lucky she was that he'd even looked at her. One evening, when he was sitting around having a few drinks, he found out that Sophie was doing a cross-country that day and was bringing in a plane later that night. After another drink, he decided he would go over and meet her and try to talk a little sense into her—tell her to stop playing so hard to get. He knew she wanted it. Besides, that's why most of them were here anyway.

Sophie was tired when she pulled in and just wanted to get back to her bay, crawl into bed, and go to sleep. She walked out of the hangar, headed over to make her flight report, when Harris was suddenly beside her. He grabbed her by the arm and slammed her up against a wall. "Hey, baby, what's your hurry? Come here, I wanna talk to you. Why are you being so damn snooty? You don't even know what you are missing yet."

Sophie tried to get away and push past him, but he pinned her arms down and kissed her roughly on the mouth. "Stop it! Please . . . don't!" she said, but he wouldn't stop, and before she knew it, he had ripped open the top of her flight suit and was groping her. She fought him off as hard as she could, but he was over six feet tall and strong. She screamed "No! Stop!" She tried to scream again, but he put his hand over her mouth, and pushed himself up against her even harder. He was going to win that bet one way or another. And it would always be her word against his.

Suddenly a man's voice said, "Hey, what's going on out here?" And he aimed a flashlight at them. It was Elroy Leefers, the mechanic, who had heard her calling out. Harris looked around, saw the scrawny little mechanic, and said, "Get lost, Hayseed, we're busy here."

From the look of terror in Sophie's eyes, Elroy quickly figured out what was about to happen, and he reached into his belt and pulled out a heavy metal wrench. "Let go of her, Harris, or I'll knock your brains out all over this tarmac."

Harris loosened his grip on Sophie for just a split second and she managed to break loose and run toward Elroy. When she got there Elroy put her behind him and looked at Harris. "Come on, flyboy. I dare you. Let's see what you've got."

Harris stood there and thought about it, but figured it wasn't worth the trouble. He was out of the mood now, anyway. As Harris walked away, Sophie collapsed in Elroy's arms. "Oh, thank you, Elroy."

"Aw, it's all right, honey, don't let it get to you. He's just a bad apple is all." Sophie didn't tell anyone what had happened. She had only a little more time left and didn't want any trouble. She just wanted to get on with life and raise her baby. She managed to avoid seeing Harris for a little while.

But a few days later, the guys in Harris's unit were flying formation, and one spotted the plane below them and recognized the red hair and he said over the radio, "Hey, lover boy, look downstairs. There's that redheaded gal who's so crazy about you. Why don't you go and say hello?" Harris heard the guys laughing, and he broke formation. That was the last time the guys saw him that day.

When they arrived back at base two hours later without him, they were told that he had been forced to make an emergency landing because of a mechanical malfunction, but that he was fine. It wasn't until later that night that they heard that another plane had crashed and that the female pilot had been killed.

At the investigative hearing, Bud Harris testified that they had, in fact, by mutual consent, been flying in formation, when the WASP pilot suddenly—and for no apparent reason and without warning—pulled up, causing the tip of her right wing to scrape the underside of his plane, ripping into his landing gear. He assumed she had pulled up and away and was in control and did not see her crash.

There was just one witness. A farmer said he was out in the field and heard a loud roaring noise. When he looked up, he saw two planes flying close together, and then the smaller one suddenly flew off to the right and went into a spin. He watched it spiral slowly down and crash. The plane exploded on impact and burned, and there was little left to determine the exact cause. After an investigation, the crash was declared accidental, and no charges were filed.

He hadn't meant to do it. Harris had thought that now that Sophie was alone and didn't have that hayseed looking out for her, it might be fun to throw a little scare into her—let her know just who she was dealing with. He would teach her a lesson about flying she wouldn't forget in a hurry.

So he circled around and flew in behind her and pulled up beside her. But in his zeal to have her see who he was, he'd pulled in too close, too fast. When she suddenly saw the plane right up on her, she pulled up sharply, trying to get out of his way. As she pulled up, the tip of her wing scraped the bottom of his plane, and he heard the sickening sound of metal meeting metal.

Harris worried that the scrape might have done some damage to his landing gear, so he did not stick around to see her plane spiral down to the ground and crash.

One of the other fliers in the air that day was a friend of Fritzi's and told her what he suspected had happened. Harris had been known to be pretty reckless.

Fritzi had flown into the base on the day of the hearing and tracked Harris down in the waiting room, just outside the inquiry room.

She threw the door open, and when she saw Harris sitting there with his feet up on a desk casually smoking a cigarette, her eyes filled with tears of rage.

"You no-good, lousy bastard! You just killed my sister, you sorry no good son of a bitch. I ought to kick your ass all the way to hell and back. Was it worth it? Showing off for your pals?"

He looked up at her. "I don't know what you're talking about."

"No? I swear to God, Harris, if I had a gun right now, I'd blow your Goddamned head off."

"Hey, lady, it wasn't my fault. She pulled up."

"Keep telling yourself that, Harris. You know damn well whose fault it was," Fritzi said. "You're not worth killing. I hope you *don't* die. I hope they throw you in the brig for life, and that you remember what you did every day for the rest of your lousy, stinking life."

An officer opened the door, motioned for Harris, and said, "They're ready for you in the other room." Harris put out his cigarette, stood up, and walked out.

A collection was taken up among the other girls to take Sophie home, and Fritzi rode all the way to Pulaski with her coffin. Gertrude May flew in from Camp Davis in North Carolina, and Wink got a leave of absence and flew in from England.

The entire town—every man, woman, and child—attended the funeral that day. And even though Sophie wasn't officially in the army, the local VFW draped the American flag over her coffin anyway, rules be damned. As far as they were concerned, she had died while serving her country.

As a tribute, they had this inscribed in bronze and placed on her tombstone:

> *She has climbed to the peaks above storm and cloud*
> *She has found the light of son and of God,*
> *I cannot say, I will not say*
> *That she is dead.*
> *She is merely flown away.*

> —*James Whitcomb Riley*

NEW YORK CITY

—

MARCH 1945

AFTER THE WASPs DISBANDED, FRITZI'S FRIEND WILLY HAD GONE home to Oklahoma, but like all the girls, she found herself restless and took off for a trip to New York to see Pinks and catch some shows. One night, while having drinks with some friends, she looked over and happened to see Bud Harris sitting at a table across the room with a bunch of other pilots. She excused herself and walked over to the table. "Hi, good-looking. Wanna dance?"

A few hours later, in a very exclusive hotel room, Harris had done exactly what he had been told to do by the sexy dame from Oklahoma. After he had removed all of his clothes, he smirked at her. "Will I do?"

Willy, still fully dressed in her steel-tipped cowboy boots, smiled and said, "Oh, yes. Come here, big boy." As soon as he got close enough, she hauled off and kicked him as hard as she could, and Harris fell to the floor, clutching his pride and joy and screaming in pain. Willy calmly strolled over and picked up his shoes and all of his clothes and threw them out the twenty-second-floor window. She left him lying on the floor, naked and writhing in agony.

Willy never told a soul what she had done, but she figured it was the least she could do for Fritzi.

POINT CLEAR, ALABAMA

SOOKIE WAS GLAD TO BE HOME. SHE WAS EVEN HAPPY TO SEE CRAZY old Lenore and actually called and asked her to lunch.

Lenore showed up at the restaurant looking radiant in a beautiful lime green dress with a long white scarf flowing behind her. "The prodigal daughter returns!"

"Hello, Mother. Don't you look pretty."

"Why, thank you. I think this is one of my best colors, don't you?" she said as she waved to a friend across the room.

LENORE MUST HAVE MISSED Sookie when she was gone, because she was pleasant all through lunch, until the very end when she said, "I don't mean to burst your bubble, Sookie, but I don't think you lost a pound at that spa. I'd ask them for my money back if I were you."

AFTER SOOKIE HAD BEEN back for a few days and had time to think about everything that had happened, she realized that this had been the most important trip of her life. She had learned so much that she never knew, and mostly about herself.

She was a lot more than Lenore Simmons's daughter. She was beginning to be somebody else, and she liked who she was turning out to be. Thank God, Earle had urged her to go. He was right. She wouldn't have missed this trip for the world.

Just a few months ago, she had been ready to sit back and take it easy, and now her life was just beginning again. She was learning so much—about Wisconsin, California, the WASPs, Polish food, Danish food.

Sookie ordered five copies of *A History of Poland,* and gave one to each of her four children. Then she sat down and read it herself. She was just in awe of how brave the Poles had been and at all the hardships they had endured.

Why hadn't she known all this before? She looked down at her arm and thought to herself, I have proud and brave Polish blood running up and down in all my veins. How wonderful! The next time she and Earle went over to the Oyster House, she did something that she had never done before in her life. She ordered a dozen raw oysters—and not only that, she ate them! She would probably never do it again, but at least she had done it once. Mrs. Poole was beginning to branch out in the world.

OF COURSE, WHEN SHE got back from Solvang and told Dee Dee her real father's name, Dee Dee immediately hired a professional genealogist to trace the Brunston family in England and find out if James Brunston was still alive. The lady found out that they had all died, except for one of his daughters.

Dee Dee wanted her mother to contact her. "She's your half sister, Mother!" But Sookie decided that there was really no point in contacting the poor lady at this late date. It would only mean having to divulge unpleasant information about the woman's father. Why upset her? She would just let that be. But they did find out that James Brunston had lived to be almost ninety and had died of natural causes. That was all she really needed to know.

Since meeting Fritzi and studying so much about history, Sookie had begun to look at Lenore with different eyes. She began to see how being a female and growing up when she had, with so many restrictions, must have been very frustrating for her. If she had been allowed to go on the stage, she probably would have been a star. And given all of Lenore's organizational skills and her ambition and drive, had she been a man, she most likely would have been a CEO of some big company. It really was sad to think that if Lenore had been born just a little later and gone into politics, who knows where the woman might have wound up?

Thank heavens, Sookie's girls could be almost anything they wanted to be. And it made her happy to think that her birth mother and two aunts had helped open doors for the women who came after them. As Carter said, "How cool is that?"

BLUE JAY AWAY

LIFE WAS FINALLY BACK TO NORMAL AGAIN, WITH ONE EXCEPTION. DR. Shapiro was very pleased with Sookie's progress and said he felt she was well on the way to making a new life for herself, but his practice in Point Clear was not growing. It seemed nobody wanted to see a psychiatrist, and if they did, they certainly didn't tell anybody about it. And so he and his wife had decided to move back to New York, where seeing a psychiatrist was a status symbol. His only regret in leaving was that he would miss Sookie. He would never have told her, of course, and she was an older lady, but in the past months, he had developed a little crush on her. She was probably the nicest person he had ever met, patient or not.

SOOKIE WAS FEELING BETTER, but she still missed seeing her smaller birds. She hadn't seen a nuthatch or a chickadee all spring. Day after day, she sat in her greenhouse and watched the blue jays. She studied their feet and the way they landed on the rim, and she began to do sketches of bird feeders and try to figure out the measurements.

She was trying to come up with a better smaller feeder with wire mesh, so just the tiny bird seeds would filter through, with a smaller ledge that curved up just enough for the smaller birds to land.

Walter Dempsey was a handyman they used from time to time,

and he could fix almost anything. He had a small carpentry shop where he made all kinds of gadgets. After Sookie had drawn a sketch with what she hoped were the correct measurements, she drove over to his shop and walked in. "Hey, Walter. I have a little drawing of a bird feeder. Do you think you could make this for me?"

He looked at it for a moment, then said, "I think I can do this up for you. When do you need it?"

"As soon as possible." It wasn't as if she didn't like blue jays. She did, but she felt she had to do something or else the little ones would just stop coming altogether.

ONE WEEK LATER, SOOKIE sat in her greenhouse and waited. In about five seconds, a big fat blue jay swooped in and tried to land on the rim of her new bird feeder. He kept fluttering around, trying to balance himself and eat the bird seed at the same time, but eureka! He couldn't do it, and after about three or four more attempts, he finally gave up and flew away. Soon several more blue jays tried to land, but because the ledge was so narrow, they, too, had a hard time balancing themselves, and they gave up and eventually flew over to the sunflower seed feeder.

It took a while for the little birds to understand, but the next afternoon she received a visit from a tiny titmouse, and as she watched, he was able to perch on the rim and feed. Success! She immediately called Mr. Dempsey and ordered five more bird feeders.

The following Monday morning, Sookie ran into the house and called Mr. Dempsey. "Oh, Walter, we had three more house finches, an indigo bunting, *and* a chickadee! I just can't thank you enough."

"Well, you're welcome, but it was really your idea. I just followed the plan. I think you may have invented a really useful thing, Mrs. Poole."

"Really?"

"Yes, ma'am, and you know, Mrs. Poole, I was thinking. Maybe you should get a patent on that design. I figure I could knock out at least twenty of these a week. I talked to Mr. Nadleshaft over at Birds-R-Us and told him about the success you'd been having with your feeder, and he said if I made some more, he'd be happy to try and sell them for us."

Sookie was delighted. She and Walter took her design to a lawyer in town, and they drew up a business agreement for their new company that Sookie named Blue Jay Away. They would split the profits fifty–fifty. Within a month, Sookie and Mr. Dempsey were so busy they could hardly keep up with the orders. In just six months, they hired an assistant and a bookkeeper, and the business grew from there.

A year later, they branched out even more and hired an advertising company. Pretty soon, they had ads running in *Southern Living* magazine and in all the bird-watcher magazines, featuring a photo of the feeder.

"Tired of all those pesky blue jays eating your smaller birds' feed? I know I was. But with the Blue Jay Away feeder, finches, titmice, and all my small bird visitors can now feed in peace."

—Mrs. Earle Poole, Jr.
Point Clear, Alabama

Pretty soon, the company had its own website, www.BlueJayAway .com, and much to their surprise orders started coming in from all over the world. As Sookie said to Earle, "I didn't even know they had blue jays in China. Did you?"

When the local paper did an article on her, they referred to her as "Mrs. Earle Poole, Jr., housewife and inventor," and she couldn't have been more pleased. Life was so amazing and full of surprises. All of her life, she had thought she was stupid, and now she was an "inventor."

Not only that, but with the way sales were going, Earle started considering retirement. As the next few years went by, the company pretty much started running itself, and she and Earle had time to enjoy being alone again.

Sookie did have one big scare. One Sunday afternoon, Earle had been on the phone talking to a friend of his, and as she passed by the den, she overheard him say, "Yes, but deep down, I really would like to have another Great Dane."

Oh, dear God, she thought. Why not a small horse or a cow in the house? Please, dear God, let this just be a passing fancy. She loved Earle, but having one Great Dane was enough for a lifetime.

THE STRAWBERRY BLONDE

BOTH UNCLE BABY AND AUNT LILY HAD DIED AT PLEASANT HILL IN their late eighties, but at ninety-three, Lenore was still going strong. Unfortunately she had outlived Angel, her live-in nurse. After much pleading, she finally agreed to go to Westminster Village, but only temporarily, until Sookie and Earle could find another nurse. However, to Sookie's surprise, during her last visit, Lenore seemed pretty happy. "I have to say, Sookie, I am enjoying my step-in tub, and the food here is quite adequate, but I could just kill Conchita for up and dying on me."

A WEEK LATER, SOOKIE had just come in from the store when the phone rang, and when she picked up, she heard a woman's voice. "Mrs. Poole? This is Molly from Westminster Village, and I'm calling because your mother has just had what the doctor thinks might be a slight stroke, and he thought maybe you should come over."

When she arrived, she was told that her mother was in the intensive care unit, but that she was to wait before she went in. Dr. Hindman came out and said, "Mrs. Poole, before you go in, I just want to warn you: She's still very disoriented, so don't be surprised if she doesn't recognize you." He entered the room before her, walked over to the bed, and indicated for her to follow. Sookie walked over to her bed, and the doctor said, "You have a visitor, Mrs. Simmons. Do you know who this is?"

Lenore opened her eyes and looked up. She smiled, then took Sookie's hand and said, "Well, of course I do. This is my daughter, Sarah Jane, and she's the best daughter in the whole world, and I love her."

Sookie looked down at the old woman lying there, so small and helpless, and squeezed her hand and said, "I love you, too, Mother." And she meant it from the bottom of her heart. Lenore squeezed her hand and dozed off again.

Sookie sat by her bed as Lenore slept, and she didn't know if her mother could hear her, but as she sat there, she quietly sang to her, "Casey would waltz with a strawberry blonde, and the band played on. . . ." As Sookie watched Lenore sleep, she was amazed that even now, as old and as helpless as she was, she was still so pretty.

THE DOCTOR CAME BACK a few hours later and told Sookie to go on home and get some rest, and he would call if there were any changes.

That night, they called with the news that her mother was gone.

THE NEXT MORNING, LENORE's lawyer knocked on the door and said, "Mrs. Poole, I'm so sorry about your loss, but your mother said I was to deliver this to you in person within twenty-four hours of her passing." She opened the envelope, and inside was a letter.

Sookie,

Not that I am planning on going anywhere anytime soon, but just in case, I thought this might be helpful.

OBIT

LENORE SIMMONS KRACKENBERRY
Born January 20, 1917, Selma, Alabama
Passed (Date and time to be filled in), Point Clear, Alabama
She was the daughter of the late Mr. and Mrs. William
Jenkins Simmons of Selma.

Grieving survivors include: (to be filled in).
She was a member of (list clubs, organizations, etc.). She is
to be remembered for her devotion to family, her innate
Southern charm, and for her high degree of integrity in all
of her volunteer tasks.
Memorials would be appreciated. Please send to:
Point Clear Soldier's Rest Cemetery Care Fund
Point Clear, Alabama

MEMORIAL FAMILY AND FRIENDS RECEPTION:

SITE CHOICES

1. Grand Ballroom, Grand Hotel
2. Lakewood Country Club (in the big room)
Day: Saturday or Sunday, 3 P.M. to 5 P.M.

- Food and beverages: Coffee, iced tea, a light punch, finger
  sandwiches, assorted sweets, cheese straws, nuts, etc. (Mrs.
  Busby has the list.)
- Seasonal, tasteful flowers at each table.
- Greeters to arrive at 2:30 for assignments from Mrs. Poole.
- Greeters are to be stationed at entry doors and/or lobby
  and stairs area.
- A simple white lapel flower should be worn by each greeter.
- Guestbook(s) to be placed in the room, NOT entry area.
- I do not want people just running by and signing the
  book—only serious mourners.
- Greeters are to move about and mingle with the guests.

Sookie, don't bother with the church service. Rev. George
already has all of his instructions. You will busy enough with
out-of-town guests, arranging special parking, etc.

Mother

At three o'clock that afternoon, the phone rang, and it was a man
from the local monument company. "Mrs. Poole, I have instructions
to deliver the headstone. Where would you like it placed?"

"What?"

"Your mother ordered a headstone . . . and it's pretty large."

"How large?"

The man told her that Lenore had ordered a five-foot white marble statue of a weeping angel for her gravestone and said, "to bill her in care of you."

"My God, when did she do this?"

"Oh, about ten years ago now, although she came in every so often and made changes. She was quite specific. It had to be carved out of Alabama marble only and had to have absolutely no flaws."

Sookie nodded. Of course. That was Lenore. Gone for good, but still calling the shots. Sookie thought, "Well, okay, old gal. Why change now?" As usual, Lenore got her way in the end, just as it should be.

SOOKIE WAS AMAZED AT all the flowers and tributes that were paid to her mother at the funeral. So many people said such lovely things about her. But the one that meant the most to her was sweet old Netta, who took her hand and said, "She was a lot of trouble, but it's going to be a dull old world without her."

It was a beautiful service, just as Lenore had wished. Of course, it all cost more than they thought it would. The weeping angel statue was so large, they had to buy two full cemetery plots. As Sookie stood at the graveside, she had many mixed feelings, but she realized the woman they were now lowering in the ground would always be a huge part of her life. Whom the heart first loves does not know or care if they are related by blood. The fact was that her mother—the only mother she had ever known—was dead. That impossible woman had driven her crazy and caused her much heartbreak, and yet, despite it all, she would miss her every day for the rest of her life.

Lenore Simmons Krackenberry
1917–2010
A true daughter of the South,
gone home.

LENORE'S LEGACY

—————

POINT CLEAR, ALABAMA

A FEW WEEKS AFTER THE FUNERAL, SOOKIE WALKED OVER TO THE house to start the process of cleaning out all her mother's things. When she unlocked the front door and walked in, the faint fragrance of her mother's perfume was still lingering in the air. She half-expected to hear Lenore's voice calling out from another room at any second, but it was eerily quiet. As she made her way back to the kitchen and looked around, it was so strange to see all the small things left behind— little objects that once would have meant nothing, but now seemed so important. She looked at the notepad on the wall and saw her mother's handwriting. "Tell Sookie I need more coffee." The sight of the handwritten note made her realize what a cruel trick death really was. One moment, a person is here, alive and talking, and the next, presto, she's vanished into thin air. Death was still the great mystery, the question that no one can really answer. She wandered around the house and wound up in the dining room. She opened the large mahogany breakfront drawer, and there it was: all that silver . . . just waiting.

She sighed and walked into the kitchen and came back with a rag, her mother's white cotton gloves, and the silver polish and sat down at the dining room table. What else could she do? She could almost hear Lenore's voice as she polished: "Remember, Sookie, nothing says more about a family than good silver and real pearls. The rest is just fluff." It was such a big house, but Lenore had filled every room. Now without Lenore, she felt so small, but she kept polishing.

That afternoon, Sookie picked up the phone. "Dee Dee, it's Mother calling. Honey, I've been cleaning a few things out, and I wondered if you would like to have Grandmother's silver?"

"The Francis the First?"

"Yes."

There was a pause, then she said, "No, not really. It would be kind of useless to me, and I'd never use it. Unless, of course, you'd let me sell it and buy something else, and I know you won't let me do that."

"No, Grandmother was insistent that it be handed down to someone in the family."

"Why don't you ask the twins? Maybe they want it."

"I can't. I promised her that I would never split it up, and I can't give it all to just one of them."

"That's true, and you know Carter doesn't want it."

"No. Anyhow, I was thinking that if you really don't want it, would you mind very much if I offered it to Buck and Bunny?"

"No, not at all. I think that's a great idea. Knowing Bunny, she'd love to have it."

Sookie was not a real Simmons, nor were any of her children, and so by rights, Buck and Bunny were the ones it should go to. Besides, Bunny was now the most Southern person she knew. In the past few years, she had developed more of a Southern accent than Sookie had.

A week later, Sookie packed the car and drove up to North Carolina. Bunny, as expected, was over the moon. "Oh, Sookie, you just don't know how happy I am to have it, and, of course, you can always borrow it anytime, but I can't tell you how much I've always loved it," she said, caressing the large soup ladle. "I think it was one of the reasons I first fell in love with Buck. I had never met anyone whose mother had a complete set of Francis the First. And now that it's ours, I feel like a real Simmons at last." Bunny gasped when she realized what she had said. "Oh, Sookie, I didn't mean it like that. I just mean . . . well, of course, you are a real Simmons. Oh, I could just kill myself for saying that."

Sookie shrugged it off. "Oh, Bunny, don't worry about it. Believe me, I'm so happy you have it."

"Really?"

"Oh, yes, and all I ask is that you promise me one thing."

"Oh, of course, anything. Anything at all."

"Promise me you won't break up the set."

Bunny suddenly recoiled in horror. "Break up the set? Break up the set? I would never ever think of doing a thing like that! Why, it would be a total sacrilege. I would sooner starve to death than break up a complete set of Francis the First." Sookie laughed and walked over and hugged her.

As Sookie was driving home, she smiled. She didn't know how it happened, but a little part of Winged Victory must have latched on to Bunny and was hanging on for dear life. Sookie had done the right thing. The Simmons torch and all that damn silverware had been officially passed on, and she suddenly felt about twenty pounds lighter.

On Sookie's first morning home from North Carolina, she was out in her garden working and looked over and saw a beautiful bright blue dragonfly with silver wings flittering all around in her flowers. That had to be a sign. If Lenore had come back to say hello, it would be just like her to be a bright blue dragonfly. Lenore was a spring, and blue was one of her colors.

A few weeks later, Sookie picked up the phone and heard Dee Dee almost screaming with excitement. "Mother! Are you sitting down?"

"No, but I will—"

"You are not going to believe this!"

"Okay . . ."

"You know that woman I contacted in London to look up the Brunston family tree?"

"Yes?"

"Well, she just found a wedding announcement in the London *Times* for your father's grandparents published in 1881, and it says that on that June twenty-second, Reginald James Brunston married the former Miss Victoria Anne Simmons at Saint James Cathedral."

"That's nice."

"Mother! Don't you understand what this means? Your real great-grandmother's maiden name was Simmons, so we are Simmonses after all!

"Oh. Well, I don't know if that's good news or bad news."

"It's *great* news, Mother. Thank God I didn't throw out the Simmons family crest. And not only that, she also found out that your real father's grandmother, my great-great-grandmother, was a fifth cousin, twice removed, of Queen Victoria!"

Oh, dear. Bless Dee Dee's heart. It was probably not the same Simmons family at all, but she was obviously thrilled to pieces with this information and would no doubt tell everyone she knew.

SHE WAS GLAD DEE Dee was so happy. It didn't make all that much difference to her except that at least now, she didn't have to feel too bad about the Kappa legacy. At least there was a Simmons somewhere in her background. She guessed her only regret was that Winged Victory never knew, and it would have pleased her so to know she had been right all along.

MARVALEEN STRIKES AGAIN

A FEW WEEKS LATER, SOOKIE RAN INTO MARVALEEN AT THE STORE, and she said, "You are not going to believe this, Sookie, but Ralph and I are dating again."

"Oh, really?"

"Yes, I realized that I really didn't hate him as much as I thought I did. It was the institution of marriage I hated."

"I see. And what does Edna Yorba Zorbra say about it?"

"Oh, I haven't seen her since she moved to Las Vegas. She doesn't do life coaching anymore."

"Oh, well, that's a shame."

"Yes, she's promoting a new line of jewelry now, made entirely of feathers."

"Really?"

"Yes, she's one-quarter Native American, you know, and they just love their feathers. Anyway, so far, it's been going pretty well with Ralph, so we're thinking about just moving in together and having sex. That's the only reason I married him in the first place. He was always great in bed. Of course, he's not as young as he used to be, but being a doctor, he can get all the Viagra he wants."

"Ah. Well, I'm glad things are working out for you. I've got to run, but great to see you."

"Yeah, me, too. I'll keep you posted. See you later."

Oh, Lord, Marvaleen. She always offered far too much personal information, or at least more than Sookie wanted to know. Ralph was Sookie's gynecologist, and now she would never feel the same way having a pelvic again.

BUT THE GOOD NEWS was that she and Dena finally did get to the Kappa reunion, and to her surprise, even after she told them the truth, they elected her chairman of the following year's reunion committee.

But then, so many surprising things had happened. The town mayor who had once sued Lenore for calling him a carpetbagger and a horse thief had been convicted and sentenced to jail for embezzlement. Dee Dee finally left her husband for good, and had promised Sookie that if she ever did marry again, it would be only a small courthouse affair. Both Ce Ce and Le Le were pregnant. And Fritzi had just sent her a photograph of herself that had appeared in the Solvang paper. She had won the senior's cup at the Alisal Golf Tournament.

Later, when Earle and Carter went on their once-a-year camping trip, she missed Earle, but it gave her a little time to reflect. She realized that thanks to Dr. Shapiro, she had learned that being a successful person is not necessarily defined by what you have achieved, but by what you have overcome. And she had overcome something that, for her, was huge. She had overcome her fear of displeasing her mother and had married the right man. And no, she wasn't a leader in society, or a rich and famous ballerina, but her husband and her children loved her. And, really, what more could a person ask for?

That night Sookie sat out on the pier all by herself and smiled. She sat there until all the stars came out, and the church bells from town rang up and down the bay.

ALBUQUERQUE, NEW MEXICO

DEE DEE HAD BECOME SO FASCINATED WITH THE HISTORY OF THE WASPs that when she found out that they were having a World War II military plane exhibit in New Mexico, she bought two plane tickets, and she and Sookie went.

Sookie told the man at the gate, "My daughter and I have come all the way from Alabama to see this today. Thank you so much for having this exhibition."

"You're welcome, ma'am. Glad you could come."

Sookie and Dee Dee stood in line to tour the B-17 Flying Fortress, the last one flying in the world. First of all, she couldn't get over the size of the thing. It was huge. As they walked around it, she read all the names written on the sides of the plane of the pilots who had flown it. She looked for her mother's name, but did not find it. There were only men's names.

Dee Dee was snapping pictures and called to her to get in line to go inside the plane. As they stood there waiting, a man affiliated with the exhibit was holding court, explaining to another group of men how he had flown one just like it at the end of the war, when most of them were sold to Russia. Sookie walked over and listened for a while, and then she said, "You know, women flew this plane, too. My mother and aunt flew this model right from the factory."

The group of men looked at her in surprise, and one said, "Really? A *woman* flew one of these?"

The man with the exhibit who was lecturing looked at her and, without much enthusiasm, said, "Yeah, a few of them did," then continued his speech to the men.

As Sookie and Dee Dee climbed the stairs and entered the plane, she could not believe how raw and stark it was inside—nothing but open sides of dark green metal and corrugated metal floors. They moved through the plane, and she was amazed that everything was so hard, with no softness anywhere. This might have been the same plane she had been flown to Houston in that night with Fritzi and Pinks.

When they reached the front of the plane and looked in at the crude cockpit and what looked to her like a hundred levers, instruments, and dials and the huge metal pedals on the floor, she was completely awestruck. My God, how could a 120-pound girl possibly fly this thing? Where did she ever get the nerve? Sookie couldn't imagine what it must have been like flying in the blistering heat of the day and in the freezing cold.

As she stood there, she suddenly became overwhelmed with the enormity of courage it must have taken, and she burst into tears. It was one thing to read about it and see photos, but to be standing inside the exact plane the girls had flown gave her a sense of overwhelming pride.

IT HAD NOT BEEN easy getting in and crawling from the front to the back of the plane and climbing down the narrow, hot metal steps. When they came out the other side, both Dee Dee and Sookie had grease all over their hands from holding on to the metal sides. There sure weren't any frills or comforts on this plane.

Later, a few people who had paid a lot of money were able to go up in the B-17. The noise was deafening as it taxied down the runway and took off, and Sookie was nervous that it would never get off the ground. But at the last minute, it lifted up and flew out, headed over the mountains. If she had had any courage at all, she could have gone for a ride in it, but she was not brave enough for that.

As they left the exhibit, they stopped by the man seated at the long table who had taken their money and stamped their hands, and Sookie thanked him. "Oh, it was just wonderful to see those planes in person and actually get inside one."

The man smiled. "I'm glad you enjoyed it."

Sookie looked back at the plane for the last time. "I'm just in awe at the bravery and skill those fliers must have had."

Then Dee Dee piped up and said, "You know, you really should tell people going through that women flew these planes as well, especially the little girls. I think they would like to know that."

The man's smile hardened ever so slightly, and he looked right past her, as if he hadn't heard a word, and motioned for the next person in line to step up. It was quite obvious that he had no intention of mentioning that fact.

Then Dee Dee did something that shocked her mother. Dee Dee looked at the man and said, "Asshole," and turned around and walked away.

Sookie did not like bad language, but she heard herself add, "Macho asshole," and followed her daughter, and they both burst out laughing.

They left the airport that day with a feeling of tremendous pride and with a deeper appreciation of what the WASPs had done. And now she had a clue as to what it must have felt like, risking your life day after day, and not even being appreciated. No wonder some of the gals were bitter.

Dear God, thought Sookie. Even after all these years, after so many of these women died flying for their country, these men still didn't want to acknowledge it ever happened. Some things never change. Thank heavens for the younger generation.

THE REUNION

Point Clear, Alabama

THE MOMENT SOOKIE PICKED UP THE PHONE, SHE RECOGNIZED THE voice.

"Hiya, kid!"

"Hello!"

"I'm calling to see if you want to come home with me."

"When? Where?"

"To Pulaski."

"Oh . . ."

"I just got off the phone with Pinks, who's organizing it. This year, we're having the WASP reunion in Pulaski. Can you come? There's going to be a parade, and yours truly is grand marshal, and I want you to ride with me."

"Oh, my gosh . . . well, yes! Of course! When?"

"August fourteenth."

"I'll be there."

Sookie was so excited. She had wanted to go to Pulaski, but she hadn't wanted to embarrass anyone by just showing up. Now she had an official invitation from Fritzi.

* * *

ON AUGUST FOURTEENTH, SOOKIE flew into Green Bay. Everybody was staying at the big Hyatt, and Sookie's plane was late, so she was told to meet them at the hotel dining room, where they would be having lunch. As she walked in the door, she looked over and saw a group of women at a table in the corner and stood and watched them for a moment.

She realized that to a stranger, they would look like any group of old ladies having lunch. One would have no idea who they were or what they had done. The maître d' came over and took Sookie over to the table, and Fritzi looked up and said, "Here she is! Pinks, Willy, this is Sarah Jane."

She would have known them anywhere. Pinks looked just like her photos, and Willy was, of course, older but still a beauty. Later, she met her Aunt Gertrude, now a nun called Sister Mary Jude, for the first time. She had a face like a chubby angel on a tree, and she grabbed Sookie and hugged her. "Oh, you look just like her. Oh, you darling girl. Oh, if only Momma could have seen you!"

Someone sent over a bottle of champagne, and Fritzi lifted her glass and said, "Well, now that we are all here, here's to all the great gals who have already gone upstairs, and here's to us. We may not be as young and spry as we once were, but by God, as the song says, 'We're still here.'"

"Hear, hear," they said as they all drank a toast.

"And here's to Sophie's girl, Sarah Jane. Welcome home."

The next day, Sookie and all the ladies in their uniforms were picked up early in the morning and driven to Pulaski. As they drove into town, they were greeted by crowds of excited people, lined up on both sides of the streets, waving little American flags, yelling and applauding as they passed by. After the parade was over, they all went to the large auditorium at the Knights of Columbus Hall, where the official ceremony was to take place, and both walls were filled with large photographs of Avenger Field in Sweetwater and the girls and the planes they flew. Right in the front, on the right, was a large photograph of Sookie's mother, Sophie, smiling, standing by her plane.

* * *

AFTER EVERYONE WAS SEATED, Fritzi got up and welcomed all the WASPs and their families to Pulaski and then sat down by Sookie in the front row.

There were a number of speeches from the mayor, the governor of Wisconsin, a few senators, and other dignitaries. After the governor spoke, everyone assumed it was over, but, suddenly, Pinks came out onstage with a twinkle in her eye. She looked like she was trying her best not to smile and said, "Ladies and gentlemen, there is someone backstage who has flown here today in order to deliver a special message."

They all looked down at the program, but this speaker was not listed, so they wondered who it could be. As soon as the woman walked out onstage, there was a loud gasp and then spontaneous applause. They all recognized the U.S. astronaut immediately. She smiled, looked out at the crowd, and then said:

"Good morning, I'm Sally Ride. I came here today to say something long overdue on behalf of all the women in the military who are flying today, and that is . . . thank you. At a time when your country needed you, you stepped up to the task and proved that women could fly and do it magnificently. You faced and overcame seemingly insurmountable obstacles with grace, bravery, and courage. Your sacrifices, determination, and refusal-to-fail attitude opened doors that now allow women like myself to fly higher than we ever dared to dream. And so as those of us in the space program today and in the future head off for the moon and the stars and beyond, know that you and all the WASPs were truly the wind beneath our wings. God bless you."

As she walked off and waved good-bye, the recording of Bette Midler singing "Wind Beneath My Wings" started playing over the loudspeaker.

What a day!

That night, the town threw a huge party for the WASPs out at Zeilinski's Ballroom. The place was packed, and when the band leader saw Fritzi walk in, he stopped the music, and everyone applauded as she made her way through the crowd. "Hiya, pals!" Sookie didn't know if they knew who she was or if they were just the friendliest people in the world, but she had never been hugged so much in her life. Pretty soon, the music started up again, and a large, jolly woman with a gold tooth grabbed Sookie, and off they went on the dance floor, dancing the polka. She *guessed* that's what it was.

Later, after Sookie had a chance to catch her breath, she noticed the long table laden from one end to the other with food. And she thought Southerners ate a lot! She grabbed a plate and started eating the most delicious something with mustard and sauerkraut. She didn't know what it was, but it was all good. She watched as Fritzi and all the others danced. They looked like they were having the time of their lives.

After being grabbed and whisked around the room by at least a hundred different people, including one eight-year-old boy, Sookie realized she couldn't blame her failure at ballet on her genetics. The Polish were very good dancers.

About an hour later, a man approached the bandstand and said something to the bandleader, and after the next song, the bandleader went up to the microphone and said, "Ladies and gentlemen, we have a special request for a song. Where is Sister Mary Jude?" The crowd roared and applauded. Sister Mary Jude was eating, but being a good sport, went up to the stage, took the accordion, and started a rousing rendition of "The Wink-a-Dink Polka." The next thing she knew, Sookie was out on the floor again, dancing to "The Oh, Geez, You Betcha Polka."

FRITZI'S SURPRISE

THE NEXT DAY, AFTER THE FORMER WASPS HAD GONE HOME AND ALL the banners were taken down, Fritzi called Sookie at the hotel, sounding as chipper as ever.

"Hiya, pal, did you survive the evening?"

"Oh, yes, but I'm still in bed. What a party!"

"Well, get your duds on and come on downstairs, because I have another little surprise for you."

When Sookie reached the lobby, Fritzi was outside in a car waiting for her. "Get in," she said.

Sookie said, "Where are we going?"

"Ah-ha. That's for me to know and you to find out."

The old Phillips 66 filling station had been closed for years, and all that was left was the shell of a building and the cement ramp where the gas pumps had once stood, but as they drove up to the front, Sookie suddenly heard the Andrews Sisters singing "Boogie Woogie Bugle Boy." Then she saw the huge banner draped across the front:

WELCOME TO THE ALL-GIRL FILLING STATION

Then the three women and one lone man who had been waiting for them came over to the car, all talking at once. As Fritzi and Sookie got out, Fritzi was grinning from ear to ear and said, "Sarah Jane, I want you to meet your Aunt Tula. This is Wink's wife, Angie, and you know Sister Jude, and this one old geezer is Nard, Tula's husband. He just came over to set up the speakers. He's not staying. No men allowed."

Nard laughed. "Okay, Fritzi, I'm leaving, but it sure was nice to meet you."

Tula just stared at Sarah Jane and then burst into tears. "Oh, honey," she said. "You look so much like Sophie." Then she grabbed her and almost squeezed the life out of her. Fritzi said, "Don't kill her, for God's sake."

When they walked around to the back of the station, Sookie saw that the ladies had set up a big table full of more food. Fritzi explained, "Every three or four years, the gals and I try to get together for a little reunion."

Tula chimed in, "And this year is so special, because you're with us, Sarah Jane."

Fritzi looked at the table. "Yeah, usually we don't get Tula's homemade sausages or her cabbage rolls."

"Or her paczki . . . oh, boy," said Gertrude, eyeing the plate piled high with homemade Polish doughnuts.

After Sookie sat down, she said, "I just want you to know I'm honored to be here, and thank you so much for inviting me. Life is so strange. A few years ago, if someone had told me that I would be at this reunion today, I wouldn't have believed them in a million years. . . . And yet, here I am!"

"And we're so glad you are here. When Fritzi told us about you, we were all just dying to meet you, but she didn't tell us how much you look like your mother," Angie said. "Oh, Sarah Jane, I wish you could have known her. She was so pretty."

"And she was twice as sweet," said Tula.

As they sat and ate, they told Sookie all about what it was like when the station had been up and running. Tula said, "I know it's hard for you to believe now, Sarah Jane, but God, this place used to be so busy. The house was right on that lot over there, and all you would hear day and night was ding, ding, ding . . . people in and out. Momma said no wonder we were all a little ding-y. That's all we heard."

Angie said, "I'll tell you something else you wouldn't believe. Gertrude and Tula used to fit into the cutest little roller-skating outfits, and what a show. They would come flying out of that station, and boy oh boy, they would whip around those cars so fast, those poor customers didn't know what hit them."

Gertrude laughed. "That's true. We were pretty fast."

All afternoon, Sookie heard the most vivid and wonderful stories about what those war years had been like, the dances and the kissing booth, and how all the boys used to hang around. Sookie said, "Oh, it sounds like it must have been wonderful fun."

"Oh, it was," said Tula. "I never knew how much until it was over. But you know, life goes on. Then the boys came back home, and after that, it was a whole different life."

Later, as she and Fritzi were driving away, Sookie turned around and took one last look at the old station, and just for a split second, she could have sworn that she heard a bell dinging, and she saw the station as it used to be, with all the girls moving around happy and busy, young and pretty again.

THE NEXT MORNING, BEFORE they left for the airport, Fritzi drove her by the church and the school that her mother and all the family had attended. It was so strange for Sookie to think that she might have been brought up here and gone to that same school. Then they went to the cemetery, and she saw her mother's grave. And she saw those of all the other Jurdabralinskis she never knew.

WHEN THEY SAID GOOD-BYES at the airport, Sookie said, "Fritzi, you will never know how much this trip meant to me."

"Well, I wanted you to see where you came from and know that you had a family. Hell, you still do. You've always got me, kid, and don't you ever forget it."

"No, I never will."

WHAT?

POINT CLEAR, ALABAMA

Sookie had just come home from her Pulaski trip and was looking forward to a nice long rest when the phone rang. It was Carter.

"Hi, darling, how are you?"

"Fine, Mom. Is Daddy home?"

"No, honey."

"Well, good, because I really wanted to tell you first. Are you sitting down?"

Oh, Lord, she hated when people said that. "No, but should I? Is it bad news?"

"No, it's good news, I hope."

"What?"

"Well, you know how you always said that someday I would meet the One?"

"Yes?"

"Well, I have."

"Oh, honey, how wonderful!"

"Yes, it is, and the thing is, we're getting married, and I want you and Daddy to come."

"Well, of course. Oh, my God, I can't believe it. Do we know her? What's her name?"

There was a long pause. "That's just it. Mom, his name is David."

"What?"

"I know this must come as a terrible shock to you, but I wanted you to know."

"Your friend David? The one you brought home that time?"

"Yes. I didn't tell you about it before, because I didn't want to upset you." Sookie sat there preparing to faint at any moment. "And it's not just a spur-of-the-moment thing. We've been together for quite a while, and you liked him, didn't you?"

"Well, yes, he was a perfectly nice person, but . . ."

At that moment, Earle walked in the door accompanied by a large black-and-white Harlequin Great Dane, who proceeded to leap up on her good Baker sofa, walk across her lap, and jump over the other side, with Earle looking at him with eyes of love. "Isn't he wonderful, honey? He's a rescue dog, and his name is Rufus," he called out over his shoulder as he followed Rufus, who went galloping through the dining room, knocking over one of her mother's good Queen Anne chairs, headed for the kitchen area.

"Mother, are you still there? I am so sorry to tell you over the phone. I should have come home and told you in person. Are you just terribly shocked?"

Sookie sat there, phone in hand, and thought for a moment. She took a deep breath and realized that, to her amazement, she was not shocked.

"No, honey. I'm surprised, of course. But I've had so many shocks in the last few years, I can honestly say that nothing shocks me too much anymore. And if you are happy, then I'm happy."

"Oh, Mother, you are the very best. Could you tell Dad? I just hope he understands and won't be too upset."

After she hung up, she sat there in a daze. She heard the back door slam and saw Earle wave at her as he and the dog ran by the front window, off to romp and play in the yard. She would have to tell Earle about Carter, and that would certainly not be easy, but she knew he would come around eventually. The girls would not be a problem. They adored Carter. Then a terrible thought hit her. She liked to think of herself as a modern and accepting woman. She had watched *Oprah* and read articles about these things, but she had absolutely no idea about protocol. When it's two grooms getting married, just who pays for the wedding, and most important to her, just who is considered the official mother of the bride? Oh, God. She suddenly wished Winged Victory was here. She would have known exactly what to do. Oh, well, onward and upward, and next year, on to Poland to see the family home. As she sat fingering Lenore's pearls, watching Earle throw a ball for Rufus, she had to admit, he certainly was a *pretty* dog.

EPILOGUE

Sookie had to laugh. It was ironic. After all of her worrying, she had just turned seventy, and she still had all her marbles. Now and then, she had a few little aches and pains, but as Earle had said to her that morning, "Honey, the good news about hitting seventy is at least you know you didn't die young."

No, she had not died young, and that was good, because she now had five darling grandchildren she was busy spoiling and Rufus the Great Dane and her birds.

After Lenore and Fritzi died, Sookie had experienced some moments of regret, wondering about how different things might have been and who she might have become if she had known the truth about herself earlier.

But now, after all these past years, sitting in her greenhouse, trying to figure out all the reasons, whys, and wherefores of life, she had finally come to a conclusion: No matter how crazy her life had been, she was exactly the person she was always meant to be and living exactly where she belonged.

Now, as to whether or not her theory was true really didn't matter to Sookie. All that mattered was that she was happy. And *yes,* she was still decorating Great-Grandfather Simmons's grave every Memorial Day. She knew it was probably silly, but it was the least she could do for Lenore.

As for her real mother, the one she'd never had a chance to know, some sixty years after the WASPs were disbanded, something wonderful happened. And today Sookie's most precious possession, now proudly displayed over the mantel in the living room, was the framed Congressional Medal of Honor awarded to Sophie Marie Jurdabralinski for service to her country.

This book was written in loving memory of Nancy Batson Crews, Teresa James, Elizabeth Sharp, and B. J. Erickson and all the other WASPs who came to the aid of their country in a time of need.

And also with my very special thanks to the four fabulous women, Joni Evans, Jennifer Rudolph Walsh, Kate Medina, and Gina Centrello, who made this book possible.

—*Fannie Flagg*

ABOUT THE AUTHOR

FANNIE FLAGG is a bestselling author and has been an actress, TV producer, speaker, and performer. Her book *Fried Green Tomatoes at the Whistle Stop Cafe* became a major bestseller, as well as a heart-winning major motion picture. Flagg's script for the film was nominated for an Academy Award and a Writers Guild of America Award, and won the highly regarded Scripter Award. Other bestselling novels include *Welcome to the World, Baby Girl!; Standing in the Rainbow; A Redbird Christmas; Can't Wait to Get to Heaven;* and *I Still Dream About You*. In 2012, Fannie Flagg was the recipient of the Harper Lee Award for Alabama's Distinguished Writer of the Year. She lives in California and Alabama.

ABOUT THE TYPE

This book was set in Garamond, a typeface originally designed by the Parisian typecutter Claude Garamond (1480–1561). This version of Garamond was modeled on a 1592 specimen sheet from the Egenolff-Berner foundry, which was produced from types assumed to have been brought to Frankfurt by the punchcutter Jacques Sabon.

Claude Garamond's distinguished romans and italics first appeared in *Opera Ciceronis* in 1543–44. The Garamond types are clear, open, and elegant.